Theo and Matilda

THEO AND MATILDA
Rachel Billington

HarperCollins*Publishers*

Acknowledgments

The quotation from *A Brief History of Time* by
Steven Hawking is reprinted by permission
of Bantam Press, a division of Transworld Publishers Limited.
Copyright © Space Time Publications 1988.

The quotation from T. S. Eliot's 'Burnt Norton'
from *The Four Quartets* is reprinted with
permission by Faber & Faber Limited.

This book was first published in Great Britain in 1990 by
Macmillan London Limited.

FIRST U.S. EDITION

LIBRARY OF CONGRESS CATALOG CARD NUMBER 90-55962

ISBN 0-06-016483-2

91 92 93 94 95   HC   10 9 8 7 6 5 4 3 2 1

To my brother Paddy,
with love

PROLOGUE

Love, all alike, no season knows, nor clime,
Nor hours days, months, which are the rags of time.

John Donne – 'The Sun Rising'

The sky came first, like clear blue glass behind the clouds. The clouds were separate, smoothly riding along one behind the other, rising and falling too, like horses on a fairground. The sky had been there when the valley was first thrown up into its folds. The valley, with its long gentleness, its swell and ebb as if imitating the sea that had created it, was ancient too. But it had never known another sky. The sky was the valley's setting, its maternity.

Matilda stood on the hillside and her head felt high and airy. The breeze moving the clouds seemed to be blowing through her. She could feel it coming out of her nose and mouth and ears, even seeping through her eyes. She closed them for a moment and her head spun dizzily.

'Where are we?' she muttered.

The estate agent from Walter Croke and Co. began to speak. 'It's called Abbeyfields. The history is fascinating. It started life as a monastery but, of course, that came to an end in Henry VIII's reign.' He looked up as if for encouragement but, receiving only a grunt from the man and a blank stare from the girl, he continued anyway, although at such speed that it was hard to make out the words. 'It was a ruin for years after that until a Victorian millionaire built a vast house out of anything remaining, but that didn't last long either and then it became a private hospital and finally, after the war, it was taken over by the county.' He paused, took a gulp and finished in a breath. 'All their modern additions have been removed, just leaving enough of the old bits to give character.'

Matilda had not meant all this. She could feel the past. It was the past that the wind blew through her head until it spun. She turned to Theo, Where are we? It was a silent appeal which Theo missed because he was staring at the ground, stubbing his foot continually on the thick clods of earth. His head was not in the air.

The estate agent studied his clipboard. 'There will be twenty-five dwellings altogether.' He sneaked a look at his BMW parked in the lane and, imagining himself speeding back to the office, he took heart. 'Predominantly for first-home buyers like yourselves, although the idea is to have a mixed income range.'

Since the girl still faced away from him across the valley and the man seemed to be obsessed by the texture of the ground, he continued, again hurrying. 'I should point out the site's useful proximity to one of the least, er, spoilt hamlets in the West Country.' Since he thought the whole place horribly remote and depressing, he smiled unconvincingly. 'You might also note its position in its own landscaped gardens with exceptionally fine trees.'

'I'm glad it's spring!' Matilda, unable to suppress herself any longer, gave an awkward hop, clapped her hands and then clasped them tightly together. Perhaps it was spring fever she was feeling, the exhilaration of a new year, the start of her new life with Theo. 'Oh, Theo!' If only Mr. Walter Croke and Co. would vanish. Go, she commanded inwardly. Her hands shot apart again and a blush rose up her face.

'I expect you'd like to walk around?'

'Yes, indeed.' Theo looked up for the first time. His face made Matilda feel weak and excited and happy. He patted the top of his conker-coloured hair and she imagined sparks flying.

'The garages will be an important feature of the design,' began the estate agent.

Matilda thought of murder, of running a dagger into Croke's heart and, suddenly catching Theo's eye, gave a yelp of laughter. He always liked to know what she was thinking and when he didn't know, he caught her up and hugged her and kissed her till she gave up the secret.

'You needn't hang about,' Theo said to the estate agent but continued to look at Matilda. He took a step closer to her. 'Just put our names on your list and leave us to wander.'

Theo and Matilda stood side by side and watched Croke and Co. hurry away. They watched as the red car reversed too fast down the hill and wound its way, ever more distant, along the valley road.

'They won't have finished building till autumn,' said Theo. 'There'll be no primroses then. Like stars in the grass, you would say. No leaves so bright and fresh.'

'In the autumn we'll be married.'

They stood halfway up the side of one valley looking across to the other. The hefty limbs of an oak tree spread above their heads. Matilda gazed upwards and saw tiny fronds uncurling. 'Have we been here before?'

'Seventh child of a seventh child.' Theo took her hand and spread it out in front of his face. He held it up higher and watched the sun shine through its pallor. 'You're a witch. Your hair is long and black like a witch's.'

'You know I'm not.'

'You behave like one.'

'But I have been here before.' Matilda frowned at a lamb bleating from the other slope of the valley. She watched as it dashed with mock hysteria for its mother.

They walked arm in arm, noticing the light, so different from their town, even though it wasn't such a big town.

'If you've been here before,' announced Theo, who had a loud, booming sort of voice, 'then I have too.'

'Of course I meant we'd been here together.'

'Now or then?' asked Theo, showing unusual indulgence.

'Then,' replied Matilda. 'If you mean another time.' She wouldn't use a word like reincarnation. She didn't believe in such things.

And he certainly didn't. 'So many centuries to choose from. So many Theos and Matildas.'

'Getting happier each time.' Matilda was wistful, for she had not been happy until she met Theo.

'You'd better not visit when they get the diggers back in. It'll be a nasty old mess. You'll hate it.' Theo looked at the bits and pieces of the old buildings which the demolishers had left to give 'character'. There was a very solidly built stone wall, a large archway, which looked Roman to him, part of a Tudor façade, a Victorian gothic turret and various other anonymous bits and pieces. 'They should have got rid of the lot.' A stone-mason by profession, Theo thought too much of the past was left lying around the country.

'Oh, no!' Matilda ran forward and touched the stones protectively. 'This bit must have been part of the monastery. Just see the width of the wall. I'm not surprised they didn't try and knock it down.'

'Be careful. It might be dangerous.' Reluctantly Theo followed her. He didn't want to admit he felt the pull, too.

'After all,' Matilda half shut her eyes dreamily, 'there're only a limited amount of experiences that can happen to a woman and a man. In relation to each other, I mean. Falling in love, marrying, having babies, being parents, getting older, dying. It's just the same for everyone whenever they lived.'

'What about if the wife bled to death in childbirth or died in agony of bubonic plague or her husband got murdered by a Saracen or she ran away with a handsome knight driving a BMW?'

'Then Matilda and Theo's story would be unfinished. They'd have to start again one way or another. We could be one way.'

'You're stupid.' But he liked her stupidity and she knew it so they kissed each other and enjoyed the coolness of their cheeks together.

'There'll be twenty-four other houses here too,' Theo said when they had drawn apart. 'At least forty-eight other people.'

'I'm sure all the other Matildas and Theos had the same problem.' She smiled at him, showing her teeth, crinkling up her eyes. She knew he would want to kiss her again but she moved off quickly, among the stones, the shifting rubble, among the remains. 'If you don't agree with me, I won't ever let you kiss me again!' she yelled when she was at sufficient distance.

'Agree with what?' shouted Theo. When he saw her at a distance he wanted to clasp her so close that you couldn't put a knife between them. His hair stood further on end and his blue eyes narrowed like a hunter's. Her puffy pink anorak gave her angel's wings.

Matilda poised herself on a huge horizontal slab of stone. 'Agree that we are just one more Matilda and Theo!'

'No!' bellowed Theo, bull-like, unsure whether to chase or admire.

'We are part of a story that never ends!' cried Matilda, enjoying his admiration.

'Baa baa,' chorused another lamb, heading for another mother.

'I am a mother sheep,' said Matilda, losing her thread for a moment. Her head dropped. Seizing his chance, Theo was at her side with a lunge and a whoop. His jeans were tight, his jacket padded.

'Doublet and hose,' muttered Matilda before he kissed her.

'I've got to get back to work,' said Theo eventually and he stepped off the stone island.

'Me too,' Matilda reminded him with the minimum of rancour.

They began to walk back to their car. Work was a sobering reality but not, they both thought secretly to themselves, the most important one.

'I kissed you', remarked Theo triumphantly as they drove along the valley road, 'without promising anything.'

'I only let you because I knew you agreed with me.'

'Walter Croke and Co. didn't say it had been a loonybin,' responded Theo.

'Oh, I don't mind that. I knew that.'

'You didn't.'

'Didn't I?' Matilda stared out of the window with an obstinate expression. She was beginning to feel silly. The further they drove from the site, the less she knew what she was talking about. 'I am not just . . . just me.'

Unaware of the tears in her eyes, Theo smiled. 'In a moment you'll start talking about God.'

'God is more in your life than mine.' Theo spent a great deal of his working day cutting gravestones.

They were reaching the final turn in the valley. Matilda twisted round in her seat. 'Stop!'

Theo pulled into a space by a gate and Matilda was out of the car in a flash. He followed her slowly. She stared back to where the remains of the monastery and house were silhouetted against the pale afternoon light.

'I saw something.'

'A bird? A sheep? A fly?' Theo mocked her.

'No. Up there. In among the rubble. A picture. Writing. I don't know.'

'It's lucky for you I'm madly in love,' Theo grumbled as he turned the car and they drove back.

It was easy to find the horizontal slab of stone. It lay on its own like a foundation stone.

'There!' Matilda stood on it once more and pointed.

'It's just a bit of newspaper left by the builders.'

'No. It's not.' She crouched down and her fingers scrabbled among the grit.

'I don't know how you can be so certain.'

'It's smooth, smooth as a baby's skin.' She held it on the palm of one hand and stroked it clean. 'Look,' she said, 'some of the letters remind me of the sort of thing you cut on your headstones.'

Theo bent his head and repressed a shiver. It was so old, elaborate black letters on a single sheet of vellum. 'We should take it to a museum.' Why was the past always so much stronger than the present? He wanted the sheet to be locked up in a glass case where it would be stared at by tourists and lose its power.

'I found it,' said Matilda. 'If I hadn't found it, it would have been buried in the foundations and lost for ever.'

'It would still be there,' said Theo. He told himself he was cold because the clouds had thickened above their heads. 'It's going to rain.'

'I've saved you.' Matilda addressed the letters as if they were alive. 'Whoever you are, wherever you came from.'

'We should take it to a museum,' repeated Theo. He thought of the gravestones he carved, which would last centuries after he was dead.

PART ONE

In this monastery of Streanaeshalch lived a brother singularly gifted by God's grace. So skilful was he in composing religious and devotional songs that, when any passage of scripture was explained to him by interpreters, he could quickly turn it into delightful and moving poetry in his own English tongue. These verses of his have stirred the hearts of many folks to despise the world and aspire to heavenly things. Others after him tried to compose religious poems in English but none could compare with him; for he did not acquire the art of poetry from men or through any human teacher but received it as a free gift from God. For this reason he could never compose any frivolous or profane verses; but only such as had a religious theme fell fittingly from his devout lips.

Bede, *A History of the English Church and People*, 731

Chapter One

In 770 or thereabouts . . .

Theo sat on a pile of dung and thought of his mother. It was fairly dry so he did not run too great a risk of dirtying his tunic and he felt an irresistible need for its comforting odour. The association with his mother was no insult to her but merely a comment on his farm upbringing and even a compliment to her affectionate motherly qualities. Theo, now a strapping fifteen-year-old, had been taken into the monastery when he was eight and not seen home since.

Theo sighed and shifted his position so that his angle of vision was a little different. Rethinking, he gathered his robe between his legs and jumped down, ran a few yards and settled on top of a wooden post. Now he could see past the farmyard and through the orchard, where he should have been gathering apples, to the dark forest trees beyond. If he moved just a fraction more, the forest would no longer present an impermeable wall of green but reveal a pale slit, like a parting in bushy hair. And at the end of this parting, which was really a track, he would see, if the light was right, a corner of those ruins, those remains of giants. Theo's heart pounded as he screwed up his eyes hopefully.

It was this time last summer that he had first seen the stones, the great walls, the arches, the wide courtyards. At least he had only seen a corner of this but his imagination, encouraged by the rays of evening sun, had painted the rest. He knew he was seeing one of the ancient cities of which men sang in darkened rooms. Now he could sing for himself.

> Thus the Creator of men laid waste this habitation,
> Until, deprived of the revelry of the citizens
> The old works of the giants stood desolate.

Aelfric had written it down for him and praised him for his understanding of the fleeting nature of this earthly life. But he had not understood it. He did not understand it. Theo jumped down from his post and returned to his pile of dung.

The poems just appeared. From where he could not guess. It had been like that from the first. Sometimes he wished he had not been born with such a gift for it was the reason he had been taken from his home and brought to the monastery. 'The Creator of the world is like a tree that grows branches. And we are like the birds who perch on them.' He had sung that when he was seven and a year later the monks had summoned his parents and said that their son would be educated at the monastery. It was then that he had been christened Theodore – gift of God – whereas before he had been merely Wulfstan as his father. Theodore had been one of the great bishops of the early Christian church and it was a great honour to be called after him.

It took the monks four years of beatings and scoldings and prayer to admit their mistake. Inside he was still Wulfstan, a peasant's son. He could not understand how the words that came out of this head could be the same as the little black squiggles the monks wrote down on vellum. Worse still, the monks sometimes changed them into another language they used for their prayers. He was glad when they gave up and sent him out to join the other field workers.

It was the abbot, Eata, who had ordered his release. He was usually too busy with the concerns of the monastery, which was more like a little village, to concern himself with the fate of one boy, but Theo's case was special. The abbot asked Aelfric, 'How long have you been teaching Theodore?'

Aelfric answered, 'Four years, in the Name of God.'

And the abbot continued, 'Does he now read and write?'

To which Aelfric, who had come to believe defeat in this matter a triumph for the powers of evil, could only answer, 'No, Father Abbot, he neither reads nor writes.'

But this was not enough for the abbot, who was a fair man when he had the time. 'And does he make songs to the glory of God, Brother Aelfric?'

To which there was a long silence and a reluctant answer. 'He is little more than a serf, Father Abbot.'

'So was that great singer of songs, Caedmon,' said the abbot but he sighed and turned away.

The truth was that Theo had not sung for several years. There hardly seemed time with all the lessons and the prayers and the

6

beatings. His head had been blocked with paper words that meant nothing to him. So it was with a joyous sense of relief that at the age of eleven he was pronounced an illiterate and uneducable and sent out to join the other boys in the garden and the fields. He would rather have been sent home but the abbot would not allow that, for working in the monastery was considered a secure and privileged life and he did not wish to be accused of abandoning a boy just because he was stupid.

The abbot was a fair man. It was sad that he had not lived to hear Theo begin to sing again. Three years ago he had begun to have fevers and his belly, which had been as large as a beer barrel, shrank to the shape of a soup plate. He had died just before Theo had seen the giant's stones and sung his song. He had gone to weep for the abbot and perhaps it was for him he had sung. But it was Aelfric who had written down the words and Aelfric, who at very least did not like him and probably hated him, who had been made abbot in Eata's place.

Theo patted the dung under his hand. Oswin and he had once had a fight, throwing great raw pats at each other. Afterwards they had lain in it together and rolled over and over till they were all filthy and smelt like the devil's crowd. Or so they had been told. They had been thrashed so that they could not move for a month and put on a diet of water and stale bread. But they were young and cured quickly. Nine months ago Oswin had begun to sweat and waste like the abbot and a week ago he, too, had died. Dung and death. Not at all suitable for a song. 'The Creator gathers the good apples off his tree and preserves them.'

Aelfric had, quite rightly, not been much impressed by this attempt. He pointed out that apples are Hellishly difficult to preserve and, indeed, famous for their rottenness. Theo thought of pointing out that this could be seen as an argument for reinforcing a belief in God's all-powerful capabilities. What was a human, after all, but a soft brown apple riddled with worms? But he decided it was not worth the trouble. Anyway, he had brought in apples because he liked the idea of the energetic Oswin being turned into a mug of strong cider, golden and bubbly. But he had sense enough not to try that. Aelfric only countenanced the making of cider because God's works must not be wasted and he could not think what else to do with the apples. Maybe he would cut down the trees.

Gloomily, Theo set off back to the orchard. Normally, picking apples was one of his favourite jobs. But Oswin's death had spoiled it for him. Last year they had raced each other, filling the baskets so fast that the two brothers whose job was to empty them into the barrels begged them to slow down. How beautiful the plaited baskets had looked, piled high with rosy apples! Some were still decorated with shapely green leaves at the stem, although that was not how it should be done. Everything had its proper way, everything its proper rule.

Theo's steps, which had unconsciously speeded up as he neared the orchard, slowed down again. It was no wonder Brother Aelfric (he could not call him abbot) was so pernickety when you considered the daily rules. Hardly an hour passing without prayers – even in the fields he knelt – and the bell ruling all. Ding, dong. The monks were proud of the bell. When it swung, the wooden frame from which it was suspended staggered like a man who had drunk too much mead. Ding, dong. Ding, dong, ding, dong, dung.

Theo began to run and in a moment was under the first tree and then up it, squatting like a big brown bird in its central fork.

'Who's that?' One of the other workers looked up, squinting against the low evening sun.

'Cock-a-doodle-doo!' crowed Theo.

'It's only Theo!' cried another worker.

'Avoiding work as usual.'

I am privileged, thought Theo, unworried by their reaction. I have the gift of song, which is both a blessing and a curse but at least it means I don't have to line up with all those pecking black crows down there. 'Cock-a-doodle-doo!' he called again.

'You come down,' grumbled Penda, who was old and whose back ached. 'You may not be in the service of God but you shouldn't waste your days in idleness.'

He was right. Theo felt shamed, although not enough to get him off his tree. If he did not want to read or write or pray in the smelly little church every hour – they had terrible problems with bird droppings from swallows who lived in the thatch – then he should find something else to do. He used to want to go home, back to the little warm hut and his mother and his brother and his sisters. But even he could see he was too old for that now. He was a man.

If he left the monastery he could find a woman and make his own warm hut and have his own children. The woman part was exciting, too dangerously exciting to contemplate now, but the general picture was not inspiring. He knew enough about the world to realise that he would never find a better place to live than where he was. In the monastery, he was free. The eorl could not make him work on his land. The King could not call him up for

8

military service. He was free as a bird. Holding out his arms so that his sleeves flapped as wide as an eagle, he gave a great shout and leaped out of his tree.

'What an idiot!' Old man Penda, who knew about cures for every kind of illness, stumbled across to where Theo lay unmoving on his back. Probably only concussed, head hit on a low branch. Well, God punishes those who look too high.

The other workers gathered round, glad to have an excuse to leave their baskets. They formed a circle about Theo, who lay on a bed of fallen apples. They seemed to steam, smelling like cider. Wasps and other insects swirled above him.

'He misses Oswin,' said a young man who was managing to eat a rosy apple with a look of pleasure.

'Death is the joyous gateway to God's Kingdom,' Penda crossed himself.

'Oswin was not ready.'

'Death comes like a thief in the night. We must be ready at every moment.'

This thought had a generally depressing effect on the company, who began to drift away. Theo was breathing. He would soon jump up and be up to his tricks again. Perhaps he was only shamming. There was a damp coolness in the air now. If they did not finish their baskets soon darkness would come and they would forfeit their evening meal, crusty bread and cheese as white as the Holy Virgin. Ding, dong for the evening meal.

A wasp stung Theo and he opened his eyes. He did not mind the sting – sometimes he had as many as half a dozen round his neck and ankles – but it had propelled him too suddenly into consciousness. The world had an eerie unreality about it. Above him were the criss-crossed branches of the dark tree with the last glow in the sky splicing them. By its light he could see the farm buildings and, to their right, the monastery to which the outside workers were slowly processing. The bell must have rung already but that had not woken him, only this wasp, the last wasp of the day, for now the air was clear above the apples, no movement, no sound.

Theo settled himself more comfortably – the damp troubled him as little as the sting – and watched his companions. It was certainly no act of friendship to leave him lying alone at nightfall, quite possibly near death, while they went to their rest. They had an air of contentment – the same look, thought Theo, as the herd of cows called in for milking, or of sheep crossing the hills for a better pasture.

9

The monastery buildings were not impressive, hardly more than huts made of lath and timber. Perhaps because they were on the south-western intersection of the bishoprics of Winchester and Sherborne, they were left to fend for themselves. They were said to have a Royal Charter with a grant but what little money they had seemed to come from the small villages round about. A corner of the hall was being rethatched, having suffered one of the fires that started every few weeks, particularly in a long dry summer such as God had given them this year. Theo crossed himself. God gave everything that was on earth, both good and ill. On the other hand, those monastery buildings were frail constructions, unworthy for a place of worship.

> Thus the Creator of men cut down waste
> Until, deprived of the revelry of the riotous
> The ruins of the giants stood desolate.

The giants had used blocks of stone as big as barrels. Or perhaps they were bigger, or smaller. It was hard to tell from such a distance. It was a place of evil spirits, inhabited by the souls of the dead who could not find the doorway to the Kingdom of Heaven.

Theo found he was shivering more violently than the cold of the ground warranted. He stood up quickly, too quickly for his bruised head which whirled for a moment into blackness, this time pulled back by the resonance of a single bell. The meal was finished and the monks were at prayer. 'To God, the Highest and the Head of Heaven, I, the most humble and heartsick, offer my life.' Theo bent his knee among the mushy apples. He would not be like the others.

Dawn came thin and grey, the sun shrouded in mists like a woman who hid her face. By the time it had risen high enough to leave the veils behind, Theo was out of sight of the monastery. He had taken last night's bread from the kitchen and a pouch full of water because he knew how hunger could gnaw at the stomach like a demon. Now he stopped, partly to look back with pride at how far he had come and partly because he had seen a trailing length of ivy, which was just what he needed.

From the hood of his robe he produced two smooth sticks, which he placed one on top of the other and then deftly bound together. He held it up, pleased with his work. Now he had a cross to guide him to a safer journey. The spirits of the fallen city would respect him and understand he came in the Name of the Lord. Or if they were evil spirits, they would be put to flight. If only Oswin could see him. But of course he could, as could the abbot and all who had departed this dark earth.

Theo began to run and although the path towards the forest was uphill, he was delighted to realise he was hardly puffing at all. Field work had made him fit whereas learning to read and write would have made him as pale and weak as an onion.

Once Theo had passed the meadows and the corn stubble, which marked the boundaries of the monastery lands, he came into a wide area of furze and scrub leading right up to the first of the great trees. It would hardly have been difficult to clear this land and put it under the plough but no one had come to claim it – whether out of respect for the monastery or fear of the city beyond the forest, Theo did not know. He had seen boys from neighbouring homesteads playing there but they never stayed long and always left before dusk. Besides, village boys began to work almost as soon as they could walk and it was far enough away to invite a beating. It was easier and more fun to steal the monks' apples or chase their sheep.

So Theo was alone, trotting through the patches of stony ground where hardly anything grew but low creeping heathers, jumping a bed of brambles as if daring a long prickled arm to rise out and catch him, slowing down to penetrate the groves of emergent trees and bushes. His progress may have been solitary but it was hardly quiet. Apart from the noise of his breath and feet, there were insects that buzzed round his head, and birds that flew up from his feet and bees that hovered above the bramble flowers. They seemed too big to have come from the monastery hives. What honey they could make, thought Theo, who had always had a sweet tooth, and what mead of the honey, enough to make his head sing and praise God in his song!

> Praise the Creator of all creatures
> The busy birds and the buzzing bees . . .

Oh dear! Theo slowed down. Not one of his best efforts. Perhaps it was better to leave poetry out of it, concentrate on going forward at the same speed. Poetry was for leisurely afternoons under a haystook or to enliven too-lengthy prayer sessions on a cold morning.

Theo reached the edge of the forest at midday and collapsed

thankfully under the shade of the first large tree. It was an oak, spreading comfortably above his head. To his left there were signs of some felling, proving that others had been here before him, probably to get timber for the monastery buildings. But his tree was massive, too large for even the strongest and most skilful woodcutter. Theo drank his water and ate his bread and then made the mistake of lying on his back and staring upwards at the layers of branches and leaves, laced together over a background of bright blue sky. From further inside the forest a woodpecker beat as regularly as a hammer from the forge.

Early afternoon was the least busy time at the monastery. The monks had their prayers to say and the field workers took the opportunity to loll about and, if they were the right age, to dream about women or, if they were very energetic, to find a woman from the village with whom to do their lolling. Even the young boy oblates, who should have been studying their Latin, escaped to the fishponds where they tried to catch the silver trout. So when Theo woke up and jumped to his feet and saw the monastery lands as swarming with activity as any hive of bees, he knew he had wasted a good part of the afternoon in sleep. From the edge of the meadowland the cows were starting to gather together, knowing it would not be long before they were called in for milking. The sun was still hot and high but at this time of year it fell as swiftly as a swallow diving for water.

Aha, thought Theo, that picture I like. And, spurred on by his own brilliance, he set off at a steady jog through the trees. At first the light struck through to the ground, falling, he thought, like polished war-spears. But as he penetrated the deeper growths, the light was reduced to splatters of irregular brightness, hardly sunshine at all, and finally he was surrounded by a dim greenish glow, which reminded him of the church when the bushes had grown across the windows.

Theo told himself that the dark and cool was a pleasant relief in a mission requiring so much hard exercise. But the truth was that he found it eerie and, despite his image of church, the sort of place where evil spirits would be happy to lurk. He jumped and yelped as a large pale creature blundered across his path. It was a swine, he saw almost at once, doubtless gone astray from the monastery herd and now living wild. Given the emphasis in the gospels on evil spirits living in just such stupid beasts, he might still have had his suspicions, except that it was quickly followed by a trail of baby swine, which seemed too small and silly to be an appropriate home for even the most junior devils.

12

After they had gone, grunting and squeaking with anxiety, Theo sat down for a rest. He then remembered the path through the forest, running as straight as a hair parting. In his haste to get on his way after his sleep, he had forgotten his plan to skirt the trees until he found the path. Now he was in the middle and, unless he was very lucky, he would never find it. Certainly, God did not help the stupid. Raising himself up again, he resumed his steady jog. At least the going was easier now, for nothing, neither sapling nor shrub nor plant, grew under the trees and his feet fell on the soft bed of successive years of fallen leaves.

Theo was young and strong, bred to long days in the fields, but as he went on and on, hour after hour in the half-darkness, he entered into a gentle delirium in which the increasing pain in his legs and chest left his head feeling light and airy. After a few hours more he began to see what he first thought was light striking low through the trees. Then he realised, with a thrill of terror, that it was a whole army of warriors throwing gleaming spears towards him. In his right mind he would have known this to be impossible, that it was actually a cheerful indication that he was reaching the other side of the forest, but in his state of delirium, he lay down until the warriors should stop shooting or pass by. Immediately, for the second time that day, he fell into a deep sleep.

The sun, which had shone so bravely all day – more as if it were July than the first week in September – at last sank in a rosy glow. At the monastery Theo, who had been missed two or three times during the day, was missed again. But such was his position there, neither fish nor fowl, that when his absence was reported to Abbot Aelfric, he merely shrugged and said snidely, 'Doubtless he is composing great verse while asleep on a bed of hay.'

Aelfric was reeling under the news, brought by a messenger in the afternoon, that he should expect important visitors the following day. Such a warning was unusual, for it was the duty of the monastery to play host to travellers, but it reflected the stature of his visitors. They were a daughter of King Cynewulf of Wessex with her new husband and doubtless a greedy band of eorlmen and armed retainers. Aelfric, who unlike the last abbot was frugal in his habits, knew he would be compared unfavourably to his predecessor unless he entertained them lavishly. His visitors would expect fish from the fishponds, pies from the larder, ale from the cellar. His monks would witness the shocking example of such liberality and would probably become drunk, too. The quiet order of the monastery would be disrupted – even if they

13

only stayed for a day or two – and the last royal visit, which, although it had happened twenty years ago, he remembered only too well, had lasted for two whole weeks. That royal personage, a warrior brother of the last king, had so enjoyed himself that he had toyed with the idea of leaving the world and joining the ranks of God's servants. Luckily a rumour of a disturbance on the easterly bounds of the kingdom near the great uncharted forests of Sussex had galvanised him into action. Or perhaps it was the rain, which had suddenly deluged down. The monastery was a dismal place in rain, with water falling through the thatch and washing in at the doors.

Blessed with a happy idea, Aelfric summoned the monks. 'Let us pray together that God, the Creator of all things, may bring the heavenly water to our parched and burning lands.' The monks would think it was to water the autumn radishes and beets. He would know better.

When Theo woke it was neither darker nor lighter than it had been before. The swords of sunlight had been replaced by swords of moonlight. But now he had regained his senses and could see them truly. He could have waited until sunrise – his present bed was more comfortable than his usual straw pallet – but he felt strong and eager to move. Besides, he liked the idea of seeing the ancient city by the light of the moon. What a song he would sing!

Out from the tall dark trees, Theo strode, a purposeful figure but made dwarflike by the forest behind and the ruins in front. The pale stones stretched over a far greater area than Theo had ever imagined. Indeed, it was of a scale beyond the imaginings of someone to whom the monastery and its outbuildings were already three times bigger than any village he had ever seen. Certainly, it was the creation of giants.

Yet, strangely, he was not afraid as he had expected to be. Perhaps he had dissipated his fear in the forest, for now, as he walked slowly touching the stones, he felt a sense of deep peacefulness as if the previous inhabitants were pleased to welcome him. It was not hard to recognise the plan of the town, the roads, the alleyways, the roofless houses and grander halls and palaces. There were indications of odder shapes, too, for which he could not imagine the use: a large half-circle, formed in steps up towards the sky. He stood at the top and felt his head near to the stars. It was an exhilarating sensation for a boy with a poet's imagination and for a few seconds his vision seemed to alter, so that instead of the ruined town he saw monastery buildings, but monastery buildings as unlike those he had left behind as a stag is unlike a mouse. He saw a tall tower and a square courtyard and buildings as fine as palaces, all of them built of stone.

Squeezing his eyes tightly shut for a second to clear this image, Theo continued walking. Soon he could see the remains of an enclosing wall and rampart, through which he spotted the road that led sure and straight through the forest. That was their road, which led downwards off the plateau where they had built their city. Although he had not reached the further side, Theo could already imagine that this was an encampment built on a vantage point where any approaching enemy would be seen from many miles distant. He could imagine the war-cries, the rush and the clatter as the sentries warned the soldiers and the soldiers ran to their posts. Theo had no experience of war but even monks knew the tales of heroism and adventure. One evening a few years ago a traveller had sung for them the great pagan story of Beowulf. The abbot, who believed in the Christian values of charity and peace, became angry and sent him on his way but Theo had never forgotten his stirring words.

Wessex was lucky to have had a line of strong kings. The laws laid down by King Ine, who had lived over fifty years ago, were still in use. The old abbot had said that the King of Wessex was the most powerful king in the whole country and to be under his protection was nearly as important as being under the protection of God. Aelfric had frowned furiously at that. But, in Theo's view, Aelfric was a kill-joy and an old woman and as sour as a dish of three-day-old goat's milk.

Spurred on by such enjoyable irreverence, Theo began to jump up and down with childlike glee. This was a mistake. He happened to be standing on a patch of earth which in daylight he might have seen to be insecurely grounded. With his third jump his feet went through the soil and he dropped straight down into the darkness below. His home-made cross broke apart and followed him.

Theo landed on what felt like a stone floor and pondered on the quick ways of God. Aelfric must be in greater favour in the heavens than he would have imagined. Since he was not hurt and he had not fallen far, he assumed it would only be a matter of climbing out. Nevertheless he had had a nasty fright and would remember not to underrate Aelfric's celestial influence in future. He began to feel that it was quite pleasant sitting there with the moonlight slotting into the hole made by his falling body. He did not imagine that there would be any particular problem in climbing out.

After a few moments Theo stood up and it was then that he saw

15

his hard floor was ornamented with figures. It gave him quite a fright, the two naked figures, one holding a musical instrument and the other contorting himself into a strange dance attitude, were life-size and life-like. Theo lifted his arms and jumped up at the ragged edges of his hole. At once a small landslide of clods of earth and small stones sent him reeling backwards. When he had cleared the grit from his eyes and dared to look up again, he realised that he was lucky not to have buried himself and that climbing out was not the easy proposition he had assumed. He sat down again. But he felt uneasy now, partly because of the naked youths who must be relations of the giants and who just might spring up alive, and partly because he had no idea how to get out.

As Theo sat unhappily on the mosaics of Apollo and Marsyas, the moon swept its graceful curve over the sky until it disappeared beyond the horizon. Theo watched it for want of anything better to do and when the stars winked out, he remembered his vision of the new monastery. It was not such an absurd idea after all, he decided, when you considered all the stone lying up here unused. A while later, birds began their noisy matins and soon after they had quietened the day began in utter peace with the palest of silken grey spreading above the deserted city.

Dawn was nothing special to Theo. He knew this early pallor, which, if the day was to be fine, would soon be tinged with gold and then blue until the colours were as garish as the paintings on the church walls. He knew the noises, how the birds would start again in twos and threes and be joined by the insects and soon the animals. He could tell the time of day with his eyes shut. But as, in this most hushed and pregnant time, he tried to say a few much-needed prayers, he was disturbed by an unexpected sound. If he had not known he was in the middle of a nowhere place, he would have said it was a horse whinnying. Theo crossed himself hurriedly and shifted his position so that he was no longer sitting on the musician's face.

The city was not quite such a nowhere place as Theo imagined. Travellers passing southwards had long ago discovered the road through the forest. In earlier years they had even picked through the fallen stones, looking for useful material or even some more valuable Roman remains such as pots or swords or jewellery. At one time, vandals had even dared the burial place and dug down deep enough to remove some gold or silver. But the area had been quiet in the last eight or ten years and the monks, living so far from civilised society, retained some of the superstitions of the peasants around them. It was as if they were afraid to cannibalise the city. After all, it had belonged to an alien race, a race of giants whose spirits must surely be dangerous.

Theo's monastery, although it was the whole world to him, was actually quite small with only seventeen monks at present of whom just two were consecrated priests. Nor, despite Abbot Aelfric's pretensions, were they very learned. They were too deep in the countryside, too remote from centres of true culture. Not one of the monks, for example, had ever been on the pilgrimage to Rome – although the old abbot had been to France and trodden in the great Bishop Boniface's footsteps. 'They smelled as sweet as a spring rose,' he always said so that the young boys giggled and tried to smell each other's large dirty feet.

The sun had appeared over the serrated rim of the forest and shone on the ruined city, which had once been called Casertum. On the far side, where Theo had not reached, a line of four horses, accompanied by a dozen or so men on foot and four or five dogs, skirted the fallen stones. The horse that had whinnied still looked restive and continually made little sideways darts, which its rider, a figure draped in a billowing blue cloak, found hard to control. Of the other riders, one wore black robes similar to the monks and two also wore cloaks, although one was short and red and bounced across its owner's back.

'There's something wrong here.' The woman in the long blue cloak spoke crossly as if she were not used to being thwarted.

Her attendant, the second long-cloaked figure, crossed herself nervously. 'The spirits of the dead, my lady.'

'Nonsense!' Matilda, who was the King of Wessex's favourite daughter and therefore not amenable to explanations from stupid women, shouted quite loudly and jerked hard at the mouth of her horse, which repaid her by giving such a buck that she only just remained seated.

The man in the red cloak, her husband of six months, laughed loudly causing her to glare ferociously. They were all bored by the journey, on each other's nerves.

'The monastery should be less than a day's ride,' said the monk soothingly.

'You said that yesterday!' snapped Matilda.

'You've got a temper like a goat.' Wilfrid smiled at his wife. He was a fine figure of a man with fair flowing hair, a thick beard and wavy moustache. Their journey, to seek a marriage blessing from the holy hermit, Dunstan, who lived on the Western Isle, had been amusing when they had faced the danger of Pictish bands but now

17

that they were once more in the safe south was unbearably dull. He consoled himself with the thought that in a week or two he would be back to his favourite pastime of hunting wild boar. The marriage had been arranged to cement the relationship between his father, a leading ealdorman, and the king. The bride-gift would make his family poor for a year or more and all he had gained was the wildness of a headstrong, young girl. Now and again he dallied with the idea of sticking a lance into her. She would squeal as well as any boar.

'This city has hardly been touched,' said the monk. He was called Cuthbert after the great saint and he was pretty much at the end of his tether, too, but at least had the consolation of offering it up to God. 'In so many places now,' he continued in a calm rather pedantic manner, although it was doubtful whether anyone was listening, 'in so many Roman cities, people have made their dwellings or at very least used the stone for their own buildings. But this seems almost untouched. It is a strange sight and a pity we cannot stay here long enough to search round.'

'No, thank you!' Wilfrid kicked his horse and put it at a rubble of fallen wall.

At the same moment, Theo, gathering his wits and lung power, shouted at the top of his very loud voice, 'Help! Help!'

By now the cavalcade had circled round to the hole. The wall Wilfrid chose was only a few yards from him so that the desperate shouts gave the horse such a fright that it reared and shot its master down its back straight on top of Theo.

All was confusion. Theo could hardly make out what had hit him and Wilfrid felt equally bewildered. Finally, Matilda handed her horse to an attendant who was cowering and crossing himself over and over again. She went to stand at the edge of the hole, whose sides had fallen in further so that it was considerably wider than it had been before.

'Two for the price of one!' she exclaimed, seeing the two men standing side by side, her good humour quite restored by the drama and her husband's discomfiture.

'I might have been killed!' bellowed Wilfrid, who was filthy and hardly recovered from his fright.

'Rightly we should have both been buried alive,' agreed Theo, joyful at the prospect of rescue but dazed by the woman's face staring down at him. She had eyes the colour of her dark blue cloak and on her shoulder a large brooch glittered with rubies, pearls and gold. She must be a very important person. And so, presumably, was the man at his side, although he was so covered with dirt and spoke so roughly it was hard to tell. 'I apologise, your honour, for frightening your horse.'

'So you should. You nearly killed me.'

Matilda smiled sweetly at this youthful inhabitant of a hole and then turned to her husband, 'He might also have saved your life by providing a nice soft landing.'

'Rubbish,' grumbled Wilfrid, who was beginning to feel like a bear caged for spectator sport. He shook three gold bracelets down his arm and brushed earth from his beard. The men, the monk and the serving maid were all peering down now with more curiosity than concern.

'Do you live down there?' asked Matilda, pursuing her train of thought. Despite the earth smears he was a beautiful young man, with sunburned skin, strong features, and shiny chestnut-coloured hair.

'I fell in too, Princess.' Did she think he was a mole or something?

'So you think I'm a princess, do you?'

'Stop that silly chatter and get me out of here!'

Theo turned to Wilfrid sympathetically even though he was shocked by his rudeness. It was no pleasure being in their situation. 'We'll need a rope,' he said, 'or the sides will cave in. I fell in last night and not all the prayers of St Christopher, patron of the traveller, could help me climb out again.'

The monk nodded at this little speech, pleased that they were to rescue a Christian and unaware that Theo had just noticed his presence and included this speech entirely for his benefit.

Theo noticed his approval and wanting more – and from other sources – he recited in his sweetest tones:

> 'Glory to God who gives us all goodness
> Saves the soul-bearer in a safe ship.'

'Ah. So you are a singer of songs!' smiled Matilda admiringly. Oh, how bored she had been all these months with her oafish husband and that dreary black crow Brother Cuthbert! She could hardly stop herself skipping childishly with the delight of finding a beautiful young poet in a hole.

'I live at the monastery the other side—' began Theo, before he was interrupted by the enraged Wilfrid.

'If you don't get me out in two minutes I shall kill somebody!' And he produced a gleaming jewel-handled dagger, which he waved in Theo's face.

'Spare me, my lord.' Not exactly cowardly but knowing when

he was beaten, Theo dropped out of sight at his feet. There he found himself face to face with the player of the lute. His mosaic eyes were big, wide and sympathetic, only partially covered by dirt. His mouth was completely revealed. Theo kissed it passionately, half-conscious that he was expressing a need awakened by the beautiful princess's face but also hoping that the warlike monster who had fallen on him would not stoop to kill a man grovelling face down in the dirt.

Meanwhile, the servants had at last produced a rope and heaved their master out of his trap.

'Let's get on now!' he cried the moment he got to the top and, after beating his disobedient horse with the rope, he jumped back on to it.

'Help!' cried Theo, hardly believing what was happening.

The monk's face reappeared. 'You wish to come out?' He seemed wistful.

'Of course I wish to come out!'

'You, as a singer of songs, could live like a hermit in your hole. The hermit is dear to God.'

'There's already one singer here,' said Theo, rudely, perhaps, but with some excuse.

Cuthbert, who had been prepared to leave, for Wilfrid had the rope and Wilfrid would not save where he threatened to kill – all life, after all, is in God's hands – turned back. 'Another singer?'

'A picture. On the floor – the most beautiful picture I've ever seen!' Theo cried hysterically. Would the princess, who had looked at him so admiringly, really leave him to die?

Cuthbert, who had been to Rome and was very interested in the art of mosaic, immediately crouched so close to the edge of the hole that Theo felt the devil tempting him to pull. Surely they would not leave a monk behind? Instead he scrabbled frantically at the floor so that the sunlight picked out the two figures and the lyre as the moonlight had for him.

'Apollo and Marsyas!' exclaimed Cuthbert, in a hushed voice so that at first Theo thought he was unimpressed. But soon he had summoned back Matilda and Wilfrid, showing a determination only possessed by certain quiet people with an intellectual passion.

'This is a beautiful example of a Roman mosaic floor. Pagan, of course, but none the less exquisite for that.'

This idea shocked Theo, who had been brought up to believe that nothing pagan could be beautiful but he did not wish to question the reason for their return. It had struck him that there was a reason why he would be more useful outside the hole.

'I know the old way through the forest!' he cried. 'The path straight as an arrow.'

The sun had grown higher over the city. The attendants basked on the warm stones. Two of them threw knuckle-bones, making a trickling noise like fast-running water in a pebbled stream. When they were ordered to hoist out Theo they did it so lethargically that he scraped and scrabbled against the side. The dogs raised themselves and began to bark.

'Put the rope round his neck,' ordered Wilfrid when he reached the top. 'And then if he can't find this so-called straight-as-an-arrow path, I shall only have to pull it tight.'

The procession of horses and men set off again, but this time it was led by Theo with a rope around his neck. Some dark birds had collected above them, giving ugly and, in Theo's imagination, threatening noises. He soon learned to keep an even speed so that his lead did not tighten, although even then Wilfrid, who held the other end, could not resist some unprovoked tugs. It would be wise to find the path quickly.

Matilda had fallen into the dreamlike state she adopted on long rides. It was typical of Wilfrid to spoil anything she admired. Now that beautiful youth with the gift of song had been turned into something less than a dog – indeed, the dogs that ran with them clearly thought of him as a rival and every now and then one ran up to snap viciously at his heels – she would not look at him or think of him. If he managed to survive the day's journey, then she might ask him for a song on suffering and endurance.

Matilda loved songs, although more along the lines of adventure stories than hymns to God. She wondered what the Roman singer, whom Cuthbert called Apollo, had sung. Certainly something gracious and noble. Matilda knew enough of the Roman way of life to envy their ease and comfort, their sophistication and artistic talent. If she had been born into their society she would have held court in a large pillared room with running water, mosaic floor and a troupe of dancers and musicians and singers to entertain her. Some had been Christian, she understood, because there were stories of terrible deaths, of limbs torn off by lions, of eyes burned out with flaming torches. Matilda shuddered with pleasure. This was the unfortunate side of her nature that had led her to accept Wilfrid in marriage. She had seen him kill a man, no one important, just one of his serfs – and the sight had excited her so that she had turned red and trembled like a child. Later she had confessed her feelings to Cuthbert but he had been unhelpful, merely stating that the devil was a crafty bedfellow. Now she had Wilfrid as a bedfellow who was just as bad as the devil. The worst thing was that in order to enjoy his attentions she had to imagine that moment when his sword plunged into the man's chest and the crimson blood flowed. She had hoped their holy pilgrimage might have exorcised the incident, which at low moments she had begun to see as something of a curse. But a couple of nights ago when Wilfrid had thrown her on a bed of peat the same image had risen to excite her. Death is part of life, she knew, but no one should revel in it. Sometimes she thought she was actually worse than Wilfrid for, whereas he was unconsciously cruel like a child (he really was very stupid and uneducated despite being of such good family), she had been brought up to know better in a nunnery run by her aunt the abbess. There she had learned to read and write and embroider and spin and say her prayers morning, night and day. Oh, it had been dull!

Matilda stabbed her heels into her horse's sides and cantered off, shouting in taunting tones, 'Come on, you old women! Some of us want to eat before sunset!' There was no doubt of Matilda's royal selfishness, for the result of her mad dash to escape her thoughts was that Theo was overtaken by Wilfrid and then tugged along behind like a sack of turnips. By the time he had managed to reach a knife under his tunic and cut himself free, he was bruised, cut and half strangled. However, his luck hadn't entirely deserted him, for as he lay, unattended and doubtful of his survival, he spotted light in the undergrowth of woods beside him. This was the path. It also proved he was alive – unless, of course, he was seeing the path to the heavenly kingdom but that would have been dazzling bright, uncamouflaged by elder and ivy.

'The path,' he muttered through broken lips. By now the servants had caught up with him. 'The path,' he repeated half raising his left arm. The servants, glad of the rest, sat down. They were rough men, more soldiers than servants, and they felt warmer towards Theo now that he was hurt and not singing. Not that they volunteered any help but at least they accepted his word and sat down companionably to wait for their masters to return. Their presence had the effect of scaring off the dogs, which scuffled round Theo slavering at their chops.

Cuthbert returned first and tut-tutted round Theo but again to no effect. He was a strong lad, he would soon recover. Besides, a little scourging of the flesh never did anyone any harm.

'The path!' he shouted, flapping his arms. And soon Wilfrid and Matilda, eyes shining from her ride, hair flying like black cobwebs, came racing back.

'God save him,' said Matilda when she saw Theo bloodied on the ground, and then blinked a few times as if to banish the sight.

'At least he's found us the path now!' crowed Wilfrid. 'Turn him loose.'

The morning sun did not follow them far into the forest. It was as it had been for Theo the day before, first the splatterings of light and then the translucent green – except that then it had been tranquil and now the trees echoed with the horses, the men's voices, the dogs barking. Theo could track their progress as they drew away from him. He crawled a little and then hobbled painfully since one of his legs seemed strangely crooked.

Matilda, leading the cavalcade with Wilfrid, turned her eyes upwards but it was impossible to see the tops of the tall dark trees. Why was it that all the moments of glitter and exhilaration should be associated with blood and suffering? Now she could only see Theo's battered face. Even the Christian church, which preached love and salvation, had death and a cross at its centre. Reining back her horse until she was on a level with Cuthbert she asked, in conversational tones, 'Is it true the Romans had a way of heating a room by putting fire under the ground?'

Aelfric looked at the sun, falling now from its height, and then back at the young monk in front of him. 'If the bread doesn't rise,' he tried to sound patient but saw his failure only too clearly in the stupid man's frightened face, 'it is not because the devil has got into it but because you have not put enough yeast in it.' When he had taken over as abbot he had never considered that he would be forced to take responsibility for every petty matter in the monastery. Abandoning any attempt at patience, he threw down the sample loaf that had been offered to him. It hit the baked mud at his feet like a stone. 'Try again, brother!' he cried. 'And pray that God may give your hands inspiration.' He wanted to lead the monastery in prayer not baking.

Yet if the bread was hard, and if this odious princess reported back to King Cynewulf that his hospitality was lacking, his small enough royal grant might no longer be forthcoming or, worse still, he might be subjected to enquiries from the bishopric or even summoned to the next synod. Aelfric hurried after the retreating cook and gave him an encouraging pat on the back. 'Remember the example of the Israelites who, finding themselves starving in the desert, prayed to God and manna dropped down on them from heaven.'

This was the best consolation Aelfric could muster under the circumstances. However, it occurred to him that if the manna had been baked by this poor dolt, it would have squashed the Israelites flat before they could eat it.

Chapter Two

The moon rose slowly over the monastery buildings. For a while it hung above the monks' fishpond giving the interesting impression of a round pale face staring at its reflection; then it moved onwards towards the forest. To Theo it was the kindliest light he had ever seen. It meant he had left the dark trees, which on several occasions had seemed as if they might be his tomb, and reached a more hospitable land. The sound of a cow mooing almost made him burst into tears.

It was not one of the cows, who were all sleepily chewing cud, but a bellow from the refectory. The mead had been flowing for several hours now, much to Aelfric's consternation, and most of the men, Wilfrid in particular, were becoming more beastlike by the minute. There had been some conversation earlier, some dramatic rhetoric and Theo's poetry had been called for. But now vain boasting had turned to vain grunting, the occasional bellow, and even the monks had to cling to the benches when they stood up. Indeed, everything had proceeded according to Aelfric's worst fears and his store-rooms would be empty for months.

'The biggest, the brawniest, the bravest!' roared Wilfrid, obviously referring to himself.

At least Aelfric could console himself that his guests were satisfied with their welcome. Tomorrow the moon would begin to wane, which often, please God, brought in a period of stormy weather. He would hint as much to Wilfrid in the morning when he was sickened by his feasting. Or perhaps he could raise the matter tonight with the Princess Matilda. She had retired with her woman to the far end of the hall and looked as frustrated as he felt. It was no good talking to that miserable Cuthbert; he had been snoring for several hours. No possibility they would see him at matins.

With such bitter and, as it happened, slanderous thoughts – matins was the aesthetic Cuthbert's preferred time of prayer – Aelfric began to work his way carefully down the table. He did not wish to attract Wilfrid's savage attentions. Unfortunately he had hardly edged more than half-way down when he saw the blue cloak slide from his vision and realised that Matilda, leaving her companion asleep at her place, had gone outside.

Matilda was depressed. Here they were, arrived at last at the monastery to which she had been looking forward as a centre of civilisation but which was hardly more than a group of mud huts, peopled by a stingy old abbot who knew little Latin and less Greek – Matilda admired learning even if she did not possess it – and a group of ignorant country peasants who seemed as keen to lose their senses in mead as was her husband. Animals, that's all they were. Animals! With difficulty she restrained herself from slamming the heavy door for it would never do to bring Wilfrid rampaging after her.

Theo saw the light as the door opened. He had crawled as far as the little meadow where the monastery bee-hives showed in a dark pentangle. Five hives for the five wounds of Christ, thought Theo, crossing himself with an intensity of religious feeling heightened by his survival. He could not move further for his exhaustion was even greater than his pain but in the morning old Penda would come and straighten out his knee and put poultices on his wounds. Now he could afford to become unconscious. Despite seeing the yellow light at the open door Theo lay back and closed his eyes.

Matilda walked slowly. The air was soft and the beginning of an autumnal mist clung damply to her forehead – refreshing after the stuffy hall. After she had walked far enough to judge herself free from prying ears she sat on a pile of straw placed bench-like beside a wattle fence, and burst into unrestrained sobs.

Matilda liked to cry. It was a harmless outlet for her emotions that made her feel better. However, in a world dominated by masculine strength and aggression she realised it was a shaming symptom of feminine weakness and made sure to hide her outbursts.

Matilda sobbed and the tears ran down her face like a spring stream bursting its banks.

Theo watched, amazed. The noise had woken him from his stupor and at first he thought he might be dreaming or delirious. Was it possible that the haughty princess, caressingly lit by the rays of the moon, should wail and rant like a three-year-old child?

Matilda became aware that instead of her tears bringing a warm sense of relaxation as they usually did, she was beginning to shiver with tension and cold. They were becoming real tears, expressing not a child's desolation but an adult's realisation that her life was making her miserable. 'What is the point of being married to that oaf, my husband?' she might have said. Or 'Have I nothing to look forward to but dutifully taking the ale-cup round the table or spinning and weaving till my fingers grow thick? Then childbirth with all its pain and danger? Motherhood with the certainty of separation? And death later, or more likely sooner?'

Theo, from his bed beyond the bee-hives, even through the suddenly nearly unendurable pain in his leg, recognised the change in the tone of her crying. She no longer sounded like a little girl but like a ewe bleating over a dead lamb. In his weakened state he found tears in his own eyes. Stretching a hand in her direction he croaked,

> 'Weary from the world is the woman's heart
> Happy is she who turns to the home giver, the god-
> head.'

The words did not penetrate beyond the battlements of bee-hives, which was a pity since under the circumstances they were creative pearls, but Matilda's eyes, however water-logged, caught sight of Theo's hand movement. Thinking it a rat or a fox or some other unattractive marauder, she jumped off her straw. It was only then that she saw a man's shape on the ground. This made her rather more frightened since only those doing the devil's work lurked on the edge of home pasture.

Theo saw her poised to flee, tried to repeat his consoling poetry, on which he must be recognised, but found himself unable to frame the words. His gallant wave proved the last straw for his battered body and he fainted.

The moment he fell backwards, Matilda guessed his identity and sprang between the five wounds. Her tears flashed behind her and so did her misery. Here was a suitable diversion, a man who had nearly been killed by her husband – with some help from herself – but yet had survived.

'How unpleasant you look!' she said, grimacing and bending over him. Theo, still in a faint, naturally made no defence. 'Oh dear. Are you dead? In front of my eyes. What a reproach!' At this Matilda began to feel rather dismal again.

Theo groaned.

'You are alive. I'm so glad. I like your songs, you know. When I have my own establishment I shall patronise a singer of songs. Perhaps it could be you, perhaps I'll dress you in an embroidered cloak and give you a lyre and on long winter nights . . .' Here her voice trailed away as she imagined Wilfrid's attitude to such a plan. 'Anyway,' she continued in a grittier, less whimsical tone, 'one day I shall live as I please and he can go and pull a goat's leg.'

This defiance addressed to a semi-conscious man seemed to restore her sense of a just world for she now settled quietly on the ground. Even the bees slept.

Judging by the diminishing level of noise from the hall, thought Matilda, Wilfrid would soon collapse into swinish sleep. Once again her thoughts became morose. Why could she not conduct her own life? Why could she not have chosen her own husband? Someone gentlemanly who appreciated her qualities.

Theo opened his eyes. He felt refreshed by his sleep. The dew was so heavy it lay on his brow like a cool poultice. It was always like this at the end of summer, the start of autumn – his favourite time of year, he sometimes thought, although the approach of winter made him melancholy, too. He sat up and only then remembered the tearful princess. There she lay, asleep now, more beautiful even than that picture he had kissed on the floor of his hole. But that had been a boy and she was indisputably a woman, although she seemed much younger now, perhaps only sixteen or seventeen, hardly older than himself. Her lips looked dark red, almost black in the moonlight, and her skin as white and cold as the stone of the giants' city. She had come out of that city, making everything good and bad in the day that was over. He wondered if he dared touch her.

Matilda felt the tentative finger on her cheek. It tickled and made her want to laugh. She was not sleeping and could see Theo quite clearly through her eyelashes. Rather too clearly, actually, as his face was still a nasty mess.

'Why ever don't you wash your face?'

Theo jumped back at her voice and then yelped from the pain in his leg. Would she punish him for presuming to touch her?

'Here. I'll do it with this straw. The dew's made it soaking.'

Theo did not dare move as she cleaned his face none too gently.

'At least you don't look like a Grendel now. Are you going to lie here all night? You're lucky to be alive.'

Matilda sat back like an excited child looking at her doll. That's what I am to her! thought Theo. A plaything. But then he remembered her tears and felt more sympathetic. 'Why were you crying?'

'Crying indeed! I never cry.'

Since this was clearly absurd, Theo closed his eyes again.

'If I cry, it's my business. Why do people usually cry? Because they're unhappy. What's so unusual about that? Everyone's unhappy. You should know that, you're a poet. Although, I must say, you don't look very poetic at the moment.'

Matilda's voice was high and beat in Theo's head like the hammers of the silver workers who had once visited the monastery. 'You are rich,' he said, 'and young. What more do you want?'

'You are stupid. I thought perhaps you weren't but you are. What is being rich and young to do with anything?' She emphasised the last word with heavy scorn so that her voice sounded like the hammer that made the hoops for the casks of mead.

'You are married to a strong thane.' Hardly had he got out the words before he felt himself blown back by a breath of fury.

'What do you know about that? You boy! You half-serf, half-monk! You nothing! You less than a piece of dung! You – you slave!'

Theo cowered. The wind of anger might blow itself out as quickly as it had risen. He watched her as she screamed and then closed his eyes.

'Open your eyes!' she shouted, but with less conviction.

'Not until you stop screeching.'

'I'm a king's daughter. You must do as I say.'

'You're unhappy.'

'I command you to open your eyes.'

Theo half opened one eye.

'Both eyes. Please.' Her voice tinkled prettily again.

'When I lay on that floor in the giants' city I decided to do something special. Something lasting.'

'You already write poetry. You're so young and hopeful.'

Theo thought this an odd comment on a man in his condition. He was finding it very difficult to keep both his eyes open owing to the swelling in the lids. However, he understood the spirit in which she spoke. What she resented was the freedom of his manhood. Women were always nearer to being slaves, even if they were kings' daughters. Yet he wanted to tell her about the vision he had seen in the giants' city under the stars. 'You've seen our monastery. Such as it is. Hardly a decent stone, so much rubble, wattle and daub, not much better than a peasant's cottage and certainly not a place to worship the Creator of all things.'

29

'Now we must praise the guardian of the heavenly
    Kingdom
The powers of the Creator and his thoughts
The works of the Father of glory . . .'

Matilda recited in a sing-song voice. 'Did you write that?'

'My songs are known only to a few.' Theo was dignified. 'The
abbot does write down the best but he goes nowhere so they go
nowhere either.'

'Then tell me your idea.'

'I want to bring down the whitest stones from the giants' city,
the whitest, the purest, the smoothest, and build a church that
reaches up to the candle of heaven!' Theo felt his voice rise with
the excitement of his vision. The church would have a tower that
would reach up higher than a bird could fly. He could no longer
see Matilda's face, partly because she had turned away from him
and partly because his eyes were so swollen that it was like looking
out of the slits in a warrior's helmet.

'There were no giants in that city.' Matilda's voice was matter-of-
fact. 'They were Romans.'

'It doesn't matter what you call them,' Theo mumbled sulkily.
His mouth was hurting him now, probably where she had rubbed
it with the straw. How absurd to try and explain a dream! The best
escape would be to faint.

'Don't you do that!'

What was she doing now? Prodding her fingers into his eyes.
The vixen. 'Leave me alone.'

'I won't have you keep shutting your eyes!' Now she grabbed
his shoulders and tried to shake him awake.

'Can't I faint without you pulling me around?'

It was a strange sight, the battered and bloody youth trying to
keep off the girl with her spidery black hair and inky blue cloak.
Even the moonlight could not make much sense of it. In fact, quite
opposite to the reality, it began to look as if they were thrashing
in fond embrace.

So busy were they that neither heard the ding, dong of the bell
for matins. Unfortunately, it stimulated Wilfrid. Stumbling out of
the door, he sniffed the cool air, relieved himself (right in the path,
with no thought for others) and then decided to take a reviving
little stroll. It would serve the double purpose of avoiding the
monks' chanting. Inevitably his steps took him towards the sweet
meadow where the bee-hives stood.

'What? Whatever? Who?' Self-expression had never been

Wilfrid's strong point. The sight of his wife in the arms of another produced a string of incomplete interrogatives followed by another of his infamous bull bellows.

Theo, just disentangled from Matilda, looked up to see an enraged Wilfrid charging towards him. Now surely it was death. So young. So undeserving. He could not even stand. Lord have mercy.

Matilda, too, looked up and her heart swelled vengefully as had her husband's. She could have expressed herself perfectly well in words of disgust, hatred and derision but the time for that was past. Screeching like the spirit of Thunor she ran forward. In her hand she held a dagger, jewelled prettily at the handle and cruelly pointed of blade.

Wilfrid did not wish to kill his wife (the death of a king's daughter would bring terrifying retribution) but neither did he wish to be killed by her. Turning sideways to present less of a target, he aimed to grab the knife and shoulder her to the ground. But Matilda was light on her feet and had not drunk a cask of mead. Neatly side-stepping, she allowed Wilfrid to crash forward. Then she came at him once more, dagger high. She laughed, the blood of warriors running strong in her veins.

By now they were among the hives, standing so peacefully, so quietly, with not a sound from their snug occupants. Probably Wilfrid did not realise what they were, for he made no attempt to avoid them as he swayed and lunged round Matilda's dagger.

'Coward!' she shouted, voice returning. 'Bully! Lion in a sheep's clothing!'

'When I catch you!' grunted Wilfrid.

'Baa baa!' mocked Matilda.

Ignoring the knife, Wilfrid threw his body at Matilda like a battering ram and, missing her once more, made heavy contact with the nearest hive.

'The bees!' warned Theo, who had too much at stake to enjoy the spectator sport.

The hive rocked and then fell. For a moment everything seemed stopped. But then as Wilfrid, who had half fallen, tottered backwards, a terrible noise filled the spot where he stood and the noise turned into a mass of wicked black bees. In a moment his head was surrounded. Flailing his arms, he rushed away, only to crash into another hive, which, like its fellow, tipped over and released its furious occupants. Screams and shouts rose above the buzzing. Wilfrid could be seen no more, except as a moving outline of bees. He was encased in the insects like a man encased by lightning.

'The bee-keeper!' hissed Theo to Matilda. She had run to him when the first hive fell and now lay beside him panting, knife held to her breast. They, too, were in danger and must not draw attention to themselves. 'He will be at matins.'

But, after all, Matilda needed not move, for Wilfrid's cries had penetrated the holy chant and here came the bee-keeper, robe tucked up, head bound in netting. Behind him, the other monks approached warily. Aelfric wrung his hands when he saw the scene. What a thing to happen to his guest, however uncivilised. And where, it struck him now with fresh horror, was the princess? Her attendant, too, looked for her mistress.

Theo felt Matilda put the dagger back under her robe. Her body was shaking.

'Will he die?'

'Brother Edwyn is a good bee-keeper. Look how he has drawn the bees away. Look, and you will see your husband.'

Matilda's view of Wilfrid was now blocked by the monks who gathered round. Bending low they prepared to carry him into the monastery.

'Old Brother Penda has more poultices than a bird has feathers.'

'I killed him.' Matilda spoke fiercely.

'He knocked over a hive. He was drunk. He didn't look where he was going.'

'I wanted to kill him.'

'That is not the same thing. Besides, who says he's dead? A big strong thane like that won't die of a few stings.'

Matilda did not answer. The moon was lowering itself and she felt as if her passion were going with it. It was her anger that had entered the bees. Why else should they swarm on to Wilfrid like that and leave her alone?

'You must go carefully,' said Theo as she stood up. 'They will be angry till morning. They will try to go back home to their queen but the darkness makes it difficult for them.'

Matilda ignored his warning and walked away from him through the thinning veil of bees. When none stung her she felt even more convinced of the truth of her statement. She had killed her husband.

As a pale dawn light washed across the meadow, Edwyn, who had stayed in case of further trouble, spotted Theo. He was a good sort and came over at once. 'Are you stung?' he began and then stopped as he saw Theo's face.

'Stung by a man,' replied Theo. Edwyn was not as handy with

healing herbs as Penda but Penda was otherwise occupied. 'Will you help me? In Christ's Name,' added Theo more forcefully as it struck him he had been waiting too long for attention.

'Your leg's broken,' said Edwyn. 'You'll need Penda to set it.'

'He's with the thane.'

'So you were here, then.'

'The thane it was who stung me.'

'The devil's sting,' commented Edwyn, who was known in the monastery for his simple belief in the power of God; he had prayed earnestly over the bees before separating them from Wilfrid. 'The thane stung you and then the thane was stung. Even at the end of such a hot day I was surprised that they should have attacked. Blessed is God who is in every living thing!'

Grateful though Theo was for Edwyn's taking his side, he felt more strongly than ever the need for medical attention. If Wilfrid had died, Penda could come to him.

'I will see if Penda can come to you.' Edwyn had a way of reading minds. 'The bees will not harm you. Look, light is clearing the darkness.'

For the second morning, Theo lay and watched the sun come up in less than pleasurable circumstances. One day stuck down a hole, the next crippled and unable to move. It seemed a very long time since he had lain in the warm dung and decided to visit the giants' city – the Roman city as the Princess Matilda had called it. Yet he had his dream and he must not regret paying the price for it. He did regret telling the princess. She was filled with black spirits who brought bad luck to all around her. Thinking it over, she was probably absolutely right in believing she had killed her husband. If he was dead.

Wilfrid was unrecognisable. He lay in the quarters reserved for guests – hardly more than a stable – and very occasionally groaned. Matilda, who was sitting with him, thought his face was as red as a lump of meat. It was a terrible sight, bloated, inhuman. Penda, however, was optimistic.

'He has not been stung in his mouth, which is a miracle. Thanks be to God. He has not been much stung on his body, thanks be to his tight leggings and the leather of his jerkin. It is his face, head and neck we have to worry about, towards which our prayers must be directed!'

'O Lord of all things, if it please you, let my lord live!' Matilda prayed so fervently that shivers ran down her back. If he did not die, she had not killed him.

Edwyn came in on this scene. The dawn light illuminated the

contrast between the pale and beautiful face of the young woman and the monstrous distortion of the man. The true spirit reveals itself in physical form, thought Edwyn. Because of this man, his happy bees were bewildered and upset.

'He lives,' he noted with some regret as he saw Wilfrid's chest rise. 'The stings do not turn to poison in his body?'

'We will see,' said Penda, placing a cloth over Wilfrid's entire face. 'He is very swollen.'

'Will the skin split?' asked Matilda anxiously.

'His skin is like a boar's.' Penda flicked a finger against the thane's neck. 'It's the blood that matters. In some the sting turns to poison, in others it irritates but does not kill. It is all in the will of God. There's nothing more I can do. He has drunk the herbs.'

'Theodore's leg is sticking out like a badly laid wattle,' said Edwyn in a matter-of-fact voice. 'Soon it will stay that way. His face looks nearly as bad as this bee-disturber's.'

Penda smiled slightly at this description of his patient – he was old and could think what he liked – and then gathered the skirts of his habit together. 'Is he, too, stung by bees?'

But Edwyn did not answer, leading him out silently to where Theo lay.

Once they had gone, Matilda dropped to her knees and, sensing her attendant hovering nervously at the door, called impatiently, 'Come, Juliana, join me in prayer. Quick!'

'The whole community is praying,' said the girl. 'No work is being done. Everybody is on their knees praying for the life of their great and noble lord.'

'Noble lord!' repeated Matilda with heavy irony. 'Noble lord, my nose!' But then she saw the girl's shocked face and remembered herself. 'Yes, we must pray fervently.'

The sun's rays splintered Theo's face. It was a useful diversion from Penda, who with the help of Edwyn was trying to straighten his leg. Edwyn sat on his thigh while Penda, huffing and puffing like a sow, pulled and twisted. Why couldn't he faint now? Theo wondered, and at that minute the sun shot into rays of green and blue and red and then turned altogether black.

Matilda could hear dim waves of monks' chanting. What would she tell her father, the King, if Wilfrid died? People died all the time but not in such ridiculous circumstances. Stung by bees. It was not a death for the great warrior Wilfrid thought himself – although there had been no attacks from outside England for many years and he had only been involved in putting down minor rebellions. What he really liked was hunting in the forests with his friends. Hunting and drinking. Both acceptable men's sports, she knew, but hardly entertainment for wives and sisters. What would she tell her friends? The humiliation of his death would reflect on her.

Matilda pulled herself up again. She was supposed to be praying, not investigating trivial matters of status and pride. What she must do was own up to her own wish to murder him. She must repent of that. Suddenly she saw that God was waiting. She must not only admit evil action but then repent of the spirit that had moved her to it. She must learn to love Wilfrid, to honour and obey him. She must promise God to be a good and humble wife to Wilfrid for the rest of his life. She had placed him in the jaws of death and now it was her responsibility to rescue him.

With this in mind, Matilda leaned close to the raw, swollen face and clasped her hands in fervent exhortation. But to her horror her good intentions were immediately blotted out with an immense hatred for Wilfrid. She loathed and despised him. She thought how he used her body, how he pushed himself into her with only a sense of his own pleasure; she thought how he enjoyed hurting others, how he had tortured that young boy outside, how he had only married her because she was a king's daughter, and she hated him more than ever. There was no possibility here of love, honour, and obey.

Bending her face into her hands, she began to sob passionately. The truth was that she still wanted him dead.

A hand touched her shoulder. 'Yes,' said a gloomy voice, which she recognised as Cuthbert's, 'he has gone to his judging. He has gone to face his Maker. *Requiescat in pace.*'

At first Matilda was unable to grasp what he was saying. How silently he must have approached. And then she understood. He thought she was crying because Wilfrid was dead. But he had died at her wish. She had killed him not once but twice.

The screams of the grieving widow penetrated the church where the monks prayed and caused them to stop in mid-chant, readjust and begin a new set of prayers. Faint, but still discernible, the cries reached Theo where he lay, comfortably now, under the shade of an apple tree. His leg was bound, his wounds dressed and he was even considering a composition on the theme of 'God's protection for his every lamb', perhaps. But now he listened, understood and tried to feel the proper emotion. 'Brute,' he said, softly enough not to startle a blackbird on the bough above his head. 'She is better off without him. May his soul find peace.'

The screams came again, even stronger and more agonised.

Chapter Three

Matilda fell into a dangerous fever. Penda said, 'She gives off as much heat as a bread oven.' Even when the hot weather – which had partly caused her husband's death for bees never attack in the cold – broke with a tremendous thunderstorm that delivered Aelfric's prayed-for rain, she remained burning.

'It is her husband trying to drag her down to hell with him,' commented Edwyn dourly.

'The King will not like to lose a daughter,' Cuthbert pointed out gloomily. 'He will look to blame someone.'

'Us,' said the abbot. 'We must pray harder.'

'If the fever doesn't burn itself out soon,' continued Penda, 'there'll be nothing left to pray for. She's like a set of knuckle-bones already.'

'We must sing.' The abbot sounded desperate. 'Tell Theodore to compose a special hymn.'

As Matilda sank deeper into her self-induced furnace of remorse – still, she could not feel proper contrition – Theo became stronger every day. Now he could even put a little weight on his bad leg, although he rather enjoyed hopping along with his sturdy ash plant.

However he could not help dwelling on poor Matilda's unhappy situation. The events of the night of the bees' attack were not at first very clear to him. After all, he had been partly unconscious with pain. But gradually his memory cleared and he saw her weeping, her confession of unhappiness, his confession of his dream, which she had received so disparagingly, and the arrival of Wilfrid. Afterwards Matilda had said she wanted to kill him and that had disguised what now concerned Theo: she had initially risen to attack her husband in defence of him, Theo, lying on the ground wounded and at his mercy. Matilda had actually saved his life. And now here he was, strong as the young ox he had always been (Theo had never looked like a poet), and there was she, according to Penda, with hardly more than a few days' fight left in her. There must be something he could do to help.

The call for a suppliant poem unlocked a torrent of words. In a matter of hours he had finished and even Aelfric's face lightened a little as he listened. He did not thank Theo but he did shout, 'Quick! Everyone! Into the chapel! As you are, as you are! God will overlook earthy feet in an emergency.'

Little from the outside reached Matilda's consciousness. She still had strength enough to struggle against Penda's drinks and her attendant's desire to keep her clean. What was the point when she planned to die? But otherwise she ignored everything and everybody. Only when Aelfric held the cross above her head she cried, 'No! No!' and turned her face away. No one had ever retreated so fast as poor Aelfric.

Now she lay, hot and malodorous, in the darkening room. Theo came beside her as silently as a cat.

'Princess.'

Matilda had almost forgotten the existence of the peasant boy. It was her husband's red, bloated face she saw night and day. She half opened her eyes and saw a youthful, smooth-skinned face pressed close to hers.

'You saved my life.' Theo's voice was gruff with sincerity. But he could see her expression did not change. Her eyes, which had dimmed to a greyish colour, stared at him vacantly. Somehow he must get through to her. He could hear his hymn being sung in the chapel and he was glad he had made it long because that gave him more time to be with her.

'You saved my life.' Theo repeated, in place of any other inspiration. Still no reaction. Kneeling down, he grasped her fingers, as brittle as dead twigs. 'You said you killed your husband.'

Even as he spoke Theo knew he had said the right thing. Matilda's eyes were no longer vacant but sharp with pain. How was he to know that Matilda had told no one of the terrible sin that had cast her into her fever?

'I killed him.' Her whisper was hardly comprehensible. 'And I could not pray for him to live.'

Theo pressed home his advantage. 'Whatever you did,' she seemed too convinced to make it worthwhile to argue about it, 'whatever you did, you did to save my life. Without you there, he would have killed me. You acted in my defence. You saved my life.'

From outside Theo could hear his hymn working towards its glorious climax.

'For the smallest bird looks to you for its protection.'

It sounded cheerful and made him suddenly irritated by Matilda's sick lassitude.

'God gives life and God takes it away.' He paused and then added severely, 'The sickness you are suffering from is the sin of pride.'

Feeling that he had done his best, repaid the debt he owed her as well as he knew how, he hobbled briskly from the hut.

Not long afterwards the monks and all who had sung, because even the labourers had been called in from the fields, came bustling out of the chapel. They were exhilarated by the sounds they had made and Cuthbert, usually so restrained, actually chased after Theo, who was heading for his beloved apple trees – which he now used as a rather inefficient shelter against the rain, for the leaves were crisping and a few had already fallen.

'Well done!' cried Cuthbert, clapping Theo on the shoulder. 'Crude, of course, for you are certainly the least educated poet I know, but powerful. I suspect Princess Matilda's sickness will reach a climax today and, with God's will, the fever will break.'

'And then you can go home,' said Theo. He could not have spoken to any other monk like that but he and Cuthbert had formed an unlikely friendship. The old scholar had discovered Theo's romantic feelings for the past. He had said more than once that if he were the abbot he would have taught Theo to read and write long ago. Unwilling to spoil his enthusiasm, Theo had thought it best not to reveal Aelfric's early and unavailing attempts.

'Yes. I'll leave as soon as I can,' agreed Cuthbert, his long, sallow face, which had grown longer and sallower over the last weeks, brightening with thoughts of educated converse. 'Being here is like living in the fifth century. But before I go I want to visit the Roman city beyond the forest and for that I will need the rain to stop and you to walk with the even beat of a soldier instead of hopping like a stork.'

'If that's your only problem!' cried Theo. Swinging his arm, he flung his ash plant with such force that it crossed a hedge and landed in the middle of a flock of sheep, who careered off as if the devil had entered them. 'Now I can walk,' boasted Theo, putting his bad leg firmly down. The twinge he felt hardly counted as pain. 'And in two weeks' time I shall run at least as fast as those sheep and certainly faster than you.'

Cuthbert gave a croaking laugh. 'You are a child but you have dreams, which is why you are a poet. Everybody else here only knows how to raise their eyes to heaven or down to their bread.'

Matilda knew she was getting better and although she had not exactly willed it, she did not combat it either. As Theo had said, she was in God's hands. She had tried very hard to die and if she had not succeeded perhaps it was not his will. However, she did not give up her special position at death's door easily and might have lingered on indecisively for some time if Penda had not caught sight of her trying to shoo out of the door a late butterfly. This was not the act of a sick woman.

'You are recovering,' he announced firmly and fetched her a particularly revolting gruel of stewed turnips and rue.

Soon he had forced her out of her bed and pushed her to the threshold of the hut where she could sniff the autumn smells. She had lain in her self-imposed exile from the world for seven weeks and now she could only stand, trembling and supported by Juliana, for a few moments at a time.

In her illness she had been uncooperative, and positively rude. In her rebirth – for that was how it felt to her – she was gracious and even, most unroyally, grateful. Her looks, too, had changed. She was skeletally thin and her mane of black hair had been cut to her ears, but it was not the revelation of bones under the white skin that surprised but her expression. Whereas before her face had been notable for its restless mobility, its moods alternating between joy, boredom and anger, it now generally showed the calmness of a much older woman. Her voice, too, which had been high-pitched and often shrill, seemed to have dropped several tones in register. She spoke slowly and only when she had something to say.

Cuthbert found her one afternoon standing near her husband's grave. The rain had at last stopped and a cool yellow light shone on the ploughed fields and the short cropped grass. The trees in the orchard were losing their leaves fast now and those remaining had more colours than the illustrations in a Bible. Matilda was probably looking at these. But Cuthbert had his own plan.

'The head-piece is hardly impressive.' He indicated the wooden cross set above Wilfrid's grave.

'No,' agreed Matilda.

'I am planning to visit the Roman city,' said Cuthbert, trying not very successfully to hide the strength of his feelings. What if she wanted to leave next week or the week after? 'Perhaps I could bring some stone or perhaps marble? A thane's death should be noted.'

Matilda looked at him in her new, thinking way.

'That is if you do not wish to hurry home.' Disconcerted by her silence, the monk blurted his fear.

Matilda continued to gaze at his face. 'I will not be leaving,' she said.

Thrilled at these words and assuming her to mean 'I will not be leaving yet', Cuthbert began almost to gabble, behaviour most unlike his usual self. 'I shall take Theodore and the men. They have been eating gluttonously and doing nothing. I will be as quick as I can but I must camp there. I must see—'

Matilda held up her hand, eventually halting Cuthbert's flow. 'Bring me Theodore,' she said. 'I wish to talk to him.'

Since the princess's recovery, Theo had become a celebrity. His poem begging God's mercy had been copied into the flyleaf of the gospel book which sat on the altar. Even his enemies could not disagree that it was on the evening of the singing of his songs that the princess had stepped backwards from the jaws of death.

Naturally Theo did nothing to disabuse this notion. After all, his words might well have done the trick, even if not the words sung to the greater glory of God. Although it was all in His hands anyway . . . Theo was light-headed with the joys of recovery and longing to start the trip to the city. When Cuthbert told him to go to see Matilda, he jogged along, singing heartily as he went.

He sobered up a little as he saw where she stood among the graves. But all the inhabitants of the monastery had become used to the cloaked figure wandering in their midst. She passed among them like a ghost, looking into no one's face and no one looked at hers. That was a surprise saved for Theo.

'Thank you, Theodore.' She gazed at him seriously.

'I wasn't busy.'

The old Matilda would have been impatient with his cheeky unwillingness to understand but now she explained quietly, 'Thank you for coming to me when I was ill.'

Theo ducked his head, embarrassed. He was an unlettered peasant, after all, and she was a king's daughter. Besides, she was a woman, so dignified and remote. Before it had been different. First he had been in such pain. And then she had been dying. 'Thanks be to God for your recovery,' he recited, piously.

'Yes. Indeed. I do.' She paused, rubbing her hands together in what Theo failed to see was nervousness. 'Brother Cuthbert tells me he is going back to the Roman city. And you go too.'

'God willing.' He knew he was safe with God but the urge to

clown was irresistible. He began to hop on his bad leg. 'See? When I can do twenty, we're off.'

Matilda bent her slow gaze to his knee. 'It's not healed very straight.'

'It's strong. It bends. What more do I need?' Like a child he demonstrated these abilities, bobbing and kicking.

But Matilda turned away sharply. She was hiding a wave of colour that covered her face from forehead to chin and part of the way down her neck. It was the sight of his legs, naked under his short tunic. They were still sunburned from the long summer and covered with a fuzz of golden hairs. They were a boy's legs, not sinewy like Wilfrid's, which she could only think of with a shudder, and yet the sight made her blush more than any part of her husband's body. Matilda put her hands to her head. She was weak, that was all, weak in the head as well as her body.

Seeing he had lost his audience, perhaps offended her, Theo stopped dancing. As he stood still, her emotion communicated itself to him, not precisely as regards his legs but enough to make him feel self-conscious. This, in turn, made him cross. What did she want of him? Why did she not speak?

'I want some stone.' Her voice was stilted and loud.

'Stone?' Theo stared stupidly.

Matilda shook her head impatiently. A scarf that she had taken to wearing over her shorn head slipped backwards showing the hair trying to spring black and curly again. 'You know. Your plan. Your dream. It's all your idea.' For a moment the old petulant Matilda reappeared. Then she returned to sober precision. 'I need a great deal of stone. The very best stone. We will have to find ways of bringing it here. I shall send for stone-masons and other craftsmen. Here, in this remote valley, we will build the most beautiful church in Wessex. It will be a memorial. It will be my penance.' Here she paused and gave Theo the sort of flashing look which was easily interpreted to mean 'and you'd better not ask me any questions about that'.

But Theo only stared. She had stolen his dream. He did not know whether to be pleased or furious. With her in charge, the dream would certainly become reality; she had power and money and, he now saw, determination. But it would not be his any more. Yet she was bringing it to him and, besides, how could he say no?

'I'm only a poor boy,' said Theo temporising. 'Hardly more than a serf.'

'Ha!' A contemptuous snort came surprisingly from her pale set face but it cheered Theo.

'What do you want from me?'

'We have to do it together. I shall become a nun and dedicate my life to God. Soon my presence will attract other well-born women and then I shall become abbess. My aunt in whose nunnery I studied began in just this way. Brother Cuthbert shall go to Rome to seek papal authority and I shall beg grants of land from my father. It will be a double house, however, because I do not want to destroy what there is already here, even though on so meagre a scale. I shall take over the running of the whole abbey.'

'You are so sure,' interrupted Theo, putting his words like pebbles in the face of a torrent.

'My aunt looked to emulate the great Abbess Hyld of Whitby and so shall I. Everything will be perfectly regulated. You will become a monk, of course. And in time, you will take over the monks' side of the monastery. We will live separately but join together in our praise of God. While you are exploring the Roman city with Brother Cuthbert, I shall travel to my father and get his royal permission. He will be thrilled, as it happens. He always thought me out of control and will be amazed and delighted that Wilfrid's death has affected me in this way. Besides he is a great believer in "prayers for the King". That will be your second job – after organising the stone. You will write a splendid "Prayer for the King". It will be splendid but not long since we will say it constantly.' Matilda paused, looked at Theo's stunned face and gave him a ferocious glare. 'You must show yourself worthy of my trust. You have become my confidant. Sometime you will be my confessor.'

Theo sat down. He had jumped too much and his knee hurt, but it was more than that. Theo was allergic to authority. At the first sign of someone trying to organise him into a consistent and useful form of activity, he felt a violent need to do the opposite of what was wanted. That was why he had never been able to learn to read or write and why he sat down now. Sitting down, in the most relaxed and passive attitude he could assume, instinctively presented itself to him as the reaction most directly in opposition to Matilda's domineering speech.

'Stand up! Who said you could sit down? Stand up, will you?' She had not shouted like this since Wilfrid's death. How could this common boy insult her so? Her only wish was to elevate him. And what did he do but sit down! 'You're sitting down and smiling! Don't you realise what I'm saying is important? Don't you understand?'

Still Theo refused to stand up or pay attention. Let her say what she liked. He might not be a nobleman but he was also a free man, not a slave. And a maker of poems. She was a royal widow who had become confused in her mind. Although she talked of serving God, she thought only of herself.

Abruptly Matilda sat down. She sat erect, her thin back as straight as a rod. She stared ahead.

Theo, sneaking a look, thought her nose was as thin and white as a sucked chicken bone. Her chin, too, was nearly as pointed. Clearly, she would not give up easily. And she had sat down.

'The grass is wet, my lady,' he said deferentially.

'Don't call me my lady!'

'You are still not well.'

'If you're implying that I am not well enough to make important plans for the future, then you are a foolish child. Not, as I imagined, a kindred soul.' The words 'kindred soul', came out from between her twig-snapping lips more like an insult than praise. Theo was impressed nevertheless. 'Kindred soul' would sound well in one of his poems.

'Surely you know', continued Matilda, set to make up for all her weeks of silence, 'that people only achieve great and unusual feats when they are in a great and unusual state of mind. It is true that I am not well. I am physically decrepit and mentally unstable. However, this has allowed my spirit to float free – and my spirit fixed on your dream of resurrecting the pagan stones in the cause of Christianity.'

'Is that what I said?' murmured Theo, forgetting to be quiet in admiration at his own inspiration.

'Not really.' Matilda leaned forward. 'Your ideas were confused. But', she continued hurriedly as she noticed Theo's stubborn look descending again, 'without you I would never have thought of it. We are, in God's eyes, kindred spirits.'

That again. Theo sighed. She was probably right. God would be on her side. Anyway, she had a stronger will than he. Besides, he really was worried about the wet grass in a graveyard that everyone knew was bursting with unclean spirits. 'If you stand up, I'll stand up.'

'Certainly.' Matilda bobbed to her feet with an energy that would have astonished Cuthbert.

Side by side they stood facing the valley. It was dusk now; the sun had dropped behind them and a white mist was curling up from the fields even to the edge of the woods. It was a scene of absolute peace.

'If I become a monk,' said Theo thoughtfully, 'I won't ever be able to have a woman.'

'Oh, please!' Matilda frowned, but that was partly because she felt that blush beginning again. 'You can't be so – so base.'

'It's all very well for you, you've had a husband.' Theo spoke simply. It was surprising that he found himself able to talk to her about these things. Perhaps it was the darkness. Perhaps it was because they were 'kindred souls'.

'You should be glad to keep the purity of your body unsullied.'

'Anyway,' continued Theo, who was pretty sure that his purity was sullied already, 'I'll never learn to read or write, so I can't become a monk.'

'We will see.' Matilda used the voice of one who knew she had won the war and was not willing to risk victory for the sake of another battle. 'Just tell me you will dream for me as well as yourself when you go to the Roman city, please.'

Theo looked at Matilda's face. Under the ever-darkening sky, it looked as pale as a cooked fish and her eyes, which he had used to think blue and then grey, now seemed as black as pools of water on a moonless night. 'I have to dream,' he said, 'and I will do what you have asked me. But you must not try to make me into something other than myself.'

'I promise,' said Matilda solemnly. 'Give me your hand. In the Name of God, let us clasp hands.'

Theo held out his large square hand. In a second he felt Matilda's hand, cold and fragile, slip into his. He was reminded for the second time that evening of a fish but this time of the little silvery trout that he used to catch from the monks' ponds. He was a boy then and enjoyed the feeling of power over a living creature. Now he closed his warm fingers tenderly.

Matilda, who had thought she was holding out her hand in Christian and businesslike confirmation of their agreement, felt his fingers tighten round hers with the most powerful emotions. Her heart thumped, her legs became weak and she had an irrepressible desire to shut her eyes. Yes. That must be it. She was still ill. She had stayed up too long into the dank night. The warmth and steady pressure of his hand had caused her to relax and if she closed her eyes she would certainly faint.

'Ah.' With a slight exhalation of breath, Matilda shut her eyes and drifted downwards to the ground.

She had fallen across the fresh bump of her husband's grave. Theo looked at her for a moment, thinking that her posture seemed to dedicate their cause to Wilfrid, its inspiration. Then, after making a careful sign of the cross, he lifted her in his arms and carried her back to her hut. After all, she was weak as a woman as well as strong as a warrior. He would bring her fresh milk each day and tell her that if she did not drink it she would never become an abbess. Abbot Aelfric, for example, had never missed a day through illness and the old abbot, though unwell for a long time, had never allowed himself to miss even matins. He could not imagine her getting up in the middle of a cold winter night, or fasting for the length of Lent, or staying on her knees for hours at a time. Physical strength was not everything, of course, but it did help.

Matilda, becoming conscious, listened to the steady beat of Theo's heart and tried to convince herself that it was the church bell calling the faithful to prayer. Soon the bell would hang not in a crumbling timber frame but a solid stone tower. Cuthbert had told her that in Rome when the time came for nones, bells rang from all corners of the city, 'ad majorem Dei gloriam'.

Theo heard the murmured Latin and his faith in her was partially restored. She was educated and a king's daughter. What she willed would take place. 'For the wonders of God's work are beyond our understanding.'

'Amen,' rejoined Matilda piously, although she did not ask to be set down.

Chapter Four

Abbot Aelfric was a holier man than his irritable temperament made him appear. Monastic orders had not brought him peace, as he had hoped when young, but anxiety. Prayer was helpful but he still felt himself dragged down by the daily burdens of organisation. The odd thing was that he had drawn the burdens on himself by becoming abbot. He had been elected, of course, but he was not so popular that he could not have withdrawn. He was a worrier by nature, critical of himself and others, a perfectionist in an imperfect world. 'O Lord, who knows all things, make me humble to your will, for you know best at all times!'

When Aelfric heard and understood Matilda's plan he saw that God had at last sent him a cross that would enlarge his capacity for anxiety into real suffering. He was to be deposed, that was what it came down to, by a young woman whose idea of communication with her Maker was as profound as a sheep's. Cuthbert was another matter, of course, and Cuthbert had been sent to break the news to him.

'We must think of the good of the monastery,' said Cuthbert, his hands furled inside his sleeves. 'At the moment you are a small isolated community, hardly separate from the peasant villages—'

'Oh, brother!' protested Aelfric.

'Your calling is different, I admit. You are monks, good and prayerful monks. But your manner of existence is rudimentary, unfitting to followers of the Order of Benedict.' Here Cuthbert paused and looked enquiringly, 'You do follow St Benedict as far as I can determine?'

'Yes. Quite,' agreed Aelfric, a little confused. The truth was that he was not absolutely certain on the point. It was so long since he had travelled from the monastery and the last abbot had ruled more on personal authority than any written ordinance. 'We had a fire,' said Aelfric, against his will, sounding apologetic. 'The books—'

'That's it.' Cuthbert seized on the point enthusiastically. 'Where are the books, the pictures, the holy relics which distinguish a well-run monastery?'

'I teach the postulants myself.' Aelfric found some dignity at last in the thought of the illiterate boys he had taught to read and write.

'But what is the use if there are no books for them to read?'

'We have the Bible. We have the psalms. We have all that is necessary for a servant of God.'

'Yes. Yes. Necessary. But is that enough? Monasteries should be a centre of study. Of deepening knowledge. Of beauty. Of culture—' Feeling himself becoming carried away, Cuthbert stopped abruptly.

'We have no money,' said the abbot sulkily. Oh, how right he had been to fear the arrival of the princess and her husband! Yet never had his deepest fears imagined such a conversation as this. Somewhere in the back of his mind he knew there was an argument against Cuthbert's but it was only later on his knees in chapel that he remembered that Christ himself had only been a poor carpenter's son. The trouble was, he, Aelfric, believed in learning. When he was young he had made a pilgrimage to France and there seen a great library. He knew what Cuthbert meant by culture. It meant worrying more about the doctrine of the Holy Trinity than why the barrels of mead were leaking.

'We are small,' he said, 'only seventeen monks, and because we are small in number, we are only given a small sum by the King. May God give him long life.'

'Amen,' agreed Cuthbert. 'But that is my whole point. God has seen fit to give you an opportunity to be a leading light in a great new venture. The princess is loved by her father. When he hears her plans for honouring her dead husband, he will press on her money. He will be inspired and so should you. I am planning a long trip to Rome in order to collect fine paintings and sacred relics – and books, of course. You, too, might plan something of the sort. It is easy to become out of touch in a place like this. The river of holy Church runs wide and deep but we must not allow ourselves to be left behind on a piece of brackish side-water. Gird yourself, Abbot Aelfric! God has challenged you to a great undertaking!'

Faced with such eloquence, Aelfric demurred no longer. 'As God wills,' he said bowing his head. 'However,' here he raised his eyes to Cuthbert's, 'it will be appropriate, I think, for me to accompany the princess to her father, the King, and substantiate her plea with mine.'

'But I—' began Cuthbert, who had allocated this role to himself.

'You are off to look at stone in the Roman city. We must not delay the project. Besides, you are right. I have been here too long without outside contact. I shall leave a deputy to watch "the brackish side-water" and take a swim nearer the centre of the river.'

'As you will,' agreed Cuthbert, not without admiration for the quick learning capabilities of what he had previously seen as a dim pastoral prelate. 'We must pray for good weather and no heathen raids.'

'There have been none here in my lifetime,' said Aelfric firmly.

'Ah, but what reason do they have to come here? However, we must remember we are soldiers of Christ and take heart.'

'Amen. Amen.'

The wet autumn hastened the cold, cheerless days of winter. The monastery was not well situated. Wind and mists became trapped in the valley as the sun did in the summer. The first frost of the season coated the grass and blackened the more delicate plants and remaining vegetables. It was not a good time to travel with early mornings, long days on the move and nights on the hard, cold ground. It was particularly unwise to travel if, like Matilda, you were recovering from a debilitating fever.

'You are not sensible, my lady,' advised Cuthbert, who still had an eye on his own chances of getting back to the court.

'You are right,' said Matilda, 'and I am proud of it.'

They spoke at a meeting held in the refectory. The princess had taken her seat at the head of the table, causing the two monks, Aelfric and Cuthbert, to sit on either side of her. Further down sat Juliana and other senior monks. Refusing to sit down, but somewhere in the dark corners of the hall, Theo watched.

'With the help of God, we will make a new future for ourselves,' said Matilda.

I'm surprised she didn't conduct the opening prayers, thought Aelfric dourly. And then executed the subliminal sign of the cross, which helped him in time of selfish anxiety. 'Amen,' he said aloud.

'Amen,' echoed all the other monks.

Matilda frowned. She could 'Amen' with the best of them but they had already spent nearly two hours of spiritual preparation in the church before reaching this point. She began again firmly, 'We shall build a new church, and a dormitory and refectory for my nuns. We will pray in the church together but otherwise our lives will be separate. The abbess and abbot only will communicate about matters that affect the running of the community. Even then there shall be an iron grille between us. However, we will both attend the yearly synod. We will be a centre of learning attracting scholars from all over the country, and as such we must keep in touch with the outside world. Brother Cuthbert has promised . . .'

From his dark corner, Theo coughed and rustled a pile of old ashes. Speeches bored him. Sermons were usually given in Latin so he was able to ignore them and work at his compositions. But Matilda spoke in the vernacular. She was standing now, her pale drawn face brightened by enthusiasm. She had exchanged her blue cloak with its brilliantly jewelled brooch for a plain black woven robe similar to the monks' except that she wore a white kerchief under the black hood. The effect was striking, as if a magpie had landed in their midst. If it was supposed to disguise her royal beauty it did not succeed although it accentuated her beaky nose, which winter cold had tipped red. Her attendant was wearing the same garb as if it were a uniform.

'. . . also the art of illustrating the texts in which some of our countrymen have become so proficient . . .' continued Matilda.

Theo had a strong urge to run out of the hall and throw himself into the cold night air. He was not afraid of frost and damp: there was always a cow to huddle against. He had only just passed his sixteenth birthday. What frightened him was learning and libraries and proficient illustrators and women who talked and talked and talked. Bang. Bang. Bang. Theo began to kick the wall. Sensibly, he used his good leg for he wanted the strength to kick away some nice chunks.

Matilda, in her exhilarated state of mind, was the last to hear the noise. What she noticed was that she had lost the attention of her audience, although they were too polite actually to turn their heads. Her brain was pounding with ideas but this, she had to admit, was an exterior thump.

'Theo!' She swivelled, stared, was scandalised and pointed an accusing finger. Another lump of grit and plaster fell from the wall.

Theo stirred it with his toe. 'Rotten,' he said, with a calm that did not accord with his violent actions.

'Yes.' Matilda pretended to understand his point. 'We will hope to rebuild this refectory at a later stage. There is much to be done and many years in which to do it. We must—'

Thump. Thump. Thump. Theo had begun again, this time with even more effect. Loosened rubble fell down the wall.

Everyone turned to watch. The abbot, who might have felt it a duty to control him, did nothing. After all, the princess had made it clear who was in charge. Let her deal with the bumptious youth. No one else could.

'Theodore is a very important part of our plan,' began Matilda in a flustered manner quite unlike her previous dogmatic dignity.

Thump. Thump. Thump. Theo did not look up. It was doubtful if he even heard.

'Theo will learn how to become a monk—'

'What?' interrupted Aelfric, and then, giving a slight smile, was quiet.

'Theo has God's ear,' continued Matilda, sounding both flustered and defensive. 'Theodore has God's ear and God's voice and God's inspiration. It was his idea that we should bring down the great stones to make a glorious shrine to Christ. He and Brother Cuthbert will travel to the Roman city.'

At this, Cuthbert shook his head. Of course he knew the princess never listened to a word he said but she must have some recollection of his lesson: it was he who had told her the source of stone for Winchester, Tewkesbury, Salisbury. Still, it was true, those were all large centres and here they were in a backwater. If it had been Theo's idea which made perfect sense, then he deserved credit.

Thump. Thump. Thump.

Was that why he was kicking the wall? Apparently not, for Matilda's kind words had had no effect.

'I shall travel to my father and ask for his support.'

The monks had settled into the thumping now. They were used to Theo's ways. Penda was glad to be sitting down at a time when he was usually in the fields. Edwyn was worrying about how the proposed building would disturb his bees. By the sound of it, it could take years. Most of the other monks wore a placid expression not far from an open-eyed sleep.

Matilda walked over to Theo. Juliana followed her. The two women stood, one behind the other, facing the kicking man.

'One for sorrow, two for you.' Theo, foot moving a fraction more gently, looked round at Matilda mockingly.

'What is the matter, Theo?' Matilda put her hands together in an attitude of prayer or supplication.

Aelfric leaned across the narrow table till his round tonsure was an inch from Cuthbert's long narrow one. From above they made two interlocking circles or a figure of eight. 'Why does she sweeten him?'

Cuthbert did not answer immediately. He had seen more of the

51

world than Aelfric. He liked Theo and he had known Matilda since she was a child. 'They are both young.'

During this whispered conversation, little had changed by the wall. Theo was still kicking, although more gently, and Matilda, with her lady behind her, stood as before, although silently.

Several more minutes passed like this, in which the squeaking of the starlings in the roof could be heard as a descant to the thumping. Then Matilda turned to the monks. 'We shall meet again, God willing, after our journeys.' She turned and, still followed by Juliana, walked swiftly from the room. The monks, who could track the direction of any footstep in the area of the monastery, heard her pass by and enter the church. There was a collective sigh of relief.

The moment she had gone, Theo stopped kicking and sat on the floor. He rubbed his big toe for a moment or two – he had tried to use the sole of his sandalled foot but not always successfully – and then began to fill up the hole in the wall. He did it carefully, without haste.

Those monks who were not asleep watched interestedly. No one quite understood but on the whole all felt the rightness of Matilda's humiliation. Humility, they all knew and it had been a hard lesson to learn, is the first requirement for he – and for she – who wishes to become a servant of God.

The forest was no longer black. Cuthbert, Theo and their companions rode under a whirling canopy of colour. The trees were predominantly oak; their frilly-edged leaves, turning every shade of gold, floated across the horses' path. But there were also a few beeches, their copper leaves clinging tenaciously to the branches, and now and again they came across a yew, as mysteriously dark as ever, or an ash, from which the leaves tumbled like water. The light, for it was a clear day with a sky more white than grey, struck through the emptying branches. When they sat down at midday for a hunk of bread and cheese, Theo looked at Cuthbert with wistful eyes. 'If we stopped for an hour or two, I could compose such a verse!'

'You would catch a cold on the damp ground,' replied Cuthbert tartly. 'Besides, such a verse as you are imagining has already been written.' Standing up with his hands joined and his face upturned to the falling leaves, Cuthbert declaimed:

'Praise we the Fashioner now of Heaven's fabric,
The majesty of His might and His mind's wisdom,
Work of the world-warden, worker of all wonders,
How He, the Lord of God everlasting,
Wrought first for the race of men Heaven as a
    rooftree'

Here he paused and pointed solemnly upwards before continuing.

'Then made He Middle Earth to be their mansion . . .'

'That is a great song.' Theo spoke slowly. 'I have never heard such a song.'

'You know nothing. You are a poor boy who has been blessed with a gift. This singer was also unlearned but when he recognised God had chosen him as his mouthpiece, he was humble. He studied and became an obedient and holy monk.'

'A poet and an obedient monk?' Theo jumped up and looked around him wildly as if he would have liked to run.

Cuthbert took his arm. 'We are given the right of free will.'

'You are setting a trap for me. You. The abbot. The King's daughter. Even the beauties of nature are a trap set to catch me.' Here he broke away from Cuthbert and ran a few paces before turning round again. 'Don't you know, a caged bird never sings!'

'Rubbish!' called Cuthbert with equal energy. 'Caged linnets sing at the lintels of a thousand humble cottages. If you wish to use poetic imagery, always be sure it is based on the facts. Besides, and most important of all,' he shouted this even more loudly as Theo looked likely to disappear in a confetti of golden leaves, 'the smallest cage is as spacious as earth itself to him who entrusts his life to . . .'

But Theo, muttering and groaning like a madman, had finally escaped.

'. . . God,' finished Cuthbert, crossing himself. He expected this expedition to last for at least two weeks, weather permitting. There would be plenty of time for further interesting conversations.

Matilda expected her journey to last five days. She was not strong and her father's palace was many miles south-east. Wilfrid's men accompanied her and they expressed their joy at escaping the monastery in much the same way as his dogs, which were also coming. Bounding and leaping, running low and fast, stopping short suddenly with their legs braced, all the time yelling and bellowing and barking.

Matilda, Juliana and Aelfric, who were the only three on horseback, watched them without comment. Matilda did not like to see their wiry bodies; they reminded her of Wilfrid. She would make the new monastery in his name but she did not like to think about his body. Her own body, though so wasted from illness, had become curiously swollen round the middle, which made her graceless and uncomfortable on a horse. She contrasted this ugly distortion with her companion's all-over roundness. Juliana's body looked equable and beautiful. Such thoughts, particularly the desire to be beautiful again, made her ashamed because she knew they were unfitting for one who was to devote her life to God.

Apart from her own unsatisfactory body, her husband's dead body and Juliana's pretty one, there was the problem of Theo. Since his knees and legs had first caused her to flush, she had been caught out in the same way at least once every day. Gradually she had come to realise that God was using the devil to tempt her. It was a test. Theo was strong and young and handsome, a pure, simple boy who had never touched a woman. She might have to turn away from him but he never turned from her. His far-seeing eyes looked at hers, unveiled. This, she told herself, was cold water on her ardour.

However, it was a relief to know that she would not be seeing him for several weeks, even if the relief carried with it a sense of disappointment. The day would be less bright without him.

'I hope your men won't become out of control,' said Aelfric dubiously. He was nervous; his heart beat as fast as a woodpecker's beak. Why ever had he wanted to leave the safe routine of the monastery?

'If necessary I'll whip them.' Matilda was calm. It was her will that carried them steadily further from the peaceful valley. 'But it won't be necessary. These men belonged to Wilfrid. They are loyal to him beyond death. They will do whatever his widow tells them. I am carrying Wilfrid's sword to the King. He will receive it and decide on their future. Until then, they will serve us.'

'That's all very well,' began Aelfric fussily – if only his heart would slow down – 'but they look terribly over-excited to me. What if they—' He interrupted himself with a scream of fright for two of the men had taken out their swords and were racing towards them.

'They're like children,' commented Matilda as the men saluted her with a volley of battle cries. 'Just remember they're on foot

54

and we're on horseback. By tomorrow they'll be walking with about as much enthusiasm as old Brother Penda.'

'That's true.' Reassured, Aelfric took his hand away from his heart. 'After all, we must all place our trust in God.'

'Amen,' echoed Matilda reverentially but her heart did a sudden turn bringing a strip of red to her pale cheeks. The movement, the men's excitement, noise and shouting after so many weeks of holy quiet had made her realise she was going home. She was going to her father, the court, her friends and kinsmen. Digging her heels into her horse's side, she bolted away from the surprised Aelfric.

It was dark when Theo and Cuthbert arrived at the Roman city, a bad time to set up camp in strange surroundings. The two strong lay brothers they had brought with them and the two peasant boys showed their unease by making a huge fire on the edge of the forest. They had never seen such a place. To them the fallen stones looked as if they might come alive and march towards them like an army of ghosts. The fire gave them warmth and light and protection. All six fell asleep with flames reflecting in their eyes.

Theo was woken just before dawn by a venomous hissing. Before he opened his eyes, he imagined a snake as long and green as Eve's tempter. With eyes half open he thought he saw an adder darting under the nearest stone. When he sat up he saw the rain hissing as it fell on the embers of the fire and he felt the drops on his bare head.

Since the others slept untroubled, he did not bother to wake them, but stood up, stretching and yawning. The water was refreshing, the bounty of God. He said his prayers as he walked, pleased with the prospect of a day among the ruins. With Cuthbert as his guide, he would learn such things. As soon as it was light enough he would pay a return visit to Marsyas and Apollo, the pagan gods who had nearly been the scene of his undoing. Would it be wrong, Theo wondered, to re-use such a magnificent floor somewhere in the monastery? After all, they were only young men and one, like himself, a singer of songs. He must ask Brother Cuthbert this and other points. It was true, what the monk had said, he was an illiterate boy who knew nothing. Despite all his dreaming he did not even know, for example, in what shape they should build the church. An arch was about all he could imagine, an arch pointing to heaven. He had actually seen one still intact standing in this city on his last visit.

Cuthbert woke in an extremely bad temper. He was cold, stiff and very wet. I'm too old for this madness, he told himself. It would be hard enough in the summer but at this time of year it was foolhardy. He became even crosser when he noted Theo's absence. He should have made up the fire, cooked the eggs they had brought with them, put out bowls to collect water. Cuthbert stood up, stamping noisily to wake the others. But then, suddenly, like a vision, the ruins of the city appeared out of the misty dawn, and he found all his ill temper vanishing. After issuing a few orders, he too wandered off into the city, lips moving with his morning prayers, although with the mechanical speed of a life-time's familiarity.

Theo had found an arch and stood under it while the rain fell on either side in silver sheets. It was thus that Cuthbert found him and registered severe misgivings.

'Theodore!' he called, his voice echoing among the mighty stones. 'What are you doing?'

'I've found an arch,' replied Theo joyfully.

'But why are you standing under it?' Cuthbert came closer and waited for an answer. The boy was not serious, that was what worried him. He was a striker of attitudes, he had no depth, no conception of thought. He acted not out of principle but out of an instinctive sense of what would be most effective. He made pictures out of life, rendering everything superficial. He made pictures with his poetry, too, but there at least the pictures were dedicated to God. Would such a man ever be fitted to be a monk?

'I'm standing under the arch . . .' replied Theo with no idea of how to finish the sentence. Then he waved his hand and laughed. It was funny that neither of them had considered one perfectly good reason. 'I'm standing under the arch so I don't get wet. You should join me. This is an enormous arch, big enough for the middle of our church. Can't you just imagine how grand it will look, Brother Cuthbert?' This time his laugh turned into a whoop and he sang out:

'Praise we the Fashioner now of Heaven's fabric,
The Majesty of His might and His mind's wisdom . . .'

'At least your memory's good.' Cuthbert joined him resignedly. 'Just look at the size of these stones. We'll need a long team of oxen to transport them.'

'Work of the world-warden, worker of all wonders . . .'

56

'Yes. Yes. We'll have to see how deeply the ends are buried. A few hours' digging will soon bring you down to earth.'

'Then made He Middle-Earth their mansion . . .'

'You skipped two lines.'

'I'm hungry. I'll dig after breakfast for as many hours as you want. Brother Cuthbert?' Theo paused for a second.

'Yes, Theodore.'

'Will you teach me my letters so I can read?'

Perhaps it is only youth that makes him so high-spirited, thought Cuthbert, following slowly behind Theo's flying figure. He had never asked to be taught anything before. Or perhaps it is his youthful energy and beauty, which make me assume his reactions are nearer to an animal's than a mature man's.

'We should wait to transport the stones till spring, if not summer,' said Cuthbert wearily, 'or the oxen will sink in the mud.'

'We can lay wattles.'

Theo was inexhaustible. Each night he saw arches and walls and stained-glass windows grow in the fire. Each day he leaped up to discover new areas for plunder. Between times he tried to make out the letters in Cuthbert's psalter.

'I am your master,' Cuthbert sometimes muttered, rubbing his chilblained hands together. 'You must let me take decisions.'

'And the first shall be last and the last shall be first,' suggested Theo. He respected the monk for his learning but also thought he was cowardly and old womanish. He would be just as happy to make careful notes of everything they had seen and then leave it to crumble into dust. Theo had sometimes caught a look of reluctance in his face when the men had taken their tools to dismantle a wall. He was more interested in the past and thought it more important than the future. 'We should make use of this cold dry weather. Who knows when the rain may return – or even snow?'

'I am old,' admitted Cuthbert after a long pause. 'I am a monk, not a mason. I shall go back to the monastery and await Princess Matilda's return.'

'Tell them to prepare the oxen,' said Theo, and then added, to cheer up Cuthbert who indeed looked old and sad, 'Leave me your book and I shall study when my arms are tired. Perhaps I'll even write my own songs by the time I return.'

'You are a good boy, although hardly likely to become a scholar.' Cuthbert pulled up his hood over his head. The day had been bright but now a cool mist was rolling out of the forest and creeping in furled white waves over the ruins. He shivered and turned to look where the fire burned in dull embers. After their evening meal they would make it blaze nearly as high as the trees. 'Tomorrow I will go early. Three of the men can come with me and bring back provisions.'

'And the oxen,' said Theo, clutching his arm. 'And we'll need eight or nine or ten more men. As many as can be spared. There's not much to do in the fields at this time of year.'

'I'll do what you ask.' Cuthbert bowed his head. He fought against a longing for a cell, a bed and a crucifix.

The monastery was quiet without Aelfric and Theo. The monks remaining followed Cuthbert's scholarly rule obediently but found ways of disappearing to mend the wattles or watch that the folds were properly cleaned out. They were all of humble stock, picked by the old abbot and not used to more civilised ways. When Theo made his first return with three cartloads of stones, they stood about him gaping.

'They are right, you know,' said Cuthbert. 'You will never put this together without a master mason. You will have to send to Gaul. There they have such people and glaziers too.'

'Princess Matilda will bring us everything we need,' said Theo obstinately. He was tired. His feet and hands were sore and itching from the cold. He looked at the pile of stones tipped out on to a flattish area by the already existing church. They had seemed so many on the journey; now they seemed so few. 'We will go back for more after a few days of rest,' he said.

'And prayer.' Cuthbert shivered and put his hands in his sleeves.

Theo had made four more journeys before any word came from Matilda. As his piles of stones grew, he hoped on each return to see the princess standing beside them, but on his last journey he found that Aelfric had come back without her.

It was cold now and they sat in the hall, crowding close to the big fire. On the long table were piled some of the things Matilda had sent: a carved chest filled with linen suitable for well-born nuns, a portrait of St Catherine, an iron grille to cover the window through which the abbot should speak to the abbess, a newly made silver chalice for the altar, several lengths of embroidered material for vestments and an intricately worked censer. Around the table were a set of ten chairs for the nuns' refectory and a statue of the Virgin Mary.

'Where are the books?' asked Cuthbert as Theo looked and

wondered. He had never touched cloth that felt silkier than a calf's flank. He put it down lest his rough fingers tore it.

'You are to arrange that.'

'And the stone-masons and glaziers?'

Theo came over to the fire. 'They are being sought.'

There was a long silence. The question that both Theo and Cuthbert wanted to ask hung heavily in the air.

Aelfric stood up and crossed himself. 'The princess is with child.' He walked to the table and picked up the censer. He sniffed it a little and then turned back so that his pinched face was only a few inches from Theo's blank amazement. 'She will have Wilfrid's child in the spring.'

'Ah,' said Cuthbert, putting his hands to the fire. 'Wilfrid's child, and this church is for Wilfrid. What a lot he has started. More in death than in life, you might say. In the spring I will start my travels to Rome, God willing.'

Theo left the hall and went outside into the cold light of December. It was late and what little sun there had been was now hidden by the rise of the valley behind him. The cows were already in and soon the sheep would be folded. A terrible sadness filled Theo, which was deepened by the sight of his many mounds of stones.

How could Matilda carry inside herself that monster's child? It was a mystery too deep for him to understand. Nor could he understand his own reaction. Surely he was building the church for the honour and glory of God? For the same reason he was wrestling with paper words and a quill pen that sprinkled blots like flies on a summer's day. Then why did he feel so abandoned, so desolate? Slowly he passed by the stones and entered the old church. For once he welcomed its dingy familiarity; he knelt humbly on the mud-baked floor.

'O Lord, bring Christian hope not pagan despair.'

He looked up and saw the eye of a saint crudely painted on the wall watching him questioningly. It reminded him of the picture of St Catherine lying on the refectory table – although that had the life of a real woman – and he realised with happy inspiration that Matilda would come back. Why else would she have sent a set of ten chairs for the nuns' refectory.

Chapter Five

'It's a bad omen,' said Theo, looking at the sky. His eye was suddenly filled with a large raindrop, which spilled over and rolled down his cheek like a tear.

'Only pagans talk about omens.' Aelfric spoke severely but he, too, looked upwards and shivered. It was a horrible day; the clouds were low enough to touch and, although it was reasonably warm for March, the rain gave a chilly sense of gloom.

'It should be such a glorious, cheerful day!' wailed Theo.

'You talk too much.' Aelfric glanced at the hooded faces of the monks gathered round him. They did not talk. Not even Penda, who loved a good grumble. Perhaps their order should become silent. But, then, Theo was not yet a monk, neither fish nor fowl. He had worked, though, studying his books while he directed the construction of the church, that must be admitted. 'We are here in God's name,' the abbot began in a sing-song voice. To make it more impressive he held up his Bible, high like a crozier, 'to ask that He should bless this first stone of our church and that the devil's works shall . . .'

He had thought she would come. Theo always found it easier to think his own thoughts than listen to official words. He was still expecting her. Women had babies all the time whether they wanted to or not. But how many women can choose to found a great church, a nunnery, and take their place close to God? All winter he had worked as hard as a slave field-worker, and, although he did not do it for her – after all, it was his dream – he had been sure she would come. Particularly on this day. It was not as if Wilfrid's baby could mean much to her.

Aelfric stopped speaking and surveyed the expanse of mud around them. If the rain did not stop soon it would turn to a lake. At least the foundation stone over which they prayed would not float away. It had taken six oxen and a specially reinforced cart to bring it down. It stood now nearly as tall as a man but Theo planned to sink it deep into the ground so that it would stay there for ever and ever. Even if the church became a ruin the stone would continue to exist. The altar was to be built around it so that they prayed towards a symbol of eternity. Not for the first time Aelfric wondered where Theo, the son of a family whose idea of time was a growing dung heap and a lowering turnip pile, had found his ideas. From God presumably, as with his poetry. God's ways are curious to know. He had even managed to teach Theo to read and write which he, Aelfric, would have said was impossible.

The monks dispersed across the field and Aelfric, still staring thoughtfully, found Theo had more talk in him still. 'When do you think Brother Cuthbert will return?'

Aelfric looked into Theo's pleading eyes and saw he was not really asking about Cuthbert. He was only a boy, yearning after a princess who had forgotten about him. 'Brother Cuthbert is not strong and he was planning a long journey. With God's help he will even get to Rome. We can hardly expect him before next autumn. And if he misses autumn, he will probably wait until the following spring.'

'We are lucky to be already endowed by the King,' said Theo, and again Aelfric saw in his eyes questions about the King's daughter. Cruelty is not the way of the Lord. 'The princess should be in childbirth any time now.' Yet he did not wish her to return and would not encourage Theo. 'A woman was created by God to continue the race of man.'

He had hardly finished before Theo cut in fiercely, 'There are other uses for women. Just as there are for men!'

'Yes. Yes.' Aelfric spread his hands. 'I am a monk,' he said simply. 'But the Princess Matilda was married and now she is a mother.'

'No!' Theo screamed, the cry of an animal. 'She had a higher calling! You'll see! She'll come here! Look at the linen she sent, the furniture. She'll come! After the baby! When the weather's brighter! You'll see!'

Aelfric pursed his lips, turned away and then turned back again. Theo stood quivering violently like a horse that had galloped too much. 'You must pray that God's will may be done. You must pray for the peace that prayer brings.'

'No!' shouted Theo, clenching his fists and stiffening his legs.

'Yes,' said Aelfric quietly. 'Now kneel down so that I may make the sign of the cross over you.'

For several seconds Theo did not move and so wild was his expression that Aelfric even wondered if he might feel one of those fists on his nose, unimaginable though such action would be towards an abbot, a superior. But then, with a movement so slow as to be almost imperceptible, Theo relaxed his tense posture, and little by little bent his knees.

Aelfric watched him till his legs were lapped around with mud. Then he leaned forward and touched his wet hair. 'In the name of the Father and of the Son and of the Holy Ghost.'

Theo heard the words but was even more conscious of the rain washing down his body and joining the muddy lake around his legs. The feeling was comforting, joining him to the earth and soothing his inner restlessness. As Aelfric finished speaking, he lifted his eyes to the huge stone which heaved up in front of him and said in a firm but calm tone, 'Amen. I dedicate myself to you, Lord, and give my life to this long work of building your church.'

'Amen, to you,' replied the abbot with satisfaction. Perhaps he would make a monk, after all. It was only later when he woke in blackness and continuing rain for matins that it struck him as odd that Theo, in this most inspired moment of his life, had spoken in prosaic words, rather than calling on his glorious gift of poetry.

'We need glaziers. We need another stone-mason or two or three. We need a foundry where we can cast a bell that makes a sound worthy of our church.' Here Theo paused and put his hand against the wall beside him. Already it reached his shoulder and was nearly as wide. Since the spring rains had passed they were progressing fast and would go even faster if they had more men who knew how to cut stone. And he needed to know how tall he could make the window at the back of the church without the glass falling out. Above all, he needed to remake the great arch he had taken to pieces in the Roman town and brought back stone by stone.

Theo's mind was so full of building plans that his hours of prayer and study, as ordained by Cuthbert before he left, were beginning to suffer. At least he had no time for any self-indulgence. It amazed him when he considered the hours he spent doing nothing less than a year ago. Now he left dung heaps to the rats.

'I've sent messages. You know I have.' Aelfric's voice rose to a wail. What was the hurry? Why did Theo have to push him all the time? He was a monk. His time was committed to a life of regular prayer. Everything else was subsidiary.

'Then why has the King answered none of our requests?'

'Perhaps he has lost interest.' Aelfric stared at Theo. He was so tall now, tall and thin and determined. It was time to teach him another lesson in humility.

'Lost interest in his soul?' Theo was scornful. 'This church is his safeguard against the perils of hell. We offer prayers for him daily. He should keep his side of the bargain.'

'King Cynewulf is a good man. Don't speak about him as if he were a merchant. As if his soul were a piece of horn. Maybe it is his daughter who has lost interest.'

Theo turned away and looked at the busy scene in front of him. The spring sun glinted on pieces of metal embedded in the stone. His men worked industriously; the noise of the mason's chipping was beating the cheerful rhythm of progress. He was not creating this for her. But she had set it in motion and she should honour her pledges. The messenger who had brought the single mason, not the glazier, had told of her baby's birth two or three months ago. She should no longer be preoccupied.

'You should go and see Princess Matilda.' Theo went close to the abbot and put his hands together in the attitude of prayer.

But the abbot only smiled. He flicked the top of Theo's fingers. 'You should pray more. More prayer and less action.'

'Then I'll go myself.'

So his humility was as thin as a sheet of spring ice. Aelfric said nothing but Theo checked himself. He stood in front of his superior and bowed his head. 'If you command me and God wills it I will go to the palace and bring back what we need.'

He waited for the abbot's response. Aelfric calculated that it would take Theo two or three weeks' travelling, which, plus the time he would need at the court, would mean he would be away for a couple of months. Such an absence was too tempting. Besides, he would learn the realities of royal patronage and also, perhaps, the reality of a mother's love for her child.

'After all, you are not yet a monk,' he said.

'But I have dedicated myself to God's service and the service of this monastery.'

'You've certainly done that.' Aelfric smiled wryly. 'Go and do what you can. Although you had better realise that an illiterate boy like yourself can hardly expect much of a royal welcome.'

'I will go as a messenger of God.'

'Oh, yes.' Aelfric was getting tired of the conversation. Why did Theo have to conduct everything at such a level of intensity? 'I'm sure you're a veritable Angel Gabriel but just keep your wings hidden on the journey or they may be torn. Not everyone appreciates a self-declared, self-made saint.'

Again Theo bowed his head but this time Aelfric thought he spotted the acting.

'Go!' he cried even more waspishly. 'Then perhaps there will be some peace here and we can find our own way to God!'

Theo arrived at the King's court like a stray dog looking for shelter. He was a nobody, neither thane nor churl, monk, nor serf. He had come on business, God's business as it seemed to him but to others might seem more like his own. When he saw the huge hall and all the other buildings around it, his obsession, which was his shield and spear, suddenly left him. He was merely a young boy emerging from the spring green wood with none of the effrontery necessary to approach a great king. Leaving the path, which was muddy with horses' churning hoofs, he sidled along the edge of the trees hardly daring to emerge into the sharp sunlight. It was mid-morning and he could hear and partly see all the busy occupations of a large settlement, a town no less, nearly as large as the giants' city he had left behind. The thought gave him courage enough to step closer. At once he was struck by the realisation that most of the buildings – even the hall, which was nearby and a church behind it – were built of timber and thatch. There were some stone blocks low down in the walls but here was no magnificent monument to the Creator as he was planning. Here was no stone arch like a rainbow across heaven. He had come to beg, indeed, but he would do it in the name of a worthy cause.

Holding his head high, Theo walked towards a building on his left. The choice was not accidental for it was issuing a pleasant smell of newly baked bread. A bakery was just the place to eat, rest, listen to the gossip of the court and prepare himself to meet the King. A day spent like this would not be a day lost and he might hear news of the Princess Matilda.

The hall was only half full. Many of the King's warriors had left that morning on an expedition northwards where there had been rumours of a band of rebels pushing their way south. King Cynewulf believed in knowledge before action and kept a close watch on all the borders of his kingdom. The men would return without fighting. A group of monks was passing through on the way to a synod but they were unused to communication and huddled together at one side of the feasting table.

Matilda sat at her place beside her father. From there, she would rise and pass the ale-cup down the table. It was a dull evening, she thought: few young men, mostly women and children, servants and the sick. She would prefer to be with her baby, Ethelburga. She had been born quickly, out of the darkness of a

65

short spring night and like spring her birth had torn away Matilda's past and opened her to a more hopeful future. When Matilda clasped her fat little baby her heart beat faster than if she held a lover.

Other noble ladies soon passed over their babies to foster mothers but Matilda had a bower of her own where she and Juliana and the nursemaid slept and tended Ethelburga. At last Matilda had found she could love someone outside herself and her ambitions in life went no further than her daughter's warm, soft skin.

Matilda's gaze, wandering slowly down the long table, reached near the bottom and then stopped at the bowed head of a young man. His head was so low that he seemed to be praying over his milk pudding. For want of anything better to do, Matilda watched this man who seemed to be not quite a stranger.

'What we need is a song to cheer us up,' said King Cynewulf. He said it quietly at first but then, thinking it a good idea, repeated the words with a bellow of royal command.

Theo lifted his head and stared to the top of the table. Matilda's attitude, bored and languorous, suddenly changed. Her expression was agitated, she looked away, back, away again and then as if making up her mind, she raised herself in her chair. 'He will sing!' she cried, pointing to Theo. 'We have a visitor, a maker of songs, he will cheer us!'

Theo looked at Matilda. She was as he had first seen her, beautiful, headstrong, pitiless. Her hair was long and black again, her body filled out and strong. He understood she was issuing a challenge to him – which could also be an opportunity. Yet since he had dedicated his life to building the church and bowed his head to Abbot Aelfric's authority, he had not written any poetry. It seemed that the free spirit which used words to paint pictures in the air could not exist side by side with the man who struggled to put one stone on top of another.

'Find a man to accompany him on the lyre,' ordered Matilda. She stood up as if to do this herself and then, remembering, sat down more regally.

'And bring him closer, closer,' said the King. 'I can't bear not being able to hear the words, particularly when I don't know the song.'

Theo stood up and approached the top of the table. The lyre player followed unenthusiastically; he would have liked to sing as well as play.

'My lord. My ladies.' Theo bowed to the King. He bowed to his daughters and to his daughters-in-law. He bowed to the thanes. 'My lords.' He made no sign that he knew anyone there. He was stern and straight and handsome and unlike the usual singers.

Matilda found that her heart was jumping like a silly young sheep. Her cheeks were burning, too, as fiery as twin furnaces. Was this because she felt guilty at abandoning this churl in his faraway monastery with his faraway dreams? She thought of her peaceful little room where Ethelburga lay sleeping and the silly sheep's patter slowed down a little.

'It's that boy from the monastery.' Juliana, sitting at her mistress's side, nudged her knowingly.

'Sssh!' Matilda frowned, which only made Juliana smile. She had always wondered about her mistress's true feelings for Theo.

> 'I sing of a place that is my pleasure and my pain
> But unknown to you as God's plan is unknown,'

began Theo in the informal way he usually approached a story.

'Louder!' shouted a thane who liked his ale. But the King was intrigued and the monks gratified by the early mention of God.

'Do you know if he has a good story?' whispered Cynewulf to his daughter.

'Oh, yes,' Matilda replied, although she did not know, and was already wondering what on this earth had made her call forth Theo. With a flash of understanding she saw that he was the spirit of disquiet. He had come into her life when he had lured her husband into a hole; he had caused sleepy bees to sting poor Wilfrid to death and finally he had blackmailed her into nearly leaving her duties as daughter and mother. What could he sing that she would wish to hear?

> 'God was worshipped, the wonders of the world;
> But the words were weary and the voices weak.'

King Cynewulf sighed. Although a reverent man and a true Christian, he found songs in praise of God tediously repetitive. What he enjoyed was a good adventure story about brave warriors attacking fiendish monsters. This young man should never have left the monastery of which he was painting such a dismal picture. He gave Matilda a reproachful look that she missed but Theo caught.

> 'Then across the town where the dark gods reign
> Came a warrior, a spear-holder and his lady wife.
> Strong as a stag killer, radiant as a sunray,
> They came to the cave where the boy-churl lay.
> Oh, how bright was the glittering of thane and horse
> How high their heads; how far their fall . . .'

Now both King and princess were sitting up and attending. The King smiled – this was more like it – but Matilda bit her lip and then her finger. 'Radiant as a sunray' was a pretty compliment for some woman but not if it was supposed to be her, if Theo was daring to tell their story.

'Deep in the dungeon created by giants . . .'

continued the poet's voice inexorably. The lyre player, resigned to his supporting role, extemporised with some threatening chords.

Matilda saw that her suspicions were correct. She half stood but her father waved her down angrily. She looked away longingly but saw only Juliana's smiling face. She must listen. And what a story Theo made of it! The lyrist, too, became quite carried away and moved from the boy-churl's tortured groans to the buzzing of the enraged bees with horrible imitation. Wilfrid's death brought tears to the eyes of many of the listeners and when 'his lady' became ill too, the hall was silent with concern. There was an audible sigh of relief at her survival. It was a great song, exciting and emotional. But how would it end?

Now Theo told of the joyous plan of thanksgiving, of remembrance and atonement. The city of the pagan giants would be used to create a new church for God. A great king would be its sponsor thus bringing honour and grace to his family.

'Don't you understand?' whispered Matilda, who could bear no more, to her father.

'I understand,' Cynewulf replied without moving his head. 'And you bring me shame.'

For now Theo sang of the less than half-finished church, of the walls to his shoulders but no further, of the royal promises that were given and not kept, of the short memory of the lady 'radiant as a sunray' who had promised to found a convent but instead decked herself with gold and jewels.

Matilda gathered her skirts and, jumping off her chair, ran out of the hall. Reaching her bower, she snatched the baby, who had just awakened, from the wet nurse and clamped her to her own breast. They were joined into one being. No one, however cleverly he sang, would part them.

The next morning King Cynewulf came to the doorway of Matilda's bower and wagged his finger at his daughter. 'You could have arranged for money to go as I promised, for masons, for glaziers.'

'I sent him a mason. It's not that he wants. He wants me! He wants me to go with him, to dress in black, to live enclosed in darkness. He wants me to leave Ethelburga.' Matilda talked wildly. She bit her fingers continually and would not sit down.

'You're behaving like a child or a fool. No one, except God, can make you become a nun. It is an honour to be chosen which few refuse. But your case was strange. This boy is only a humble emissary. Only God can tell you what you should do. You must pray.' Cynewulf took her arm and tried to look into her eyes but she ducked her head. 'There is nothing more to tell me?'

'Nothing. Nothing. Nothing.' Matilda shook her head repeatedly. 'My baby is everything.'

Finally irritated, the King shouted from the door, 'She is only a girl, this baby you talk about so much, not a god. Not even a boy. Hand her over to those whose business is to look after such a creature and pray for proper guidance.'

Matilda went to Theo. Juliana had told her he was only staying one more night while arrangements were made for the continuation of his building. Matilda left Ethelburga, sleeping so rosily, so divinely, and crept across to the great hall where Theo lay with the other retainers and servants. She shook his shoulder roughly but Theo only rolled over and gave her a sleepy smile. He looked as if he were in the middle of a happy dream.

'Come out with me!'

Obediently, Theo stumbled after her, eyes still half shut.

'What do you mean, trying to separate me from my baby?' Her hisses seemed louder in the dark air.

Theo blinked.

'What am I to you? To you, a churl!' She was like a madwoman.

Theo dropped down on his knees.

'What are you doing? Trying to make fun of me again? Isn't once enough, in front of all my people?'

'I kneel at your feet, my lady,' said Theo. The sight of his handsome, innocent face, staring up at her, infuriated Matilda further. 'Tomorrow I am returning to the monastery,' said Theo bowing his head like a slave. 'Your father, the King, has been generous.'

Matilda would have liked to kick him, but he spoke again in what she saw as falsely humble tones.

'What shall I do with the linen you sent for your convent, the chests, the furniture, the silver?'

'Dump them in the river! I don't care. And get up!' She had hold of him again, pulling on his cloak. But underneath the wool she could feel the warmth and strength of his arm. Why did he make her aware of such things? It was horrible, horrible. Whimpering, Matilda ran off into the darkness.

Theo had always thought summer the happiest season. He had liked to see the leaves growing heavier, the grass longer, the cattle fatter, the corn more golden. He had enjoyed watching the sun rise so high and set so red and round. The months that changed fragile lambs into sturdy sheep, that hatched out butterflies as big and brightly coloured as the flowers they sucked, that turned cygnets into swans and fluffy chicks into egg-laying hens must be a source of pleasure to someone who lived as close to the country as Theo. Each summer since his childhood he had looked forward to warmth and longer days. But this summer he was sad.

This was despite the progress of the church which, thanks to royal aid, sped upwards and outwards. Cuthbert had not yet arrived in Rome but they had word of books that would be brought from France.

When Theo told Aelfric the story of Princess Matilda's defection and his visit to the court, he commented somewhat severely, 'Jesus Christ taught us to honour a mother. Pray to Mary for greater understanding.'

So Theo felt unable to discuss the matter further, although he suspected it was at the root of his sadness. He and Matilda had planned their dream together. Now he was alone. The abbot had positively beamed when Theo had told him that Matilda would not be returning.

'God always knows best,' was his infuriating way of expressing his satisfaction.

The summer was not as hot as the year before and there were thunderstorms that beat down the corn and caused the river to flood into the fishponds. When the water receded, several fish flapped helplessly on the meadow grass. Theo found them there early in the morning and stared at them with a feeling of gloomy solidarity. That's what I am, he told himself, as he carried them one by one to the pond, a fish out of water. But there's no water for me and no one to carry me if a pond appears. I'll just have to bear it, carry on with my studies, become a monk and fight the sin of . . . What was his sin? Theo popped back the last fish and wiped his hands on the grass. Despair was a sin. But he was not despairing. Merely unhappy. Unhappiness was not a sin. Just as happiness was not a virtue.

*

'If it falls, it will crush you.'

Theo laughed at Aelfric's warning tones. He became more of an old woman every day. 'If I've survived all those stones, I'm hardly likely to be killed by a door!' But the door was heavy, solid oak, carved from a great oak tree they had felled for that purpose. He had wanted to raise it himself, complete the building of the church, but he saw how it was foolhardy pride for he was still young and narrow-shouldered. What he needed was three or four of the oxlike peasants who had lifted the stones, one on top of the other, as if they were pebbles. Gently he eased the door back to the ground.

'You're right,' he cried to Aelfric. 'I shall watch and admire from a position of safety.' The two men stood side by side, their old enmity had almost completely disappeared over the two years it had taken to build the church. Theo, discounting his inner sadness, had bent his will to the task and in doing so had found he could accept the abbot's authority for the first time. He recognised him now as the representative of God's will on earth and only scoffed at his personal weaknesses. Physically Theo had changed, too; his boyish agility and unpredictable movements, which had made him seem nearer sometimes to an animal, had steadied into a duller beat. He moved more slowly, spoke more slowly and thought before he did either. His slightly coarse features had become more refined and his strong skin colour had seeped away in the long hours spent in church.

Aelfric, seeing the change in Theo who had always been so rebellious, thanked God for the intervention of His grace. Soon Theo would take holy orders and become a monk like all the other monks. Aelfric looked behind him and saw they had been joined by most of the community wanting to share in the glorious moment. Yesterday, they had mounted the new bell cast especially in a foundry in Winchester, next week they would have a service of dedication, today the brothers gathered in happy fellowship.

'Oh, if only I could sing,' cried Theo suddenly and in such a powerful voice of emotion that Aelfric jumped.

No, Theo was not like the other monks. He had been wrong. Not yet. 'We can all sing,' Aelfric said, purposefully misunderstanding. 'Credo in unum deum . . . factorem caeli et terrae.'

Theo bowed his head. It had been a childish outburst. He had faced the fact that the subordination of his will had killed his creative gift. Obviously it had not been a gift of God but a selfish expression of himself. As such it was better gone. He would follow the line of black monks and sing the plain chant just as they did. 'All for the honour and glory of God.'

The day had been a fine one and the sun lingered on the horizon in the tantalising way of early spring evenings. Just as it disappeared, but while there was still light in the sky, a group of horsemen was seen slowly winding its way along the valley.

Three of the boys who worked in the valley came rushing to the abbot. He was eating his evening meal but visitors were far more interesting than beans and bread, rarer, too. In a moment, followed by a line of equally curious monks, he stood in front of the hall.

'Not a grand visitor,' he told his neighbour, with some relief. They had invited a royal representative to the dedication of the church but the messenger had returned quickly with news of an epidemic of the plague.

'Five people,' said his neighbour.

'Women,' added another monk in a shocked voice.

'Prepare hot food,' ordered the abbot, pulling his hood over his head. He returned to the hall where Theo and half a dozen others still sat over their wooden plates. 'Five travellers,' he said, breaking his bread into several pieces. He looked at Theo. 'Two or three women.'

There had been a time when Theo had acted as a look-out for the monastery, always expectant. But that had stopped more than a year ago. 'I'm glad we have visitors for the church,' he said. 'They will spread the news that it is completed.'

It was almost dark when the horses came softly and slowly to the monastery buildings. Their riders bowed wearily and in silence slid to the ground. Two servants held the horses while a woman, heavily cloaked, approached the abbot. He stood at the threshold of the hall, hands folded into his sleeves, hood low on his forehead.

'You are Abbot Aelfric?' The voice was soft and she looked nervously at the abbot who indeed might have been a sentinel of death, standing there so black and still.

'I am Abbot Aelfric and in God's Name welcome you. There is food inside and a room for you to sleep.'

The woman bowed and entered the hall. It, too, was dark but a huge fire lit up one corner of the room. Theo, who had just thrown on a log, stood beside it, his profile clearly visible against the leaping flames. The woman went over to him. She stood quite humbly before him and then carefully drew back her hood so her face was revealed.

'I have come back,' she said.

Theo stared foolishly. He could feel the fire beating in waves of heat behind him. It made Matilda's face as red as a sunset. He was conscious of dread and anger and something else more frightening still but he was so used to disciplining his emotions that his expression hardly altered. 'Where is your child?' He spoke severely.

Matilda felt the warmth of the fire burning and cauterising. She swayed forward as if drawn by its power, as if she were hardly capable of resisting its pull. 'Two years ago I had one death on my conscience. Now I have two.'

'Why have you come here?'

'I have come back to the service of God.'

'Yes.' He had no right to judge. God directed the footsteps of each one of his creatures.

Again Matilda swayed. Theo took a step forward as if to support her but then stopped himself. Behind her he could see a movement of disturbance, of whispering and frowns among the gathered monks. It had started after the words of the two servant women to Aelfric.

Matilda turned to see what Theo was looking at. She understood at once and put a hand out to Theo. 'My daughter died of the fever but I do not have it. Nor my companions. We have been travelling for five days since then and the time for it to show itself is past.'

'If the fever killed your daughter, why do you have her death on your conscience?'

'I should have kept my promise to God and returned here. I put human love before the love of God.'

Now Theo turned away and put his hand to his face. The dread and fear were weak allies. How could he disguise any longer the joy that was making him glow more than any fire? 'Your church is finished,' he said, putting his hands together as if in prayer.

But Matilda was not deceived. She saw the triumph in his attitude. For a third time she swayed forward, this time actually taking a step towards the flames.

Now Theo reacted. He said, loudly enough for anyone to hear, 'We have the things you sent safely kept.' His tone summoned the abbot to them.

'Bless me, Father, for I have sinned.' Matilda sank down at his feet.

Aelfric, prepared to reject, was cast in the role of confessor, Christ's representative. He laid a hand on her head. 'We are all sinners. The Lord is our only judge.'

73

Theo took his hand from his face and watched the scene, clear-eyed. An enormous happiness made him want to shout and sing.

'Give praise, sing gloria, shout alleluia, Lord.
Thy lady comes.
Sing gloria, shout alleluia, give praise, lady.
My Lord is with us always.'

The words flowed from him without conscious effort.

Chapter Six

At this time there were double monasteries throughout England, at Coldingham, Hartlepool, Whitby, Repton, Ely, Barking, Minster, Wareham. A double monastery, 'double' because it encompassed both monks and nuns, brought all sorts of advantages. The men did the work most suited to their talents and the women that suited to theirs. They met to pray. Soon, a nunnery was laid out on the southerly side of the church and at a distance of a few hundred yards. The construction was under Theo's direction, and although they used little stone that which they did was decorated with a vine scroll pattern, bunches of grapes and tendrils on which birds and insects pecked. The buildings were spacious enough to be worthy of a king's daughter and even included a courtyard or garden where the women exercised in privacy. Matilda unpacked her chests, clothed herself in black and settled herself for a lifetime as abbess.

This did not mean she wished to cut herself off entirely from the outside world. That may have been her first instinctive reaction after the death of her daughter but a year or two later she had different ambitions. The monastery, and her convent in particular, should become a centre for wisdom and learning. She would model herself on the Abbess Hyld, who taught justice, piety and chastity. From three nuns (who were quickly reduced to two when her maid, Juliana, fled back to court after the epidemic had passed) the number rose to ten at the end of two years and thirty-five at the end of three. Moreover, many of these were aristocratic ladies who for one reason or another – often because of their religious beliefs, but not always – shunned marriage. They brought with them dowries of land so that the monastery no longer needed to look to the King for money. Like a good school or college, it was recommended in the right circles. Mothers knew their daughters would be well looked-after there. Older women whose lives left something to be desired came there to make atonement and to find a holy death.

In this way Matilda often knew more about her father's kingdom than he did himself. He would send messages to her for advice and even visited the monastery once for a short retreat. Worldly in this sense, Matilda's rule was also founded on the strictest adherence to religious observance. Her noble ladies might be allowed to sleep comfortably but they were expected to rise for midnight matins, just as the monks did, and then attend prime at six o'clock in the morning. The psalter must be read, the litany recited and such helpful scriptures as St Paul's letters to Timothy and Titus read with close attention. Nowhere was the Gregorian chant, with its double choir singing in harmony with reciprocal responses and antiphons, performed more nobly. Matilda had always been filled with energy and now she had found a suitable and useful outlet. The sleepy monastery, whose bell had reached no further than the cows grazing the other side of the valley, spread its influence through Wessex.

Aelfric was abbot in name but well aware as to who made the decisions. Strangely, he found he no longer resented the imposition of a woman's rule. Besides, he had begun to spend more and more time with the books Cuthbert had sent. Each morning he read from a copy of the four gospels, written in letters of gold on purple-dyed parchment, and in the afternoon he studied the works of Gregory the Great. (Cuthbert himself did not return, dying in a French monastery on a second venture at the two-thousand-mile trip to Rome.) Usually Matilda and he talked about necessary matters through a little window with a grille, for the men were segregated from the women everywhere but in church. But one day, about eighteen months after her arrival, he asked her for an interview.

They met in a small store-room, often used as a confessional. Matilda wore a defensive air of defiance. Aelfric blessed her, for he would always be a priest and that she could never be.

Matilda bowed her head. Aelfric had changed. He had always been small and wiry but now he looked pinched and fragile.

'I am old,' he said. 'My span of life is nearing its end. Soon you will need a successor.'

Matilda said nothing because, although so much in charge, she still revered the old man.

'I have been asking for guidance on this subject and I have had my answer. Theodore is now a tonsured monk and a holy priest. The wildness of his youth is long past. The monks must vote, it is true, but I shall recommend that he should take my place.'

At the mention of Theo's name a ripple had seemed to pass over

Matilda's face and body as if a wind blew on water. 'It is your choice,' she said as the abbot waited for a response.

Aelfric coughed and tried to see Matilda's expression behind the ornamental ironwork. With all the changes at the monastery, he was one of the few people who still remembered the relationship between the old Theo and Matilda. Now they only saw each other on either side of the church when monks and nuns sang the antiphon at mass.

'I know nothing of Brother Theodore,' said Matilda.

'That is true, Abbess,' said Aelfric. 'But you knew him once and if he became abbot you will know him again.'

'There is no reason why I should object to him as abbot,' said Matilda, her quiet tones beginning to ring a little as if with suppressed emotion.

'He will be your confessor.' Aelfric leaned away from the window and put a hand to his head.

'Christ is my confessor.'

'Of course. Of course. Then it is decided.'

This conversation, carried out in Latin as with all the business of the monastery, echoed in Matilda's head through the weeks following.

She found herself trying to pick out Theo from among the black-cowled figures. Her body, which since her daughter's death she had trained to be subordinate to her mind, began to make its presence felt. Her breasts tingled, her thighs pressed against each other, the narrow suppleness of her waist demanded that she swayed a little as she walked. Try as she might, the severe uprightness of the nun dedicated to God flowed outwards and tried to break the bounds.

In church when the newly trained voices of the nuns reached upwards in the highest notes she found tears gushing into her eyes and overflowing down her cheeks. This was not religious ecstasy, unless a seeking after love could be included under that term. Terrified of allowing herself to think about Theo, Matilda's thoughts turned again to that period when she had had someone to love. But the joy of the baby Ethelburga had been destroyed by her death. Apart from that first moment of arrival at the monastery when she had accused herself of being the cause of the baby's death, she had talked about it to no one. But now it became an obsession, linked to Wilfrid's terrible death also caused by her. She realised she had never asked for absolution; she was still guilty, still unworthy.

Rational in the running of the monastery, kindly to the problems of the nuns, calm and fair, inside Matilda burned the fire of self-loathing. Pray as she might, she could not resolve it. At last she decided to talk to Aelfric. Perhaps he could cool her spirit.

Matilda sent him a message. But the message came back that the abbot was dead: he had been found that morning in his cell, on his knees with his crucifix between his hands. It was a death much to be wished for.

'I cannot bear this!' cried Matilda, astonishing all those around her. 'It is unendurable!' And falling on her knees, she tore off her wimple and beat her head on the floor. Her companions went to restrain her but she pushed them away screaming, 'Leave me alone! Leave me! Go!' So they went, still amazed, and thought perhaps she was ill. Why should she care so much at the old abbot going to his just reward?

Theo did not wish to become abbot; inside himself, he felt no different from the opinionated peasant boy. He had become a monk and a priest because of his dream of a fine church built with the giants' stones. But now that dream was complete and he had been chosen by Aelfric. In life there was no chance to go back, so forward it must be, however unwillingly. Nor could he escape by pretending to be a scholar for that he would never be.

It was early autumn, and as Theo walked out of the monastery and along the upper reaches of the valley he stared longingly at the farm workers bringing in the last of the harvest. Making sure no one was looking, he took off his sandals and splayed his feet on the warm grass. They were white now but still strong and straight. The grass tickled his instep and made him smile.

Now he must think about how becoming abbot would bring him into contact with Matilda. Theo pressed down his foot harder so that the grass was flattened and no longer tickled. He knew all about the sins of the flesh, the devil's cravings that young postulants brought to him for forgiveness and absolution. Was that what he had felt for Matilda? It must be that and that would be simple to control for it did not fly in the face of God. Then why did he feel it was something more dangerous which dared to compete with his love of God?

Before Theo became abbot he was summoned by the Bishop of Sherborne, who perhaps wanted to see what sort of man was to play second fiddle to the Abbess Matilda. In his absence, Matilda became more peaceful, although she was still troubled by thoughts of the death of her baby. For that she could not forgive herself. But in the three months Theo was away, she taught herself to think of him as an abbot, a priest and a monk. Once he was no longer a man but purely Christ's representative on earth, she would be able to ask him to help her.

On their first meeting, in the dark little room with the grille in the middle, when business matters had been completed, Matilda lowered her voice. 'I would like your advice on a matter of conscience, Father.'

Theo lifted his head slightly to show he was listening. All gestures were small in the monastery, a conscious denial of the ways of the body.

'Once I had a baby girl whom I called Ethelburga. She was a plump healthy baby, like a puppy in her easy, happy ways. I loved her so much that I forgot everything else. Even my father, the King, had to remind me to carry the ale-cup. I thought of nothing else every minute of the day. When she smiled, I smiled. When she cried, I cried.'

'I know this story, Abbess,' said Theo. Yet it was not true because he did not know how a mother could love a child. But listening was painful. 'Where is the sin? You are looking for absolution, I assume?'

'Oh, Father!' Matilda's voice raised a note and then quickly relapsed into her previous expressionless monotone. 'I made the baby into a god. And yet she was of my flesh.'

'You were a young mother. A ewe bleats for its lamb.'

'I had broken my oath to God. The death of my husband had lain on my conscience . . .' Seeing Theo was about to speak again, she interrupted herself and hurried on. 'God had given me a particular work to carry out.'

Theo, who had been sitting more upright in his chair, relapsed again. 'You are carrying out God's work now.'

'Yes. Yes. But at the time of which I am speaking, I worshipped my child and it was only her young death that brought me to my senses. She was the sacrifice for my soul but I did not recognise that. Worse.' Matilda paused, and taking her hand from where it was wrapped in the other sleeve passed it slowly across her face.

Theo watched, fascinated. The fingers were so thin and white they were hardly more than bones, gleaming in the pale beam of wintry light. As they touched her face, he saw they trembled. Led by them and the new low light to her face, he realised that despite the cold in the room, perspiration stood on her forehead and long pink-tipped nose. A warning glow of what he knew to be human love caused him to half close his eyes. 'Speak, Abbess. Remember, I carry with me the power of Christ.'

'I had left the King's court with my baby,' said Matilda. 'I fled to the coast with her nursemaid and my attendant. I thought the plague would be made clean by the salty winds blowing in from the sea. I did not realise she was already ill. She was so good. She never cried. But her skin began to burn to the touch and although she tried so hard to please me, she couldn't eat or drink. I knew she was dying then and my anger with God made no prayer possible. Instead I lit a funeral pyre and when she lay still, I took her out and put her on the flames. I watched her burn until her ashes were mixed with the ashes of the branches I had piled beneath her. Then I took both and walked for three hours until I reached a high cliff which descended to a rough and tumbled sea. I threw the ashes as far outwards as I could, the miserable remains of my sin both in her living and her death. They rode out to sea as if on a pagan burial ship.'

As Matilda spoke the sliver of light dipped below the small window and when she had finished a bell began to ring for evening prayers.

Theo stood up. She was not looking for human comfort and he must not give it to her. 'Come to me again tomorrow.'

Silently, they each left by the little door behind them. The monk waiting outside for Theo noticed nothing particular in his face and fell in behind. But the nun accompanying Matilda saw her haggard looks and laid a hand on her arm. Impatiently, the abbess shook her off.

On the following day, seeping rain had come to join the December darkness and cold. Theo blessed Matilda as she entered the little room. 'Pax Christi vobiscum.' Matilda sat down. As before, she did not try to look at Theo's face but waited with a resigned humility for what he might say.

'King Anna had a daughter called Ethelburga,' he began.

Matilda stared ahead, stiffly upright. A scarlet wave of colour surged across her face and disappeared upwards under her wimple.

'Ethelburga was a nun and preserved with strict self-discipline the glory of the perpetual virginity beloved by God. She became an abbess and began building within her monastery a church in honour of all the apostles, in which she wished to be buried. But when the work was only half done she died. Once she was safely buried in the unfinished nave, the brethren became engrossed in other matters and discontinued the building of the church for seven years. Eventually they decided to move Ethelburga's bones into another church already consecrated. When they opened the

80

tomb, they found the body as untouched by decay as it had been by the corruption of sinful desires.'

Theo stopped speaking and the sound of the drizzling rain took the place of his voice. He had spoken slowly for his Latin was not very fluent and at each hesitation, Matilda had stiffened expectantly, waiting, perhaps for condemnation, explanation, absolution. But as the story continued to unfold, a story with no explicit reference to her own situation, her mood changed. She understood what he was telling her; it was the same message he had given her when she had tried to die after Wilfrid's death. Yet she would not show him she knew.

'How sad that they did not finish the church,' she said.

'That is not the point of the story.' A serene expression came over Theo's face although he still did not look at Matilda.

Matilda sighed. She could see he was waiting. 'I threw my daughter's ashes to the pagan gods of nature,' she said. 'I killed her body and then her soul—'

'No,' interrupted Theo. 'You cannot do that. No human has the power to do that.'

'And then I gave my life to God.'

'Yes,' nodded Theo. 'That is all God asks: repentance.'

Matilda felt tears come into her eyes but she did not know if they were of anger or resignation. She had never cried for Ethelburga. First she had been mad and then she had come to the monastery. She remembered how she used to cry for anything, in a luxury of easy emotion. But the tears she felt coming now, building up in her body, were not as water, hard as steel. Her body was tortured by the pain, as if with childbirth.

'I don't want to give her up,' she whispered. 'She is all the human love I had.'

Theo now looked up and watched the woman struggling in front of him. He wanted to inspire her with Christ's spirit, to talk of His suffering on the cross, but he was taken aback by the physical aspect of the youthful woman in front of him. Even behind the black criss-crossing of the grille. Even in the distortion of deep emotion, she was beautiful. He turned his eyes down quickly.

'How can I go on?' gasped Matilda. Even now she did not forget she was an abbess and that the nun who waited outside must not hear the breakdown of order.

'God gives us all strength. Let us say the *Pater Noster* together.'

But this was not possible, for at last Matilda's tears came flowing silently. She shuddered with relief and Theo, eyes firmly downcast, said the prayer as slowly as possible so that she had time to recover.

The regularity of life in the monastery changed the nature of time. The Benedictine emphasis on continual prayer as well as Theo's and Matilda's position of authority over a large body of people – the majority young – gave them almost no opportunity for private anxiety or self-doubt. Time passed both very quickly and yet stood still. Meeting constantly over a period of two years, Theo and Matilda did not feel a progression or ageing in their relationship with each other because they only recognised their relationship with God. But the human need for affection from a fellow is not so easily discounted.

Not only did the community of nuns rapidly increase in number but also the monks. Among the novices who came to learn the rule of St Benedict was a youth called Thomas. He was red-cheeked with black curling hair and such a jolly disposition that he had often to be reproved for singing when he should have been reading, and talking when he should have been singing. Theo, who believed an abbot should not separate himself from his monks, showed Thomas the proper behaviour in a monastery. He taught him the humble jobs such as filling little bowls with beeswax so that they could have a light burning through the night; he taught him Latin so that he could read the gospels and understand the importance of their teaching. More and more Theo was reminded of his childhood friend, Oswin, who had died so young and so suddenly. He came to love Thomas like a younger brother. He looked for his cheerful face at the church services and missed him if he was sent to do some work away from his side.

Another new member of the community was a young monk who had been born in the north and trained in a French monastery. He came to the monastery as Theo's deputy. He had a particular gift for oratory and when Leofric preached a sermon the atmosphere of the usually sleepy church quite altered. His words flew round the vaulted stone building like birds seeking escape. Sometimes he would fix his fierce eyes on a particular brother. The recipient of such attention would soon show all the signs of a haunted man, squirming around and on several occasions being so overcome by his own sinfulness as to throw himself down on the stone floor where he would lie prostrate in the traditional attitude of penitence.

One Sunday Leofric was emphasising the difference between spiritual love and earthly love. Theo, who had never really controlled his childhood inability to listen to anyone who spoke for more than a few minutes, was looking at Thomas where he sat in the novices' pews. Sunlight from the high narrow windows lit up the freshness of his innocent, eager face. He was listening with great concentration; his mouth was slightly open and even seemed to move now and again as if mouthing Leofric's words made him better able to understand them. Suddenly Theo felt a tremendous wish to touch those red soft lips.

The thought was so shocking, so obviously direct from the devil, that he bowed low, cursing himself frantically. When he had sufficiently recovered to return to an upright position, he shifted his angle of vision so that he faced away from Thomas. At once he became aware of a face turned towards his. By his avoidance of Thomas he had found Matilda. Severe and pale, eyes hardly blue they were so dark, she stared at him. Had she seen his expression when he looked at Thomas? Is that why she seemed so reproachful? Why else was she looking at him so fixedly?

There was no stripe of sun on Matilda's face as there had been on Thomas's but the white edge of her wimple made lightening round her upper face. Trembling still from his brush with Thomas and the devil, Theo felt his body become empty and vertiginous, as if he stood on the edge of a high cliff. It was deep, passionate, human love he saw in Matilda's grim concentration. She loved him and, instead of turning away ashamed, as he had, she was allowing him to see her longing. It was dreadful, unbearable, far worse than the spark of desire he had felt for Thomas. She must turn away or he would faint.

With shaking hands Theo pulled up his hood closer and shut his eyes. The persistent voice of Leofric, which had slipped into the background, slowly reasserted itself in his mind. 'And the purity of Christ is as far above man as man is above the beasts in the field . . .'

'*Mea culpa! Mea culpa!*' Rising distractedly from his pew, Theo stumbled out to the aisle there, in front of the whole congregation who peered forward to see who was today's sinner, and spread-eagled himself on the hard floor. What a blessed relief it was to press his burning cheek against the cold stone! What an ecstasy to sublimate his torturous thoughts into humility, reverence and repentance! Soon Leofric, who could speak for upwards of an hour without pause, returned to his words. But now they filled Theo with joy, washing over him, giving him back his purity.

As soon as he could after this service, Theo summoned Leofric to him. 'I am base-born,' he said. 'Hardly more than a beast in the field.'

Leofric looked sympathetic. He liked good use to be made of his words and the abbot was never a moderate man.

'I have risen too far, too quickly. I suffer from pride. If you'll take my place for a month or two, I would like to return to work with the animals.'

'But, brother Abbot,' Leofric looked less sympathetic, 'you are needed for more onerous tasks. You are good with the novices. You read. You write. You understand the ways of the monastery.'

'I beg you.' Theo knelt. Humility gave him pleasure. He had tears in his eyes. He thought with longing of the green meadows, the white sheep, the trees with their red apples, the sun, the rain, the birds' song, the insects' sting, the dung, the earth, the mists, the dark.

Leofric, being an emotional man himself, could never resist tears. 'Just for a little while, then. We must not run away from temptation.'

'We are taught to avoid the occasion of sin.'

'That is true.'

A few months, no more. I shall attend matins and nones. Each day I shall battle with the devil and do penance.

'There are many who would be thankful to avoid responsibility.'

'Thank you, brother.'

Realising he would be acting abbot and, unlike Theo, not without ambition, Leofric could not repress a small smile.

As if reading his thoughts, Theo commented, 'Abbot Aelfric should never have made me his successor.'

It was June when Theo left the monastery and went into the fields. It was the busiest time of year and the other workers, many of whom he had known since childhood, were at first sceptical that he would stand the pace. 'Your hands are soft and white,' one said. 'Your face is like an egg, it is so pale and smooth. Your body looks more ready to fold up into a sitting position than chase the bull off the cows.'

'And it's not as if you did any work when you were one of us,' added another.

Theo was pleased by their reproofs. It made it easier to convince himself that he was not taking a holiday. 'I used to spend my time thinking up songs,' he told the workers. 'But now I'm here to do penance so I'll be working longer and harder than any of you.'

In order to keep his promise more easily and because it made him happy Theo slept in the cowshed. He rose at dawn when the cows were milked and taken out to the fields. At night-time he set himself the task of cleaning out any of the unoccupied sheds. With that and the nightly services, he hardly slept more than two or three hours. This, too, made him happy. Sometimes he would allow himself an hour in the hottest part of the day when he would find himself a patch of shade under a hayrick or a tree. The heaviness of his limbs, exhausted in the service of the monastery, gave him more satisfaction than all the books and learning. Once, just before he slid into sleep, he found himself addressing Matilda just as if she stood before him. 'You should never have made my dream become real,' he told her. 'You should have left me alone to be what God had made me.' He was asleep before he heard her answer.

The real Matilda was not thinking of Theo, for the day after he handed the running of the monks to Leofric a messenger brought the news that her father, King Cynewulf, had been killed. Such an event, in times of relative peace, threw the whole kingdom into disarray. More than ever, her counsel for a peaceful solution was needed. Sometimes one nobleman's visit followed another as if she were a queen in her court.

In August, Theo joined the long row of workers with scythes who harvested the wheat. There had been an unseasonable week of rain, which had beaten down much of the corn so that instead of facing a field of cheerfully waving golden heads they saw a bent and fluctuating row of brown stalks. It was hard to work up a proper rhythm, hard to lay it on the ground in smooth swaths. After a few hours they were all glad to stop and drink the ale that had been brought to them. Theo had been accepted back among them. Like them, he wore only a tunic. Once more he was sun-burned, his tonsured brown hair glowing like a ring of copper on his head. But today his imitation of animal health did not reflect his inner mood for Leofric had called him for a discussion the night before.

'You must return after the harvest,' he had said.

'Let me work through the autumn. I'm needed at the farm,' Theo pleaded. Already it seemed inconceivable that he, the peasant, should ever have been abbot to this educated and trav-elled man.

'The abbess remarked on your absence.' Theo looked up and catching Leofric's eye looked away quickly.

'The abbess cannot understand why you wish to pretend to be something you are not. Neither can I.'

Theo could see that the monk waited for an explanation but did not have one to give. Why did Matilda – why did the great abbess wish to torture him? 'At least let me stay till the end of September.'

'I will let you know.'

He would follow Matilda's instructions.

'The abbess is anxious,' continued Leofric, just when Theo had assumed the interview was over and had half risen to go. 'The abbess has heard from Beorhtric, the new king, that Viking ships have been sighted not just along the north and east coast as is usual but along our southern coastland. It is only a day's marching to us here and we are very unprotected. The abbess is anxious and wants to talk to you.'

'Why me?' Theo was standing, close to flight.

Leofric was taken aback. 'Why you? But you built the monastery.'

'Abbot Aelfric built the monastery with the King's money. I was merely their servant.'

'As you say. The abbess wishes to see you. Come to the small hall after dark. I will also be present. And wear your proper robes.'

'Yes, Father.' Theo had bowed and been blessed as if indeed Leofric was abbot. But now he lay in the field uneasily. These months of peaceful subjugation of his mind to his body seemed to have left him as vulnerable to his emotions as before.

Matilda sat in the abbot's elaborately carved wooden chair. They could have met in her room but she wanted to be on neutral territory. It was true that she wanted to consult Theo about creating some sort of fortification for the monastery but it was also true that she was indulging her increasing wish to see Theo face to face. She knew only too well why he had gone to the fields like a dog licking its wounds but she wanted to see it in his eyes. She needed him. In the church at night it was too dark to make out his face and he had started missing nones. She had found a life in which she could conduct herself with honour. However, she was now forced to recognise that Theo was part of that life and his absence made her feel vertiginous and feeble. Even now, as she waited for him, she was quite ready to burst into tears.

Theo entered the room. He bowed to Leofric and Matilda sitting by his side, like a king and queen although, and he quickly repressed a smile, Matilda had appropriated the grander chair. Now he was in her presence all his anxiety was drowned in a flood of contentment.

'Good evening, Abbess.' They could have spoken in Latin to

each other now. Perhaps they should have. *'Dominus vobiscum.'* *'Et cum spiritu tuo.'* But it was a pleasure to speak simply as they had at the beginning. Leofric started in surprise as they used the vernacular but said nothing for he was an observer.

Matilda leaned forward and her face, as pale and translucent as the inside of an oyster shell, stared at him intently. She too, was happy. She began to speak about the new King Beorhtric who had none of the power of her father and the danger of foreign attack but her tone and her expression said something else.

Leofric became aware of the atmosphere and shifted uneasily in his chair. It was inconceivable that there should be any intimacy between these two – for one thing he had become Matilda's confessor and knew there was not. They shared a past, he knew that, too, but she was so austere, so dignified in her royal holiness, while Theo was sensitive and puritanical in his examination of his conscience. Nevertheless, he decided to interpose his voice between them, remind them of his presence.

'Viking attacks have always been directed towards Mercia and the Humber. Their homeland lies northward. Why should they take all the trouble to sail round to the south?'

As he finished, Leofric became aware that both Matilda and Theo were gazing at him with the same air of bewilderment. It was not what he said, which could be no surprise, but the fact of his speaking. They had forgotten his existence. He frowned comically.

Matilda made an effort. 'We are not talking of attacks such as in the past. This is on a different scale altogether. This is an effort to take over the whole country, kingdom by kingdom.'

'Then we can do nothing. We are soldiers of Christ. Our best defence is prayer.'

'At least we must protect our books, the gospels, the Bible, the silver from the altar.' She paused before adding, 'Most of all, the holy relics.'

Theo felt stifled. He told himself the room had no vent for air except one small window and whereas the other two were used to life indoors, his peasant's dislike of small enclosed spaces had resurfaced over the last few months.

Matilda saw that Theo's face was reddening. Sweat ran down his brow like snow melting off a rooftop. He was still standing for there were only two chairs in the room. She stood up. 'We will walk as we continue our conversation.'

Leofric walked a pace behind the abbess and Theo. She was right to lead them out into the open air even if the sight of a monk and a nun walking together might cause scandal to any spying eyes. Although it was nearly dark, the hot day had left a glow in the sky and a balmy warmth in the air. They walked in the yard where the nuns came to read and take exercise. Soon it would be time for compline and then to bed. Leofric shivered and pressed forward a little. Warm summer nights were dangerous.

A small cat, black with white markings, dashed across the corner of the yard. Suddenly changing direction, she pelted straight towards Theo. Unable to resist, he bent and picked her up. He held her, wriggling, towards Matilda. 'Black and white, like you,' he said, unsmiling. Furious, the cat clawed at her captor's hand and leaped down.

Matilda looked at the blood on Theo's sunburned skin. 'There are too many cats here,' she said. 'They run wild.'

Theo put his hand to his mouth and sucked off the blood. 'They are outside God's law, I suppose.'

'Yes.' Now it was Matilda's turn to shiver and look about her nervously. 'I must return to my community.'

'Amen,' agreed Leofric fervently. Perhaps, after all, Theo should stay out in the fields as long as he felt he needed.

Theo stood in the fishpond, up to his waist in cold muddy water. He was trying to emulate St Cuthbert, who had crept out at night to stand in the icy sea and pray. One night an inquisitive monk had followed the saint and discovered this proof of his great holiness. With no sea close by, Theo had first tried standing in the long wet meadow grass but that had turned out to be an entirely pleasurable experience, the sweet-smelling grass seeming to caress him lovingly. The fishpond was a lot nastier but he was afraid he might get into trouble with the keeper of the fish, who was notable for his protective attitude to his charges and for his fiery temper. It was not easy to do penance without being noticed in such a small community. No wonder St Cuthbert had headed for the sea.

After the meeting with Matilda, Theo had realised that he must humble his body. The life of a farm worker, even though he had hardly slept, had merely encouraged it into greater health and energy. The sun made his head ache and the work made his limbs ache but they ached with a physical satisfaction that was dangerously close to sensual enjoyment. He now allowed himself no ale and only bread twice a day. This regime had already made him tremble when he lifted the heavy bundles of straw so now he was attempting a more specific penance. His body was wild, like an animal's, filled with unconscious longings; it must be tamed.

At the same time he must not make himself unfit for work. God would help him to find the right balance.

Theo looked down at the water and saw that he had been standing so still for so long that the mud had sunk away and the water was clear as glass. He could see his naked feet, planted among the weeds like a giant's among trees. Between his pale legs fish swam in and out, silently gliding. As he watched, one opened its little pink mouth and nipped at his leg. It was a ridiculously tickling sensation making him want to laugh.

'My God! My God!' Theo flung his head backwards and cried out in shame. Would he manage to turn every penance into pleasure? For a few moments he kept his eyes shut and that was better, a negation of living. But soon he realised he was beginning to sway and would have to open them again if he did not wish to fall. Eyes open, Theo stared at the sky and the cloud covering, which had been streaky and not particularly distinguished, shredded smoothly apart revealing a young moon, silvery and tender as a little fish.

Desperately, Theo bowed his head down again but, worse and worse, the whole glory of the sky was reflected at his feet with the wonderful addition of the wavering fronds of weeds and the real fish, more ghostly than their celestial imitator but superior in their sinuous motion. Theo had never seen a natural sight more beautiful. It made his heart beat faster and poetic words begin to push their way into his head.

'Is there no help?' With another cry, Theo clambered furiously out of the pond. For a moment he stood naked and shivering, undecided what to do next. But even that was pleasurable for the warm weather was continuing and the water was already drying off his skin. In the east an early lightness on the horizon suggested it would be another glorious day. Picking up his clothes and holding them close to his body, Theo sent up a fervent prayer for guidance.

Almost at once the answer came to him – so obvious and so painful that it had to be right. He must leave this monastery, where he had been happy and unhappy and where Matilda ruled, and go to another. There he would shut himself in the cloisters and have no other reason for his existence but his devotion to God. Leofric would make a far better abbot than he could ever be.

With limbs like lead and hands weak and shaking, Theo began very slowly and methodically to dress. He must go immediately while he still had the knowledge and the strength.

*

Matilda lay awake in her little room. She always felt closest to God in this dark hour between matins and prime. It was supposed to be the devil's hour, she knew, when man was at his weakest. But her devil's hour came later in the day when she felt her woman's blood singing through her body. At two or three in the morning, she was weak and frail and nearer to virtue and God. Now she should sleep a little as St Benedict prescribed.

Eyes closed, Matilda listened to the night-time sounds of the countryside, the fluting of a nightingale, the faraway bark of a fox. Then, half asleep, she became aware of a different sound, more of an echo really, the faraway shuffle of many horses' hoofs, advancing slowly, in order. Assuming it was a dream, for as a king's daughter she knew well the sounds made by a cavalry column, she did not raise her head or look from her window.

Theo had only realised that the lightness on the horizon was not an early dawn when he saw the first rider silhouetted against the glow. By then he was already six or seven miles from the monastery. Turning at once he began to run back the way he had come. If the monks and nuns were warned quickly enough they might have time to escape to the woods.

For the first time he properly appreciated how his fasting and lack of sleep had affected his strength. After two miles he was in danger of fainting. His broken leg, which he had not thought of for years, began throbbing and burning. He could hear his breath, gasping and whistling and sobbing. The horsemen, whom he estimated to be at least a hundred, would overtake him before he reached the monastery. Clearly they were planning to arrive before dawn.

If the community could not flee, the only hope was to make terms. In effect, this would mean buying their lives with the altar silver or anything else of value. But that would depend on how disciplined a horde rode behind him. They came silently and in line but that might mean nothing when they found their prey. Theo knew all the stories of stealing and rape, of torture and murder. Besides, although Leofric might feel it his duty to negotiate for the lives of the novices and monks in his care, he could not see Matilda, the hot-headed daughter of a king, easily handing over her dowry. Death would have more appeal for her, both for reasons of pride and of Christianity. Death is the gateway to life. Martyrdom would suit Matilda.

With such thoughts racing through his head, Theo found new energy and entered the peaceful fields outlying the monastery ahead of the soldiers. Perhaps they had stopped at the sight of the monastery in order to plan their attack. The farm buildings were nearest along the valley and partly hid the monastery. But the tall stone church stood proudly, part of the way up one side of the valley, visible for miles around, declaring a tempting prosperity by its noble size and design. Even now that Theo saw it was likely to bring a harsher fate to its faithful than its humble predecessor, he still felt proud to have been part of its creation. Kneeling for a moment, partly to get his breath back, he crossed himself and asked forgiveness for his sins.

Matilda turned from her window and put on her wimple. When she went outside she found most of the community already moving towards the church. No one spoke. The only sign that anything was wrong was that the monks and nuns were not in their separate columns but mixed together, heading in one stream towards the church. Their calmness was deeply touching to Matilda for some of them were very young, hardly more than children, and must have known what dangers faced them. Methodically, she looked along the line of black hoods for Theo but could not find him. Perhaps he was already inside the church or perhaps he was sleeping outside somewhere as she knew he often did. Perhaps he was already captured, taken from under some haystack or perhaps he had escaped.

Matilda stood at the church door and looked down the valley. The horsemen were in six columns, approaching unhurriedly. In a moment they would reach the farm buildings. Just now a group of farm workers dashed past her searching for sanctuary, their undisguised terror causing a disturbance within the icy tranquillity of the church. Theo was not among them either.

Matilda went inside the church and ordered the sacristan to shut and bolt the great oak door. It was like being inside a fortress. Light coming through the window behind the altar silhouetted the central arch that Theo had brought, stone by stone, from the Roman city. Matilda's spirit was strong enough to face the cruellest enemy but her treacherous woman's imagination pictured Theo as he had been before he became a monk. She saw his shiny untonsured hair, his strong arms and straight legs.

'We will say prime?' Matilda's thoughts were broken by Leofric coming to stand beside her.

'Yes,' agreed Matilda, with her eyes still on the arch, 'and after prime we'll say mass and after mass, nones, and after nones, vespers and then compline and then, if we are still here, we will start again. It is an excellent opportunity for fasting and abstinence. We are particularly fortunate it's Friday.'

'Quite,' said Leofric with creditable conviction for he could not help thinking that 'fortunate' was hardly the way he would describe their present situation.

'We must hide the gospel book under the altar stone.' Matilda moved away briskly. 'It will be safe there.'

Theo was equidistant between the horsemen and the church but he was climbing uphill and, although he knew the shortest way, they were catching up again. He had seen the little dark figures of the farm workers disappear towards the church and guessed that that was where everyone would gather. He thought with satisfaction of the huge blocks of stone, each one chosen by him, transported so carefully and built by expert masons.

Now he passed the farm buildings and then the soldiers had reached them too and were driving the animals out before setting fire to the barns and stables. The fire would give such a brilliant light that he could hardly hide. And yet the church was so close now. He even imagined he could hear a faint chanting. Or was that inside his head?

The soldiers behind him were no longer quiet. As he had expected, the excitement of action had called forth the harsh cries of battle, more frightening because they were in the guttural syllables of a foreign language. He also realised that only part of the force was mounted and then often two to a horse. More ran beside them. That explained their slow progress. Presumably they only had the horses they had captured on their way from their ships. They must have put in at Dorchester. Theo was surprised to find that he could think so analytically and then realised that this was because he had given up hope. There was nothing he could do that he had not already done by building the church for the monastery. Pulling up his hood so that his tonsure would not give him away, he crouched by a bush. In a moment the Northmen were around him and picking up the pace of the running men, he joined the horde. For a while, at least, he would be safest hidden among their ranks.

Prime usually lasted about half an hour – although both Leofric and the abbess noticed they were rushing. It was towards the last prayers

> Quantus tremor est futurus
> Quando iudex est venturus
> Cuncta stricte discussurus

that the Vikings reached the doors. For a moment the chanting faltered and then picked up again at a louder and shriller pitch.

There was an air of hysteria growing within the church, which started with the weakest but, like a bad apple in a box, soon began to infect the others. They were packed so close that each could feel the trembling of his neighbour.

After ten minutes or so of futile battering at the door accompanied by bloodthirsty cries there was a momentary silence. This was more frightening than before. Several young novices began to wail loud enough to be heard above the chanting. They were on to mass now; also taken rather faster than normal.

'*Mea culpa, mea culpa, mea maxima culpa.*'

At least Leofric's voice was steady. Matilda clasped her hands tightly and prayed for a good death.

It was almost a relief when they heard a noise above their heads and realised the roof had been set alight. Strangely, the quick crackling sounded more like fast-running water than fire. This gave Matilda some consolation for water was a sign of purity and salvation while fire was horribly linked to hell and damnation.

However, when the first burning beam fell to the floor, she, like the others, found herself screaming and cringing back. Even though she immediately stopped her cries with her fist, there was no good pretending that she could preserve calm around her. Some wished to live above everything. The noise and tides of hysterical movement began to dominate the inside of the church. Leofric told his young server, who happened to be Thomas, to take shelter from the falling beams under the stone altar. In a moment he was joined by a rush of others, bigger than he. His shrieks as he was crushed against the stone made Matilda put her fingers in her ears. Leofric, who had put him into what had become his coffin, looked on with horror.

Theo heard the singing change to screaming. At first he thought the attackers planned to burn the church and its inhabitants, his proud stone useless. But then he saw that they had ladders and realised they were merely making a way in for themselves.

The faces of the Vikings, many blackened by smoke and some wearing helmets decorated with horns, appeared over the rafters. They looked like devils and were seen as such by their prey below. Groups of the terror-stricken religious, reminded of their beliefs again, fell to their knees. Soon, more and more followed suit. So it was that the first fifty or so invaders were presented with the sight of a church in which every person knelt. No one had the courage to raise their voice but many lips moved in silent prayer. Matilda found she was closely holding a nun on either side of her.

The Vikings dropped down from the rafters. It was a long way but their fall was broken by the monks and nuns beneath them. The impact was too much for Penda, the oldest inhabitant of the monastery, who groaned softly and rolled sideways. The man who had landed on him, laughed at this humble sound of life giving way to death and, as if out of sheer good spirits, stuck his sword into a monk on either side of him. This was the signal for a rise of noise, for a death here, a blow there, a shriek, but the killing was still casual as if it were not the real purpose. Killing was unimportant. Silver, treasure was what mattered. This they could carry to their ships and sail back the way they came. For these men were not the spearhead of an invasion but merely a chance landing, a chance attack.

A group of warriors, led by a fair young man in a fur cloak, was already on the altar. Leofric held the silver chalice. His arms moved. For a moment, Matilda thought he was going to hand it over but instead he looked up and stretched up his hands. 'Hoc est enim corpus meum.'

The sword cut off his head cleanly and for a grisly moment, the chalice remained held by a headless corpse. But then the fur-cloaked man was waving it cheerfully at his companions. He was like a man at a good feasting, sure of himself, unthinking of suffering. Suddenly Matilda was reminded of Wilfrid. In just that way Wilfrid had lived his life.

More were coming over the roof and through the door, too, for it had been opened from the inside, and the atmosphere had changed again. There were too many bodies in the church and not enough treasure. Matilda could smell the men, sweat, dirt, smoke, blood and lust. Wilfrid over and over again. For herself it did not matter but the young nuns in her charge were so tender, as white and delicate as new stripped vellum.

But now the fur-cloaked man who seemed to be their leader was bellowing a name. He came towards the nuns, shouting, pointing his sword. Matilda realised that he was looking for someone and then recognised her father's name. They were looking for the King's daughter. Of course they would. This was not a band of mere vandals, or they would have massacred them all by now. The villagers must have told them about the King's daughter who was an abbess. They would kidnap her and use her as a bargaining point. Cynewulf or Beorhtric, they would not know her father was dead. How tempting death seemed with this as an alternative! Matilda struggled to loosen the terrified grip of the girls on either side of her.

Theo came through the door as Matilda put herself into the

hands of the Vikings. He saw her lips move as if in prayer and could not guess she said, 'Wilfrid.' He had always thought of Matilda as a tall woman but at this moment she seemed tiny. The soldier pulled off her wimple and put his hands over her face as if looking for evidence of royal blood. He grimaced slightly as he touched the bristles of her cropped hair but then smiled as he found the emerald cross on her bosom. As if satisfied, he picked her up. His behaviour to her, like that of all the other soldiers, was rough but almost good-humoured. The effect was more obscene than if they had been raging with hatred.

The entrance of the church was now cluttered with men leaving and entering, a few dangling a nun as they might a chicken. There were also horses, led or ridden right up to the door. It was to one of these horses that the leader carried Matilda. He set her in front of him where she sat proud and straight, making no resistance.

Up to now Theo had not moved since he had seen Matilda. In all the confusion he had been able to stand, staring, and no one had bothered him. But suddenly he realised that in another moment Matilda would have gone and he would have made no attempt to save her. This was not a holy death she was facing but a dishonourable death in life. Battling his way like a madman, he reached the leader's horse level with the doorway. Grabbing the horse's reins, he began to shout, senseless words but with her name over and over again.

Matilda saw him and bent forward. Her face was white and gaunt like an old woman's but as she spoke, a scarlet flush changed her into a parody of her youthful self. 'Don't you see?' she screamed. 'It is Wilfrid come back to get me!' She waved her arm at the black figures, swaying, kneeling, running, dying. 'I will go and they will live.'

'No! No!' Theo knew she was wrong. That was not the choice. This pagan murderer was not Wilfrid. It could not end like this. They could not part like this.

But the horseman had now realised that his way was not blocked by crowds alone and pushing aside Matilda, reached forward with his long sword.

The blade went deep into Theo's side. It felt not like a knife, thin and sharp, but like a hammer blow to his heart. Knowing he was facing death he tried to pray, but as well as the hammer there was a sense of loss so strong that it made his head light and his stomach sick. The loss he dreaded was not his own life but Matilda, who was going from him into the dawn leaving him behind. Bent over but still standing, Theo tried desperately to catch a last glimpse of Matilda. But her captor's back was broad and he had not even noticed the colour of the horse.

Theo slipped to the ground. Behind him he felt something hard and realised he was lying along the oak door. He put out his hand and felt the carving. They had not burned that, then. Nor would they ever be able to destroy the stone foundations of the church. It had been his dream in which Matilda had shared.

Theo rolled over until he lay face downwards on the floor. He tried to put out his arms in the attitude of penitence, but could not manage it. And yet how long he was taking to die! 'Into your hands, we commend our spirit, O Lord!' Still the thought of Matilda returned, reminding him that, although she had left him now, it was not many hours since he had set out to leave her. Even so, they had come together again. Their fates were linked. But fate was a pagan idea.

'*Mea culpa*. My dear heart. My dearest. My sweetheart. *Mea culpa.*' A breeze as sweet and fresh as any new dawn touched Theo's eyelids. At last the hammer stopped pounding and Theo lay still.

PART TWO

Sir, I have written to the King's Highness to be good lord unto me, and am as loath to ask anything out of his coffers as any creature living, beseeching you to help me to some old abbey in mine old days. I have no trust but God, the King, and you.

Letter from Lord Lisle to
Thomas Cromwell, 16 March 1536

Chapter Seven

In 1540 or perhaps a little earlier . . .

Matilda woke up for no reason. There was no fire, no flames leaping skywards as if hell were trying to burn heaven itself. There had been fires like that in other parts of the country – the stories had come even to their remote part of the world. They were not usually started by King Henry's agents, who were more concerned to take a monastery's treasures and beat a hasty retreat. It was the local people who started the fires, as if it were fun to be festive in the place where they used to keep respectful silence.

Matilda put her feet out of bed and carefully drew back the hanging. Something had woken her – not a noise any more than a red sky. The quiet was as intense as the black, so black that it was hardly worth opening her eyes. She bent down and felt for her slippers and then pulled her wrap off the end of the bed. Something was drawing her out of the house. She could picture herself already, creeping down the wooden staircase, unbarring the heavy front door, making her way carefully along the rutted road. She could see the abbey now, the dazzle of its flying walls, the bell tower, like the crest of a bird the jewel-like pattern of its cloisters and monkish buildings. She had known it for ten years since she was sixteen and first come into the house where she now lived. She had been married there, had her baby christened there, heard a requiem for the same child and two years ago heard another for her husband. The abbey was witness to her adult life, a part of herself, whose presence she could feel wherever she was, whatever she was doing. Perhaps that was why she was drawn there now at three or four o'clock on a dank November morning.

As the mistress of Abbeyfields Manor crept out of her door like a thief, the agents of the Crown went about their business inside the abbey as slowly and deliberately as if they had nothing to hide. It was hard to appreciate, thought Theo, who was watching with all the other monks, that they were committing an act of sacrilege, of desecration. The two of them wore a particular expression, really an absence of expression, which seemed to say, 'We are acting under orders, doing a job, you have no quarrel with us.'

Theo folded his arms. The men were on the lady altar now. They were examining the image of the Holy Virgin to see if she were ornamented by precious stones. When they found nothing they let her fall to the ground. It was the first sign of irritation and the smashing sound of plaster on marble echoed round the great church. The agents were lit by torches held by servants but the monks stood in darkness. Even so, Theo sensed a movement of protest, of shock. They had stood impassively when the tabernacle had been broached, the chalice containing the Body of Christ removed, the gold doors studded with jewels dismantled. Yet now they shivered, even groaned, at the breaking of a painted effigy.

The agents were whispering to each other. They frowned and seemed to argue. Obviously they were not satisfied with their loot – such a big church should have more treasures. The leader approached the monks.

'Where is the treasure room?'

'You have been there already.' It was an old monk who spoke. He was too old to fear death.

'There should be more. Did your abbot take the key?' The second man seemed to have a list. They were calm again, men paid to do a job, temporarily frustrated.

'The abbot retired with the King's permission.' The old monk spoke. 'He has a pension. A house. He has no need of a key.'

The men became impatient. They had a quota to fill, a schedule. They wanted this church completed before dawn, before the people from the village awoke and made scenes. Scenes were none of their business. They wanted to have done with it, take a few hours' sleep and then move on to the next place on their list. The leader indicated one of the youngest monks to his servants. The men brought him forward, roughly but without too much threat.

'Where is the key?'

'There is no key.' Theo spoke, for the young monk believed stories of murder and pillage and had no wish to become a martyr. In Theo's view they were in no danger at the moment, although that might change in the morning when the bad elements in the village and countryside around came to pay off old scores. The monastic servants would have no pension, no job. 'We're a poor community,' he explained. 'Only eleven monks left, as you see, and this huge building. The gold and jewels went long ago to pay for its upkeep.' He did not add that it had paid more for the

102

abbot's upkeep than anything else. Although he thought it. This monastery had been dying before experiencing its death blow.

The agents whispered again and spoke to their servants. They were hard men, after all. They flung the young monk to the floor in disgust and, taking up staffs they had leaned against the walls, they raced about the darkness of the church. Wherever they found a statue, they knocked and bruised. Though only three, their rampaging turned them into an army.

Matilda hesitated outside, but there were no cries, only the violence of shattering objects. Unseen, she came through the door. The noise stopped as suddenly as it had started. Everybody was exhausted. Even the servants panted and hung their heads. Matilda looked for the monks and found them, a row of black figures as closely grouped together as if they were bound by a choir stall. She tried to make out Theo but he was neither a bent old man nor a thin-shouldered youth. The old monk, Penda, was receiving a document from the agent. It held the King's seal and pronounced the end of the monastery. It was in too remote a place to be saved as a local church. This was the final act of its life.

Matilda pictured how it had been on her wedding day, the brilliance of the wall hangings, the shining of hundreds of candles, the singing raised to the vaulted roof in the glory of God. Then, there had been nearly fifty monks as well as lay workers and a dozen or so nuns from an associated nunnery. The church had not been full, of course – that had not been the case for a hundred years. Then the monastery had housed several hundred monks and had been extended to its present size. But it had a life, an energy – a Christian life and energy.

After the marriage the abbot had returned for dinner to the manor. He had brought with him his deputy and a young monk. The young monk, called Brother Theodore, had eaten few of the twenty or more dishes served and only spoken to say grace.

Matilda shut her eyes for a second and then opened them. Now she saw the dark church again, the bulk of the pillars obscuring her view like occasional trees in a half-pillaged forest.

Theo shook hands with the two men and wondered as he did so whether he should lecture them instead. But the time for that had passed years ago when he should have stood up to the abbot and said, 'You are living like a country squire, a landowner, instead of a servant of God.' But he had been too scared, too young, and by the time he was bold enough, he had grown to like the abbot, even respect him. He was a kind and generous man. Sympathy for venality in his fellows was the other side of his love of blackbird pies, of geese stuffed with prunes and fine Bordeaux wine. When Theo had come to him with a theological problem, he had listened gravely and then answered with a kindly pat on his shoulder, 'Good brother, don't be so upset. If God had meant us mortals to understand his meanings, he would have created things very differently. Remember how often he asks us to become like children. Be humble, sing his praises but do not seek to understand. Lucifer fell from the sin of pride and his was the greatest fall of all.' The abbot had stood to signal that the interview was over. 'There, now. Does that make you feel better?'

It had seemed churlish to deny him the satisfaction of the successful comforter. Besides, he was a great man, dressed in furs in winter, the finest linen in summer. He had always seemed most at home in the neighbouring manor where he was treated with deference and gave advice about the proper baking of the sturgeon for the fast days or the need for regular exercise. It had been good of him to take one young monk's problems so seriously. Now he had become a country squire, abjured his monastic calling and taken up residence in a large house about twenty miles away.

Theo stood back to let the agents pass but the second stopped suddenly and turned back. 'Where is the altar of St Aelfric?' He was addressing Theo, who immediately ducked his head as if deaf or stupid. But he had spoken earlier so they knew he was neither. 'We need the bones. We don't want people to think we're only here for the gold and silver.'

They almost made Theo smile, despite everything. Did they think people, even peasants, were so stupid? King Henry needed more income so he raided the churches. After he had finally repudiated papal authority in 1534, almost all had acknowledged him as Head of the Church so there could hardly be any serious religious reason for wiping out what communities remained.

'The bones are buried under the altar.' Theo pointed. 'They haven't been moved for seven hundred years. The stone above them weighs as much as three millstones. Without gunpowder you'd never stir them.'

The servants shuffled excitedly and Theo wondered for a moment if he had made a mistake but the agents were not inclined to take so much trouble. They contented themselves with a sudden show of anger. 'You and the other monks must disperse. Leave. Go. This is no longer your home!'

'We understand.'

'We'll rest in your dormitory till first light.'

'Of course.'

The monks, still in line – how would they manage when they had to stand on their own? – turned to watch the agents of their dispersal make their exit. But the figure of a woman stood in their way. Heavily draped and completely motionless she recalled the same image to everyone's mind. Was this the Virgin Mary whose plaster form lay shattered on the floor? The younger monks crossed themselves, the servants took several paces backwards and even the agents, hardened to scenes such as they had just directed, stopped and stared.

Only Theo recognised Mistress Matilda Whitfield and took a step forward. However, when he understood what the others were thinking he moved back into line.

'It is the end, then?' Matilda spoke, her voice clear as a bell.

One of the servants literally jumped with fright. Theo could see his feet leave the ground. But the agents were made of sterner stuff.

'It's only a woman.'

'Who let a woman in here?'

'I come from the manor.' So she was a lady. Ladies did not make trouble, particularly in these times. But her presence was odd at four in the morning. Too tired to wonder further, the agents pushed through the oak door and went out into the night.

The old monk followed after them. His voice, as he led them to the dormitory, quavered unhappily. He had seen the Virgin Mary and hoped she had come to strike these violators dead. It had been an unChristian and unlikely wish, he realised, but at least it had raised his spirits. Now he felt truly dejected. Perhaps if he spoke kindly to these King's men they would find some priestly role for him somewhere. If only he had been closer to the abbot he might have been invited to join him in his grand house as confessor. But that had never been his style. 'Mind the steps. The moss has made them as slippery as an eel's back.' Probably death was his best bet or his widowed sister Mary. He was too old to become a vagabond, whipped and beaten. He used to hand out bread to those people from the monastery's kitchens and now he had become one of them.

Once the servants had followed their masters and the door closed behind them, the atmosphere in the church changed entirely. The monks, who had been so stately, began to chatter like magpies. Matilda, who had been a plaster cast of holy virginity, dashed up the marbled aisle. 'What shall we do? Oh, what shall we do?' She took Theo's arm with such force that he was whirled round. His sandals went flip-flop on the floor.

'It's too dark to talk,' said Theo. 'It is not a woman's place.' Her urgency made her seem mad and he did not wish the other monks to notice.

'Look what they've done!' cried Matilda, distraught. She abandoned Theo and ran about the church picking up fragments of stone. Some she laid back on the floor as if they were parts of a puzzle.

'It's too dark for that.' Theo sounded calmer than he felt. 'We should leave as the agents instructed us.' The old monk had already gone and when he looked round he saw that three of the youngest monks had left as well. They were not yet priests and would find it easy enough to move back into the country villages from which they had come. That left seven men including Theo, two old enough to find retirement somewhere and four, like himself, in their twenties.

Matilda stood at the head of the main aisle. Her eyes were full of tears, which affected her speech so that the words seemed to bubble from her mouth. 'I will receive you in my home. Those of you who wish. There are beds, there is food and you can stay for the moment.'

Theo thought of the times he had accompanied the abbot to the manor. He had been disapproving and ready to criticise, although he had said nothing. Mistress Whitfield, young and obstinate, had forced him to speak, raising erudite matters of theology about which he knew little and she less. Then he had been made her confessor, a position of greatest formality and greatest intimacy. He had not wanted to know about her relationship with her husband. Mostly it had been shocking, although by the inference of his sins, not hers. *Mea culpa.* Now she waited, poised in the middle of the bruised and battered church, waited for an answer to her invitation. The other monks stared silently as if uncomprehending or merely hoping that he, Brother Theo, would take the initiative. They were all more used to accepting commands.

Matilda raised her arm. As if at this signal, a sliver of light edged through the narrow window behind her and stretched out hesitantly towards her head. She could be one of those saints depicted in stained-glass windows, Theo thought, her skin as clear as colourless glass, her outline so sharp and strong. The manor had been built on the foundations of an ancient nunnery attached to the monastery and he imagined the purple cloak she was wearing transformed into a nun's black robe.

Matilda was exhilarated by her act of generosity and did not expect to be turned down. Cradling a piece of a carved stone angel's head, she started to march down the aisle. Obedient now, the monks fell in behind, Theo following last and most unenthusiastically. Withdrawing his attention from Matilda for a moment it struck him that once they left the church, they could never rightfully return. Besides, the church itself might no longer exist. He turned back, his eyes fixed on the altar, and then, indecisive, frowning, followed Matilda once more.

Outside, the dark sky was lightening as gradually as if one veil and then another was being pulled away. Certainly there would be no sun today. Matilda looked up and shook her head free of its hood. She had not stopped to put on her headdress and a wind that was blowing up along the line of the valley caught her black hair and blew it about her face so fiercely that for a moment several strands stood almost upright on the top of her forehead. Now she looked more like a witch than a nun. Theo, still hanging back, sighed nearly as frantically as the wind. He should run now, along the yew avenue, past the manor, past the farm buildings, down the grassy valley, run and run till he reached the next village and then the one after that and after that a very large town where an ex-monk with Doubting-Thomas beliefs could hide for a year or ten.

Matilda was walking quickly, at the head of her monkish procession, through the muddy courtyard where the agents had been led to the dormitory, and out on to the tree-lined track that ended at her house. Her speed was an excuse for her beating heart, her flying hair disguised the agitation of her features. She was concentrating on her Boadicean qualities. Now and again she even went so far as to cry exhortations, which flew behind her and astonished the following monks. If she had stopped for a moment since she had woken in the black night and felt for her slippers, she would have had to face the truth: far from being a warrior queen saving her troops from destruction, she was Eloïse seeing her chance to snatch Abelard.

'Aha!' Matilda halted as they came in sight of her house. From the three tall chimneys smoke twirled out energetically. 'The servants are up and have lit the fires.'

The five monks immediately behind tried to look appreciative although they were too dazed to do so convincingly, and Theo, who still lagged behind, showed no sign of hearing her words. As they paused he stared down the valley with longing eyes. Matilda saw where he was looking and, sensing the possibility of defection, set off again at a brisk pace.

The door to the manor was held open by an old manservant.

He crossed himself as he saw the monks but then spoiled this reverential attitude by half shutting the door once his mistress was through so that those behind must squeeze by in an undignified manner. It was at this point that Theo said loudly, 'I think I'll go for a walk.'

Matilda heard it quite clearly even though she was inside the door. 'Fish-face!' she ordered the old man. 'Throw that door as wide as if the King were coming.'

Theo stood on the threshold then, polite but not entering. 'Poor man. What does he want with a flock of carrion crows? I'll walk a bit. It's past the time for sleep.'

'But not for breakfast.' Matilda stood defiant. Now that it was light or at least grey, her cloak no longer disguised that she wore her night-smock underneath. Fine linen, muddied like froth at the end of a dark sea, swirled about the hem.

Theo took a step towards her. Like his fellow monks, he was used to being obedient. Now he could smell woodsmoke, dried herbs and, stronger than anything, frying bacon. 'I am hungry.'

The meal was set in the kitchen as if the servants understood their mistress's will but would go only so far in complying with her. Making no comment, Matilda left them and went up to her bedroom. Once there, she dropped her cloak to the floor and flung herself on her still rumpled bed. A little red and white spaniel curled up on the end squealed protestingly and then came to lick her face.

Oh, the joy of tears! Tears, like physical action, blocked out rational thought. The only trouble was that if you went on too long, they resulted in a headache. After five minutes of sobs fit to drown a whale (but not a little dog who licked them so gallantly) Matilda sat up. She must dress and be efficient again. Her sister-in-law, Bridget, would be awake soon if not already. Between five and six was her normal time of rising, and then there would be battle cries.

Matilda pulled her heavy night-smock over her head and, still wearing the thin shift that was like a second protective skin, walked towards the wash-bowl. She splashed her face with the cold water and then paused to look through the leaded panes of her window behind the washstand. It had started to rain, a sheet of drizzle that spread up the valley's trough. She went round behind the basin and peered closer. Now she could see small figures approaching behind the rain. Brother Theodore and she had discussed this possibility. She had always said that the countrymen were too imbued with the spirit of God to want to

108

destroy anything associated with him. But Theodore pointed out that the villagers had their own church and their own priest down in the valley and the monastery was less associated in their minds with God than with fat capons and barrels of ale.

'But do you accept that?' Matilda had asked, indignant on his behalf.

'We give food to the poor.' Theodore had not answered directly. 'We rise during the darkest hours of night to say our prayers. We say matins, prime, tierce, sext, nones, vespers and compline. We pray seven times daily. We live communally, owning nothing in our own right.'

'But not the abbot,' Matilda had not been able to resist commenting.

'The abbot is a great man, a nobleman. He is not like us.'

Matilda had not pursued the subject further for she was afraid of being told she was a noblewoman. She was a gentlewoman, certainly, the owner by marriage of a smallish manor house, but she was also a lonely woman, a woman alone.

Smiling, Matilda returned to the present and turning from the window drew her shift over her head. How white she was, as white and plump as a plucked turkey. She had goose-pimples too, starting along her arms and moving across her breasts. Matilda bent over and pinched her thigh; the flesh felt agreeably firm and warm. 'Deliciously juicy,' she pronounced appreciatively, splashing more water over herself.

'Whatever are you doing?'

It was typical of Bridget to barge in without knocking and then be shocked by what she found.

'Washing,' replied Matilda, nobly resisting the temptation to throw the basinful over her tiresome old sister-in-law.

'And what is all that noise downstairs?'

In order to annoy, Matilda made no effort to cover herself. 'The King's agents came to the monastery, so I invited whoever felt the need to breakfast.'

'Ha!' snorted Bridget. She was a stalwart woman whose face would have looked better on a man.

'And now I can see the peasants coming up to pillage the remains.' Matilda turned to the window again.

'Ruffians.' Bridget came close beside Matilda. Too close for comfort for her breath smelt of last night's onion. Besides, Matilda was still naked and suddenly felt vulnerable rather than defiant. She dressed quickly throwing her clothes over her head and then feeling behind herself to do up the complicated rows of ties and buttons. 'You should get Annie to help you.' Bridget watched disapprovingly.

'She takes twice as long as me. Her fingers are as thick as sausages.'

'Then use a maid. And what about those monks downstairs? They'll never go once they've found a comfy resting place.'

'This is my house.' Matilda, who was twisting her hair with one hand and holding a cap in which to stuff it in the other, glared at her sister-in-law.

'My house. My house!' Bridget grumbled, but she had heard the line too often since her brother's death to take much notice. 'These monks aren't destitute, you know. They all have pensions.'

'You call four pounds a year a proper pension for an educated man?'

'If they're so educated, they'll find it easy enough to find other employment. I heard they were getting five pounds.'

'And the abbot four hundred and fifty plus a house and land.' Matilda dragged her gable hood on top of her cap so that not a strand of hair could move into sight.

'He's old. You can't expect him to find new work.'

'He's never worked, that's the truth.'

'And who are you to talk, my rich young widow?' This was an unexpected gibe from Bridget. Usually she was so intent on stopping Matilda from doing anything unsuitable – or that was how it seemed to Matilda – that she would never suggest she had any duties beyond a little spinning or embroidery. As if she had shocked herself she turned her back on the bedroom and stared out of the window.

'What can you see?' Matilda bent over to buckle up her shoes.

'They've come for something. I can see empty carts, sacks and barrels.'

'Bridget!' Matilda's voice rose to a scream. 'The books!'

'What do you mean? Books! What do you care about books? Where are you going?' Bridget's voice also rose to a scream.

On the landing outside Matilda's bedroom, Annie, the old nurse turned serving maid who often felt it her duty to take up position behind closed doors, found herself knocked to her knees as her mistress raced past. Just as she was rheumatically heaving herself upwards, Bridget knocked her back again. She, however, stopped at the top of the staircase and said loudly enough for anyone to hear but clearly with the main object of relieving her soul, 'If she's determined to make a fool of herself I'll not be the one to stop her!'

Once more Annie's safety was threatened as Bridget stamped

across the landing but this time she stopped in front of the old woman. 'What are you doing crawling about on the floor?'

Annie raised her eyes to heaven, indicating that any explanation was beyond her and then, deciding the same about upward motion, she crawled clumsily through Matilda's bedroom door.

Bridget looked down on her as if meditating a kick in the huge expanse of her rear. Now and again when she saw that Annie was more animal than human, and stupid animal at that, she remembered the horrible truth that she had been suckled by her as a baby. Those monstrous breasts had given her her first sustenance. Without them she would probably have been laid in the grave with her mother. Such thoughts gave her an even greater wish to kick the bottom attached to the breasts that had fed her.

Impervious to such ingratitude Annie continued her way along the floor. Her eyes were fixed on Matilda's slippers ahead of her. Already she could see the caked mud and worse. 'It's enough to make you cry.' She mumbled and grumbled.

'Oh, do get up! Do!' Even though Bridget's attitude to Annie ranged from fury to irritation, she could not help finding it odd that Annie took more trouble over Matilda, whom she had only known since Matilda married and who showed her total contempt and had not even managed to produce a baby that lived for more than a few months.

'She's been outside in her night-clothes.' Scandalised, Annie heaved up her bulk by holding on to the bedpost.

'And now she's gone racing to those greedy monks like a madwoman.'

But Annie was an old woman and only crossed herself with this news. 'They'll be needing help for a day or two.'

'A household of sentimental women.' Talking to herself again, Bridget's curiosity conquered her disapproval and she trod so firmly down the wooden stairs that each one squealed a protest.

The monks watched Matilda rather as a herd of bullocks grazing in a field lift their heads at the appearance of a human being. She was an interruption to the pleasure of their breakfast but undeniably interesting, if incomprehensible. Only Theo rose above this bovine lack of understanding. He was not hungry after all and glad of a chance to push away his porridge.

'Everything is agreed,' he said, standing up but keeping his distance from Matilda. 'The monastery is handed over to the King's government. It has nothing to do with us.'

'Nothing to do with you any more than that mob coming up the valley? They'll be here in five minutes.'

'The abbot took most of the valuable books and the commissioners took the rest. The door of the library is locked.'

'Ha!' Matilda's loud snort caused one of the eating monks to bend low over his plate as he disguised a giggle.

'The value lies in the sheep and the land.' Theo continued to make quiet rational comments, although his heart was banging like the bell, which had not rung for prime. 'Wait!' he called with more energy as he saw Matilda swirling about and whisking away.

I am in a passion, thought Matilda as she sped out of her house for the second time that morning. I recall, with passion, the books that have belonged to the monastery for hundreds of years. They were painted by artists of genius, they were held in the hands of saints, they were handed down in trust from one century to another. As a woman, I am privileged even to have laid my eyes on them. Such books are priceless. 'Sheep indeed!'

This was flung over her shoulder for the benefit of Theo who was fast behind her. The rain had stopped falling and dawn, such as it was, had cleared the sky. But the trees of the avenue were dark over their heads and the air was as wet as a sponge. The ground, which had been sticky before, was now saturated and splashed up behind their legs. Theo caught hold of Matilda's shoulder. She stopped immediately. He had never touched her before. When she confessed there was a grille between them, and when they walked together he clasped his hands behind his back or bundled them in the sleeves of his habit. His fingers were strong and wiry and actually rather disagreeable. Matilda tried to shake herself free but Theo held on tenaciously.

'You have a plan?'

'My house has been linked to the monastery ever since it was built. I want some books for my library.'

'Oh, I see. You want to do some pillaging for yourself.'

'Thomas More insisted that men and women were equally suited for a proper education.'

'Thomas More had his head chopped off.'

By now they had stopped, poised face to face like two fighting turkey cocks, their red faces reflecting their boiling blood, their ears deaf and their eyes blind to any events outside their own passionate arena.

'Stand away, numbskulls!' Two horsemen could hardly believe a monk and a woman blocking their path, standing so idiot still in the river of mud.

Just in time Matilda sidestepped, pulling Theo with her. Even so, the horses' hoofs sent up fountains of brown filthy-smelling ooze, which settled over them like glue. 'It's sickening. The country in winter.' Matilda shuddered and smeared a blob of mud across her face. Theo looked behind her. Along came a cart drawn by two stout mules and piled high with the monastery's most prized possessions. A band of servants, although they were nearer soldiers than servants, followed on horses as bushy as shires. This was all by order of the King and agreed to by the abbot, Theo reminded himself. The second surge of flying mud seemed unimportant.

'It's started to rain again,' said Matilda dismally.

Theo turned back to her. 'Well, what about these books, then? The men will be on us soon.'

'Some of them will be my tenants.' Matilda's enthusiasm sank lower.

'Yes, you are a powerful woman.'

Without answering, Matilda began to walk towards the monastery. She kicked her feet like a child so that Theo jumped to avoid being further swamped, although as the dirt squeezed up between his sandalled toes, he did wonder if it was worth the trouble. With this kicking and jumping, they arrived quite speedily at the library building where they were surprised to find the way open and unlocked. Without looking at each other they entered the dark silent corridors, the discipline of the cold stone.

Matilda allowed herself to be left by Theo for she was beginning to think the whole operation was a dismal mistake. Theo's fingers on her shoulder had hurt as much as her husband's marital grip. Men were nasty insensitive brutes and there he was now striding off into the murky darkness. How he had stood it here for so long it was hard to imagine. Probably the experience had warped his mind.

Theo looked up at the vaulted stone ceiling and thought they would be hard put to pull that down. He walked round the alcoves where he had spent so many years silently reading. There were books scattered about the floor, some splayed open like tents, some broken apart so that a vellum leaf lay exposed. He bent and picked up one which was richly painted with the Virgin Mary in a bower of roses.

'They wouldn't have liked that one,' he commented to Matilda who had crept up behind him.

'Let me see.' She held it gently between her least muddy fingers. 'Even saving this one picture made our visit worthwhile.'

'Yes,' Theo agreed calmly. He was in a state of shock; he could hardly believe any of this was happening. Even she hardly seemed real, although up to a few minutes ago she was making as much fuss and noise as a wild pig.

Making up his mind, Theo left Matilda among the books and went back to the church. Crouching behind the altar, he remained several minutes heaving and pulling until a stone tumbled out beside him. Carefully, he drew out a book, not large but thick, with a cover once richly ornamented but now battered and pock-marked as if some inlaid objects had been removed from its surface.

Matilda found him sitting on the floor. In the dusky light, she could hardly see what he held. 'What is it?'

'The gospels. The jewels have gone but the gospels remain. It is the bones I was speaking of to the King's thieves.'

'Bones? You mean the holy relics.'

'Bones. Words. Bones. It's all the same.' Reverentially, Theo turned the pages. This was real treasure and the abbot had left its future in his hands.

'Bring it then, quickly.' Matilda was nervous and therefore impatient.

'Look.' Theo turned back to the beginning of the book. Instead of the neat Latin script filling the rest of the book, here was a page of black letters leapfrogging elegantly across the flyleaf.

'The writing's different.'

'Anglo-Saxon.' Theo stroked the smooth white vellum. 'It's supposed to be a poem by a monk pleading with God to save the life of the original abbess.'

'It is beautiful.' Matilda saw its beauty and felt rather than saw Theo's emotion. But now she could hear the irregular baying of the approaching crowd.

'They're not ruffians.' Matilda peered down the length of the aisle.

'Of course they are. You mustn't confuse charity with common sense.' Hugging the book of gospels, Theo followed her into the nave.

'I can hardly walk.' Matilda looked at him over a pile of books so high that only her nose and eyes were visible.

'That's ridiculous. Give me some and put some in your skirts. And don't take so many. They might still be here tomorrow.'

Slowly they walked from the peaceful darkness to the shouting and light and rain. Together they stood beneath the arched door-way and stared out at the courtyard.

'Well, what a lot of people!' Matilda tried to sound light-hearted but her voice shook and she looked as terrified as she felt. Surreptitiously she let three or four books slide out of her skirt. It was

114

strange, thought Theo, how unrecognisable and even threatening ordinary men become when they are doing unexpected things. Surely that man, for example, throwing down lead from the roof, was an honest fellow called Richard Ford, but now he was turned into a wild brigand as likely to hurl a lump of lead at Theo as to the ground.

'Shall we stand here for ever?' complained Matilda in a whisper. Her shaking had now progressed down her body as far as her knees.

'I was thinking,' began Theo but then, seeing Matilda's expression, understood she was unreceptive to philosophy. His sense of unreality had the useful side-effect of making him without fear. 'We'll take advantage of their thieving preoccupation.'

Theo and Matilda edged out along the wall. Everybody was preoccupied. Dark stumpy men in boots and padded jerkins, whisking about in the excitement of what they might be able to lay their hands on. One man carried a plaster candlestick in front and dragged a long white altar cloth behind him. The dark mud fell on it like splashes of blood. Neither object seemed likely to survive their journey or to be of much use to him if they did. Behind him a man staggered under the weight of a stone pedestal which he threw into a cart. He seemed surprised and mortified when it broke in half. The man with the lead was more successful and soon had a chain of workers methodically stripping the roof. In one corner a group of three or four boys had started a fire on which they were hurling anything that might burn. For a moment the atmosphere seemed more carnival than dangerous and the sticks and implements that had turned them into an army from the distance had either never existed or were now laid down.

Matilda and her black-frocked companion slunk swiftly along the wall and were unnoticed until they reached the far end when Matilda made the unfortunate mistake of bumping into her chief dairyman. He was the man who brought the cheese and butter to be sampled at the house and it was hard for either of them to pretend non-recognition. But he was piled high with stolen tiles and she was laden with stolen books so that they might have made an attempt had not one of Matilda's heaviest books taken a sudden dive sideways and hit Jack Butt's toe.

Automatically, Matilda halted her progress, so suddenly indeed that Theo bumped into her so that, weighed forward already, she tipped over on to the ground. Mistress and servant now found themselves face to face in the mud. The dairyman was still holding his foot and moaning.

'Stop that caterwauling,' said Matilda coldly, forgetting her fear, 'and help me up.'

But now the strange sight of the spreadeagled woman and the curiously unsteady monk had drawn attention and in a flash Jack was joined by a whole crowd of farm workers, most of them tenants to the monastery although Matilda thought she recognised one or two faces from her own estate. Ignoring Theo's hoarse 'Run!' she faced round with noble disdain.

'You are thieves and scoundrels,' she declaimed, 'with no reverence for the things of God!'

This might have been a good line were it not for the books scattered about her feet and the monk at her side.

'Black crow! Black scavenger!' shouted a leprous fellow with a hole for a nose.

Why are troublemakers always ugly? thought Theo.

'Oh, you're all so stupid! So stupid!' screamed Matilda, who was now on her feet again.

Attack may be the best form of defence, thought Theo, but they will not hurt her and they might easily consider me good target practice. Two seconds later a lump of stone hurtled through the air and cracked against his forehead. Heavenly light and stars, thought Theo, as he crumpled, senseless to the ground.

'You've killed him! You've killed him!' screeched Matilda, almost drowning the triumphant whoop from the crowd.

But now that the monk was down and clearly not likely to be up in a hurry, they began to lose interest. In a moment there would have been no one but the dairyman left and that only because Matilda had a grip on his arm.

'You must help me carry him to the manor!' shouted Matilda. 'You, Butt, and you, and you.' Her finger stabbed towards various shrinking youths. 'And make no mistake, if he dies, I shall take the case to King Henry himself!'

Her determination probably had more effect than the King's name, whose power was much diluted before it reached this remote part of his country, and soon a halting procession began along the manor road.

'He weighs more than a stone coffin,' grumbled Butt, who had been elected leader.

'It's the devil in him,' contributed a misshapen youth, giving a shaking heave.

'Go carefully,' commanded Matilda. 'He isn't a mat to be dragged along the ground.'

In fact, it was the pockets of the black robe that were dragging

116

and the books in them which were making the men's task onerous. Realising this, Matilda laid the robe and its contents over Theo's stomach and then, suddenly remembering her own load lost in her fall, dashed back to the courtyard. But there the carnival was becoming more chaotic, two more fires already started, which burned brightly despite the drizzle and her books were dispersed in the mud. She dared stop no more than a moment and picked up only the nearest volumes. Even then, one was so heavy that she had dropped it again before noticing it was Theo's gospels. With fingers made clumsy by panic, she opened the book and wrenched out the flyleaf, which she pushed inside another smaller book. From there she dashed back to see what her pall-bearers were doing with Theo.

She found them sitting on the grass while Butt steadily relieved Theo of the contents of his pockets.

'I didn't tell you to stop,' protested Matilda, 'I didn't tell you to steal.' But they all knew she was crying in the dark.

Without answering her, the men hauled up the lightened Theo and continued on their way. She was lucky, their attitudes made it clear, that they did not dump her odious cleric and get on with a jolly morning of redressing their wrongs.

Clasping what books remained to her, Matilda trailed her way home.

Chapter Eight

'But why is he in your bed?' Bridget's tone of distaste, disapproval and malice cheered Matilda.

'You wouldn't want him in yours.'

'In mine? In mine! I sometimes think you're becoming deranged. I've hardly got rid of one lot of monkish mouths when—'

'You've got rid of? You've no right! No right!' Matilda now sounded as furious as her sister-in-law.

Theo opened one eye and then shut it again. Really, there was no incentive to vision. The sensual feel of the comforts around him was pleasure enough and if he could have plugged up his ears he would have been happy to lie there for ever. O God, thank you I did not die, despite seeing the heavenly wheels of St Catherine and the stars of your glorious upper firmament. Theo floated off into contented unconsciousness once more.

'You must move him to the back room,' said Bridget severely.

'What have you done with my monks?' squealed Matilda, who had undergone enough difficult and exhausting experiences to exasperate anyone.

'I'm not answering,' said Bridget, suddenly calming down to give Matilda an infuriating look of older sister patronage. 'You're in one of your moods and when you're in one of your moods I don't speak to you. Now I shall get Annie and the servants to remove this person.'

'Aaaahh!' Matilda's scream of frustration penetrated Theo's otherness and his face distorted as if in pain.

'Just look at that!' Bridget pointed to him almost admiringly. 'If you scream like that you'll kill him.'

Matilda flung herself down on the end of the bed and wound her arms round herself as if physically to contain her fury. This rather surprised her sister-in-law who usually managed to goad Matilda out of all control so that she made as much sense as a dancing bear.

'Brother Theo is staying here,' Matilda's lips clacked briskly, 'at present in my bed and then,' here she paused to glare at Bridget, 'after the physician has been and given permission, he may be removed to the back bedroom. Meanwhile, you may leave me and ask Annie to come up.'

Bridget left. She thought to herself that Matilda had soon forgotten about the other monks and smiled cynically. Annie, hovering as usual outside the door, caught the smile and was reminded of Bridget's father, her old master, when he was planning a touch of marital mischief, dalliance you might call it. It sat very oddly on Mistress Bridget's features, which were both hearty and virginal – untouched by human hand at least.

'Now, now, now,' said Annie, bustling into the bedroom, although her energy rose more out of curiosity than a wish to be helpful.

'His head needs washing,' ordered Matilda who stood again, like Anthony over Caesar's body. Her heart clanged inside her chest like a bell-clapper going at double time. She had Theo in her bedroom and she had routed Bridget.

'He needs washing all over,' commented Annie, 'and, if it comes to that, so do you.'

Matilda never listened to Annie so this bit of impertinence passed her by. She bent over her captive and inspected the contusion on his forehead. It was deeper than she expected and the bruise had pushed up a bulge as purple as a sea anemone.

Theo dared to open an eye once more. There she was, her face distorted by its closeness. The mud had dried, blotching her skin like a skewbald but she was beautiful none the less, a beautiful young widow.

Theo sighed and closed his eye before she noticed. They had first met, if that was the word, on her marriage day. Although there was a village church further down the valley, the manor had always been linked to the monastery, indeed had owned it and the lands surrounding it a hundred and fifty years ago. The present noble Whitfield had quarrelled with the then abbot. Arbitration had gone to King Edward III, who had sided with the church and given much of the estate into the hands of the monastery. Land was power and money. Almost at once the status of the manor declined to the level of one of the thousands of country houses tucked into a fold of green hill. From nobility, they became landed gentry and their duties to king and country diminished accordingly.

As their star fell, the monastery's rose, symbolised by the sheep that spread across two or three valleys. Not the sort of flock Jesus had talked about, Theo sometimes thought. By the time he joined the monastery, there was money coming in from six or seven farms, not all near at hand, and the abbot enjoyed several manor houses into which he moved according to the season. One year recently, he had spent no more than eight weeks in the monastery. Theo sighed again.

'I think he's conscious,' whispered Matilda.

He had been one of a double black line at her wedding. They had sung the mass for her and afterwards saw her leave on the arm of her husband, Wilfrid Whitfield, who had inherited at the age of twelve and never done anything against his will since. No one, except perhaps Bridget, mourned his death.

'He's certainly not dead. Look at the colour of his face.' Annie wiped his cheeks clean of blood with a cloth she pulled from her wide skirt. A sickening smell of bitter rue, sweat, sweet crumbs of biscuit and now blood mixed with dirt caused Theo to wrinkle his nostrils upwards in disgust.

'Look at that, twitching his nose like a mongrel dog. He's shamming if you ask me.'

'Take away that disgusting rag and go and fetch water and a piece of clean linen!' Matilda pushed the old woman so hard that she rocked backwards although she was far too solidly based to move further. Grumbling and wheezing she made as slow progress as she dared to the door.

The moment the door had creaked shut behind her, Matilda crouched beside the bed like a tiger about to pounce. 'And now you must speak to me.'

Theo kept his eyes firmly shut and sighed for the third time.

'And don't keep sighing. I can't tell you how irritating it is. I save you from the jaws of death—'

'You led me into the jaws of death.'

'I did not. I merely . . .' began Matilda, and then changed her tone. 'I'm so glad you're feeling livelier. Now do open your eyes.'

How charming is a woman's tone, thought Theo, who hardly knew a woman, when she wants something.

'We have talked over serious matters,' continued Matilda in the same mild way, 'and I'm sure you don't mean to shut me out now that the momentous ending has actually happened.'

'I am a priest.' Theo gave in and opened his eyes. 'I am a man of God. I have dedicated my life to God.'

'We all do that,' replied Matilda bracingly, 'every morning in our prayers.'

'Is this a serious conversation?'

121

'I didn't ask for platitudes.'

'I didn't ask you to bring me here. First, render me unconscious and then put me in your bedchamber?'

'Oh, Theo.'

'Brother Theodore.'

'Sorry. Oh, Theo. Sorry, I should think of you with more reverence.'

Theo and Matilda stared at each other and tried not to laugh. They were young, after all, and the situation was ridiculous. Besides, Theo was partly right. She had taken him when he was too weak to resist.

'Does your head ache?'

'Yes. I saw black stars and comets and planets and meteors edged with gold and sending out scarlet spikes. I thought I was dead.'

'In heaven or hell?'

'Perhaps purgatory.'

'Why do we have to see everything in terms of God?' Matilda gave up her animal crouch and came to sit on the bed.

'It's my work. You don't have to.'

'And who's your employer? Ah, you see my point.' Matilda wagged her finger triumphantly. 'For several years now you've been employed by another human being. A king, admittedly, but no less human for that. In fact some might say more so.'

'Oh, make your debating points. I won't argue. You're right, anyway.'

'Of course I am. The moment the church broke with Rome was the moment you should have made your decision.'

'I am not a saint or a martyr. Besides, the abbot made the oath of allegiance for us.' Theo groaned.

Matilda frowned. 'I suppose you think I shouldn't bully you after a knock on the head.'

'We used to have an excellent barber-surgeon at the monastery. When he had finished shaving our tonsures, he tended our bodily afflictions.'

'Barber-surgeon,' repeated Matilda crossly. 'What you need is a proper physician.' Suddenly angry, she stamped out of the room. After sending a servant to search for the man who called himself physician, although if the truth be known, Annie brewed better cures than he did, she went out into the formal garden. There, among the dark clipped yews and hollies, once long ago the nunnery's place of exercise, she had sat to consider her husband's death. It had not been sudden, a snake bite which had festered, a leg become gangrenous and eventually removed, a weakening of the body and the spirit. He had never fought death, merely been angry that such humiliation should come upon him. He had not admitted he was dying even as the abbot put the oil of extreme unction on his forehead. His less than glorious passing out of life continued his way of living it. He had been a vain, lazy and irresponsible man. A week before his death he had been charged with not providing the statutory two men for four days' road repair duty.

Matilda pouted gloomily. It was no wonder she had never loved him, had not deeply mourned the death of their baby, his heir. After that death, for which he blamed her, he had turned against her, taking village women whose existence he did not trouble to hide, trying to degrade her with the filth of his personal habits. Bear-baiting was his favourite sport or, better still, setting dogs on a blinded, tethered pony.

Forming a friendship with a monk was not exactly a recipe for happiness but it had given her a sense of joining herself to something better than lust and selfishness. And now Brother Theodore's life had exploded apart and for a moment she had him in her grasp.

'O salutaris hostia
Quae coeli pandis ostium . . .'

Matilda sang softly, swinging her legs below her wooden seat.

Theo felt exceptionally young and virginal lying on Matilda's wooden-frame bed. He pitied himself, so innocently at the mercy of a world of marauding women. Opening his eyes, he forced himself to imagine this becoming his bed, his house. That was what Matilda wanted he was sure. But his imagination failed to rise to the occasion. Becoming aware of a scuffling sound, he turned his head sideways and saw Annie's large staring bulk.

As she met his eyes she crossed herself reverentially, but her look had been assessing and worldly.

'Go away,' said Theo and added to himself, 'I'm thinking.'

Surprisingly, she left at once, although first laying a neat fold of white linen on his bed. Did she not dare place it on the priest's forehead? Reminded of the white cloth laid on a baby's head to symbolise purity at his baptism, Theo frowned and groaned. If only he could remember why he had become a priest in the first place. But he had been so young. It had been such an honour, he could remember the pride in that. The monks had taken the

123

place of his dead parents, given him an education well above his background. They had taught him to read, write and sing.

'Laude, laudate, dominum . . .'

Like Matilda, Theo sang a little Latin under his breath and at the end of it decided he must let events take their course. Feeling that his wound exonerated him from further brain-torturing decisions, he then fell into a heavy sleep.

The rain stopped while Theo slept and a greenish sun spread across the valley. Light at this time of the year is so precious, thought Matilda as she watched the physician's horse break through the cobweb rays. Rising to find him food, for he would certainly expect abundance coming on such a day, she found her body had stiffened like an old woman's; she must have sat for hours. After he had gone, she would press close to the fire and let the warmth soften her through.

The house was so quiet. Night-time could not be so noiseless. Theo, woken for the physician's visit, was offered a choice of blood-letting by a puncture in the vein or by the sucking of leeches. He chose the latter, thinking it a greater penance for it was bad blood that must flow, sinful blood. But when he saw the little black animals, he cried out, like a baby. 'They are devils! Take them away!' So the doctor, grumbling loudly, took out his needle. After he had gone Theo tipped quickly back into unconsciousness and only woke again as the last rays of the sun made a feeble attempt to penetrate the thick panes of leaded glass. He watched their efforts lazily for a while, his lassitude matching theirs and magnified by the silence. Any movement must make a sound and break the peace, which, he thought, after the riotous disturbances of the night and morning, might be healing.

Here he opened his eyes more positively. He should without doubt rise and flee. As soon as he finished thinking this, his glance fixed on the heavy door which was swinging slowly open.

Matilda glided forward like a ghost, the most vigorous movement coming from a spout of steam which twirled like a tornado out of a bowl she held between her hands.

Not speaking at all, in Theo's experience a most unusual occurrence, she set down the bowl and sat on a chair by the window. Perhaps she thought he was asleep, but his eyes were wide open, or perhaps she, too, was humbled by this weird silence.

The rays of sun gave up the battle and receded below the

window frame so that the room was dark. Still Matilda did not speak.

Theo examined his physical condition. No headache, no distorting vision, no pain, no need to linger. He sat up and began to eat his soup.

'Delicious,' he said. 'Nutritious,' he continued as Matilda failed to respond. Although he could not see the expression on her face, her immobility was beginning to feel threatening.

'I'm not censorious,' said Matilda suddenly as if reading his thoughts. 'I'm just unhappy.' She stood up, looked out at the darkening sky and then turned back to the bed. 'I suppose you'll go when you've finished your soup,' she said in a matter-of-fact voice, 'and then I'll have no one and nothing.'

Theo put down his soup, which had begun to taste nasty, and carefully slid off the bed. He approached Matilda and whether because he had spent too long horizontal or out of fear of her intentions, for a moment, she disappeared into blackness.

'Hold me.'

He must have swayed for Matilda gripped his arm. Together they sat on the edge of the bed. Theo took Matilda's hand and remembered to say what he had planned. 'Your dream is too big. It is like the earth and the sky put together.'

'Yes.' She looked down sadly at their fingers curled into each other. 'I even dreamed of having your child.'

Theo used his free hand to stroke her cheek. It was burning hot although the room was cool. Why did he find her so much harder to resist in this defeated docility?

'Kiss me!' murmured Matilda, causing Theo to disengage both hands and stand up in terror. Now he could flee. He would go to the Bishop Gardiner at Winchester, who had been a guest at the monastery in more secure times. Noble and powerful, even now a friend of the King, he would find a place for him. Theo turned back to Matilda, who had bowed her head again in the way he found so appealing.

He thought that, after all, a farewell kiss was in order. Strangers kissed on meeting, knocking their ugly noses, vile. How his mouth met Matilda's was a mystery. And once they met, they clung. It would have taken a chopper to slice them apart. One flesh. Such comfort, such joy! And there was more where it came from. Theo's hand, snake in the grass that it was, uncoiled along Matilda's body until it met the smoothness of her neck.

Matilda began to imagine falling backwards on to her down-filled mattress. Like two statues she saw them toppling and then resting gently a moment before further efforts towards conjunction.

But Theo was leechlike, sucking, clinging, drowning. He saw black again, mostly because his eyes were closed but also because his wound had begun to pulse and throb. Agony and ecstasy.

Feeling something tickling her cheek, Matilda flickered open her eyes and then opened her mouth even wider and screamed. Blood was on her cheek, blood spattered down Theo's face.

The wound had opened, gaped as if with malicious laughter. Theo's farewell kiss had a contradictory result. In a moment he was back in bed again, with the ever-watchful Annie through the door like lightning and holding out a cotton pad.

'He has had a reversal,' announced Matilda coldly, because her scream had drawn in Bridget who looked more distraught than necessary. She had been with Walter Croke, the steward who had followed her half-way up the stairs. Entering the room she examined Theo as if he were a side of beef.

'It's only a little blood,' she announced scornfully. She bent low with a fat beeswax candle making Theo jump nervously as a hot drip scalded the back of his hand.

'There's no need to burn him to death,' snapped Matilda.

'And there's no need for you to scream like that. I had thoughts of murder,' returned Bridget. 'Croke pulled out his dagger.'

'You like thinking of murder.' Matilda took the candle and set it down by the bed. Theo closed his eyes against the light and other things. Despite the circumstances, his mind wandered – not very far, however. He remembered how this house had always seemed to bulge with women. Even at the monastery they were aware of it. Wilfrid Whitfield was surrounded by his mother Elizabeth, his unmarried sister Bridget, another sister who had later married and moved away, his wife Matilda – oh, Matilda! So ferociously beautiful through the confessional grille. Then there were troops of women servants. They also came to confess – usually with more reason than their mistress.

It was an irregularity, thought Theo, trying to squeeze his ears shut as tightly as his eyes for Matilda and Bridget were hammering words at each other, an unfortunate irregularity, due to historical precedence and geographical propinquity, that the inhabitants of the manor were permitted to use the monastic church and the services of the monks. The abbot was to blame as well. Such a thing would never have happened if they had not been so cut off from a good organising bishop. This valley sometimes seemed to be a little kingdom all on its own. If they were nuns, he thought, recalling the existence of an abbess who had once ruled a joint monastery, it would have made more sense. But they were not nuns. Particularly not Matilda.

'The linen is laid out in the back room, if you please, madam.' Annie used the kind of mock servility which indicated that she had the upper hand. Theo would stay the night but he would spend it in the back room.

Suddenly, Theo found himself hoisted upwards.

'Put him down!' cried Bridget. 'He's only got a bump on his head.'

'Light as a baby,' crooned Annie, cradling the poor monk in her arms that were as strong as they were fat.

'Put him down!' shrieked Matilda, snatching first hood and then cap off her head so that her hair tumbled down. 'Do with him whatever you like. I've had enough!' With a witchlike swishing of skirts, she flew from the room. Two large dogs who had parked themselves at the doorway, followed by the little red and white spaniel, bounded up at her, yapping and barking. Walter Croke, a bulky portentous man, found himself whirled ahead of her down the stairs.

'I can walk,' said Theo, stepping decisively out of Annie's cradle. But he had misjudged the distance and stumbled, falling heavily on the floor. One of the dogs, which had been kicked backwards by Matilda, bounced about with a pink tongue dangling warm and smelly above his head.

Theo discovered he was less well than he had judged. Again, blackness, although lightened by tongues of fire as in those holy pictures illustrating the coming of the Paraclete, swept over him.

'He's gone again,' said Annie smugly as Bridget stamped her foot in frustration.

Theo became delirious. For several days he did not know where he was or who looked after him and when Annie entered the room he cried, '*Ave*, Brother Thomas!' and when the physician returned for more bleeding he sat up and took his fat old hand. 'The bees need a queen,' he said earnestly, 'I've told you that before.' But when Matilda paid a visit, he turned his face to the wall and sighed deeply. The back of his head, she noticed, previously smoothly tonsured, was now covered with a thick chestnut-coloured stubble.

Matilda, who was not patient, spun wool for a few days, watched the milk drip into cheese for a few more and then attacked the so-called physician. 'He won't recover, will he?'

'Recover? Recover?' replied the physician good-humouredly. He was good-humoured owing to the rich jellies and sweetmeats that accompanied his every call. 'He's a strong young man. Recovery is certain. What's not certain is in what form or condition he'll recover. Just listen to his mind. Oh, fine. Oh, fine. He'll recover all right but he may not be the same.'

This idea of a recovered but changed Theo terrified Matilda. She ran after the physician who was heaving himself on to his horse. It was a cheerful early afternoon with a wind blowing puffy clouds around a blue sky. The horse's mane whipped into Matilda's face and that or her anxiety brought tears to her eyes. The physician was surprised for he had seen her watch first her baby die and then her mother-in-law and then her husband with a noble lack of sentiment. Since Matilda was holding his stirrup, he stirred his well-fed bulk to satisfy her wordless appeal.

'He needs to confess,' he said, smiling with the truth and simplicity of it all. And since Matilda made no response, he added, 'Priests can't confess themselves, you know. They can't cut their own tonsures either. Impossible. Against nature.' Then, since Matilda had lifted her hands to her head thus freeing his stirrup, he trotted off with a self-satisfied farewell wave.

Once he had gone, Matilda began to walk swiftly in the other direction. Anger cheered her. What a totally idiotic sponger he was! Not only could he not cure Theo, but now he suggested religious expedience calculated to ruin all her hopes of happiness. Allow Theo to fall once more into the hands of priests? Never! In his weakened state he would be like mud in their hands. They had had fifteen years of his life, now it was her turn. Angrily striding, Matilda found herself half-way down the road to the monastery. She had not returned there since the escape with Theo and felt a morbid curiosity. Really, proximity to a monastery was the cause of all her troubles.

It had been wet that strange morning, mud flying up from the ground like frightened sparrows. Now the ground was dry, the wind blowing up the avenue of dark yews and making them creak and sway. But the sun was bright, dispelling mystery, dispelling gloom. Matilda came out from the trees and entered the monastery's precincts.

Already there was a sense of decay. This was partly due to the removal of most of the lead roofs and guttering, but also to the sheep who roamed with a somewhat bewildered look among the high stone walls. Behind, and towering above the other buildings, the church still retained its dignity. Feeling guilty at facing it in defeat, Matilda proceeded towards it cautiously; an ancient church was not something lightly dismissed and there were stories that there had been a church on that same spot for eight hundred years.

As she came nearer she saw that the massive oak door had been removed leaving a black hole, mouth open wide in protest. But whoever had accomplished the onerous task of getting it off its hinges had been defeated in the end for it lay abandoned a few yards from the church. Going to examine this symbol of closed authority she started back, for a patch of dried blood lay at its edge. Obviously it had fought back, battering its thieves.

Putting away such superstitious thoughts, but sure all the same that that was why the door had been left, Matilda approached the church again. She was annoyed to find her heart beat louder and more irregularly than it should. She had taken books and stone but that had been for their own protection. The real prize she was after was far greater.

The black mouth gaped, furious and unforgiving. Matilda approached steadily, telling herself there was no harm that these vacated chunks of stone could do her. The sun, lower now, but still clear and bright, shone into her steady gaze. But she had not reckoned with the mouth speaking, with a great dismal bellow coming from the fathomless hole.

'Oh, God! No, please!' Filled with terror and quite unable to move, Matilda crossed herself over and over again like any priest-thralled peasant.

The bellowing stopped and out of the blackness stumbled a cow. Black itself, like the hole, it lifted its head once more and cried out but this time, released from the echoing stone walls, it merely sounded as a mournful moo.

A mournful moo. Mooing mournfully. Matilda staggered about with laughter, tears ran down her cheeks. After a few minutes, she felt so weak she went over and sat down on the oak door. That was all there was left in there, a cow separated from her fellows, from her calf perhaps.

Rediscovering her energy, Matilda leaped to her feet and began to run back to the manor. The moment she arrived, panting and dishevelled, she gave orders for the estate carpenter to be sent to her. 'I've found the perfect piece of wood for a door,' she informed Bridget.

'But we have a good door.'

'Then we will turn it into a table or a chest or a bed-head.'

In her new positive mood, she had no difficulty in deciding that Theo should only have a priest if he called for one and since he now rambled on about a herb garden which he wanted turned into a patchwork quilt, this seemed unlikely.

Chapter Nine

Theo became accustomed to the rhythm of life at the manor. At the beginning his fever heightened every sound so that even without consciously attending he knew the moment at dawn when the servants unlocked the outside doors, the moment the whole household sat down for breakfast, the times of cleaning, washing, and paying the outside workers or receiving payment from the tenants. All this was done from the manor whose estate, though much shrunk, was still run with proper respect for tradition. Bridget's voice, which had a distinctive West Country slur not shared by the foreigner Matilda, commanded each hour of the day. Like the bell at the abbey, which Theo missed as a soldier misses his orders, her forceful tones penetrated his solitude. Unlike the bell, it did not require him to take action. He was out of all action.

'You're like a child.' Annie washed him. Annie changed his linen. Annie scolded him and ignored his flights of fancy.

'I am a heron.' Debouched from the bed, in his nightshirt, he stood on one leg and spread his arms.

'You'll be flying away soon, I expect.'

Theo dropped his arms. Annie saw through him. He no longer flinched from black monkeys on the bed-hangings nor hailed angels flying in at the windows. The world was settling back again into a recognisable shape. 'My legs are too thin.'

This was true. His legs were as white and spindly as two willcw wands under his nightshirt.

'You need exercise. Tomorrow I'll set you working.'

Matilda had abandoned Theo – or so it seemed to Theo. She had turned him over to the old nurse who, indeed, treated him as if he were a child. His priesthood slipped away under her hands and he was not at all insulted to be set mundane tasks. When he prayed now he prayed as a young child, asking God's protection and forgiveness for his sins. He did not try to say mass, partly because he could not stand up and partly because he did not

131

feel himself capable of performing the miraculous central act of transubstantiation, the changing of the bread and wine into the body and blood of Jesus Christ. As he became stronger he realised this attitude smacked of pride, for the power had been given to him by God and was not of his own making, but even so, he could not come anywhere near the belief necessary to raise the bread and cry out, 'Hoc est enim corpus meum!' No, he would rather carry logs or pound the dough. Day by day, Theo became almost a pampered servant in the house.

Matilda watched this happen with remarkable self-control. Theo's sick madness had frightened and repelled her, making her feelings unclear to her. Besides, she had never seen him without his monk's habit and he was smaller and less impressive without its bulk. Even the fashionable padding to arms and thighs (Annie had pulled out some of Wilfrid's clothes) did not give him physical substance. He was an ugly, ethereal being, skin blue-tinged in its pallor, eyes surrounded by a web of red veins, hair chopped to an all-over stubble. The first time he had come downstairs, Matilda had not recognised him and afterwards she had not wanted to.

'He must leave the back room and go into the servants' quarters,' said Bridget bossily as she and Matilda sat over their sewing. 'That is, if he's staying.'

'Uhm,' said Matilda, unhelpfully. This time after supper and before bed, when she and Bridget sat together, depressed her terribly.

'Although, of course, he is not a servant even though he's working as one.' Bridget frowned at such ambiguity. 'He is an educated man.'

'A priest!' shrieked Matilda, surprising both of them. The needle from her sewing pierced her finger and she thrust the finger deep into her mouth.

'So we used to think.' Bridget raised her heavy eyebrows in a way that Matilda always found particularly irritating. It was all her own fault, screaming out the word that she most dreaded, that gave her nightmares at night. Was she responsible for Theo's apostasy? But he made no overtures to her, slipped by as she slipped by him. One evening she had left the book she had rescued from the monastery in his room but it stayed untouched in the corner.

'He is useful to the house.' Matilda willed her voice quiet and steady. 'Put him in the upstairs room that used to be a cupboard.'

'What you need is a husband.' Bridget sighed. 'The milk will turn to gold before we find one in this part of the world.'

Normally Matilda would have reacted angrily to the idea of her needing a husband but she was still recovering from her cry. 'A widow has no need of a husband,' she eventually managed in dignified tones.

Theo found himself tucked into a little space that relied for light on a hole in the door. At night he felt like a piece of old cheese in a larder, fetid and sweating. But in the day he grew stronger. Just before dawn, which was coming earlier now and warmer, he crept downstairs and went to a side door leading from the kitchen to Bridget's neatly planned herb garden. He sniffed the air like an animal, expanded his puny chest and swung his arms a little. If it was to be a bright day, the sun rose from above the other side of the valley. At first its rays were darkly bowed by the trees that grew on the hillside but it quickly surmounted them and flew into the blueing sky.

Sometimes, for after all he was unwatched and still relatively insane, he bowed two or three times and intoned pompously, 'O golden orb, who removes the dark threat of night and replaces it by the hopefulness of day . . .'

But then he tended to peter out into silent reflection for 'pray for us' sounded inappropriate addressed to such an imperious deity and he could think of no other ending. He would like to have been able to burst into a rush of pagan poetry but he had not the gift. Instead he recited some Latin verse or, as the days passed and his legs strengthened, worked off his feelings by walking or even running down the pastures.

By then the shepherds were already out and looked at him with disapproval or even fear. He was beginning to earn a reputation as an oddity, a monk who was not a monk, a servant who was not a servant, an educated man who carried pails of water – and worse. Once he had been seen emptying a chamber pot. In particular, Matilda's steward disliked him. Walter Croke was a solid man in body and mind, whose family had looked after the estate for nearly a hundred and fifty years. He had his own solidly built house filled with a solidly built wife, a great many children and rather too many servants for a man in his position. Since the death of his master he had assumed more and more responsibilities and despite Bridget's valiant efforts to keep him in his place (Matilda did not care enough to bother) he began to strut and command as if it were he who owned the place.

'If he didn't have such a huge, healthy wife, he'd be looking to marry you,' Bridget had once remarked bitterly to Matilda.

'The King found a healthy wife no obstacle,' retaliated Matilda, for the thought of Croke in her bed was worse than that of her husband, 'and Croke's growing more like him each day.'

The steward's principal reason for disliking Theo was for historical rather than personal reasons. The manor's estate, marching side by side with the monastery's which was also managed by a burly steward, had been its rival for centuries. Depending on the whim of whichever king ruled, the lands of one had shrunk and the other had grown. Walter Croke, who was not of religious temperament anyway, never went near the monks and hated them long before it became fashionable to do so. Theo, therefore, appeared to him as an enemy infiltrated into his camp. When they met, which was often because their activities criss-crossed the day, he drew back and crossed himself. It was a reaction that startled Theo at first because he did not judge the steward to feel much reverence for the cloth. However, after a talk with the servants, he understood that it was actually an angry hint so thereafter he avoided the man as much as possible or if they came unavoidably face to face, he cried out heartily, 'Good morrow, Master Croke, your back is as broad as an ox!' or 'You stride this little earth like a Colossus!' or 'They say bulls are stupid but I say they're noble!'

Naturally this annoyed Croke even more and doubtless contributed to Theo's widening reputation as a madman. Croke, though, was suffering under a heavy burden of disappointment, for when it became clear that the monastery was to be disbanded he had high hopes of pulling at least some of the land into his hat. But gradually it was becoming clear that the royal commissioners had some other plan. There were growing rumours that they would sell the monastery and lands to the highest bidder, which could well mean a fierce new competitor. Croke began to look at his old rival, the monastery's steward who was still in charge, with less dislike. The man was obviously expecting to be thrown out for he had allowed more of his early spring lambs to die than any good overseer should and his cows had begun to suffer from milk fever, a sure sign of lack of attention. One evening, he even approached Croke, although no words had been spoken between the two communities except in dispute for over a hundred years.

'The days are longer,' the ex-monastery's steward said with emphasis inappropriate to the thought. Croke saw he had been drinking ale and understood he was wondering if there might be work on the manor estate should he be supplanted.

'The sun will rise red tomorrow.' From Croke this was almost encouragement.

'And the day after that,' responded the other gloomily.

The next time Theo met Croke their paths crossed at the dairy, where Theo had been sent to collect extra milk for the house and Croke was looking at plans for a new roof. The steward grabbed Theo's arm, spattering milk from his pan. 'You need to do some real work, a young well-made chap like you.'

Theo was surprised. Was he being bullied? Was his mad monk cover no longer repellent?

'They need extra hands fencing the woodland,' continued Croke. 'Now spring's in the air the cattle are jumping like lambs.'

Although Matilda believed Theo's presence no longer meant anything to her, she was the first to notice his absence. 'Where is he?' she asked Annie belligerently as if his departure from the house was her fault.

'He's well now,' said Annie cagily. 'Thin as a cricket but well.' It was her habit to keep secrets until they were winkled out of her.

'What a lump of old lard you are!' exclaimed Matilda. 'I asked you where he was not how he was.'

'Oh ho, lard? Is that it?' Annie sat down on Matilda's bed, which she had been tidying. 'I just thought you hadn't noticed how well he looked. Thin like a cricket—'

'If you mention crickets!' Matilda raised her hand threateningly and then let it drop with a deep sigh. She sat down beside the servant, and forced a wheedling smile across her face. 'Has he left for good?'

'It depends what you mean by left.'

'I mean', Matilda's hands twitched and curled, 'gone away, found a new spot of earth on which to place his body.'

'That's good.' Annie was enjoying herself more and more. 'New spot of earth, spot of earth. Well, I suppose in a way you might say that was true. On the other hand, how new is new?'

Matilda lost her temper. She took off her pointed leather shoe, which was studded with silver, and began to beat Annie about the head and shoulders. 'Tell me, you fat hag! I'm your mistress. You tell me what I ask you!'

'Aagh! Ugh!' protested Annie, although the cap and hood she wore were so padded and her shoulders so fat that she hardly felt a thing. 'Oh, m'lady!'

'There!' grunted Matilda, whose arm was exhausted. 'Now tell me where he is.'

'In the fields,' snivelled Annie, an unconvincing snivel since her eyes were beadily enjoying every moment. 'By the woodland the other side of the river. He's working—'

'Working in the fields?' Matilda put her shoe back on meditatively.

'A monk. A man of education.'

Annie nodded cheerfully. A skein of hair that had come loose with the battering dropped like straw from a badly bound sheaf.

'You are disgusting,' said Matilda and went to order her horse.

It was still early in the morning, a windy, streaky day with the sun's presence diffused and insubstantial. The horse was excited to be fetched at this unusual hour and skittered and pranced like a colt. The boy who held his head watched Matilda with admiration as she caught the reins tightly and flung herself upwards. The expedition, which had begun out of pique, came to seem like a very jolly idea. She was escaping the house, Bridget, woman's duties. Best of all she was on her own, for usually when she rode round her estates she was escorted by the steward who huffed and puffed on his ugly great cob and only showed her areas which proved the triumph of his husbandry.

If I were a man, thought Matilda, I would live my life quite differently. I would run my own affairs, travel six months of the year, hunt in between times and have a young wife who would be my reflection as the moon is to the sun. The romance of this image was dispelled by a rising flock of starlings which caused the horse to rear in mock terror and Matilda to bang her nose on his neck. It seemed she must concentrate on riding.

Besides, her dream was altogether self-deluding for, as a reasonably wealthy widow, she had as much if not more freedom than most men. She could have travelled, she could have entertained, even though they were certainly off the beaten track. She could have taken more interest in the land, discovered better outlets for their excellent timber, involved herself in the problem of the wool trade, made herself into a powerful woman in the country. It was possible for an energetic, ambitious widow. But she had come as a child to the manor, as a wife picked for her family credentials and dower. She had been given to her husband and learned to submit to him and then to his sister and finally even to his nurse. Her rebellions had always been childish, romantic and without real purpose. Indeed, her capture of Brother Theodore might be said to be her first truly independent action.

Matilda did not think about Theo as she pranced down the valley. She thought about the heady smells in the spring air – even the fields where the sheep had been folded smelt good to her. She thought of the horse, so strong and warm beneath her. She thought that this land which his hoofs touched so lightly all belonged to her and she felt puffed up with delight. Deciding not to bother with the bridge, she cantered towards one of the fords in the river and laughed out loud when the water sparkled up around her.

Theo had backache, which is not to say he was not enjoying himself. For three days now he had been knocking posts into the ground. His favourite moment was the *plunk* as the sharpened wood settled into its earthy hole. He worked with three peasants, who had been taken off their own land to do this job and grumbled continually in a resigned way. They all worked hard and were patient with Theo's early clumsiness. They assumed he was a foreigner, a casual labourer, brought in to help out at this busy time of year, and they were glad to welcome him. None recognised him as a monk.

On the first evening, one of them asked Theo where he was sleeping.

'Nowhere in particular,' answered Theo, who thought that a fair description of his cupboard with a hole.

'There's room with us and decent food.'

So Theo left the manor and told no one but Annie, who caught him removing the little book Matilda had taken from the sacked monastery. 'That won't make much of a pillow,' she had commented dourly.

'I never saw a pillow before I came here.' He did not say where he was going but had perfect confidence in Annie's detective powers. Which did not mean he was pleased when he looked up and saw Matilda and horse, spotlit by the spring sun. Where he stood, it was dark and dank and quite another world to her bright progress across a meadow in which buttercups and daisies smothered the grass.

The peasants stopped working when they saw Matilda approach. They recognised her, of course, she was their lady even though it seemed sometimes that the steward or their dead lord's sister held the reins. They admired her sturdy horsemanship and were so curious about her reason for riding towards them that they did not utter a word but merely stared.

Matilda stopped within an inch or two of Theo who stood stolidly in the middle of the line. Spittle dropped from the horse's mouth on to his shoe. He looked from that to Matilda's face, which was red and shining, exhilarated and determined. Theo's heart sank.

'Come with me!'

The peasants watched as Theo, horse and rider walked off round the rim of the wood. The trees curved, echoing the curve of the river, and when they had turned out of sight of menial eyes, Matilda jumped down and walked beside Theo. The horse's head, however, came between them buffeting her affectionately just as she found the right words. Theo said nothing.

'I'll tie him up,' she said. 'Then we can talk.'

But even on their own, conversation hardly flowed. As the silence between them lengthened, the noises of birds, of animals, of a countryside filled with procreative energy, grew louder and louder in Matilda's head.

'You don't love me, do you?' Her whisper was agonised and she immediately put her hands over her ears as if to avoid his answer.

Theo waited for a moment and then leaned forward and gently took her hands from her face. It was screwed up with eyes tight shut like a cross child's.

'I'm working,' he said. 'You must let me do things in the way I want.'

'But if only you'd just say something! I don't know where I am. I don't know what to do.'

'That doesn't depend on me.'

'Yes, it does. It does!'

'When I was sick you didn't want me.' Theo looked across the valley to where the manor shone pale gold in the morning sun. His eye travelled down the dark yew avenue until he saw the more formidable outlines of the monastery.

'That's different. That's . . .' Matilda tried to think why it was different and failed. She did not admit to herself that her interest in him had been rearoused by his flight from the house. She also noticed that even three days' working outside had restored his physical presence. He was still thin but a man again, not a ghost. 'You were not yourself when you were sick.'

'I must get back to my fencing.'

Matilda's frustration was beyond words. Why could she not command him like she did everyone else? Perhaps he despised her lack of seriousness. 'I expect you want me to become a wool trader,' she eventually thought of saying, but by then Theo had walked briskly away from her and she might just as well return to her horse and weep into his mane. Not that weeping came very easily this morning. She was too healthy, filled with physical force.

Plunk. Theo's hands, grimy and blistered from the unaccustomed work, thrust down a larger than usual post. Leaning against it he watched Matilda canter away. Marvelling at her strength and confidence, he wondered that she had not caught him up and thrown him across the front of her saddle. That was the reason she must be patient until he was ready, until he was as strong as her. It was not their love for each other that was in doubt. He loved her. I love Matilda. I love Matilda. Matilda is my love. Sighing and smiling, he pulled the post out of its hole and threw it across the field like a javelin.

Spring brought all sorts of changes to life in the manor. Most important it brought visitors, travellers who had been used to stop at the monastery now looking to the manor for food and place to spend the night. They came to the front door as the light faded, sometimes as many as twenty men, servants armed against vaga-bonds, gentlemen and, very occasionally, ladies wrapped in cloaks and covered in grime. Similarly the kitchen door was also besieged by would-be visitors, but these were the poor, the sick, the unem-ployed and mixed among them the thief and the murderer.

Bridget soon became distraught. 'It's not that I begrudge the food to whoever it may be but I fear for our lives. We are a household of women with only a few old manservants to protect us.'

She addressed Walter Croke, who had come to break an unwel-come piece of news and found himself confronted by a hysterical woman who had no intention of listening.

'The King has issued strong laws against vagabonds,' he said to placate her. 'The stocks first and then even hanging.'

Bridget was as competent as he and Croke knew that her anxiety was perfectly reasonable. Normally he would have enjoyed sooth-ing her and solving her problems for they had established over the years a flirtatious relationship, even though only they would have recognised it as such. But today he drank his ale quickly and merely suggested he sent up three or four strong lads from the farm to act as guards. 'Thank you,' said Bridget, raising her eyes to his with a softened look.

But Croke turned his head away. 'Soon you'll have protection enough without them.' The message he dreaded had come to him that morning: the Earl of Ryngeley was riding towards the valley with a large retinue of friends and servants. The King had granted him, for a price, the monastery and lands and he wanted to look over his property.

'Oh, my lord! My lord!' Bridget could only think of arrange-ments. 'We must brew tomorrow!' she cried, looking at Croke's mug of ale as if she might take it back. 'Lay clean rushes. Fresh herbs must be dried and spread among them. And we must summon the glazier. And the carpenter. The earl will have my bedchamber. Everything must be in order, everything, as . . .'

The steward rose as she was still speaking. He had wanted to discuss what this would mean to their estate, make a few suggestions of co-operative management, hazard the character and ambition of the monastery's new owner.

'. . . patched linen in the country,' Croke heard Bridget say as he left the room. On his way out of the house, he passed Matilda. Assuming his habitual look of disapproval – she should have a husband, be bearing children – it struck him that she was titular head of the house and his conversation of change and chance should be held with her.

Walter Croke and Matilda followed the pathways of the formal garden. It was walled and square and said to be based on the cloister attached to the old nunnery. The dark pyramid of trees stood like sentinels at the end of each line. Matilda, who knew the steward's low estimate of her, wondered why he wanted to talk. When she understood, she reacted as emotionally as her sister-in-law had reacted practically.

'Suppose they turn it into some great brick monstrosity with chimneys as tall as maypoles!'

'My own hope is they'll look, admire the scenery and then decide they couldn't possibly live in so remote a corner of England.'

'They? They?' Matilda wondered what it would mean to have such close neighbours.

'*They* is in fact *he*,' said Croke, frowning at his mistress's frivolity. 'The Earl of Ryngeley is presently unmarried and only recently inherited. He is a favourite of the King and a shrewd man of affairs.'

'Unmarried? Oh, how that will excite my sister-in-law!' said Matilda, amused by her steward's black looks. She stood suddenly still. 'So tell me, advise, what is it you have brought me here to say?'

Croke's frown deepened. 'Our estates march side by side, madam,' he said meaningfully and then added, with an insulting wink, 'Lord Ryngeley is said to be very amorously inclined. Very amorously indeed.'

Another month passed, in which the valley lost its misty veil of spring and came through clear and hard and green. The sun was too aggressive for so early in the year, everyone agreed, but it certainly helped the crops to an early start.

Theo, moved after several weeks from fencing to hoeing, found the sun had as much effect on him as it did on the turnips or the corn. In short, it dulled his mind and strengthened his body. After years of living in the dank shadows of the monastery, followed by a winter of illness and incarceration at the manor, his body was as lank and white as a plant kept from the light. All this energy had entered his mind, which burned with lunatic ideas repeating Heavenly or Hellish images until they threatened to drive him mad. That was why he had left his cupboard and, after he had strength enough, submitted to the steward's commands. The settling of the post in the earth gave him far more pleasure than the blisters or aches gave him pain. The peasants, too, with their ordinary grumbles and their unimaginative resignation to hardship, seemed rooted in the sanity of the earth they tended. Natural order, physical labour and simple companionship were Theo's doctors.

Then came the sun, offering a new level of treatment. The workers left their huts as the sun rose above the easterly side of the valley and returned when it had swung all the way round and dropped down behind the westerly flank. It had disappeared by the time they reached home but Theo sometimes stood outside and watched, marvelling at the red marbled sky and the knowledge that the same sun would rise again the next day. At such moments, life at the monastery and his priestly duties seemed of minutest importance.

One evening he saw coming up the funnel of the valley from a southerly direction a long trail of horses and men. They were antlike, not only in their size but also in their regular and determined approach. He watched on his own for a few minutes and then called out. Everybody in the valley knew who the visitors were and had been awaiting their arrival expectantly.

Matilda looked at her face in a small enamel-backed mirror. She was no longer young but the dusky light made her eyes glow and the steel face of the mirror made her skin seem smoother than it was. She, too, knew Ryngeley was arriving, an emissary from the world outside the valley. She would greet him with regal disdain as a queen in her kingdom. After all, perhaps Bridget was right. She did need a husband. An image of Theo keeping himself obstinately to the fields made her frown.

The Earl of Ryngeley was an ugly and assuming man who was interested in power realised in land and wealth. He was angry that an underestimation of the last stage of the journey should lead to their arrival in the dark. One hundred and fifty miles should never take longer than five days and they had left London over a week ago. Even though they picked up a man from the village to show them the proper path, their tired horses stumbled and what should have been an exciting discovery became a wearisome game of Blind Man's Buff. There was certainly no point in trying to see whatever remained of the monastery so they turned at once towards the manor.

'So small!' was the earl's unfavourable comment.

'Small and old-fashioned,' added his cousin, who rode beside him.

'Food and drink,' said a third man exuberantly, just before the official greeting party came out of the door to the manor. Flares, blazing as high as trees, accompanied them so that a square of night was illuminated, much like the stage in a theatre.

Matilda, enjoying the moment of drama but nervous all the same for such a grand visitor could not be taken lightly, stood distinct from the others, trying to ignore Bridget's litany of anxieties rattling in her ear. 'There're even more than I expected . . . not a woman among them . . . arriving so late.'

She stopped only as the two parties met, kissing their greeting in proper custom. Matilda realised she had forgotten about this sort of man, the heavy odours of beer and sweat and grime overlaid with some sweet perfume. His face was on a level with hers, a dark meaty colour from what she could see under beard and moustache. He was graceless, small but unselfconscious and more obviously powerful for that. His companions, on the other hand, were swaggering fellows of a kind she remembered from her childhood. Her husband, although more countrified, had been of their sort, looking for the best of everything but to no purpose – unless self-gratification counts as a purpose.

'We are very pleased to welcome you!' declaimed Matilda and, making sure her majesty was appreciated, she swept into the house at the side of the earl. Bridget had pointed out more than once that if he married her two great estates would join together and she would be a woman of power and importance.

'We are not formal.' If Bridget said it once that evening she said it twenty times. She said it in the upper chambers and at every course of the feast she had spent so many days preparing.

Matilda, who was being very formal despite the less than perfect manners of her guests, eventually smacked her hand hard enough to bring a spout of tears. 'Stop grovelling to them!' she hissed.

Indeed the amount of food prepared and consumed was prodigious: soup, brawn, three sorts of fish, capon, boiled beef, swan, baked meat, rabbits, pigeons and a pie containing more than a dozen blackbirds. Then there were tarts, custards, cheeses and preserved fruit.

'I am working for your good.' Bridget, who had not taken her place at the table until this moment and had only come within Matilda's range as she checked the supply of wine, began a horse-like whinny of despair. 'They have drunk all the French wine!'

Ryngeley, overhearing this, and who sat on Matilda's other side, pressed his face close to her so that she had a good view of his blackened teeth and cried, 'Hippocras will do as well! My cousin and I worship hippocras. A wine as sweet as a lady's purse.'

As if this request was the last straw for Bridget, Matilda suddenly found her sister-in-law hanging round her neck with a throttling force. Thrashing her arms for survival, Matilda was surprised to hear a thump as Bridget loosed her grip and crashed down on to the floor. It seemed she had not been attacking Matilda at all but merely trying to save herself from falling. In a moment she was surrounded by dogs barking cheerfully as if at a bone and drawing the attention of even the most inebriated.

'She has only fainted,' said Matilda, hauling her sister-in-law on to a bench. It was unlike Bridget, who was as strong as any mature animal you cared to name.

'Not dead, I trust,' said Ryngeley, swaying a little and peering so closely at Bridget that Matilda guessed he must suffer from short sight.

'Certainly not.' Matilda tried not to sound too cross. In the morning he would be an important man again.

'Good, good,' said the earl, retiring back to the table and ladling sugar into his drink. Death was a man's business, illness a lady's.

Bridget's eyes fluttered open a little and then her mouth but the sound came through her nose, an ugly snorting. Matilda realised she had not merely fainted and arranged for the servants to carry her to her room. This was something Bridget herself would have organised better for the servants had also been drinking and needed the strong will of authority to make them stand up, let alone carry a partially paralysed woman, fat and muscle, up the stairs. At one point, two let go at the same time and it seemed that poor Bridget might slide like a corpse down the wooden stairs.

'Hold on!' cried Matilda, near tears. Why did poor, infuriating Bridget choose this night to fall sick? Why was there no one to help her? Why did a woman have to find a husband?

When she returned to the hall, she became even crosser on seeing a row of faces like peas in a pod, staring in at each window. 'Tell them to go home!' she began to order the servants before she noticed Theo's face. He looked like a handsome gargoyle, mouth open either in awe or concentration.

Abandoning her guests, who were now stupefied with drink, she flew outside on wings of rage. The crowd of peasants withdrew demurely at her wild appearance but she managed to catch hold of Theo. 'What do you mean, spying through my windows? I am entertaining important guests, my sister-in-law is sick and you are spying through windows!'

'We all came to look.' Theo indicated his fellows, who slunk back even further into the shadows.

'We all. We all! What have you to do with all?'

'I'll say good night.' Theo would have escaped if Matilda had not been clasping his shoulder.

'I am glad to see you,' she said. 'You can lend me support. Tomorrow Lord Ryngeley looks over the monastery. You'll be just the person he needs.'

Theo's protests were interrupted by two of the earl's men bursting from the house and vomiting almost at their feet.

'What animals!' said Matilda, disgusted.

'I didn't know your food was so dangerous.'

'Food!' Matilda made another lunge at Theo. 'They'll be as healthy as cockerels in the morning and you're to be here an hour after dawn, my guide and counsel.'

Chapter Ten

It seemed a very long time since Theo's life had been regulated by the monastery. As he walked through its buildings and grounds at the head of Matilda's party he felt as if he had left it years ago – decades, centuries, millennia. He realised he no longer felt himself a priest.

'These fishponds are empty of fish,' stated Ryngeley as sombrely as any man whose liver had turned to porridge. He directed a baleful glance at Matilda, who might be indirectly responsible for the state of his liver but was certainly not implicated in the lack of fish. It was her freshness that he found disagreeable. He preferred young women to be subdued by the effects of childbirth.

'Plenty of weed, though,' agreed Matilda blithely. Her theoretical interest in the earl was waning in the face of his unappetising daylight appearance and the presence of Theo. For the first time since she had known him, Theo looked simply happy.

As well as feeling ill, the earl was beginning to sense that this expedition, started with such high hopes, was not to fulfil expectation. The monastery was further west and in a more isolated position than he had expected. Neighbourly interest seemed represented by one insignificant house of women who did not even have archery butts or a bowling green. From what he had seen, his favourite sport, stag-hunting, was limited by a countryside either too open or too densely forested. It was true he could marry Mistress Whitfield but her estates would hardly be compensation enough. Besides, she was so dowdy with her French hood which went out of fashion with Anne Boleyn. He began to see that the King's grant of this monastery and its lands was less of a gracious sign of favour than he had been led to understand.

'Does the wind always blow this hard?' Ryngeley asked irritably of the man behind him, who happened to be Walter Croke.

'Oh, yes!' responded the steward. 'Without ceasing. All the year round.' Seeing the nobleman's gloomy look, he elaborated with relish. 'This valley has the worst climate in the whole West of

145

England. Frost and ice trapped all winter through and then a summer you'd hardly notice, what with the aforementioned wind, except when the heat comes and lies over everything like a smothering rug. It's a wonder anything grows or anyone survives.'

'You've forgotten the rain,' suggested Theo, who was amused by the steward's game. He agreed, too, with his new-found cheerfulness, that no one could possibly want this repellent earl to stay a moment longer than was necessary.

'Rain? Floods would be a better word!' Croke pointed down towards the valley. 'You see that stream? A month ago it was a raging torrent. The track was impassable. We were all cut off, living on sodden bread and rotten meat . . .'

At this point even Ryngeley looked dubious. The stream, far down below, tinkled so merrily between its grassy banks, nor was there any sign of recent flooding in the flower-filled meadows on either side of it. Besides, all the large buildings were half-way up the steep slopes of the valley. For a moment he pictured the palace and gardens he could make in this little valley.

Seeing his expression, the monastery's steward who had kept quiet up till now, expecting that any word might draw comment on his ill management but who was even more keen than the rest to have an absentee landlord, suddenly whooped, 'Bees! 'Ware bees!' He might have been making it up but they were not far from a collection of bee-hives, previously carefully tended by the monks but recently left to their own devices, and a black cloud seemed to be forming over the top of one hive.

Lord Ryngeley and his followers, none of them stoics and weakened by the excesses of the night before, did not wait to question but fled at high speed.

'Like the Gadarene swine,' commented Theo.

'If only they'd fall over a cliff!' Matilda laughed a little wildly. The cool wind had come to break the unseasonably hot weather. It blew, unusually, from the north-east, the winter snow carrier but now a disperser of unwelcome guests.

'Are they so terrible?' Theo, Matilda and the two stewards, almost hand in glove now with the success of their plan, began to walk slowly along the path.

'They've given my poor sister-in-law a dangerous attack of apoplexy. She's showing as little sign of life as her bed-posts.'

'What will you do?'

'Oh, they'll go soon. This kind of countryside isn't at all to their taste. Look how they ran.'

'I was thinking of Mistress Bridget.'

'I stayed with her last night and she's resting quietly. No pain, I think, just a kind of paralysis of mind and body.'

Matilda talked sensibly but her heart beat as foolishly as any young virgin and when they walked through a field of newborn lambs, their bleating turned to silly song: 'I am walking side by side with Theo, baa baa.' When she thought of Ryngeley for a moment it was of a man with black teeth and vile-smelling breath.

Bridget's continuing immobility gave her an authority she had not possessed in her more bustling days. She indicated by a slight movement of her head that Matilda should sit by her bed.

'She's wanted you all morning,' whispered Annie – if a sound as loud as a dammed waterfall could be called a whisper.

'I took Ryngeley to the monastery,' shouted Matilda, although there was no reason to believe Bridget's hearing was impaired. Indeed, she closed her eyes as if the sound pained her.

'She wants to tell you something important,' hissed Annie.

'Leave us alone, you bag of old cheese!' Matilda saw no need to treat Annie differently because her sister-in-law might be dying.

Once they were alone and peaceful – although hardly quiet since Ryngeley's party had embarked on a boisterous mid-morning meal below them – both women temporarily gave up the idea of communication. Matilda was hugging to herself the memory of her walk with Theo before he had left to join his peasant comrades. Bridget was trying to force her thoughts to turn into words and then to make the long journey from her mouth. She also wanted them to be the right words.

'Ooo us arry tee mun.'

Matilda started guiltily. She had almost forgotten about Bridget. Now she stared at the twisted mouth, which had produced such ugly and incomprehensible sounds. She had never loved her sister-in-law who from the moment Matilda had arrived, a young and frightened girl, had made it clear that she considered her inferior in every way. The birth of her baby had been her only triumph and when he had died, she had been made to feel useless. Yet she and Bridget had lived together in great intimacy for ten years and the sight of her incapacity was shocking.

'Ooo ust arry tee mun,' repeated Bridget and this time her inner agitation was indicated by her left hand which raised itself two inches off the bed-cover.

Matilda stared at it in fascination. It was a leathery hand, blunt and worn-fingered, a hand that had worked as hard as any

147

peasant's, but its quivering impotence made it seem almost delicate.

At this point Annie, who had naturally stationed herself outside the door, lost patience. 'Can't you understand what she's saying? I can even through the door.'

'Cow! Clod! Cat's meat!' shouted Matilda, incensed by this invasion of privacy. 'You should be saying prayers for your mistress, not spying behind doors.'

'She's saying,' said Annie, entering unperturbed for the priest had been sent for hours ago and he would do a much better praying than she could. 'She's saying, "You must marry the monk."'

'If you don't leave this minute . . .' began Matilda, who never listened to Annie. 'What?'

'She said, "You must marry the monk."'

So great was Annie's satisfaction at getting across her message and Matilda's stupefaction at understanding it that neither saw the reaction in Bridget as she heard this interpretation of her words. Her mouth struggled to form a shape but the lips were becoming as rigid as the lips of an oyster shell. The word 'earl' was far beyond her capability, which was why she had been reduced to saying 'man' as best she could in the first place. But now she could say nothing at all.

'Oh, Annie!' gasped Matilda. In her emotion she fell to her knees beside the bed. 'A dying wish cannot be set aside lightly.'

Annie crossed herself reverentially and got as near to kneeling as anyone of her bulk could achieve. She had always liked, almost loved, Theo, whom she had nursed from a weakling lunatic to sturdy health.

'Poor Bridget, poor Bridget.' Matilda took the cold fingers in her hot hands. 'Maybe she isn't dying.'

Maybe she was not before but the agitation caused by the misunderstanding of her heartfelt wish inspired a further contusion of her blood. A spasm took hold of her body, released its grip and then took hold again. This happened several times and Matilda, now watching with fear and pity, became aware that her sister-in-law really was dying. She also thought that the priest had not come to give her the last rites and that the spasms were curiously in time with the shouts of the men in the room below.

'Tell them to keep quiet!' she commanded Annie, giving her a kick to help roll her off the floor.

'Me tell his lordship to keep—' began Annie indignantly before thinking it better to avoid another kick.

148

Creeping down the staircase, she dared to put her head into the great hall. Even the servants had withdrawn to the doorway where they huddled disapprovingly. The guests were throwing the floor rushes at each other. Although the rushes had been newly laid in their earl's honour, they were already filthy with food and country dirt. Moreover they tended to break so the air was filled with stalky fragments. Annie withdrew hastily. Even though the scene held a certain nostalgia for her, reminiscent as it was of the behaviour of her late master, she still felt discretion the better part of valour. In fact, almost as soon as she had left the men burst outside, shouting for their horses and their dogs, determined to go hunting, whatever the chance of success.

'We'll ride to the forests!' cried Ryngeley. 'Wild boar for dinner!'

Matilda stood at her bedroom window and watched them stream away. They were oafs, she thought, without much emotion for Bridget was dead and her last words waved about her head like a banner. Poor Bridget – so unprepared for death. Matilda dropped to her knees again and put her head in her hands. But her posture was easier to control than her thoughts.

Theo stood up imitating the line of peasants strung across the field. He stared at the trail of men wildly galloping towards the forest and thought that the young and not so young noblemen had time to make fools of themselves. He noticed too that some carried cross-bows, which was hardly the most sporting way to fill your bag.

The forest became dark almost as soon as the men entered it and the undergrowth grew so thickly that they were soon hardly able to make progress beyond the slowest walk. The dogs, tough as they were, found themselves entangled by brambles and creepers that tore at their coats, so that once or twice they even had to be cut free.

'There must be a track!' shouted the earl, slashing down and then up with his dagger. The wood seemed positively evil in its determination to resist penetration. He could not imagine that there would be much sport. As he thought this, he reached a clearer area and caught sight of a fat old sow, lumbering away followed by half a dozen terrified piglets. By what foolishness had he arrived in this God-forsaken place? Suddenly Ryngeley realised that he should never have left London. It was a mistake, in these dangerous times, to leave the King's side for a moment. He must return at once bearing presents of quail and hunting dogs and perhaps Mistress Whitfield's nice little red and white spaniel for the Queen. What had he to do with this tiny pastoral empire, apparently so peaceful but actually fraught with obstacles? His place was beside the Crown.

'There's an old track here!' cried one of his men. 'It cuts straight through the centre of the forest.'

But Ryngeley had already turned back and did not hear him.

Chapter Eleven

Annie was feeding herself a glutinous milk pudding. She ate messily, licking her fingers between spoonfuls and making disgusting slurping and sucking noises. She squatted on the other side of Matilda's bedroom door and her sensual enjoyment of her food was heightened by the knowledge that her mistress lay in bed with Theo. Annie's excessive flesh had made her unattractive to the male sex – except to those undiscriminating peasants, filthy and more like beasts than men, whom she despised. Nevertheless she retained an appreciation of the sexual act, learned in earlier days when she was a slim young dairymaid.

Apart from a feeling for sex, Annie's natural level of imaginative curiosity was so high that she could obtain as much pleasure from other people's delight as her own. Besides, she felt some responsibility for making the union now being celebrated next door. 'You must marry the monk' had been a touch of divine inspiration. Annie put down her bowl and crossed herself reverentially.

Theo and Matilda cuddled together in bed. Their love-making had left them languid and sleepy. They had been physically separate for so many years that it was almost impossible to understand that at last they had joined themselves together.

Images of ordered beauty filled Matilda's mind, of paths bordered by lavender, of the rounded top of an oak tree, of coloured cross-stitch on white linen, of a cat stretched out on a warm brick wall.

Hymns came into Theo's mind because those were the terms in which he thought of ecstasy and praise. But he recalled them without guilt because his love for Matilda was great enough to encompass his other spiritual love.

'I would like to sing,' he murmured.

'Kiss me instead.' Matilda moved her lips a little but felt too content to reach for him. They lay side by side now, although their bodies touched and their fingers twined loosely together.

151

It was a lazy summer's afternoon outside, birds, sheep and labourers huddled in leafy shade and it felt like a lazy summer's afternoon inside. Beyond the door, Annie, who had finished her slop, mouthed the kisses she imagined taking place next door. 'Kiss, kiss.' She pursed her pudgy lips and kneaded one fat shoulder with a set of fat fingers.

'If I could sing any song but a hymn in praise of God, I'd sing to you.' Theo's voice tickled Matilda's ear.

'Don't take His Name in vain,' she whispered in all sincerity. 'And go to sleep, to sleep a little, sssh.'

They had married in church after all for no one at the other end of the valley knew or cared that the fine upstanding young man was an ex-monk. Gossip in their hamlet and among Matilda's workers was another matter but neither of them thought about that. Besides, at this time there were many monks who had changed their profession. What else could they do?

'Why waste time in sleep?' Theo raised himself on one elbow and looked down at Matilda. 'I shall get to know your body inch by inch. I shall study it. You are my map.'

'A map! You call your mistress a map!' Giving up sleep, Matilda punched weakly at Theo's chest.

'A map! Indeed, a map of the world!'

Again Matilda punched him, harder this time and soon they were rolling round the bed like two puppies.

'That's the way. That's the way.' Annie rocked herself ecstatically and then, as the noise from the other side of the door quietened, she became subdued too and her arms formed themselves into a cradle.

'Rock-a-bye-baby,' she crooned and her voice for someone so bulbous was surprisingly sweet.

After the Earl of Ryngeley's rapid departure for the court, taking with him Matilda's little red and white spaniel, Matilda had watched Theo fly to her. He had come back to the house at the time of Bridget's burial, taking off his peasant clothes and replacing them with doublet and hose. He was serious with her and respectful and helped her to deal with all the arrangements usually made by Bridget.

This naturally infuriated Croke who refused to attend their wedding and even after they had been married several months would not sit down at their table.

'He is a disappointed old spoilsport,' explained Matilda. 'He can't understand why I am not concerned with power. Even though he hated Ryngeley. A true noblewoman, in these times, is bartering salt for cheese, wool for velvet, greyhounds for a word in the ear of a lord not so very far from King Henry's left kneecap.'

'You are my much esteemed bedfellow,' said Theo, stroking his wife's arm. She was supervising the planting of gillyflowers in the garden and her sleeves were rolled to the elbow. 'What do you need of such things?'

'We have never taken our place in the county,' replied Matilda as if she were using the royal 'we'.

Ryngeley's visit, although unexpectedly short, had been filled with drama. The remarkable events coupled with the great lord's unattractive looks and behaviour had, not unnaturally, obscured from Matilda that she had been entertaining someone close to the centre of power.

She might not have thought of him again at all – except to wonder how her little spaniel fared in his rough care – had he not sent a barrel of salted puffins, a silver plate and a gold kirtle for her, a young hawk and a pair of spurs for her new husband.

Croke, who had accompanied the servant who brought the gifts, was full of ironic comments at the generosity of the gifts from someone who was not even a kinsman. 'He is a wily man, that Lord Ryngeley. He has estates here now but he is not here. He is giving you thanks for your pains before you have them.'

Matilda looked at Croke with bright concentration. When Bridget was alive she had thought him a presumptuous dullard but, then, she had no interest in the estate.

'Either he must rent,' continued Croke, catching his lady's look, 'or he will cut the trees, sell the wood. If he *is* short of money, he might do both. For sure, he'll never come here again.'

'Then it is his agent we must deal with.'

'Indeed. Indeed. I know the man. With your permission I shall send him a few dozen quail.'

This conversation, brief and to the point, widened Matilda's horizons wonderfully. Everything she had taken for granted could be destroyed by the will of one man, who, after a show of welcome, she had done her best to humiliate. She could still see his stewed face as he fled the imagined bees.

'There is still some Gascoigne wine in the cellar.' She sat up in bed one night startling Theo who, even when she was quiet, found sharing a bed disconcerting.

'You were dreaming, my heart,' he supposed, sweetly reaching up to her hair which, since her cap had fallen off, lay like a dark nest on her head.

'The monastery opened its doors and gave me you.' Matilda stroked his cheek, which was as bristly as a boar's back. 'But now we must see that its ragged walls don't spring back and chew us in its jaws.'

'You are still in your dream,' commented Theo, whose new relationship with Matilda's tender and subservient body had led him to mislay the strong, independent woman.

'You sleep. You dream. I'll not while I worry what Ryngeley plans for his new property.'

Theo understood the reproach in her tone and thought to make fun. 'My ladyship's pleasure is everything to me. For what am I but a poor peasant, educated to be a monk, but more like a fish now out of his pond, flapping poignantly on the bank.'

'Poignantly!' Matilda frowned and smacked Theo's hand away. 'I am sick with worry,' she said, which was not quite truthful. Actually, she was fired by a radical sense of involvement in the world outside her emotions. 'My dearest, my sweet.' Her whole being depended on Theo all the same so she kissed him and regretted her sharpness. 'My own lord, sleep now. We'll both sleep now and in the morning we'll talk.'

In the morning, Matilda woke early but not earlier than Theo who, since his marriage, had reverted to regular communion with God. He knelt in his nightshirt and cap by the bed, which was so high that only his nose and forehead showed over the top. Matilda sat cross-legged and watched him. He prayed like a child, eyes screwed tight, mouth opening and closing soundlessly to the words. Before he had finished, Annie, bearing cloths and water, waddled into the room. Out she went again and in with clothing.

'You come in without warning, you go out again the same,' grumbled Matilda, without conviction for Annie was beneath notice. The dogs, who had removed themselves from bed to floor since Theo's advent, roused themselves lazily, wagging their tails at Annie's short legs so she stumbled and cursed. 'By the Blood of Christ!'

'Ssh. Ssssh.' Matilda, sitting cross-legged on her bed like the prow of a ship, indicated Theo, still praying.

Annie picked up the corner of her skirt and wiped her eyes, which were trickling from the cold morning air. 'Where's autumn? You tell me. A summer like the heats of Hell so that the cows can't find water in the ponds and now winter enough to freeze your toes off.'

Matilda smiled. She liked Annie being uncomfortable – odious and odorous monster – yet she took comfort from her heavy

154

warmth. Matilda felt her own firm body and wondered if childbirth would turn her into such a jelly.

'Get dressed now, before Jack Frost nips off those pretty breasts.' Irresistibly, Annie drew her hands across Matilda's body as she heaved her skirts and bodice over her head. She felt for signs of life. For two months now she had listened to love-making and it was time she felt a change. 'Aha. Aha.' She heaved on the laces, wheezing and panting. The breasts were first, always first, the darkening nipple, the smoother whiteness with the veins protruding a delicate blue. She could tell the breast of a pregnant woman within a week.

'Oh, do get your hands off me, you dirty old woman!' Matilda saw Theo had finished his prayers and went to lay her cheek against his. 'Dress. Dress. Dress,' she said lovingly. 'Today we have business.'

Annie went to the basin and wet a cloth but Matilda would not let her wipe her face. She hung over Theo as he dressed, carefully lacing hose to doublet, a testing exercise for one who had worn a monk's robe for so long. Standing partly on the largest hound to make her higher, Matilda loved him to distraction, except she must not be distracted today . . . his straight body, his strong shoulders, his thighs, his stomach, his knees, his manly scent. 'No!' she cried to Annie, who approached with a cloth. 'He wants none of your swabbing.'

Theo liked these womanly attentions. It was still so unaccustomed. He felt like bread soaked in milk, softened all through. Matilda and Theo looked into each other's eyes and their faces flushed and, if it had not been for the joy of knowing they would still be together that evening, they would have got straight back into the downy bed again.

Hand in hand, my lord and lady went down the creaking oak stairs. Slipping and sliding behind them, the dogs snapped and sniffed; soon they would be out in the brisk air, following the trail of rabbits and hares. Further behind, Annie shuffled down, balancing her bulk by the balustrade. Her little eyes gleamed as if she saw a nice stuffed partridge: a baby by May – she was sure of it – or June at the latest.

Matilda walked slowly between the row of yews that led like giant monk sentinels towards the abbey. She had just talked again with Croke and her eyes were even wider open. Bridget, God rest her soul, had worked hard for the estate – she had known about cheese and herbs and stewed magpies – but she had never seen what was happening beyond its boundaries. She, Matilda, who had come as a young bride, knew more of the world. She understood instinctively from having lived between her father's three estates that life was a balancing of people and possessions, that the balance shifted constantly, that servants must be employed to see that it stayed in your favour. Time must be spent with those that had power, money must be spent to make sure you knew who was in power. She had come as a little girl and put aside all this useful knowledge because it had not been needed by Wilfrid or Bridget. Wilfrid shouldered no responsibilities; he ran his life as if he ruled a little kingdom. They were so unimportant, so far from London, that it might have continued like that but for the closing of the monastery.

Matilda lifted her head so that the November air could cool her face. She had been woken on the night they came to the monastery by the sense that something momentous was happening. Of course, it had enabled her to capture Theo and perhaps that was where she had lost her way. But he was hers now, her husband, her lord, her beloved. Matilda hugged her cloak around her and gave a pleasurable shiver or two. Now, at last, she was released into the real world.

The abbey had changed little over the past year. Roofless and partially dismantled, it yet stood solid on its stone foundations and its sweeping buttresses still pushed it to the sky. The spire was peeled down to the level of the walls and someone had recently removed most of the flooring of the church but it provided a remarkably grand home for the sheep – hundreds of sheep, it seemed – that nibbled inside and out.

Matilda sat on a block of stone fallen from the spire and looked across to the wooded slopes of the valley opposite. Croke was right. First they would cut the trees and then the wool from the sheep and then the sheep themselves. That was the quickly realisable value of the property. But what then? How would it be for her to own the whole valley, run it as a large estate should be run so that there would be a prosperous future for herself and Theo? A prosperous future for their children.

Matilda had seen what was in Annie's eyes: that passionate feminine desire for a birth. She felt it herself – not as she had when married to Wilfrid, for he had wanted an heir, a male child, to carry on his name. That was not possible now. The estate had come to her and she would have Theo's baby, a baby who would have no name to carry on but would be the fruition of true love. They would found a new dynasty here, in this valley. But for that she must be wily, adventurous and energetic. Her will must be

156

stronger than Croke's so that he would become her good and faithful servant. He would talk to someone who would find the person who led to the King. Croke would get the right pig by the ear.

Excited by her imaginings and feeling the damp cold rising from the stone on which she sat, Matilda began to stride urgently among the various buildings. The dormitory still retained its door but nevertheless smelt as if it had been used as a cattleshed or worse. The cloister had been much hacked about with carved foliage strewn in autumn imitation around the grassy square. She could not throw off a feeling of sacrilege, walking among these places that had been so secret. Still, where sheep defiled a woman could tiptoe with good conscience. Nevertheless, as the wintry clouds closed lower over the hillside, her enthusiastic plans for the future began to be dulled by a thickening atmosphere of religious awe. Matilda tried to make herself see it as the church was, a hollow building only decorated by the luminosity of yellow ragwort and pink ragged robin. Why, in its emptiness, did it still cause her to hush her step and approach the central altar stone as if it were any more than a builder's foundation, for the altar had long disappeared? Matilda stood at the head of the nave and thought that it was on this very spot she had made her wedding vows and tried, unsuccessfully, to bend her imagination to the person she was then. But it was impossible: that person had gone for ever – which was a relief and a delight.

Happy again, she began to hum a song about a lover and his lass. Soon she heard an accompanying whistle, a blithe, sweet sound that made her turn and run out of the church.

'Theo!' she called joyfully.

A shepherd boy looked at the lady from the manor who held her skirts above her knees and ran shouting. He ducked his head and stopped whistling. Matilda walked by and gave him, in passing, a disdainful kick. She carried on a step or two and then swung round. It had begun to rain and she could see he was about to shelter inside the church. He hesitated as she stared at him, noting the bedraggled clothes that showed the outlines of the skinny body which seemed slightly deformed round the shoulders. But his eyes had the brightness of an animal's and when he had whistled he had made a blithe sound.

'Who is your lord, boy?'

'I have no lord.' He spoke with the harsh West Country drawl that reminded Matilda of her past husband. It was strange how since her new marriage there had been so much to remind her of the old.

'And these sheep. Who do they belong to?'

'They're God's sheep.'

God's sheep. What did the boy mean? Wedded bliss had not made Matilda less impatient. Was this deformed rat-faced child a philosopher or did he merely mean that the sheep had been owned by the abbey?

'Would you like to herd sheep for me, boy?'

The shepherd rubbed his leg where Matilda's kick had landed but made no answer.

Matilda did not know why she persevered except that she could still hear the boy's whistle, which had made her think he was Theo. 'I am the mistress of the lands adjoining these.'

'You be a grand lady,' said the boy suddenly and shrilly.

Vermin, thought Matilda, incapable of rational thought. Doesn't he realise how he should bow down to me and think himself honoured? 'Why do you let the sheep into the church?' she asked severely.

The rain was heavier now, the drops merging together into fine grey sheets moving across the valley. The boy shook his head so that the rain shot off the ends of his shaggy hair. The sheep, clearly acting from habit, moved steadily towards the church.

'It's not as if it's got a roof,' said Matilda. She remembered how, all those months ago, the black cow had frightened her with its plaintive mooing. Even with her hood up she was getting quite wet, and it was still not clear to her why she was continuing such a one-sided dialogue. What was it she wanted this silly boy to say?

Keeping a sideways watch on the lady, he was edging after the sheep. 'How old are you?' shouted Matilda. But before the words had battled through the rain, she knew that was the most hopeless question of all. What had age to do with his life? But she was wrong.

The shepherd lifted his streaming head. 'Thirteen summers come Michaelmas.' His voice was serious and attentive. At last!

Matilda moved a few paces and stood over him. 'Where did you learn that?'

The boy looked towards the church. 'The monks learned me.'

Aha! Now Matilda had found her link. Here was the boy Theo had been before he had been taken into the monastery, physically an inferior specimen but united by one point in their experience, in this boy an experience that ended so quickly he was cast back on to the hillside hardly changed at all, but in Theo's case a long training for a world that came slowly and then very quickly apart. After such a life how could he become a greedy lord of the manor? I am stronger, stronger, strong! thought Matilda, exultantly.

'Thank you,' she said to the boy, kicking him again but more gently. 'Tell me your name.'

'Mervyn,' muttered the boy, who looked like a sodden bundle of rags.

'Mervyn. Mervyn. Mervyn,' said Matilda, walking away fast enough for her wet cloak to form a bell. 'You are the first witness of my proud ambitions.'

Darkness came early into the valley and yet the shadows of woods and buildings were pale, swathed in dank mists, cloudy and clinging. Matilda ordered candles to be lit by four o'clock inside the house for she was writing daily batches of letters. All the relations and friends came crowding back into her picture of life. 'My lord, I heartily commend me unto you . . .' Her writing hand was so unused that she caused nasty blots on several attempts and eventually called for Theo's help. His script was small and regular, a pleasing spider across the page that caused Matilda nearly to strangle him around the neck with her hugs and kisses. She kissed him, truly, in part from fear that this act of writing would cast him back into monkish thoughts and, perhaps, regrets. He headed each letter, 'St Blaise's Day' or 'The eve of the feast of St Lawrence'.

But he patted her cheek and told her, 'I am your clerk, your lover, your servant.' Away went his writing again, forming her words of profound honour, boundless good will, desire for further contact, into an orderly progression. Theo grew more thoughtful as he wrote and when the night outside was as profound as it ever would be, he went to the narrow upper chamber which he had appropriated for his own use. His candle, guttering dangerously in the draughty doorway, threw light to every corner. In one he bent among a pile of ill-assorted possessions until he found what he wanted.

'Oh, where are you? Where are you hiding?' called Matilda from below, who felt a cold wind whenever he left her side – although she was perfectly capable of leaving him.

Theo came down again, trying not to drip wax on the pile of books he held. Matilda watched jealously as he opened the top one. 'Does it have pictures?' she asked, as a child nags her mother.

'Oh, yes,' Theo answered without lifting his head, but he was pleased with her interest.

'They're the books we brought from the monastery.'

159

Theo frowned. The illustrated capitals, some ornamented with beasts or pictures of monks at prayer or in the field, glowed reassuringly. Slowly he unfolded a sheet of vellum stuck in among them.

'I tore it out.' Matilda dared to come over now that he seemed to need her. 'It was so old and you told me the story of the abbess.'

'But you let the gospels go.' He was more upset than was sensible, his blue eyes staring and his wiry fingers combing through his hair. It had grown below his ears now and twisted and twirled like a columbine. 'How could I have forgotten? All these many months.'

'You have the poem.'

'The poem!' Pushing aside the books, he let his head fall on the table.

Matilda took hold of him and raised him from his seat. It was bedtime. In their deep warm bed they would be like two chicks in a nest. She would comfort him there. His wildness frightened her, bringing back memories of his month of madness when he had seen fiery devils and angels with straw in their wings and pitchforks in their hands. His body had wasted almost to nothing and with no human flesh and a mind trying hard to incinerate itself, there had been no one for her to love. She did not want that to happen again.

Theo submitted himself to her caresses and at last felt so weakened by her loving sympathy that he began to sob. Matilda had the good sense not to ask the reason and soon he quietened, curled up close beside her and fell asleep. Matilda sighed. She had loved him because he was different. God was the only thing that could separate them. Her worldly plans would never touch his heart. She must let him say his prayers and not complain if the crowd of vagabonds at the kitchen door threatened to make baking a full day's occupation. Perhaps she would build him a little chapel – although these were hardly the times. Lying awake for more than an hour as the night settled down around her with no more disturbance than the occasional squawk of a paranoid chicken, she could not avoid the knowledge that God had taken an important part of his heart when he was still a boy. She should be content that he had brought a human love to her and not ask for divine passion.

Chapter Twelve

The house smelt of the beeswax rubbed into the oak panelling and furniture, and of the lavender heads preserved since last summer and now piled into china bowls set on window-ledges and chests. Matilda was satisfied. This was how a proper house should look. She walked from room to room, her jutting stomach giving her a comical waddle, while the sunbeams coming through the leaded windows, bounced from one shiny surface to another. In the dining hall a great fire blazed, but the sharp brilliance of the sun made its flames seem dim. This will be the truest spring of my life, thought Matilda. My baby will come into a world where the dark corners have been swept clean of beetles, bugs and earwigs.

Although still needing to inspect the kitchens and the dairy, Matilda sat down for a moment. In a few hours' time her sister would arrive from Gloucestershire with husband, two children and a retinue of servants, including a harpist and a hawker. Alice was her half-sister, her father's daughter by an earlier marriage, so she hardly knew her intimately even if such a long time had not passed since their last meeting. But her husband was the sheriff for his shire, a man of property who took responsibility for his bit of earth.

Theo looked at the farm's accounts with a rigorous eye. They were satisfactory, only needing more land to expand their dairy produce. He had *The Book of Husbandrie*, which gave good advice on running a farm. The household expenditure, however, was ridiculously large: new linen, new silver, newer wall hangings, more imported food and wine. Entertaining, Matilda's present passion, was expensive. She, of course, said the money all went on providing soup for his beggars. Theo smiled at the thought of his wife and wondered whether her habits were a pregnant woman's obsession, as one might need pomegranate or oranges or another the taste of rosemary or coriander. When she had a baby she would not want all these people, he thought in easy self-deception. Abandoning his columns of figures, he decided to walk out in the

161

May morning sun and inspect the new archery butts Matilda had caused to be set up in the meadow. Perhaps he would even learn to draw a bow himself.

Annie saw her master coming through the hall, head high as he looked to the meadows and the sky filled with birdsong. She scuttled back and crossed herself. Theo's attention was drawn by her smell; she no longer changed her clothes and her hair hung in undressed grey hanks. She was revolting, particularly on such a clean bright morning.

'Good morning, my old nurse,' he said stifling his distaste. 'Why are you seeking dark corners?'

Annie would not answer beyond an animal-like snuffle and a shake of her greasy locks. Matilda said she was mad, beyond reason, and that they should turn her out to one of the peasants' huts where she could hide herself like a sick stoat. But Theo felt sorry for her, remembering how she had looked after him during his illness. Also, he knew what had set off her madness: two months ago Matilda had chosen a young girl from the village to be wet nurse to the baby. In order to ensure her cleanliness and health, the girl now lived with her own baby in a back room of the house. From the day of her arrival, Annie had turned into this sort of animal, spitting and pushing at the frightened girl and turning her own living area into a squalid den.

'We still need you, Annie,' said Theo, frank and free, standing in the usually dark hallway now shot through with beams of spring light.

Annie flinched further away, growling with a show of gums and few remaining teeth, like a mad dog. She had not really believed she would be allowed to feed the new baby, thought Theo. Apart from anything else she was too old. For the first time he wondered if Matilda was right and she should be made to leave the manor. Her little bloodshot eyes seemed full of malevolence, instead of that doting curiosity he used to see.

'You are not yourself,' he said and went quickly to the door where the sweet air would wipe away fearful presentiments.

Annie watched him go, sighing with relief and crossing herself over and over again. In her jealous and muddled brain, ideas, memories, images crossed and recrossed until she felt tortured as if bound in tight strings. Most of all, she feared that moment when she had falsely explained to Matilda Mistress Bridget's last words. 'You must marry the monk,' she had said when she knew it was Ryngeley whom the dying woman meant. It had been an act against God. No good would come of it. This house would be cursed because of it and she was the cause. No wonder she was being replaced by a pretty young village girl. Not that it would help them, not for a minute. Annie huddled down on the floor like a dirty rug. Soon a couple of dogs, who liked warm smelly things, flopped down beside her.

Matilda's visitors came when the afternoon shadows were doubling every tree and turning the smallest copse into a well-stocked wood. She was filled with pride as she saw the size and richness of the entourage. It wound its way rather slowly through the valley road and then started more briskly the short journey up towards the house. Matilda pictured what they would see, looking up: the solid stone-built manor with its long chimneys and dark-veined windows. They would see where the gardens, newly enhanced with flowers, lay and the farm buildings and the great yew trees. Strangely, Matilda's mind's eye did not include the ruins of the monastery, so much larger and more dramatic than the house. To her now, it was a nothing, a ghost, a building with no visibility until she decided to breathe life into it again. She had invited her sister to stay at the house and it was the house that Alice must see as she approached the end of her journey.

After the sun had set, mists came whispering up the valley and hovered over streams and pools or folded round the trunks of trees. Spring procreation was so evident in the countryside that even then the peaceful dark was constantly interrupted by squeaks and trills and murmurings. The house, lit by the extravagance of candles that Matilda had ordered, seemed part of this energetic new life, not resting until far into the night. The sound of the harp rippled across the valley, echoing in grander display the trills of the fast-flowing stream. The singer's voice, a youthful tenor, sang as clear as the nightingale, and when more voices joined with less harmony they were as exuberant as the chorus of bullfrogs that made the reeds shake.

The house was so full that most of Matilda's servants were to sleep in a farm shed. Many of the sheriff's servants also chose to go there, taking mugs of ale and whole loaves of bread. They sang, too, though more like crows than nightingales.

Annie took part in neither festivity for, hour by hour, her mind withdrew further from the outside world. She felt herself part of the terrible curse she had invented, tortured and inconsolable. Yet, although she no longer acted, her senses still functioned – in particular her wily peasant ears which picked up every sound, every word. So it was she who recorded, unconsciously but indelibly, the first word of the coming of the plague.

'We must not stay beyond a few days,' said the bodyservant of the sheriff to his master. 'We seem to have journeyed beside the sickness rather than through it and certainly it has not arrived here yet. But we should not take any risks.'

Annie, lying in her rug-dog attitude, took this in acutely. Plague was coming to the house. The information wound its way into the tangle of her mind and started a new pattern of horror.

The little valley with its forgotten monastery, its one large house and its small village had been remarkably free from the plague. It was travellers who carried the plague and, from the time of the monastery's decline until Matilda's steps towards regeneration, there had been few enough of those. The valley people looked forward hopefully to dying in their beds or at least on a clean pallet of straw.

Alice, Matilda's half-sister, was a stately woman, possessing the same fine features as Matilda but cast in a stronger mould. Matilda admired her substantial presence with a kind of childish hero worship. This was how a mature woman should be. The morning after her arrival she was already writing letters to important servants of the King who were to arrange for the education of her sons. When she told Matilda that they would only be staying three days instead of the ten days planned, Matilda felt too awed to question or complain. At least she had received an invitation to pay a return visit to Gloucester later in the summer, after she had recovered from her confinement.

Theo made no comment either because the sooner any visitor left the better for him. 'I reverence you, dear heart, dear wife,' he told Matilda, rather formally for a new husband. 'If you, like your important sister, had two chins, a nose like a church bell and feet that make the floorboards squeal in protest I could not reverence you more.'

'Ssh, Theo,' said Matilda, blushing out of an equal proportion of aggravation and pleasure – he was, first of all, her love. 'Ssh, you have no respect.'

The train of sleepy horses left very early in the morning when ground and sky and trees were still painted by the blue of night. Matilda sighed and wrung her hands when they had gone. Tears, even, appeared shimmering in her eyes. But then, to her own slightly guilty surprise, she proceeded to spend one of the happiest days of her life. Above the valley a strong wind blew clouds across the sky, not always in the same direction but always bustling and energetic. Matilda was like these clouds, dashing about the house and garden, issuing instructions for the resumption of normal order after their guests. Even the chickens were not safe from her managing energy.

'There's one laid under the kitchen table,' she cried to the cook.

'But she always does, my lady,' pointed out the cook.

'Out with you!' shouted Matilda, brandishing a brush.

Walter Croke, who had come to report on a discussion he had had with the sheriff's man about the monastery lands, found his lady would not sit down long enough to listen. Casting a baleful look at Theo, who did nothing to keep his wife in order, he retreated. Women had no concentration, he thought irritably.

The young wet nurse from the village saw her mistress's behaviour and picked up her own child with sad tenderness. Such wild activity meant only one thing. Soon her milk would flow into another baby's mouth. 'Oowhh!' wailed the baby as he felt his mother's too-loving hugs.

The wind grew stronger in the evening instead of dying away as it usually did at the end of the day. Annie stood in the shadow of the house. She smelled nothing of the dusky damp of spring but only the rank odour of plague. Thirty years ago she had known the smell intimately when her man had brought it back from a visit to town and died within a week. The smell had stayed in her nostrils for months afterwards, the cloying odour of death and the end of her own youthful simplicity. Now it was in her nostrils again, blown up the valley with such physical reality to her heated imagination that she began to see it as a mauve-coloured cloud.

Annie's body jerked and then froze, for voices came round the corner of the house and one she recognised as that of the young wet nurse. Crouching by the shrubbery, she watched as the tearful girl handed over her baby to an old woman who wrapped it closely and then set off down the path to the village. The girl stood watching, silhouetted almost to blackness by the lingering brightness of the western sky behind her. Enraged by her dignified posture and unconscious beauty, Annie sprang out from the bush and attacked her with her nails and her teeth.

The girl, who was strong and much taller than Annie, hardly bothered to defend herself but eventually gave the old woman a shove that sent her stumbling backwards. Grotesque in her fatness and rage, she lost her footing and tumbled down among the weeds and nettles. Not looking to see if she recovered herself, the girl pulled her kerchief closer over her head and returned quickly into the house.

The house was quiet inside and very dark. Facing south and east it caught none of the last rays of the sun except as they reflected on the opposite side of the valley. Matilda's room was lit by two candles, one beside her bed and one on a chest by the window. She kept her eyes on this candle, which moved continually in a draught that came through the window even though it was closed. She knew now that the baby was forcing her body to make the changes that would allow it to enter the world. She was frightened, her back ached and strange pains moved from her stomach to her thighs. But the light was cheering, dancing about the top of the candle, bending with the wind, first one way and then the other, sometimes reduced merely to a pinpoint of orange, at other times flooding upwards boldly. She liked it best when it pirouetted round and round like the last gilded leaf on a tree.

Matilda lay alone in her bed. A servant had ridden out for the midwife but these slow hours of preparation were to be spent on her own. Theo, she knew, crouched in another room reading. He never looked so engaged as when studying one of the books rescued from the monastery. He had tucked the Anglo-Saxon poem into one of the contemporary works and kept the whole pile, together with estate papers, in a stone niche behind one of the downstairs chimneys. He kept them there for security, Matilda knew.

'Aeeoiw!' A catlike shriek of anguish sent the dogs skidding across the bedroom floor. Even though she thought of Theo, Matilda had kept her eyes on the twirling candle flame and now it was out, leaving only blue circles in front of her eyes.

Theo came. 'My love, my sweetheart.' He was horrified by the thought of the suffering she must endure and it took her some time to make him understand it was the candle that had made her scream.

'We will light it again,' he said practically. 'We will light rows of candles,' and Matilda saw in his eyes the image of the altar at mass.

'No. No.' She did not want to be part of that ceremony. 'Sit with me a moment.'

Theo sat by the bed, holding his head in his hands, praying probably.

'Take my hand.'

Theo took her hand, which was hot and clammy.

'I will be well,' she said, seeing his nervous staring eyes. 'And the baby is strong enough to battle through anything.'

Again they were silent, so silent that Matilda could hear the wind insinuating itself through the window frames. If it grew any stronger the whole house would begin wheezing and squeaking.

'Shut the door,' Matilda told the midwife, who entered and settled herself at the end of the bed. But then a new thought struck her. She sat bolt upright. 'Where is Annie? Where is mad Annie?'

'Sssh. Sssh,' said Theo, alarmed by her violence.

'Where's Annie? I don't want Annie near me or my baby. Go and see where she is and send her away.'

Theo crept out of the room, calmer still in the face of her passion. He lit a candle and held it up to every place where Annie took her mouldering heap. When he could find her nowhere and the candle had blown out three or four times in the draughty corners, he returned to Matilda. 'She's nowhere inside the house.'

'You're certain?'

'I'm certain.'

Matilda sighed with relief. The pains in her stomach became bearable again. She closed her eyes and even smiled when she felt Theo take her hand. His hard fingers gripping hers were a pledge of his fatherhood, of their future together as a family. They would never be parted now.

Annie was surrounded by the stink of herself, the imagined smell of the approaching plague and the dungy earth on which she had fallen after her push from the young wet nurse. She had not been hurt but had lost another level of consciousness. She might have stayed on the ground all night had not some fresh spring insects begun to chew their way up her legs. She got up slowly and moved towards the house. Her legs were so stiff that she reached no further than a window. Confused, she saw a light moving across the room, ducking around the corners. Now that she was upright and more exposed the wind whipped her clothes and nagged at her hair. Holding on to the wall, she lumbered round the outside of the house, following as far as she could the path of light inside.

As she watched, it became magnified in her imagination and she saw a flame leaping as high as a mountain. That was it. That was the only enemy strong enough to defeat the plague. With red and blue and orange whorls dancing in front of her eyes, she dragged her way to a hidden door used by the dogs and pushed her way through. She knew the house so well that it was easy even in total darkness to find her way to the kitchen where there was a candle and fire to light it.

Although mad and not open to ordinary sensations, Annie still kept an instinctive guile and practicality. She took the candle to the dining hall, which was wood-panelled and newly hung with tapestries. It was also in the centre of the house and away from the servants. With no show of emotion beyond a careful concentration, she applied the flame to the loose ends of the hanging, persevering in her task until the material was well lit. She then moved to the cloth on the table. It was all so easy and so right. The room would soon blaze like a giant bonfire and there would be no putting it out. The plague would find nothing left for it.

Satisfied so far, Annie hurried to the hall and lit the hangings at the bottom of the staircase. Once that caught alight no one upstairs would get out. She had done her last service for her mistress.

Fires in the summer countryside were nearly too frequent for notice. Almost nightly a hayrick ignited itself, or a fire lit too foolishly in a hut sent its occupants racing. But in May the ground was dank, the plants wet with rising sap; a fire then was unlooked-for. Besides, the nights were still cool and there was no one out on the hillside to smell the acrid warning. The blaze that overtook the manor was unnoticed until it was too late to do anything. Mother, father and still unborn child were trapped in blazing unity with no chance of escape.

The fire burned all night and in the morning curious villagers came up to see what remained. They looked at the blackened stone and walked through two or three rooms that had remained curiously untouched. One of the men, wearing heavy boots, tried to count by the bones how many had died but then Walter Croke arrived and shooed them away.

An old man said, 'It was always cursed after she married the priest,' but most were merely worried about their jobs.

Later in the day officials came from the nearest town and talked to Walter Croke. They walked among the pyramidal trees now underplanted by gillyflowers and rosemary and tall blue iris.

In the evening one of the ex-monks from the monastery, who had settled in a neighbouring village as a priest, rode over. He went to the abbey first and tied his horse at the stone archway which still supported the nave. All on his own he walked down the yew avenue towards the horrible smell of a burned home. It still smouldered and no one had done anything yet about removing the bodies.

'*Requiescat in pace*,' said the ex-monk taking a cloth and holding it to his nose. He did not know why he had come but as he rode away, he thanked God for His assurance of everlasting life.

PART THREE

Men are so seldom really good. They are so little sympathetic. What man thinks of changing himself so as to suit his wife? And yet men expect that women shall put on altogether new characters when they are married, and girls think they can do so.

Anthony Trollope, Phineas Redux, 1874

Chapter Thirteen

In 1880, give or take a year or two . . .

Matilda looked at her son's red, excited face and could think of nothing to say.

'Papa had a snake in his pocket!' he repeated.

Without doubt he was right. It would be typical of Theo to bring a snake into his father's funeral service thereby expressing his dislike of the new vicar, his disbelief in the ordinances of God and his disregard of the conventions. He had, however, loved his father, although they had nothing, not even genetic features, in common. That should have given his Darwinite friends pause for thought. It did not, of course, for they were hardly interested in what stared them in the face . . .

'Mama! Mama! You're not listening.' Tom pulled at his mother's black puffed sleeve and then at her skirt. At length she paid attention but only to give his hand a sharp smack.

'And why are you back so soon?'

'I ran.' Tom retreated sulkily. 'They're all so slow.'

'It was an honour for you to be allowed to go. Boys of eight should show respect. And where is your cap?' I have too many children, thought Matilda, and this one is out of control. Why has he come to me like this on this day and started telling tales about his father as if I would be amused? It is a year before he goes away to school, unless I send him early with Edward. Edward has never behaved like this.

Tom watched his mother, upright and frowning. Her face and narrow torso were framed in dark velvet by the wing-backed chair she always chose in this small drawing room. 'I don't like you in black,' he said irrepressibly. 'It makes your nose look longer and your eyes flash like a vampire's.'

Ignoring, or not hearing, this further proof of her son's lack of discipline, Matilda rose slowly and moved across the room. She had arranged for a reception in the large red drawing room and this had merely been a moment of unaccustomed solitude, a moment for reflection. Lately, as her seven children grew older and were less easily confined to nursery quarters, she found herself longing often for the opportunity to be alone. Unlike Theo, she had no study upon which the door could be shut so firmly that there was no need of bolts. She had no other occupation than her family and household. Even when she had found the moment to sit reflectively in her favourite chair with her favourite view through the long windows to the facing green slope of the valley, she had found herself considering the problem of Cook's bunions.

Death, appropriate subject for contemplation since her father-in-law had been taken so suddenly, so unexpectedly, had not found a place in her thoughts except as a general sense of depression. Sir William Hope, Bt, had been her ally, a man of practicalities who lived within the world that God had given, who actively improved the world God had given.

Matilda raised her eyes to the ceiling of the great hall within which she now stood. The house was a showpiece, a monument to the New Hope Building Company which had made her father-in-law's fortune. Only a man of his energy could have taken possession of the ruins of a medieval monastery and turned them into a house the size of a castle. There had been a farmhouse nearby, built over the remains of a Tudor manor, but he had bought that, too, and dismantled it, taking only the good stone and one large window. It seemed that the manor had suffered from a devastating fire not long after the monastery had been abandoned. One of Sir William's axioms was 'The soul of man lives on in his buildings.'

'Mama! Mama! I can hear them coming back!'

Matilda turned to look at her eldest daughter. Tom, she noticed, had fled his unresponsive parent. 'You look very nice, my dear. Is Lily ready, too – and Hannah?'

Elizabeth replied with a look her mother understood perfectly. It said, Why should I look after my younger sisters? And then, You know perfectly well that Lily is always ready and Hannah never, so why do you ask? And finally there was a real reproach: Mother, I loved my grandpapa so why did he die?

'We will forget about the others.' Matilda put her arm through Elizabeth's and led her towards the drawing room. They would be friends and face together a life in which they were no longer protected by the splendid umbrella spread over them by Sir William.

'Oh, Mama!' whispered Elizabeth, responding immediately to

the physical contact with her mother. 'You know I will do anything to make you happy. But it did seem hard that the boys should go to the funeral and not I.'

'But I didn't go, dear,' said Matilda, finding firmness enough to stem the flow. One of the things she had found herself noticing recently was that, despite the employment, thanks to her father-in-law's generosity, of a governess, an assistant, a nurse, two under-nursemaids and an army of other servants, she was still the one to whom all complaints, however trivial, were addressed.

This particular complaint, she supposed, was not trivial. But there was no time now for a serious discussion, particularly on a subject that was probably best unaired. 'God makes no difference between you and your brothers,' she said gently. 'This evening we will all pray together.'

Elizabeth, who looked as if she had more to say, was now stopped by the presence of Croke, the butler, and two other servants for they had reached the red drawing room.

'It is all prepared, m'lady,' said Croke, making Matilda start visibly and even diverting Elizabeth. 'Sir Theodore' and 'Lady Hope' was new, not quickly accepted except by a butler.

Matilda looked at the long sideboard with the heavy glasses, decanters and plates of cakes and biscuits laid out in regular columns like an army. 'It looks very orderly, Croke,' she said, and then stood back to see the effect. It was a heavily panelled, sombre room, with velvet curtains and ornate flower-patterned wallpaper echoed in vases of tall lilies. It had been remoulded and decorated only this year in the William Morris style, which Sir William had recently favoured. He had always decided such things, even though his main residence had been in London and he had hardly spent more than a couple of months in the year at Abbeyfields.

'I expect Lily is planning to make an entrance,' said Elizabeth jealously.

The church party, consisting of Theo, his eldest son, Edward, the local doctor, Dr George Rebew, the vicar, the Reverend Oswald Plunkett, the family lawyer, Theo's secretary and one or two not very distinguished local friends, were crossing the hall. Their voices were unnaturally hushed, although talkative in the way of people recently released from a long service.

Matilda took up a dignified position by the mantel.

'My dear Lady Hope.' The Reverend Oswald Plunkett approached her first, arm outstretched. Behind him Theo grimaced. To his mind this new young vicar was both unctuous and presumptuous.

But Matilda smiled. Mr Plunkett was young, well-looking in a clean-shaven, fresh-faced way. Most important of all, he was cheerful, optimistic and filled with unselfish plans to better the world. When she was with him, her heart, tugged so tight by Theo's cynicism, lack of belief and self-centredness, relaxed and dared to beat in tune with the rest of human kind. He was, or at least appeared as such to Matilda, a good, simple man.

Theo saw his wife's smile and squeezed the neck of the snake in his pocket. How could Matty find comfort from a man who based his sermons on a privately printed volume entitled *Good Thoughts and Holy Words*, could not read Greek, and had never once questioned anything he had been taught? Theo removed his hand from the snake to twist together the tendrils of his long beard. Mr Plunkett had now embarked on condolences that were no less irritating to Theo for being heartfelt. The vicar had no right to feel for the death of a man he had hardly known.

'Mr Plunkett is a refreshing figure in the neighbourhood.' These sentiments, in direct contrast to Theo's, were expressed by Dr Rebew. He was a small, dark, thick-set man with a jutting beard and a voice that turned everything, even the time of day, into an ironic possibility. Theo liked him for that.

'His figure may be refreshing but his mind is as stale as an old cigar.'

Dr Rebew looked ironically grave. Although a general practitioner, his particular interest was in the insane and he had recently raised the money (partly from Sir William) for a small institution where he kept what Matilda referred to as 'Dr Rebew's unfortunate guinea pigs'. Theo and he often had interesting discussions about the human brain. Now he went to bow over Matilda's hands. She gave him her usual suspicious look. If he were not always so efficient with the children's ailments she would certainly have looked for another, more 'human' doctor.

As she peered over his bent head to the other mourners she thought he murmured, 'I have lost a patient but you have lost a father,' but decided that was too peculiar a comment even for him. He moved past and Matilda put her hand to her nose.

The lilies, as tall as her youngest children, were a tribute to Sir William from the gardener, and now, as guests and family moved about, their heavy scent flowed out on the eddies of air. Matilda had never liked the smell, which seemed to stifle her power of breathing, and knew she would like it even less after today. She felt herself swaying. Theo, circling restlessly, caught his wife's elbow.

'It's the flowers,' she murmured, in case he would think her falling prey to some hysterical sorrow.

'Oh, if it is merely the flowers,' replied Theo and, to his guests' surprise and his butler's discomfiture, he began a methodical removal of all the vases. In a moment the polite Mr Plunkett was there to help him and soon a chain of hands stretched across the room.

Matilda, arms folded round herself, watched as calmly as possible. There was never any point in trying to stop Theo once embarked on a course of action.

'Oh, Mama! Mama!' Elizabeth rushed to her mother, whispered in anguish. 'How can you let Father be so absurd?'

'Sssh. Eliza. You forget yourself. The scent was giving me a headache. Your father is most kind.' Her severe words silenced Elizabeth but Lily – pretty, conventional Lily – had followed her over. She felt so humiliated by her father's behaviour that the first tears of the day stood in her eyes.

'What must people *think*?' she cried.

'They will think that you two are exceedingly badly brought up. Now you must either return to the schoolroom or go and make polite conversation. I shall take a glass of madeira and join you.'

Matilda chose to talk to the family lawyer, a Mr Lapidus, who had come from London on a train the night before, an experience he longed to describe. Unlike most men of the law, he was not pompous, chosen by Sir William for that reason, but he had assumed a gloomy manner for the occasion. Matilda had done no more than accept his serious compliments on the funeral service when Theo bustled over, as satisfied as a boy with his floral banishment.

'On a day of sadness it was an act of reverence to my wife.' He addressed Lapidus impartially but, noticing who he was, he added with a quite different intentness, 'Ah, you, Lapidus. Have we arranged for the meetings? The time? The place?'

'Indeed there is the Will.' The lawyer tried not to brighten but could not entirely repress a smirk of excitement. Reading a Will, and the Will of such a man, was one of the high points of his profession.

'Not on the day of his funeral!' interrupted Matilda, with more show of passion than ever before.

'Oh, my dear, my dear.' Theo shook his head so that his beard waggled. 'The Last Will and Testament must be read and Mr Lapidus is a busy man. A London man.'

'Tomorrow morning will be acceptable,' said Mr Lapidus,

reverting to his former manner. Staying at Abbeyfields Hall was a pleasure that did not often come his way. Last night a hot bath had been drawn for him, his clothes laid out, and after dinner he had been able to retire and study his papers in bed – a luxury made possible by the excellent gaslight in his room which, he had noticed, was of the American type and did not smoke or smell.

'That's settled, then,' said Matilda, bestowing a smile somewhere between her husband and the lawyer. She missed her father-in-law so much that the effort of turning her muscles upwards felt like lifting a heavy weight. She would pass a few words with the neighbouring gentry – they were not very grand because it was August and the grouse season had taken the grand to Scotland – then she would retire.

Matilda felt herself near tears. Sir William would have managed this occasion so comfortably. Theo, on the contrary, had assumed a plotting look only a few hours after his father's death. He did not mourn, he plotted, and doubtless she would know what he plotted tomorrow morning.

Theo, watching his wife moving away with a set, pale face, was both irritated and sympathetic. She lived far too much for people; she had allowed herself to be caught in the strangling web of children and family. When he had met her she had been free. Now even her walk was controlled, yet how she suffered! He, Theo, would never allow himself to be so trapped. Even the death of his father must be turned to profit, not borne as a yoke. 'You must prepare for changes,' he told Lapidus bracingly. 'Le roi est mort, vive le roi!'

Lapidus bowed agreeably but was inwardly shocked by his client's hard-heartedness. His previous dealings had all been with Sir William, a worldly man, a man of determination, ambition and good sense, a man to whom no scandal had ever attached and who had been working on a new design for a railway station somewhat on the lines of the Red Fort in Delhi on the very day he died. Sir William had been a self-made man, a patriotic British citizen who had emulated his queen in his long celibate widowhood. Lapidus thought of his ex-client and, like Matilda, felt comfortable.

Sir Theodore, however, was exactly the opposite. Now in his late thirties, he talked and walked like a young man, an anarchist perhaps, or at least a socialist, thought Lapidus, working himself up. Yet some of his habits and his autocratic behaviour and his very long thick beard made him, on occasions, seem older even than his deceased father. He was restless and his thoughts were restless and it was pointless to make any remark to him for it would be instantly contradicted. Lapidus saw Matilda gliding among her guests, for her dress was flowing and narrow in the new artistic style, and thought it was fortunate that Sir William had provided well for his family and that Sir Theodore's beliefs, whatever they were, had not precluded him from living off the money made by the sweat of his father's brow.

Matilda had set course for the carved oak doors at the end of the room. Their design was based on that of an ancient table found in one of the outbuildings of the old farmhouse. They were carved with leaves and corn ears and garlands of strange lettering. It had been one of Sir William's happiest notions. 'I am a builder of the second half of the nineteenth century,' he had been wont to say, 'a modern man. But, unlike some, I am not afraid to look backwards and take the best from the past. In the great buildings of the past, they used stone and wood, wood and stone. None of this stucco and cheap brick. I have built my house on the site of a monastery and there are objects here, books here, that have survived from time immemorial.' Although a sensible man, Sir William favoured the bombastic in his speech. 'In three hundred years' time, my house may be changed into something else but never, never will it fall!'

Matilda sighed and failed to catch Mr Plunkett's sympathetic look. Instead the children's governess saw it and took it for herself. Since the children were trailing their mother out of the room, she might be forgiven a moment's discourse.

'I see Miss Plunkett is not here?' she began.

'She was not invited,' replied Mr Plunkett shortly, for he did not like the idea that his sister's lack of an invitation was anything to do with Miss Waterville.

'Of course her ladyship did not go to the funeral,' murmured Miss Waterville, her embarrassment taking her into deeper waters than she wished. She need not have worried, however, for even her blushing look could see that his attention was on the carved oak door as it closed behind his hostess. It was odd to leave before her guests but would be forgotten as an expression of the depth of her attachment to her father-in-law. Not noticing the governess enough to say goodbye, the good simple man of God made his way to take his departure of Sir Theodore.

Matilda slipped across a corner of the hall and entered a corridor which led, via many tributaries, to the back of the house. By the time she had reached the garden, all the children except Hannah had fallen away. Hannah, whose pocket – even on a day such as this – bulged with her present book and whose hair resembled a corn sheaf loosely tied, took her mother's arm proprietorially. 'We won't see anyone now,' she said, 'we can be quite alone.'

Repressing the thought that she could hardly be alone while her daughter was there, Matilda consented to walk arm in arm along the pathway. They were moving along the side of the gentle sloping valley up which the house stood half-way. It was the least organised part of the garden, originally planned by Sir William as a romantic shrubbery. After filling the lower part of the garden with the conventional trees of his age, the wellingtonias, the monkey puzzles, copper beech and chestnut, he had turned his attention to the upper part. He had chosen and planted all the most exotic rhododendrons and azaleas that he had seen surrounding the great houses of south-east England and the Midlands. No one had advised him that Abbeyfields Hall stood in a belt of strong lime which would quickly kill off all his shrubs. In disgust he had left further ideas to Matilda, who had planted lime trees, a grove of silver birch and a strong young oak below which sheep nibbled the grass to a springy turf.

'I'll wait for you here,' said Hannah as they reached a bench set under the oak, half-way to the top.

Matilda smiled. Hannah could never resist a book for more than five minutes.

The sun came out as she reached the top of the hill and her new trees dappled the ground with the shade of their light-coloured leaves. Below the house stood the remains of a yew avenue, probably hundreds of years old, and the walled kitchen garden, said to be on the same spot as the original Tudor garden although some said its layout was even older than that and dated back to an early monastic garden or cloister. Behind her stretched corn-fields, still not cut for the weather had been wet, but she preferred to look down to their valley. All that land was owned by Abbey-fields Hall and much of the valley grouped down around the river and a church tower. The day was so clear that she could see right along the valley and then beyond two curves of hills to the vague outlines of the nearest large town, at least twelve miles as the crow flies and longer by carriage. Yet that was the way Mr Lapidus had come, by train to the town and by carriage to the house and it had only taken him an afternoon.

Feeling in danger of arousing further anxieties about Theo and the Will, Matilda turned a more thorough gaze on the village. There were few large buildings – the church, the vicarage, newly built just before they came, a village hall and school erected twenty years ago by Sir William. Otherwise it was a mean little place with rows of labourers' cottages, a public house hardly distinguishable from the cottages, a forge, a few shops, and a couple of farmhouses and grand old barns. There were nearly as many people employed at Abbeyfields, thought Matilda, with a feeling of disquiet, as in the village. In fact, as she knew, to work at the Hall was every villager's eager hope for their child. Oh, what was Theo plotting? Unrefreshed by her hard-won solitude, Matilda started so hurriedly back to the house that it looked as if she were in flight. Surely she had enough responsibility with her children, her relations, those employed already at the Hall without worrying about the villagers as well? Yet the condition of some of those cottages was really dreadful. Holding her skirt high, Matilda fled downwards and did not even hear Hannah cry, 'Mama! Oh, Mama! Wait for me!'

Mr Lapidus, the accountant, the farm agent and Theo were having a meeting prior to the reading of the Will.

'As you know,' the agent was saying gloomily, 'eighteen seventy-nine was a disastrous year for all English farmers and we were no exception. Unfortunately, this year looks likely to be hardly much better. Barley prices have dropped to almost nothing, wheat prices have halved and the market for cheese is severely diminished.'

At this point he faltered, not because he had little more to say, with facts and figures, to prove that it was not his fault that the profits from the estate were dropping yearly, but because Sir Theodore was so obviously not listening. They had met, to mark the special nature of the occasion, not at the estate office but in the house. They sat, at Theo's whim, in the smoking room, although none of them smoked, and the vaguely Moorish decorations, the carved ceiling and wall hangings, were confusing even without Sir Theodore prowling around, touching an embroidery here, a scimitar there, as if he were noticing them for the first time.

'This was my father's sanctum,' he said suddenly. 'It smells of him.'

Now it became clear that he had been actually sniffing the decorations. Lapidus and the accountant exchanged a glance. 'It seems', he began gravely, 'that the estate finances are a source of disquiet.'

'To whom?' asked Theo, still circling. 'Not to me. I don't have expensive tastes. I don't expect my farms to pay for my hunting, shooting or fishing.'

Theo spoke carelessly but his words produced an uneasy silence. It was not the way a landowner was expected to speak. It was confusing, like the room. Even Lapidus, who kept the clearest head, felt confused. It was true, Abbeyfields was not organised for expensive country pursuits but nevertheless its running ate up huge sums of money. There were ten horses in the stable, for example, even without hunters, employing a head groom and two stable boys. But this was not the way to think.

'I do not prize possessions,' said Theo airily. 'My interests are in the natural world.'

'Of course, Sir Theodore,' said the accountant, who had properly prepared himself for the meeting and felt some comment was called for. 'Your paper entitled "The Reptile as Human" was much discussed in naturalist circles.'

'Yes,' agreed Theo, smiling cheerfully. 'You can trust snakes. They have no pretensions to a conscience, no belief in afterlife, and no ambitions beyond a daily meal. St Francis, who was the only serious Christian until he overdid his fasting and became mentally deluded, understood this. You might say I am a St Francis without religious paranoia.'

This time Lapidus did not dare catch his colleague's eye. Was his distinguished client serious? The happiest conclusion would be that he joked, but before he could question further, Theo had taken him by the shoulder.

'I'll tell you what, Mr Lapidus, let's continue this meeting in my new conservatory. Not quite complete but I think you'll find it of interest.'

The three men, led by a bouncing Theo, proceeded through the billiard room, various unused gun rooms, gentlemen's wash room beside Theo's study – for all these manly places were grouped in the fashion of the 1860s at the far end of the house – past dining room, hall and to the other wing where the sound of hammering became audible.

'Aha!' cried Theo, throwing open a door in a small octagonal anteroom. 'At last, my conservatory – or, as my dear wife calls it, without feeling the need of a visit, my zoological garden.'

The three men, out of breath and already bemused by the distance they had covered, found themselves in a huge glass building, domed once in the middle and four times round the outside like a vast flower opened above their heads. For once it was a bright day but the light had to pierce the darkness of fat-leaved plants that grew up into the roof. Lower down there were plants with sword-edged leaves and sharp cacti growing scarlet flowers and all kinds of foreign creepers and shrubs they could not identify.

'Splendid!' said Lapidus, gulping.

'Magnificent!' echoed the accountant, thinking of what it must have cost.

'Fascinating,' murmured the agent who had just noticed a fat snake curled up not more than a yard from his feet.

'But it seems to have been finished for some time,' said Lapidus, looking upwards and thus failing to see the snake. The two workmen, tools in hand, had stopped hammering at their entrance.

'Ah, yes, the glass house was built ten years ago by my father. But now I am moving in my collection.' Bending down Theo picked up the large sleepy snake, which boasted the striking pattern of an Indian python, and draped it round his neck. Its tail and head dangled below his knees. Since the three men stared, speechless, Theo continued conversationally, 'The men are working on homes for those who are less friendly than Queen Victoria here.'

Now they could see glass-fronted boxes lurking under the greenery. Some were already inhabited and others were in the process of construction. 'None of these snakes is really dangerous. We can sit here quite comfortably and talk about the falling price of corn. I must warn you, however, that after the reading of the Will, at midday I believe, none of it will be relevant – to me, at least. So perhaps our time would be more usefully spent with a short lecture on the eating habits of the dear Queen.' Here he paused to stroke the head of his snake-cowl, who flickered out her tongue and blinked her eyes flirtatiously. 'I assure you the pleasure would be all mine and I could even offer a small tour of her dinners which are kept in cages near at hand.'

This was too much. It was clear even to Theo, who was honestly speaking his mind – if with an underlying urge to shock – that the three men facing him thought he had gone out of his mind. In a moment they would be calling for Dr Rebew and one of his discreet strait-jackets. That was not part of his plan.

'On second thoughts, gentlemen, it might be best to defer our meeting altogether. I shall have you shown to the dining room where you can take some refreshment and await, or at least, those it concerns, can await', he bowed to the accountant and Lapidus, 'the reading of the Will.'

He had hardly finished speaking before the three men were out of the conservatory, which had become, in their imaginations, a gladiatorial arena, and stood with a flush of relief in the octagonal anteroom.

'You may continue.' Theo waved his hand at the workmen who had stood immobile throughout. They began hammering at once and their master turned to leave before rethinking and addressing them loudly, 'You are good lads, brave, hard-working lads and I shall consider you for my next Indian exploration!'

Under Theo's insistence, the whole family gathered for the reading of the Will. Even the twins, Alfred and Daisy, barely three years old, were brought in by their nurse. Sir William's two sisters, one unmarried and one widowed, who had been too upset to attend the reception after the funeral, came from a faraway wing of the house. Neither had inherited the love of action that made their brother so successful and they spent most of their time playing cards or eating. Matilda found them a place to sit and then resumed her thoughts. She had not spoken to her husband privately for two days, but she had heard him come late to his dressing room and pace about far into the night. She had lain awake anxiously and eventually turned to God with some heartfelt prayers for the welfare of those within her responsibility. Beneath her anxiety lay sadness that Theo would no longer open his mind to her.

Theo looked at his wife and although his mind was filled with the momentous decision he had taken since his father's death, he saw and suffered for her fear. He had been avoiding her, not unconsciously, for he knew that she would try to bind him to her and break his resolve. He still understood her and loved and respected her, too, but their lives must not be tied too tightly together if they were to thrive – if he was to thrive. Her reproachful looks might make him feel guilty but they would not alter his plans. After all, he was not unfaithful to her nor profligate with money. He merely needed occasion to travel, study and write, ambitions of which no man should be made to feel ashamed.

Thinking all this, Theo nevertheless felt an inward burning as he contemplated Matilda's pale, set face. He should have visited her in bed last night and given her proper warning. Angry at the knowledge of his cowardice, Theo banged the table loudly. 'We will say a prayer!' he said or rather shouted, surprising everyone, particularly himself. Obediently, the gathering rose, planted their hands together and cast down their eyes. 'Lady Hope will lead us,' said Theo, using his wife's new title for the first time.

Matilda stared down the table at her husband. Was this some trick? An underhand attack on her faith? Or an appeal for her support? Christian charity taught that one must always think the best of one's neighbour even if he was also one's husband and acting suspiciously. 'Let us pray', began Matilda feelingly, 'that duty and responsibility may prevail among the righteous and that the righteous may prevail over the wrong-doers,' she paused, 'or even those who are not wrong-doers but have been led astray. Our Father . . .'

Theo's conscience felt appeased by Matilda's obvious attack. It was a fair fight between them and she was as strong, if not stronger, than he.

'Before we come to the Will,' Theo continued to stand after all else sat, 'I would like to give you the reason why I have gathered you here around me . . .'

The accountant and the lawyer shifted uncomfortably. Sir Theodore Hope should not use a word like reason. It was unsuitable. Who else would have children present – one of whom was kicking the table legs – at such a solemn moment as the reading of the Will?

'In brief,' announced Theo, smiling unexpectedly, 'I am planning to sell the New Hope Building Company as soon as possible. My wife and children and dependants will continue to live here on the profits from the estate and the company's proceeds will go to finance the New Hope Indian Reptile Expedition of which I will be leader.'

'Not all the proceeds, surely?' The cry sprang unbidden from the accountant's lips. All the money he had handled so wisely and so well to go to capturing more horrible dangerous snakes! It was amazing that he did not bang his head on the table.

'You may invest any remaining money in South American railways.' Theo smiled charmingly, as if conceding a point.

Lapidus was furious; his reading of the Will had been quite upstaged by Sir Theodore's out of place intervention. If he had to speak he should have waited until after the Will. It would have served him right if Sir William had left it all to Lady Hope which, unfortunately, he had not. South American railways, indeed. A notoriously unsound investment.

Matilda, without either a word or taking a conscious decision, rose in stately fashion. She moved slowly down the side of the table and by the time she reached her husband, she was followed by a row of seven children.

'You have answered my prayer,' she said, face to face, eye to eye, 'and now I shall respond to your answer.' Raising her slim and elegant hand, she smacked Theo across the face.

As Theo saw her intention, he decided that the snakes he loved had a strong affinity with the woman he had married. If only she

185

could be like this always, cold, passionate and dangerous. In order that she should not see his desirous expression, which would have insulted her pride, he lowered his eyes and sat down.

'Mama! Mama!' wailed the twins, but no one else, not even Tom, dared speak. In silence (save for the twins now sobbing pathetically), Matilda, with her train of children, processed to the door. Let nobody think he had her blessing for his hare-brained, selfish, meaningless schemes.

'Aha,' said Theo to the remaining company as soon as the door had closed. 'We have witnessed a mother tiger striking out in defence of her young. We must make sure that their affairs are in order.'

'Amen,' agreed Lapidus, his rage subdued by shock and his gaze transfixed by a trickle of blood running into Sir Theodore's beard.

'Amen to blazes!' shouted Sir Theodore, hopping to his feet. 'We must at all times proceed without assurances of heavenly guidance. Any other route leads to hypocrisy, mediocrity and, in extreme cases, lunacy!'

Chapter Fourteen

Matilda lay awake in her huge empty bed. At first she was so enraged that she imagined herself going into Theo's room and biting and kicking and tearing his limbs off one by one. But he did not come upstairs until after two and by then the weight of the great house, the seven children, the servants, the villagers, all the things and people who depended on her, lay heavily on her once more. She had even begun to see that his deliberate and continued absence, rather than his previous occasional and random expeditions, would make her life easier. She would be in sole charge. Exhausted yet unable to sleep, she began to make plans in which, by now she was half dreaming, the nice Reverend Oswald Plunkett made a surprise appearance.

At four when she had entered a passage of green grassy calm, there was a knock at the door and Theo, like an ancient prophet with baggy nightshirt and flowing beard, stood by her bed.

'I have come to apologise,' he announced before Matilda's eyes were properly open.

'It is too late,' mumbled Matilda with difficulty.

'I know,' agreed Theo humbly, yet sitting near her as one come to stay. 'I am a coward but you are a formidable adversary.'

Matilda pulled herself up a little and tried to think of what she wanted from this conversation. They had not talked intimately for so long that she was taken off her guard. His large greenish eyes were looking at her with sympathy and even admiration.

'I am afraid I am not a satisfactory husband,' continued Theo. 'Though I think it is not I that has changed but you.'

'Of course I've changed.' Matilda found impatience came most easily. 'I've had nine children, seven living. I have a large house to run. Our circumstances have changed.'

'But I haven't changed,' said Theo with, to Matilda, infuriating gentleness.

'I know. I know.' Matilda seemed about to deliver a harangue but suddenly she fell back again into the pillows. He had not changed and she had. They both agreed on the facts. 'You are right,' she said. 'You haven't changed. You never will. So you must go and chase snakes and I will stay here and look after the estate. Good night now, Theo. I am very tired.'

But Theo was not tired at all and could still feel that unsatisfied tingle of desire. It was disappointing that Matty would not argue but she still looked charming with her dark curly hair and pale pointed face. It was hard to believe she would be forty this year. Tentatively he put out his hand.

Matilda turned her face away but rather in resignation than avoidance. Let him touch her and stroke her and hold her. He was gentle when they made love, warm and kind and comforting in a way he never was at any other time. She would not kiss him because there was still an angry knot inside her head but she would join her body to his.

Carefully Theo drew off Matilda's white nightdress and then his own. His body, so big and padded, lay down beside Matilda's fragile boniness. The bed creaked and sank.

Matilda sighed as his hands ran down her body. She remembered, not unhappily, the passion of their early married days. They would wake in the morning more tired than when they had gone to bed. But not the sort of tiredness she felt all the time now, rather an aching, smiling satisfaction.

'Oh, my dear little Matty. My little dove. My darling duck.'

Theo's endearments never changed and always made Matilda feel tender and loving. She put her arms as far round his broad curved back as they would reach and thought about a ship's smooth hull and a tree trunk's strength. It was strange that his physical presence should be at such deceptive odds with his spirit. It was this, perhaps, that had misled her early on. How could she have guessed she had married a Puck in Caliban's body? Not Caliban, though, his body was too smooth, too fluent, too sweet to her body. Nothing clumsy, nothing forced.

'Oh, Theo. Theo.' Even the knot in her head was slipping apart, opening to his loving fingers. Why did such loving and beautiful moments have to be so rare? Why did morning ever have to come, as it would, it would, and tear them apart?

Despite Matilda's fears, the night that she spent with Theo softened the weeks of his departure. The huge house dragged them apart again physically but they retained a tenderness for each other, which had a calming effect on all around them, particularly the children.

Elizabeth, the eldest, came to her one sunlit morning where she sat at her desk in the small drawing room. 'Miss Waterville is asking whether we are to see Papa on to the ship. May we, Mama?'

Matilda looked up from the letter she was writing. She paused and then took her daughter's hand. 'Shall you miss your father very much?'

Elizabeth considered, frowning. 'Will you miss Papa?'

Matilda was not too engrossed in her own depressing thoughts to hear her daughter's appeal. Every normal child wants her parents to love each other.

'Certainly I will.' Matilda patted her daughter's hand reassuringly and to her own surprise found herself adding almost passionately, 'Without him I am nothing!' With tears starting in her eyes, she was glad to see Croke standing at the door.

'Mr Plunkett and Miss Plunkett have come for you, m'lady.'

It was early in the day for callers and the vicar was full of apologies. 'I wasn't certain that you would recall . . . the school . . . you expressed a wish to visit?'

While her brother explained the reason for their call, Miss Plunkett smiled at Elizabeth. It was a fixed smile, almost a rictus, produced of nervousness, not good will since Miss Plunkett considered any girl between the ages of fifteen and twenty-five a threat to her brother's bachelordom and therefore a threat to her position. The fact that the Hopes would never condescend to marry a humble village vicar did not reassure her since she admired Oswald so completely as to assume him capable of breaking all conventions of rank. Miss Plunkett's smile became ferocious when Matilda suggested that Elizabeth accompany them to the village school – a plan she had no memory of making.

'I will get our shawls, Mama,' cried Elizabeth, pleased to be included in a grown-up outing.

'Yes, do.' Matilda looked down at her black mourning dress. 'Nothing too smart. Grandeur would be out of place.'

Mr Plunkett nodded approvingly and his sister, imitating him, made a trimming on the old-fashioned bonnet she wore flap about her brow.

'Shall I order the carriage?' asked Croke as Elizabeth tripped away.

'Certainly, the carriage.'

Again Mr Plunkett bowed in pleasure at his mistress's words. He was a natural servitor and only God came before those to whom he showed deference.

Matilda, however, saw his youth and energy and smiled upon

him cheerfully. 'What will we see?' she asked as they moved towards the hallway. 'Will they sing for us or recite?'

The village school was Mr Plunkett's pet project and he embarked on a lengthy explanation of the method of teaching, which could help the already literate children from the better homes but also include the very poor and disadvantaged who had never been allowed in school before.

'God has made all human beings equal,' cried the vicar, carried away by his schemes, 'and we must ensure that none of his creatures forgoes his true deserts!'

Matilda thought his sentence a trifle clumsy but could not criticise its content. Miss Plunkett, however, showed, by a restraining hand on her brother's arm, that she was shocked at the sentiment. 'My brother has worked very hard to help even the poorest—'

'The poor shall inherit the earth,' interrupted Oswald.

'The meek, I believe,' said his sister, with gentle or even steely perseverance.

Matilda turned to Miss Plunkett and noticed that she resembled her brother. She was fair, straight, pink-cheeked and determined. Yet the very things that cheered her in the brother irritated her in the sister. 'You are much involved, too, Miss Plunkett?'

Luckily, perhaps, any answer was made impossible by the arrival of Elizabeth followed by Miss Waterville carrying the wraps. In another moment Croke announced the arrival of the carriage and they all bundled out of the door.

Above their heads, from one of the shamrock-shaped windows in which Sir William Hope had specialised, Theo watched them go. Although he considered the vicar and his sister ridiculous figures, he was glad to see his wife taken to some employment outside the house. Unlike many or even most men of his class and time, he did not consider women inferior either physically or mentally. Recently he had feared that Matilda's obvious dissatisfaction with her life might lead her to take recourse in ill health. He would far rather she was bustling about 'doing good' than lying on a *chaise-longue* sniffing *sal volatile* or sipping laudanum.

Theo shut the window with a bang, which went unnoticed by those borne briskly away by the carriage but caused his assistant, who was waiting inside the room, to start forward nervously.

'I've not jumped out yet,' responded Theo jovially. 'Although there may be those who wish I had.'

Popularity was not expected or sought by Theo and he thought it quite amusing that his whole household, including his lawyer and accountant, believed he was behaving callously and

190

irresponsibly by selling his father's business. Their arguments, as far as he allowed them to develop, ranged from the sentimental 'but it was your father's life' to the hard-headed, 'you will sell for the worst possible price because you are selling at the worst possible time . . .' As long as Theo could remember, farming prices had been going down, yet he only had to visit a few of the big landowners to see in what luxury their so-called failing estates kept them. It was all bunkum. The sort of bunkum Theo could smell like a skunk and avoid accordingly.

'I am the son of a working man,' he said, startling his assistant yet again. 'Work was my father's god. He worshipped work. This house and estate is a monument to his enjoyment in work. But he never came here to enjoy it. Instead he popped in my wife as his representative and she, unlike him and, one must add, unlike me, takes the whole place absolutely seriously.' Here Theo turned to face the assistant. 'You might almost say the son of a working man should not marry the daughter of an aristocrat.'

The assistant indicated he might almost say nothing of the sort by walking very fast out of the room. Theo shrugged. Whenever he set his mind to consider the human animals around him, he soon found himself sinking into a morass of imponderables. Better to leave them to their devices and turn resolutely to his.

'I wish to dictate.' He summoned back the assistant who stood quavering in the corridor. 'The letter is addressed to the President of the Royal Geographical Society, the Right Honourable Lord Aberdare. My dear Aberdare . . .' On the trail, as it happened, of a good argument culled from the latest edition of *The Proceedings of the Royal Geographical Society*, Theo marched happily about his room.

Matilda, reaching the centre of the village, such as it was, the church, school house and vicarage, turned enquiringly to her escort. 'It is odd, is it not, that we are so remote from this. Abbeyfields Hall, I mean, half-way up the hill.'

'Abbeyfields Hall is an ancient site, your ladyship. In the time of its great days as a monastery, it would have been far bigger than the village. The barns that Sir William turned into stabling give some indication.'

Matilda felt guilty at being the owner of such an engorged site and her determination to pursue a charitable course grew proportionately.

'The children are waiting, I believe.' Miss Plunkett held open the door to the small stone-built house. Elizabeth, who had been admiring an angel carved in the lintels on either side of the window, hurried over. 'It's a charming little place.' She waved her hand upwards. 'Just look at the fishtail-tiled roof.'

'My predecessor was interested in aesthetics,' commented the Reverend Oswald Plunkett, not as if it were a compliment.

'And my late father-in-law's firm built it,' added Matilda, causing both brother and sister to blush in sensitive embarrassment. If Sir William had chosen fishtails then fishtails were perfect.

The school was divided into two rooms separated by a rough red curtain. In the larger room the younger children recited their alphabet and engaged in spelling bees, in the smaller the older ones bent industriously over their long tables.

Matilda was immediately struck by the scarcity of older children, almost all of whom were girls, pale and dull-looking like lumps of unrisen dough.

'Yes,' said Mr Plunkett, guessing her thoughts. 'They leave to work. It is a hard task to persuade any to stay.'

The younger children were, without doubt, a more cheerful sight, so many of them crammed on to the narrow wooden benches, each wearing a clean pinafore, hands clasped together in front of them and heads turned towards their teacher. As the party from the Hall moved up the room, the teacher raised her arm and fifty fluting voices began: 'All things that on earth do live . . .'

Matilda felt tears bubble into her eyes. They were angelic, she thought, these scrubbed-faced children who had been plucked from their dark and dirty cottages to enter God's light and the light of learning. In her emotion, she clasped Mr Plunkett's arm and gave him a look of passionate exhilaration. He, whose eyes were usually subserviently downcast, returned it so that they were drawn upwards on the same happy cloud.

'This must be the most important work in the world,' said Matilda solemnly when the hymn was finished.

The teacher smiled but was too humble to speak and, since Mr Plunkett was still overcome by emotion, it was left for his sister to add in sober tones, 'The education of young minds is a heavenly duty.'

Elizabeth, meanwhile, had pursed her lips as if her mother's reaction offended her in some way. It was true that Matilda's visits to the schoolroom in the Hall were seldom accompanied by joyous expressions of its importance. More often, she asked for a child to be excused for an hour or so in order to help her with some chore. 'Can I look at their slates?' Elizabeth asked the teacher in a businesslike voice.

Mr Plunkett returned slowly to earth, but his heart was not the same. The look he had exchanged with Matilda had caused the blood to flow through it so fast that it was as if he contained a vast pumping engine. A more worldly man would have recognised this sensation as falling in love, but Mr Plunkett was ignorant of such things and merely assumed his destiny to be linked with Lady Hope in great works of charity. Unconsciously, he put his hand over the place where her fingers had grasped his sleeve.

The remainder of the visit was filled with practical demonstrations and explanations, which were without emotional impact but gave everybody concerned, including Elizabeth, a happy sense of involving themselves in good.

'We must look forward,' said Mr Plunkett when they stood outside again. He swayed a little for his heart still rushed above its normal rate. 'There are still many souls to be sought.'

'Yes,' agreed Elizabeth. 'All the older ones who fall away. I should like to concern myself with those unlucky creatures.'

'Excellent!' exclaimed the vicar, addressing the daughter although his eyes kept sliding away to the mother. 'I am glad you do not think it a morning wasted.'

The four then parted, Matilda and Elizabeth driving to Abbeyfields and the Plunketts returning to the vicarage.

Yet virtue never went so unrewarded. Matilda and Elizabeth could hear the noise within Abbeyfields even before Croke had opened the front door. Before he could find proper words to inform her ladyship of the trouble, Tom burst through his legs.

'It wasn't my fault, Mama! Papa says I can help, you know he does!'

'Ssh. Sssh.' Matilda took the kind of deep breath employed by a soldier before facing the enemy. 'What has happened?'

But Tom now stuffed his head into his mother's skirts and began to wail loudly.

Elizabeth's usual kindhearted nature was restrained by the thought of that classroom of pale dumplings: they could not indulge themselves in such histrionics. 'What's Master Thomas done now?' she asked, addressing the butler.

This time it was Miss Waterville who scurried across the hallway, wringing her hands in agitation. 'I should not have screamed! I know I should not have screamed! But under such provocation—' Her place was taken by a panting Edward and Lily and it was Lily who managed to explain the cause of the drama.

'Tom let the snake rats escape!'

'And one got into the kitchen and Cook has given notice!'

Matilda took another breath, which was the final snuffing-out of her glow. 'Where is Papa?' she asked in menacing tones.

'T-t-trying to c-catch the rats,' sobbed Tom into her skirts. Brushing him aside, Matilda struck out across the great hall. She felt herself a gallant vessel in stormy seas, prow forward, roll under control, no idea of anything but survival.

The rats were kept in cages in an underground cellar, built of what remained of the undercroft of the old monastery. Part of it was used to store wine, part for coal and part had been lined to contain great blocks of ice. The whole was far nearer the kitchen than the snake conservatory, which often meant transportation problems. It was in this area that Theo had set up his home for the only food that his snakes relished.

'They must be live,' Theo had explained early on, 'or my poor delicate snakes will get indigestion.' Matilda, despite suffering from a difficult pregnancy, had been shocked enough to consult a book about the feeding habits of reptiles, but on discovering they indeed required a weekly feed of live mammals, decided to pretend that the cellarful of pathetic little victims did not exist.

'Oh, why do all Theo's interests lead to anarchy?' she asked herself as she battled to the end of the hall and dived down a corridor. 'And why is it always I who has to put together the pieces again?' She turned into another corridor, which was uncarpeted so she could hear the clattering of all the feet following behind her. 'Is it any wonder I look so tired and woebegone that you would think I was not the children's mother but their grandmother?'

The moment Matilda arrived at the scene of the rats' bid for liberty she saw that Theo was enjoying himself. It was true that as soon as he caught sight of her he adopted a penitent expression but before that she had heard his happy boom as he commanded the entire indoor staff to search in every nook and cranny.

'We must not let them escape,' he cried, waving a cane as if it were a marshal's baton, 'or my noble snakes will face starvation!' He turned and saw his wife. 'Ah, my dear. You have heard the frightful news!'

Husband and wife, lit waveringly by the lamps held by servants who, bent low, scurried past them, confronted each other. Theo, who was never one to diminish a drama, decided to put his penitence into action. Using his cane as a prop, he lowered himself on to one knee. 'You are a saint, my dear, to put up with such a trial as me and my snakes.'

'Oh, Papa, do get up,' wailed Lily, who never gave up hope of turning Theo into a conventional father. But her wail was hardly reaching a diminuendo before it turned into a fortissimo scream and she began hopping about and beating at her skirts.

'Ha! Ha!' cried Theo, bounding off his knees. 'It sounds as if Eliza's caught one of the little beasts.'

'I'm not Eliza!' screamed Lily, shaking out her skirts frantically.

'Eliza or Lily, silly names both of them, chosen by your mother, the best thing is to turn you upside down, give you a good shaking and let the animal drop out. You there!' he addressed one of the strong young carpenters who had been working upstairs. 'You could turn a slip of a girl like that upside down in a minute.'

Before Lily could decide which she feared most, a rat or a man, a new element was introduced to the scene.

Cook, after giving notice, had stumped off to her room where she sat smoking a pipe, her secret and treasured vice. However after ten furiously puffing minutes, she had a better idea. Returning to the kitchen she bent her corseted bulk and called in a sweetly wheedling voice, 'Puss! Puss! Pussy dear.' In a second a huge black tom-cat had bounded through the pantry window and streaked towards her. What nice fish-head was she offering him today? asked his expectantly arched back, his glistening wide-open eyes. 'You have a feast in store,' explained Cook, dangling a piece of cheese as bait. Through door after strictly closed door went Cook and cat until they emerged into the final corridor and Tom Cat smelled the most inspiring aroma in the world.

Blacker than any shadow, the huge cat flew about the cellar. At first the occupants were hardly aware of what was happening, except that Lily had stopped shaking her skirts.

'It's a cat!' bellowed Theo in the outraged tones of a man faced by a card-playing cheat or a live lobster for his dinner or a wolf among sheep. 'It's eating my rats and now my snakes *will* starve. Who let that monster down here?'

'It was an excellent idea,' said Matilda coolly. 'For now we can leave the cat to do its proper job and we can go back to ours. Come, Theo.'

Since there was no catching Tom and no stopping him catching the remaining rats at liberty, Theo decided to follow his wife. He usually did when she spoke firmly.

That evening at prayers, Theo once again handed over the prayer-leading role to his wife. He expected a divinely clothed rebuke for those who put the animal kingdom before the kingdom of the soul – Matilda was clever about this sort of thing. But instead her eyes suddenly opened wide and her cheeks flushed. 'Let us,

O Father, find the strength to help those in this world who do not have our opportunities or our strength. Let the strong help the weak. Let the happy help the suffering. Let the rich help the poor. Let us pray.'

Theo tried to see in this a reference to himself but failed. He could not know that, as Matilda looked across at her now regulated household, her children, her elderly relations, her servants, nurse-maids, governess, she experienced a repeat of her morning's exhilaration. Confident in the control of her family, she would spread her light out to dark places. Even her toes tingled at the thought.

Theo, coming to his wife's bed sometime after midnight was surprised to find her arms warm and welcoming. 'You have for-given me, dear?' he asked, unable to keep the surprise from his voice.

'Forgiven?' Matilda sounded sincerely wondering.

'The rats,' suggested Theo.

'The rats, of course, the rats.' But Matilda did not sound as if she were thinking about them at all, which indeed she was not. 'That's not serious,' she said, not at all in her usually languid night-time voice. 'Cook retracted her notice. At my age one cannot afford to spend time worrying about things that are not serious.'

'I see,' said Theo, not seeing. There was something new here that he did not understand. 'May I ask what is serious?'

'Oh, my dear Theo!' Matilda, who was emotional but only occasionally demonstrative, threw her arms round her husband's neck. For the next half-hour he had no choice but to listen to his wife's plan to turn Abbeyfields village into a model from which all England would learn. 'I don't know how I can have been so selfish so long!' cried Matilda, at intervals.

Eventually Theo began to feel sleepy, which had not been his object, until Matilda became aware that she was addressing a more or less inert lump. She was happy enough not to be upset but hugged Theo reassuringly.

Her close warmth aroused Theo to his original intent. 'How will I do without you all these months of travelling?' He stroked her shoulder and pulled her black curls down from the night cap.

Matilda did not resist for she loved her husband but as he entered her she felt once again the excitement caught from the eyes of the Reverend Oswald Plunkett.

'Ah,' she moaned, eyes closed. 'Ah, Theo,' and pronouncing his name was both soothing and deflating. He loved her but he was planning to travel far away.

'My dove, my duck, my dear heart,' murmured Theo gratefully and he pictured her as a young girl.

Matilda, though intent on doing good, was certain it would be done her way. The money would be hers, coming from the proceeds of the sale of Sir William's business before it disappeared into shares. However, Mr Plunkett won for himself a rival, although never equal, ascendancy by his shining good looks (his smooth fair skin, thick fair hair and long slim legs became more impressive on closer inspection) and by the badge he wore so seriously as Christ's representative on earth. He was not priggish but modest, despite his advantages, and even Elizabeth, who had the fifteen-year-old's longing to discover an adult's weakness, found little to criticise.

'I believe Papa only dislikes Mr Plunkett,' she confided in her mother one day, 'because of his feelings about God.'

'Whose feelings about God?' Matilda's voice was brusque. For some reason she did not like to hear Theo's and Mr Plunkett's names in the same sentence. 'Hasn't Miss Waterville taught you to affix the personal pronoun to the proper subject so that there can be no mistake about it?'

Elizabeth was hurt. She had been holding her mother's hand as she walked about the house with a little watering can but now she slid hers away. 'It would hardly make any difference to which gentleman I referred,' she said coldly. 'If it were Papa I would mean he did not believe in God and if it were Mr Plunkett I would mean he was devoting his life to God. The point of my remark was that they have a fundamental religious disagreement.'

Both mother and daughter were equally amazed by this boldness and Matilda went as pale as Elizabeth went red. Both were filled with alarm but Matilda knew she was in the wrong. A dignified apology was the only fair course and yet it was a dreadful shock to discover her eldest daughter knew of Theo's lack of belief. It was a dreadful shock to hear it on her lips, without criticism, apparently, but possibly that made it even worse.

'My dear,' she said putting down the watering can and forcing Elizabeth's hand back into her own, 'only God can know what is in a man's heart.'

Elizabeth, perhaps luckily, felt too emotional to argue further or even to speak and would have liked to throw herself into her mother's arms and be comforted like a small child for the difficulties that faced her in the world.

'You are so good, Mama!' she said eventually after they had walked back to the little sitting room where tea was waiting for them in front of a high-burning wood fire – it was early September now and the high-ceilinged rooms grew cold by the afternoon.

Matilda was satisfied by this homage, not because she was conceited enough to believe it but because she felt it was the right attitude for a daughter to hold towards her mother. As a reward she sent Elizabeth to collect the plans for the extension to the school house. Nothing pleased them more than poring over these simple drawings for an extra room. 'And in a month or so we will interview for a second teacher.'

'And the new pupils,' added Elizabeth a little anxiously. Despite all her efforts, visiting the horridest little huts, she had only persuaded two extra children to attend and that was because they were so poor she had been able to bribe them with the promise of a new pair of shoes each and a calico dress and a jacket respectively.

'As to that, I have formed a conviction,' said Matilda looking down her long straight nose to the little china tea-cup from which she drank. It was pleasantly peaceful without the other four older children who had driven out to a birthday party in the neighbourhood. 'After much thought', she looked up at Elizabeth, 'and prayer, I have realised that in order to make our school something out of the usual, we must set an example.'

'An example, Mama?' Elizabeth was quite bewildered.

'The question was which of you children should attend . . .'

A feeling of horror mingled with disbelief caused Elizabeth to choke on her toasted crumpet.

'. . . and after much prayer, I have decided on Hannah.'

'Hannah to go to the village school!'

'She seemed the most sensible choice. You are already involved as a helper. Lily – well, I just could not see Lily fitting in.' There was a pause.

'But Hannah is so clever.' Elizabeth felt some defence must be attempted. 'She's much the cleverest of us girls.'

'That is an advantage in my view. She will be such an example and is quite incapable of falling behind herself. She is also the right age and can be head of the new middle classroom.'

Further discussion was made impossible by the arrival of the twins with their nurse. As Elizabeth laid out the building blocks, which were prettily decorated with the alphabet, she wondered, almost bitterly, if these two clever little things were also destined for village life and then, hugging Daisy's sturdy round body, realised it was only she who was at risk.

Since Theo was on a final prolonged stay in London, planning for his departure, Matilda decided to burst the good news on Mr

Plunkett before informing her husband. She was making a rare visit to the vicarage, which was perhaps an unfortunate choice of location since brother and sister were so concerned that their hospitality should not be found wanting that they hardly sat down for more than a minute.

'The tea is possibly too strong?' suggested Mr Plunkett, bounding across to Matilda as she put down her cup.

'Not at all. Just as I like it.'

'The cake is crisper than you're used to?' Miss Plunkett joined her brother. 'Cook says our oven is running very hot.' This was the kind of lie to which even very good people who want to impress are drawn, for the Plunketts had no cook and Miss Plunkett had baked the cake herself.

But Matilda had little interest in food or the finer details of household management and noticed their attentions only as irritants, for the Plunketts would not keep still and listen to her exciting plans. 'Do sit down,' she was forced to say quite sternly. 'I have something to tell you but you are like two greyhounds the way you streak about. I assure you Miss Hope and I are very well provided for.'

At last the Plunketts sat down, the vicar leaning forward over his long legs with such an intent gaze that Matilda felt flustered for a moment. She began speaking in less measured tones than she would have liked. 'We must set the level!' she cried. 'We must not rule from above. We must set an example.' Soon she had spun such a web of generalities that Mr Plunkett's blue, admiring eyes had become a little glazed. By the time she revealed the part her daughter was to play 'in elevating the tone of the educational life of the village', he was hardly listening rationally. Besides, the idea was so unexpected – so almost shocking. His sister's reaction was quicker.

'Oh, but, Lady Hope! Would it be proper?' Her imagination had leaped at once to picture the inadequate lavatory facilities and the ungenteel smell that often rose from the children's boots.

'Lady Hope is the best judge of that.' Mr Plunkett turned to his sister. In a second revelatory flash, he saw that Lady Hope was a saint, a Christian revolutionary, a lady of Christlike mercy and goodness. 'We must follow whatever Lady Hope decrees,' he added reverentially.

Miss Plunkett looked at her brother with some astonishment. Although sharing his awe in the social sense, she could hardly have understood – indeed he did not himself – that she was looking at a man in love.

'Good,' said Matilda with finality. 'I am sure we will find many a shrinking violet will shrink no longer with such an example as Hannah.'

Despairingly, Miss Plunkett tried to catch her brother's eye but his was fixed on his beloved. Sensing her wish, he dashed at once from the room to summon her carriage. Mr Plunkett's heart had been fixed on God since he was eight and he had served his Master in practical ways. But his deep well of romantic love was untouched; it was dangerous for such a passionate man so lacking in self-awareness to fall in love.

Miss Plunkett waited until the carriage had left their mossy driveway and the vicar had re-entered the small sitting room before raising the question of Miss Hannah Hope. 'I gravely doubt, brother,' she touched his sleeve timidly, it was a little damp from an early autumn mist, 'whether Miss Hannah's enrolment will help our little school.'

Mr Plunkett appeared to listen. He bent his head in his usual kind, attentive way but Miss Plunkett, knowing him so well, could see that he had not heard a word.

Theo was beginning to feel the reluctance to leave his wife and family that he recognised from his two previous experiences of extended travel as being the final wriggle of breaking bonds.

Matilda was sewing, delicate little stitches in a handkerchief she was working for one of the old aunts' birthdays. She was pleased Theo saw her in such a docile occupation and there was a something of theatre in her glossy bent head and flashing fingers.

'I shall remember you like this,' said Theo.

'No, you will not!' Matilda could not resist replying. 'You will not remember me at all. You have never been the slightest bit interested in another human being unless you're face to face and even then you often contrive to avoid them.'

'Oh, Matty, Matty!' Theo rolled his eyes sentimentally. 'I wrote to you from Bombay and from Calcutta.'

'That was because you were ill and felt sorry for yourself and guilty about me. You didn't want to die without anyone knowing.' Matilda laughed and threw down her sewing.

'The Society knew where I was,' said Theo, rather huffily. He would not easily abandon his loving farewell scene. 'I wrote to you as an expression of deep feelings.'

'You did not write. Your colleague, Captain de Yonge, wrote, a very nice clear hand, too.'

'I was ill, Matilda.' Theo whined a little.

'You must be honest with yourself, Theo, dear.'

'You are a hard woman.'

'If I am a hard woman, it's because you've made me one.'

This was a thought depressing to both of them so Matilda stood up and started towards the door. Her discarded sewing fell to the floor unnoticed except by Theo who bent forward and picked it up. Still sniffing for sentiment, he saw it was a handkerchief and stuffed it into his pocket. From there, transferred from pocket to pocket, it followed him across continents, a memorial to his wife. And it was only many months later, on encountering a very good laundress in Paris, that he discovered that the little prickings he had suffered in and around his hip during that period were due to the needle still folded into the cambric.

Chapter Fifteen

With Sir William Hope dead, his business sold and Theo out of the country, Matilda found her life considerably narrowed. Previously when her husband had been travelling, Sir William's periodic visits had given reason for entertaining but now she was on her own in a houseful of women. Even Edward had returned to Eton, and Tom to a preparatory school. If it had not been for the Reverend Oswald Plunkett she would have forgotten what a man looked like.

The experiment with Hannah had begun. The new pupil sat in a corner and read a book. She was shy and did not enjoy the curtsying and bowing that greeted her arrival each morning but equally was unaware of the sly nudges and cheeky comments that arose after the novelty of her presence had worn off. The problem of sanitary arrangements was solved by Miss Plunkett taking her off for frequent rest periods and biscuits at the vicarage where Hannah enjoyed the original experience of holding one person's full attention. Since Miss Plunkett was well read, having made it a point of honour to read every book her brother read and her personal taste leading to novels, they had many interesting discussions. It was at least a kind of schooling for Hannah but not as her mother had planned.

Matilda expressed her dissatisfaction to Mr Plunkett. They were taking a turn round her rose garden since the vicar had expressed an interest in the pretty stone balustrades which edged the terrace. The weather had turned as cold and cheerless as February even though it was only 1 November – All Saints' Day as Mr Plunkett pointed out – and Matilda had wrapped herself in a heavy shawl. She leaned against the stone parapet of the terrace and addressed him seriously. 'I'm afraid you are not giving your pupils a chance to benefit from Hannah's presence in school.'

'You look like a saint!' The unlikely words swirled out with big white breaths. He added more softly, 'Or like a queen.'

Matilda stared at him. It was, to say the least, disconcerting to be addressed in such a way, particularly when she was half-way through what could only be termed a rebuke. She saw, as his sister before, that he had not been listening to a word she said. 'Hannah has been at the school six weeks,' she began again, struggling against the knowledge that she was blushing and that her puritanical vicar had his hand over his eyes in the posture of a romantic poet. 'However, she still seems quite remote from the other children. Does she, for instance, take one general class?'

Mr Plunkett had now turned his back on his lady and leaned against the balustrade, a most untypical posture, so that his voice was faint. 'So much advanced,' he said, 'far ahead of even the oldest and cleverest of the pupils.'

'I see.' Matilda took the opportunity, while his back was turned, to rearrange her cloak in more formal folds and reset her face. What did he mean by 'queen'? An irrepressibly smug smile passed – not too fast – over her face.

But the situation suddenly overwhelmed poor Mr Plunkett who, muttering something about hollyhocks – or that was what it sounded like to Matilda – dashed from the terrace and made for the open spaces beyond.

Matilda, standing still among the wintry survivors of a rose garden, heard him blundering round the bamboo canes and then saw him appearing for a moment behind a wall before finally vanishing through a side gate. She sighed nostalgically, reminded of Theo's impulsive youth, and even bent to pick a lingering white rose. But the petals fell at once, as if to remind her how awkward life would become if she were forced to recognise Mr Plunkett's loving passion. Worse still, if she must recognise her own interest. Instead she frowned and tried to imagine how she could integrate Hannah with the other pupils.

Inside the house, Hannah had just returned from school escorted by Miss Plunkett, who had been disappointed to miss her brother. 'Her ladyship took him to the garden and then I saw him hurrying away,' Croke informed her with relish and disapproval. In his view her ladyship gave far too much of the time of day to this inferior family.

So Miss Plunkett left, hastening down the drive after her brother who certainly had been behaving oddly lately, and Hannah found her favourite window-seat in the schoolroom. Unhappily, when she took up *Pride and Prejudice* to continue reading about the fascinating lives of the Bennett family, her vision blurred and her eyes began to water. It struck her, then, that she had had a headache for the last day or two, which had been gradually increasing till it was now making her whole head hot and heavy.

She wondered who to tell, but in a family as large as theirs little time was given to anything less than serious sickness.

Matilda had not been sleeping well lately and when Elizabeth came to her in the middle of the night, she was awake in a moment.

'Hannah is ill,' Elizabeth whispered, trying not to be pleased by the excitement of it all. 'She's throwing herself about the bed and the sheets are wringing wet and she's talking all the time without making any sense and her eyes are wide open. I woke Miss Waterville and Nurse but they can't do anything with her and think you should send for the doctor!'

Before Elizabeth had finished her dramatic message, Matilda was down the corridor, wrapper flung over her uncoiling hair, feet still bare. A fever, such as Elizabeth had described, was a great dread. She had lost two babies like that.

Elizabeth and Hannah shared a room, a large high-ceilinged room with little furniture and bare floorboards. Usually it smelled calmly of the trees and grass outside, for Theo insisted on open windows for his children even at night. But now it was warm and filled with the anxiety of many half-awake bodies. Miss Waterville was there and the young children's nurse and two nursemaids and Matilda even caught sight of Cook lurking along the corridor. Lily, too, sat beside her sister, trying to hold a cold cloth on her forehead.

'Out at once! Out! Miss Waterville, how could you allow such a scene?'

As Matilda approached Hannah she could feel the heat coming from her body. She was no longer talking as Elizabeth had described and lay instead in a fretful languor. 'Tell Croke to send for Dr Rebew at once and to say it's a matter of extreme urgency.'

The doctor did not arrive till eight and his dark face was drawn. 'There's scarlet fever in the village,' he said at once to explain his late arrival.

Matilda stared at him with such a look of horror that he began to explain further. After all, Sir Theodore was a friend and his wife and children all on their own. 'There's little I can do, of course, because the sickness spreads too fast and they have no space for separating those with the fever from the healthy. But, now, how can I help you? Nothing too serious, I hope?'

Speechless, Matilda led him to Hannah's bed. The child had begun to babble in the last hour and her eyes were wide open, although they saw nothing. Dr Rebew felt her forehead and looked at Matilda. 'I'm sorry.' He bent over his black pouchy bag.

Matilda stood close by him. Outwardly calm, her head was filled with a voice crying out, 'If Hannah dies, I will have killed her. For the sake of experiment from which no one gained but my own silly pride, I have exposed my daughter to a danger that could be deadly.' Slowly, because she was afraid she might faint with self-loathing, Matilda sat down again on her bedside chair. Why had not someone reminded her that charity and goodness and love must all be turned first on the family and only if there is an overflowing there can a mother afford to look outwards? God was punishing her for her arrogant presumption. She must turn to God and ask for his forgiveness. Sliding off the chair, she fell forward on to her knees and put her head in her hands. Dear Lord, spare my child for she is innocent and it is I who have sinned!

So distraught was Matilda with her self-reproaches that she almost forgot Dr Rebew, who was, meanwhile, attending to Hannah. Eventually he finished and touched Matilda's shoulder. 'You should not stay on the floor too long. Call a nursemaid and take a rest. There is nothing you can do.'

But Matilda was far too distressed to rest so she accompanied Dr Rebew down to the breakfast table where a very subdued gathering failed to eat devilled kidneys and gammon and porridge. At first Matilda did not notice the food but as soon as she did, she put her hand to her mouth and fled from the room. After finishing his piece of toast, the doctor followed. He found Matilda still standing in the hallway, as if uncertain which way to go.

'I'm afraid you are not well,' he said gently.

Matilda swung round on him. Short, dark-bearded and agnostic, she had never considered him much of a human being so it hardly mattered if he heard the truth. 'If I were ill,' she cried bitterly, 'it would be right and proper, for I it was who sent Hannah day after day to that place where washing is a luxury—'

'Scarlet fever has little to do with washing,' began Dr Rebew, who had known nothing about Hannah's attendance at school. But Matilda's conscience took no notice of medical details.

'It is my daughter who is dying!' she screamed so that her voice catapulted round the high roof of the hall. 'And I stand here as fit as a fiddle!'

Dr Rebew, blown a little backwards by her passion, only just managed to jump forwards and catch her as she fell.

Matilda came round in her own room and for a moment or two thought Hannah's illness was a dream. Then she thought she was ill, and then she remembered everything. 'Hannah! Hannah! How is she?'

'There is no change. You have only been unconscious for a few moments.' Dr Rebew stood above her looking grave. 'I presume you are aware of your own condition?'

There was no mistaking his meaning. Distraught as she was and with all her attention fixed on Hannah, she could still be astonished that a woman of her only too wide experience had not realised earlier. The truth was that she had not wanted to think she could be pregnant again. Theo was away and the Reverend Oswald Plunkett was here and Hannah, poor Hannah. Oh! It was almost too much to bear. One hand on her head – which felt ready to drop off – Matilda struggled out of bed.

The doctor did not attempt to restrain her but followed closely through the long corridors of the great house. They found Hannah quieter, perhaps sleeping, Matilda thought, and again she allowed herself to be persuaded away.

Dr Rebew and Matilda sat facing each other in the small drawing room. 'I shall stay until the crisis is passed for your daughter,' he said.

Matilda gave a little cry for she had dared to hope the crisis had passed. She had dressed and recovered herself to some extent. She was even capable of pitying the doctor's grey, exhausted expression. She could not let him leave, however, so she offered no words of sympathy.

'I will go to Hannah now.' Dr Rebew rose.

Matilda rose too but again felt faint and had to sink back into her chair. 'It would be better if this baby died.' She spoke in a ferocious mutter but the doctor heard and came back to her.

'In my hospital,' he said, 'I have children and adults and adults who are more like children, in whose existence there seems very little point.'

Matilda stared upwards at his ugly, sagging face and her instinctive dislike returned in defensive fury. Was he daring to compare, to put into the same sentence – or at least thought – her family with his dreadful godless guinea pigs?

Seeing her expression, Dr Rebew retreated hastily. Overstepping the social mark was something he recognised easily, since his strong feelings led him to do it so often.

'I shall be back shortly,' he said and left the room before Matilda could follow.

Sitting on her chair, Matilda began to imagine she was bleeding. This pleased her even though she knew how quickly it could become frightening, but she felt too drowsy to do anything about it. The house was unnaturally quiet, as if it were holding its breath in sympathy with the sick child. Despite everything, she slipped into a half-sleep.

She was awakened by a timid knock at the door, which opened almost immediately to reveal the pale, fearful face of Miss Plunkett.

'I had come to warn you of the scarlet fever in the village. But after I heard the troubling news, I thought . . .' Her thoughts, doubtless helpfully Christian, remained unexpressed for it was impossible to speak further with the face Matilda turned on her.

Matilda stood up. She was not bleeding, she noticed; there was to be no easy escape. When she had first seen Miss Plunkett's sheep's face an urgent wish to blame someone other than herself caused the expression of hatred that had silenced Miss Plunkett. But now as her dazed vision cleared and she saw the humility, the desire to serve and the well-washed gloves wrung together, she was ashamed.

'Nurse may want relieving,' she said. 'Ask Dr Rebew. He is up there now. In a moment I will follow.'

After Miss Plunkett had gone, as hastily as is consistent with a noiseless closing of the door, Matilda walked round the room in slow circles. Her sense of loneliness was profound. She knew that a letter written to Theo would take several months to reach him – if it reached him at all. The reality of his being away had never struck her so hard and she felt a bitter resentment.

Leaving her drawing room, from whose intimate order she usually took comfort, she stepped out across the hall and towards the wing which ended in the conservatory, newly housing her husband's snakes. The cold in the approaching rooms made her shiver and drag her long patterned scarf around her throat. But once she entered the conservatory, the warmth and light and sweet smells from the rare and tropical plants that grew there became suffocating.

Why had she come here? Matilda was on the point of fleeing, when the fat coil of snake nearest to her, slowly raised its head. It was a large Indian python, easily recognisable by the magnificent cream and brown diamond-like pattern along its back. As it un-coiled further Matilda, staring mesmerised for the eyes without eyelids seemed to be fixed on her, caught a glimpse of something white under the gleaming scales. The python loosened itself further, moving easily and slowly towards the front of its glass box.

Matilda moved back a little and then found herself doing the least expected thing in the world: bursting into merry, if somewhat hysterical, laughter. 'You're sitting on a heap of eggs, just like a chicken!'

It was true. Queen Victoria had removed herself enough to reveal the corner of what was obviously a pile of eggs, seven or eight, probably more. Where Matilda had expected bitter remembrances of Theo, she had found instead a good mother. It was ridiculous, quite ridiculous.

The head of the python was now peering at her expectantly. Matilda bent down slightly and addressed her fellow mother as best she was able between her fits of mirth. 'You look happy enough,' she said to the bright beady eyes, 'but, then, you're shut into a nice cosy home with every want taken care of. Now if you were in my position—'

She might have continued had she not been disturbed by the sound of footsteps immediately behind her, accompanied by a high-pitched squeaking. She rose and turned, feeling foolish and flustered.

'I hope I didn't frighten your ladyship.'

It was the keeper of the snakes, the big strong lad who carried the cage of squeaking rats once a week to their death. Not that Matilda felt sorry for the rats in theory but the terror of the jumping, scrabbling vermin in the face of the stately python was macabre and impressive. The deadly plan of nature is not usually seen so clearly.

The remembrance of Hannah's sickness returned with terrifying suddenness. What was she doing so far from her side? Why was she hesitating in this inimical domain when her daughter might be dying? Sweat, which had been slowly gathering, suddenly trickled down her neck and forehead. Gathering her skirts, she ran from the conservatory.

The snake-keeper watched her retreat, scarf fluttering behind her, with disappointment. He was an enthusiastic worker and had wanted to share his pride in the python's eggs with her. Besides, Sir Theodore usually liked to find a home for a couple in a nice warm airing cupboard and he could have asked permission of her ladyship. Disappointed, the youth put down his frantic cage of food and went to check the mother python. She would not eat while she was incubating her eggs. All around there was a faint rustling as the other snakes moved slowly forwards.

It was now light in Hannah's bedroom, but a cheerless November light that Dr Rebew saw no reason to mask. Miss Plunkett had taken over the nursing and was bathing her patient's limbs with a damp cloth.

Her action told Matilda at once that Hannah's fever had not abated. She looked round for Dr Rebew but Miss Plunkett turned to her. 'He's with Miss Elizabeth.'

Matilda said nothing but Miss Plunkett understood. She was well attuned to the sick room, having had much practice with both her parents and a younger brother and sister, all of whom had died. 'I expect she is merely tired and overwrought.' It was a relief when Dr Rebew returned almost immediately and took Matilda's arm.

'It is not good for you to stay here,' he said, his voice sounding surprisingly normal after Miss Plunkett's whisperings.

Yet Matilda lingered. She was looking at Hannah's face more closely than she had since her daughter was a baby. She had been the fourth child, three above her and three below, wedged in the middle with no chance of capturing anyone's attention. Perhaps that was why she had taken to books so readily, reading by the time she was three and never seen without a volume in her hand since she was six or seven. She had not seemed unhappy, however, or, if she were, never strove to express it. All she displayed was a doglike devotion and obedience to her mother.

Matilda stepped closer to the bed. Hannah had never been pretty. She was stalwartly built like her father but had inherited her mother's long nose. Her complexion had been muddy and her movements clumsy and graceless. Now the brilliant spots of fever in her cheeks gave her the look of a painted woman, an actress.

'I have been a bad mother, a bad mother,' she muttered, quite certain now that Hannah would die.

The doctor felt it his duty to lead Matilda away from the sick bed. This time they sat across a table in the small dining room where a cold luncheon had been laid. Matilda was amazed to see the house still functioning even when her will had been removed. Even more surprising was the presence of the old aunts. It was true that since Theo's departure they had slipped across now and again from their wing but on this day their appearance struck Matilda as a ghoulish desire to be near tragedy.

They were hearty in their feeding, tucking between their withered lips great slabs of ham, chunks of potato, rounds of stuffed eggs. Neither of them was fat, but that made the display more revolting in Matilda's eyes for they had no reason to stoke up their dying furnaces. Ah, dying! Although sitting so straight and severe Matilda's whole being throbbed with the horror of what was happening upstairs.

'You must lie down.'

Matilda jumped at the doctor's strong voice and turned on him a look of fury. Why did he keep harping on her need for rest? She was not faint, she was not bleeding and if she were she would not care. Surely he had understood that? If it had not been for the presence of the aunts, she would have shouted at him.

The aunts had almost finished now, wiping, with delicate napkins, their mouths, which seemed to Matilda more like the beaks of carrion crows.

Dr Rebew went back to Hannah again for in a few moments he must return to see his patients in the village.

'No better.' Miss Plunkett, who had not left her post even for lunch, bowed her head. She had learned to accept death as part of God's will. When she looked at Hannah and saw the young girl who had discussed with such modesty, but such eagerness too, the joy in Wordsworth's poetry, her eyes filled with tears. But then she distanced herself a little and saw Hannah, virtuous and innocent, stepping Heavenwards.

'I think we should send for Mr Plunkett,' she said, following her train of thought. If Hannah must Step Off the Top Rung of the Ladder then Oswald should be there to hold her hand.

'I will advise Lady Hope,' said the doctor who, though no believer himself, had often seen what comfort a kindly parson could bring. 'However, I would not think the child in immediate danger.'

'No,' said Miss Plunkett, inwardly disagreeing.

'I will be back in an hour or two,' said Dr Rebew.

Matilda accepted the doctor's dark face, dark beard and dark suit as part of the nightmare through which she was living. When he rapped and opened her bedroom door she hardly moved from her pillows.

He came to her, felt her pulse and said, 'Would you like me to send for Mr Plunkett?'

Matilda looked at her windows. It had started to rain. The wind blew, unusually, from the east, so that the rain, sweeping across the valley, slashed and battered at the glass. 'If my husband were a serious person, he would be here now, not chasing snakes in some Indian desert.'

Dr Rebew, whose real interest was not in the body but the mind, half shut his slightly bulbous eyes. 'Sir Theodore is a great gentleman,' he announced.

Matilda sat up, face puffing angrily. 'Don't be so absurd. He doesn't even believe in God!'

Dr Rebew could hardly restrain a smile. 'Sir Theodore, like all serious persons, is seeking for the truth.'

'The truth! The truth! What nonsense you men talk! Self-indulgence and poppycock! Laziness and selfishness! Does the truth come before human life? Does the truth come before a wife? A daughter, a son? What is this thing called truth except an escape from the responsibilities each person owes another? Did Christ hold forth about truth? He talked about loving your neighbour and obeying God's commandments which, when the cant is left out, are all about loving your neighbour too. You scientists, naturalists, zoologists who try to explain the meaning to us lesser beings who accept the explanation that God made the universe as the only important truth—'

At this point Matilda, although she had still much more to say along these lines, was overwhelmed again by the realisation of Hannah's illness and burst into loud sobs.

Dr Rebew stood where he was. He thought that her God seemed to bring her little consolation and he pictured the humble homes where parents relinquished their children quietly in the conviction they were going to Heavenly joys. This sometimes made him angry, for the parents' resignation could lead them to jeopardise their children's chance of survival by lax nursing. Lady Hope's passionate unhappiness reminded him of one or two of his hospital patients.

'Why do you blame yourself?'

Matilda became quiet at his question. She was a courageous person and always felt better when confronting a problem. 'I told you. I sent her down to the village.'

'You were trying to help those less well off than your own family.'

'I had ideas of philanthropy.' Matilda became a little more excited. 'But that was not the whole case. I was bored. I was lonely. I was angry with Theo.' Confessing was surprisingly easy. Even so, Matilda did not mention Mr Plunkett although as she spoke she saw his blue eyes looking into hers and his young golden-red skin frowning in concentration.

'If your daughter dies—' began the doctor, meaning to offer consoling words, but he progressed no further for Matilda clapped her hands over her ears. She could not bear that he could admit such a possibility.

Dr Rebew began to think he might do more good in the village. 'I may assume you would like Mr Plunkett's attendance?'

'No! No!' Matilda fought for self-control. 'Yes. Yes! Whatever you think. Yes, he must come. I must not deprive her. Oh, poor Hannah!'

Too tired to speculate further at such displays of emotion, Dr Rebew left the room, determining to arrange for a sedative for Matilda as soon as possible.

The day, which had never been bright, was darkening too fast even for the time of year. Elizabeth, now installed in Lily's room, felt that it was an omen foretelling that Hannah would not recover. She herself, no longer suffering from nervous exhaustion, sat in the bed trying to write up her journal. Lily sat in a comfortable chair engaged in the same task. Her head was bent so close to her pen that her face was hidden, all but the white dome of her forehead.

'It's too dark to write,' said Elizabeth, although, as she knew perfectly well, that was not the reason her pen stayed still. It seemed that, faced with the first tragedy of her life, she could find neither the will nor the words to describe it.

'Yes,' Lily agreed immediately, as she did about everything that had the cloak of normality, and put down her pen. 'I suppose everyone is too busy to bring in the lamps.'

There fell a sad silence, which was broken by loud and jolly noises as the twins came up the nursery stairs to prepare for bed.

Elizabeth drew back the bedclothes from her legs. 'I'm better now.' She wanted to ask what Lily had written in her journal but felt shy. The two sisters, although closest in age and sharing so many of the day's activities, had never been at ease with each other; they were too similar perhaps, each with a need for order, although Elizabeth thought of herself as far more adventurous and suffered from the jealousy often felt by an older sister for a younger. 'I can't write!' she cried impulsively. 'It seems too fearfully bad. I can't write it in as if I was talking about Nurse's greed or Miss Waterville's vanity or—' She stopped abruptly and gave her sister an expectant look.

Lily understood. She picked up her journal and held it up close by the window to catch what light remained. 'I wrote, "Today Hannah fell ill with scarlet fever. At first we did not know what it was but then Dr Rebew came . . ."'

As Lily continued to read in her light matter-of-fact voice, Elizabeth became more and more disturbed. 'But, Lily!' she cried out. 'What will you write if Hannah dies?'

Lily's agitation was still under control. 'At the end I have written down the Lord's Prayer and tomorrow I shall underline "Thy Kingdom come" and "Thy will be done" and that will help me bear it. I shall colour the words and illuminate them and even embroider a pillow, a little lace-edged pillow, so I shall never forget.'

Elizabeth could see the comfort Lily found in her plans, it showed in every line of her body, but she did not feel as if similar could help her.

'I'll get a lamp or we'll be even more dismal.' Lily rose now and bustled off so that Elizabeth had to remind herself that her sister was not hard-hearted but blessed with practical, common sense and a totally unquestioning belief in the Almighty.

Elizabeth, bred on charming tales of young heroines who faded delicately away, was horrified by the ugliness that she, like her mother, had seen in the sick Hannah. 'I don't want her to die,' she said aloud, suddenly finding a voice. 'I don't want anyone I know to die!' Her appeal, age-old and useless, was heard by no one.

The Reverend Oswald Plunkett arrived at Abbeyfields just before the usual time for prayers. He stood on the doorstep waiting for the butler to swing back the great door, and looked up at the towering pile of masonry above him. The main roofs were long and deeply sloping, interrupted by turrets, roofed conically as if with witches' hats. Most of the walls were built of stone, cleverly dressed and set but occasionally highlighted by reddish brick. There were windows everywhere, of every conceivable shape and size even in the smallest turret. It was clearly planned and constructed with no expense spared. And yet, its owner and creator, a hearty, healthy, living man, had been taken to his Maker only a few months ago and now a young inhabitant looked on the face of death.

Shivering rather, for it was still drizzling and, lacking his sister's attentions, he had been without the proper coat all day, Oswald reflected on the truth of Christian teaching and managed to avoid picturing his unacknowledged beloved, Lady Hope, sorrowing inside.

'Her ladyship asks for you to remain in the hall for a few minutes as she will be coming down shortly for prayers.' Croke showed his agitation by speaking before the door was properly closed.

Mr Plunkett knew he was not popular with the servants. Refusing the chair the butler offered him now so that his vital role must be accepted, he stood with his hands behind his back and a solemn expression on his face.

Around him the hall, although generously lit at the walls by gaslights, reached upwards in a seemingly unending darkness of

214

ceiling. He had always recognised its origins in church architecture and been both exhilarated and discomfited. Now he removed his hands from back to front and prayed that God's will should be done.

Formal prayers were a sombre matter. The family was already dressed in black, owing to Sir William's death. Matilda had to sit down half-way and was hideously pale under a veil she had assumed. Elizabeth, who had bullied Miss Waterville until she had been allowed out of bed, sobbed in irregular spasms. The servants, gathered together closer than usual, spoke over-heartily, as if in reproof of the family's faint-heartedness, and the two old aunts, who had never spent so much time out of their wing, finished every prayer a beat or two behind everyone else. Only the twins, given special dispensation to appear on this special occasion, clapped their 'Amens' cheerfully, although this caused Lily to frown and snatch their hands.

Mr Plunkett followed Matilda up the stairs to Hannah's bedroom. He must not look at her delicate heels clicking on the polished wood but pray harder that the comfort of God would descend.

Matilda felt his steps beating regularly behind her and fought against a passionate desire to turn on him and shout words of accusation. He had aided and abetted Hannah's ejection into an area of danger. She would like to see his blue eyes fill with sympathetic tears and his face redden, then pale with shame and sorrow. She would like, in fact, to cast herself on his bosom.

But she said nothing and he said nothing and soon he stood beside the sick child and prayed that God's plan for her should be fulfilled. Miss Plunkett fell to her knees on the other side of the bed. Matilda, black veil covering her emotions, held Hannah's hot hand.

Down the stairs again went Mr Plunkett and Matilda, still in silence. A servant carrying a lamp lit the long corridors ahead of them.

'Come in the morning,' Matilda said eventually when they reached the front door. She did not offer him a drink or even lift her veil to him and he stepped out into the wet night without daring a backward glance. Yet his whole being was filled with a burning desire to alleviate his loved one's sorrow.

Chapter Sixteen

Hannah, against all expectations, recovered, but the twins, the ebullient little Alfred and Daisy, caught the disease and, being smaller and more vulnerable, could not fight it off. Alfred died first but Daisy survived him by less than twenty-four hours. One day they were the inexhaustible creatures who caused a headache in everyone who came near them and two days later they were dead. All who looked at them were struck by their beauty. In life they had never stayed still enough for it to be noticeable.

The household, already in shock but still functioning efficiently, now began to show unhappy signs of dislocation. Two kitchen maids ran away in the middle of the night. Cook erroneously informed one of the old aunts, who informed Matilda, that Croke was drinking and Hannah, who had ventured downstairs once or twice, reverted to her bed. Even the phlegmatic Lily was found in tears, after Miss Waterville had told her that she was a proud arrogant girl who treated her as if she were a common servant.

Matilda knew that this was her moment. Life had not challenged her much, whatever her complaints, and now she was given the opportunity to show her worth. Sir William, her protector, was dead, and Theo was away. He probably had not received her letter yet. Alone – unless she counted God, which she was finding more and more difficult to do these days – she had the responsibility for all the people under the great spreading roof. Lying awake at night she made resolutions: she would admonish Croke, inspire Cook, support Hannah. But in the morning she felt so sick, so tired and so cold – it was a horrible winter – that she could hardly bear to leave her room. When Lulworth, the twins' oxlike nurse, came to give notice, sensible enough as she had no charges remaining, Matilda found herself unable to tell her about the new baby even though she was the best nurse she had ever had and would be invaluable. She let her go with such gloomy looks that the nurse felt she was being reproached and burst into loud defensive tears.

'I loved them like my own,' was her honest cry.

'Yes, yes, Nurse. I know.' Her agonised bellowing was almost too much for Matilda's self-control but made it even more impossible to announce her own pregnancy. 'You must not hurry away,' she managed. 'You must find a new place first.' She was trying to be kind but the idea of a 'new place' set off the nurse again so that the interview ended, as it had begun, in misunderstanding and misery.

When she had gone Matilda looked out of her window and the calmness of the green hills inspired her with one happy idea: Hannah should go to the Plunketts' house and be cared for there. Outside this mausoleum of death and among young, healthy and affectionate people, she would soon thrive. The death of the twins and her increasing pregnancy had subdued her feelings for the vicar into a kind of nostalgic glow. She thought of him as of a favoured younger brother.

The Plunketts, brother and sister, received Hannah with equal ardour but for differing reasons. Miss Plunkett had grown so fond of her during her illness that she felt towards her as a younger sister. The vicar, still burdened with a total lack of self-knowledge, never passed a minute of the day without thinking of Matilda. To have her daughter constantly under his roof gave this unconscious mental exercise a legitimate excuse, which warmed his emotions further. If he could not admit to loving the mother, he could like, encourage and give sympathetic looks to the daughter. If Hannah had been older, prettier and less ill he would certainly have fallen in love with her. As it was, he held her hands in holy communication and asked rather too often when her mother was planning to visit her.

Matilda took a cold and lonely walk among her silver birches. The confusion in her head stopped her taking any pleasure in the view across the valley. Everything seemed to have hard edges – trees, walls, hedges, the ground under her feet. The frost had bitten hard that morning and a weakling sun had failed to melt more than the top grasses, which bent with a flaccid greyness. She felt too chilled to sit and too tired to walk. Surprising herself, she pictured the jungle warmth and brilliant colours of the snake conservatory. There she could sit on her own and be warm and comfortable.

Matilda sat beside the mother python's vivarium. A chair was already in place as if it were someone else's habit to sit there. Matilda had the dislike of snakes common to most people but Theo had kept them too long in the house for her to feel any fear. Besides, she knew that none of them was venomous even though the tamest might decide to give you a nasty nip or squeeze his length a little too tightly round your neck. She had never shown much interest in Theo's passion, partly as a sign of her disapproval, yet now she found herself admiring the gleaming coils. She could only see the merest glimpse of an egg but she knew they lay there safely beneath their mother. She tried to remember what Theo had told her about the hatching of the python's eggs but could only remember his descriptions of a courtship dance between cobras, which he insisted was beautiful but she thought sounded disgusting. Becoming more curious, she left her chair and walked round the conservatory, bending at each glass box to examine the snake or snakes inside. She was at once amazed by the diversity of size and colour and even shape. The smallest, a milk snake, *'Lampropeltis doliata'* – Matilda read the label aloud – was only about two feet long and very prettily coloured with pink and yellow and black stripes. The largest was an anaconda, *Eunectes murinus*, whose body was nearly as thick as a dog's and looked as if it would unwind two or three times as tall as a man. It was slumbering apparently, as Matilda, much impressed, peered at it. Half its great bulk lay in a scoop of water and the other spread across most of the rest of its living quarters. She wondered, rather uncomfortably, how many rats it devoured to keep itself that mammoth size.

The heat in the conservatory thawed Matilda's winter chill. She sat down on the chair again and allowed herself to relax for the first time in months. She rested her head on the long chair back and gazed upwards. The jungle plants grew in a tangled canopy above her; some were fat and juicy, prodding outwards like gross fingers, others spouted downwards in fountains of green, while yet more twined and curled round each other, so clasped together that she could see neither start nor finish. It was a dramatic example of nature's fecundity, for some of the plants had only been introduced earlier that year. Theo would be gratified, thought Matilda with a sigh.

She placed her hands over her stomach. But it was her breasts that had grown, making her constantly aware of her body's change. Elsewhere she was still thin, although, knowing herself so well, she could see the alteration in the pigment of her skin, the enrichment and glow, the added lustre to her hair. Theo always loved and admired her at these times, an admiration she partly resented, knowing he liked to see her taken over entirely by the woman's role. And yet was that true? Had he not in the past tried to make her join with him in his activities? And she had refused. Had she made motherhood an excuse for separating herself from him? But she had never meant them to become so separate. Matilda sighed again, more resigned. She was warm, she was pregnant, she was alone. None of these were bad things. With guilty surprise she realised she had not thought of the poor twins for nearly an hour.

The Reverend Oswald Plunkett did not have enough to do. The village of Abbeyfields was too small for such a young and able-bodied clergyman. He should have found a living in a big town where he would have inspired the respectable ladies to new heights of churchgoing and gone among the poor as a tornado of muscular Christianity. As it was, his underused physical and spiritual energy turned inwards into a fever of love. Mr Plunkett's love for Matilda grew, like the jungle plants, with shocking speed. A few months ago it had merely caused his heart to swell and beat louder. Now it roared through every pulse of his body so that he was in a continual ferment.

For several days he even wondered if he had caught scarlet fever – which would have been a relief – but his temperature raged inside his mind and made no impression on his sister's thermometer. 'You are not well,' she told him, because it was she who noticed his flushed looks and restless behaviour. 'But there seems to be nothing wrong with you. Perhaps you need a change of air. We have been here without a break for two years.'

'But, sister,' the vicar stood and sat and stood and sat around their little sitting room until Miss Plunkett began to feel giddy. 'But, sister, you would not be able to come with me because of, because of—'

'Hannah.' Miss Plunkett completed his sentence for him, only slightly surprised that her wonderful brother should have forgotten their honoured visitor. She smiled with the smile of the fulfilled servitor. 'I couldn't come, it is true. But you could go to Uncle Plunkett. How often he has asked us! It would be doing him a charity, I know.'

'To leave my work here for no reason!' exclaimed Mr Plunkett wildly, and hit the pretty striped wallpaper with his fist.

Miss Plunkett became seriously alarmed. Expressions like 'brain fever' presented themselves to her imagination, always fertile ground for identification of illness. 'You should go away. I see it now,' she said decisively, for this was her area. 'You are over-strained. I will manage perfectly well with Hannah. She is so much—'

'But—' Mr Plunkett interrupted her, and then turned his back so that all she could hear was an impassioned mutter, including the word 'Hall'.

'You are worried. Of course, I see that leaving your duties, especially when Lady Hope has suffered so much—'

'Suffering!' squealed Mr Plunkett.

'Yes. You are so good,' Miss Plunkett contemplated her brother's sense of duty with pleasure, 'but you must sometimes think of yourself. Lady Hope will understand if you explain. As a boy you were subject—'

'Explain!' cried Mr Plunkett, swinging round. 'Yes. That would be proper. Yes, indeed. I shall explain. Is it raining?' Here he dashed to the window. 'No. Not too dark. I can be there and back for tea. Thank you, dear sister.' Here he swiftly clasped Miss Plunkett's hands and just as swiftly dropped them.

'But I didn't mean . . .' began Miss Plunkett. But she spoke to his back. Already he was outside, calling impatiently for his coat and hat and eventually finding them himself.

Miss Plunkett went to the window. She had not meant him to go off like that, dashing out as if the devil were after him. He would arrive quite unsuitably hot and flustered. He should have taken the horse another day, talked over the matter further, approached Lady Hope with circumspection. Certainly this unseemly haste proved that he was not himself. Already his flapping black coat had disappeared into the shadows of late afternoon.

Disturbed but not seriously alarmed, for nothing could seriously shake her faith in her brother's rightness, Miss Plunkett left the room and went upstairs to see if her visitor had woken from her afternoon sleep.

Mr Plunkett had never been to Sir Theodore's snake conservatory. When Croke indicated that her ladyship had been seen heading that way – his terms were vague and unwelcoming – the usually well-mannered vicar did not even wait to remove his coat.

A servant, summoned by the butler, caught up with him after he had crossed the hall and entered a second corridor, but even then he hardly slowed his pace.

'Let me go ahead, sir,' cried the servant, well trained to open doors. But the speeding figure ignored him and the corridors they had now reached, narrow and winding, allowed for no overtaking.

It was only when Mr Plunkett opened a door and found himself on the point of falling down the stone steps of a deep cellar that he stopped. Gazing wildly round, he noticed the flunkey for the first time. 'I am looking for the conservatory,' he panted out with difficulty.

'Certainly, sir,' replied the servant, also panting, although he had run no distance compared to the vicar's upward journey from his house. 'Please follow me.'

Mr Plunkett followed, a little sobered although still hardly sane. He took off his hat, at least, which had stayed firmly clamped to his head. Putting his hand to his forehead, he found his hair so soaked with sweat that it dripped on to his nose. But even that realisation could not deter him from the course decided when his sister had pronounced those fateful words: 'explain to Lady Hope'. The joy of being given permission to explain himself. Ah, now he would explain!

The extraordinary thing was that, despite Mr Plunkett's mad flight to his beloved, he still had not admitted to himself that he was propelled by Cupid's dart. The superficial part of himself, that he recognised, still believed that he looked upon Lady Hope as a noble benefactress, a distinguished lady, an admirable wife and mother. That he also longed to throw upon her tender frame his young, hot and heavily panting body did not enter his consciousness. If it had, he would never have been able to approach her again – in fact it was so unthinkable to his sincere and open nature that it would put him in danger of true madness.

'Here is the door,' said the servant, staying a pace or two back for Theo had made the place generally out of bounds.

'Thank you. You may go.' Mr Plunkett saw his knuckles tremble as he lifted them to the heavy wood panelling. The knock he gave was uncharacteristically feeble.

Inside the conservatory, Matilda lifted her head with an irritable expression. Why should her visit coincide yet again with feeding time? She would have to leave because she could not bear to see those little wriggling bodies dragged inexorably into the snakes' gullets. A rat's tail was such a disgusting sight. She shuddered and looked round for her shawl. The knock was repeated, which was odd since the keeper usually behaved as if he owned the place.

'Come in, come in.'

Mr Plunkett, red-faced, sweating profusely, burst into her presence.

'Oh, what is it?' Matilda stood at once, all tranquillity lost.

'I've come to explain—' began Mr Plunkett, but he could hardly breathe. The jungle heat of the conservatory, the sweet smells of exotic plants, the reality of Matilda's person so close to him, added too much to his already overtaxed body. Eyes rolling, legs crumpling, he saw this longed-for interview disappearing into waves of blackness.

'Quick! Sit down!' Understanding that her visitor was about to faint, Matilda pushed him into her chair. She stood over him while his head swayed towards the floor. The danger of fainting passed but he was still finding it difficult to speak and the heat inside him burned like a furnace. He could not explain anything in this state and yet his urge to speak had not diminished.

'Yes,' agreed Matilda, as he began to struggle out of his coat, 'it is very hot in here. The snakes need it, you know, but the contrast with the cold outside can be very shocking to the system. Probably that is why you felt faint.' She looked at him doubtfully. 'Can you talk now? Your sudden arrival has made me very afraid—'

She was interrupted by the vicar suddenly falling forward off the chair on to his knees. 'I want to explain . . .' he gasped in barely recognisable words.

'You're squashing your hat,' said Matilda, hardly knowing what she was saying. Ignoring the hat, Mr Plunkett was shuffling forward with the apparent intention of holding on to Matilda's ankles. 'You're ill!' she cried, smoothing down and holding her skirts tight round her.

Her attitude was so defensive that it penetrated Mr Plunkett's ardour. 'I'm not going to hurt you,' he mumbled.

'Of course you're not going to hurt me,' cried Matilda, apparently more amazed every moment – although she knew, she knew. 'Do you want to hurt me? As a matter of fact, I should like to sit down.' Stepping round the vicar, Matilda found the chair again for it was her turn to fight a wave of faintness.

'O Lord! O God! O Great Creator!' Mr Plunkett shuffled round till he faced her again.

'What is the matter?' began Matilda as she revived. It was a sad fact but she could hardly recognise in this abject creature the golden young man who had so inspired her in the past. He seemed to be in an attitude of confession. 'Do you have something to tell me? Dear Mr Plunkett.' She bent forward and patted him on the head as if he were a child or dog. Obviously he was having some sort of breakdown, a suspicion encouraged by his next action, which was enthusiastically to kiss her shoes.

'I deserve nothing,' he muttered, grovelling. 'You are an angel, a saint. I am a beast, a worm under your feet.'

The 'angel, saint' part of this address reminded Matilda unavoidably of their walk in the garden when he had addressed her in such terms and then suddenly run away. Death had come between that moment and the present. He had sat by her dead children's bedside and conducted their funeral service.

'Have you done wrong?' Matilda asked, almost sternly. 'Something of which you are ashamed?'

At last her words fully penetrated poor Mr Plunkett's seething brain. He sat back on his haunches with a comical look of dismay. 'I love you,' he said, and as he spoke tears began to roll down his cheeks. 'I love you to distraction.'

Matilda stared at him, open-mouthed. Her first reaction was gratitude for the chair, solid beneath her; she gripped its rim with either hand. His pain was a terrible reproach, although now that he had spoken a certain relief showed in his face despite the tears, which continued to roll.

'I didn't understand,' he said as if to himself. 'I didn't understand about love before now. Oh, it's such torture. Such joy!' He leaned forward passionately. 'I love you! You are my sovereign lady, my glorious dream! My Queen of Heaven!'

'Ssssh,' said Matilda in helpless tones. She could see he was working himself up further and she had so little energy. 'You mustn't say any more or you'll regret it terribly. Be quiet now and I'll tell nobody.'

But Mr Plunkett was not listening to her. He only heard this sudden magnificent voice that told him he was in love. For the first time he felt love, and the object of his affections was incapable of stopping the flow. Rising to his feet, Mr Plunkett began a triumphant caper in front of Matilda during which words of loving adoration exceedingly similar to divine worship poured from his mouth.

Matilda saw it was pointless to speak because he was not listening. She was reminded a little of Theo and wondered whether all men were mad underneath. Mr Plunkett had always seemed so calm, so sensible, so dedicated to good. That was why she had been drawn to him in the first place. How dreadful it all was!

'You are a man of the cloth!' she tried shouting. 'Your life is dedicated to God!'

But this had no effect at all, for Mr Plunkett was consumed with a desire to touch Matilda's cheek. He felt as if the whole of his life had been leading up to this moment.

Matilda saw the blaze in his eye and the determined step forward. It struck her all of a sudden that she should be frightened. Here she was, alone in a conservatory full of snakes with a man behaving oddly, to say the least. 'No, Mr Plunkett.' She put up her hands to ward him off.

'My beautiful flower! My whitest rose!' Mr Plunkett's progress forward was adoring and implacable.

'But, Mr Plunkett!' began Matilda, now seriously in fear of she knew not what. 'I'm in a delicate condition,' and since that did not cause even the smallest hesitation, she screamed, 'I'm going to have a baby!'

Mr Plunkett stopped abruptly. He was standing on his hat again but he did not notice this. Matilda had said the one thing that could pierce his armour of love. She was going to have a baby. Sir Theodore's baby. The fact of the baby introduced the husband into the room. A blank, dazed look of misery enveloped the vicar's face and demeanour. He looked down and saw the hat. Stepping off it, he put it on his head, crumpled and dirty as it was.

He uttered little gasps of distress.

'I think you should go now,' commanded Matilda, who would have felt sorrier for him if he had not made that threatening advance. But the sound of her voice seemed to reactivate Mr Plunkett for the hat was swept to the floor once more and he stamped round in a widening circle.

'That cruel monster! That evil master!'

Gradually Matilda realised he was referring to Theo. 'I don't think you should—'

But now his furious strides were lengthening and he was plunging up and down the conservatory while imprecations against Sir Theodore poured from his mouth.

Matilda clung to her chair as if it were a lifeboat and watched. His emotions were no longer directed towards her but were more violent than ever. She wondered if she could slip out and get help.

Now Mr Plunkett's violence was turning on himself. 'I love! Ah, an impossible love! I am outside the bounds! Beyond the limits! There is no hope for me! Only despair! Where can I go? What can I do? Ha! I am in darkness! Cast out! Outer darkness!'

Matilda dared to rise and had just reached the door when a loud bang and the clatter of falling glass caused her to turn round in a hurry.

'Oh, Mr Plunkett, no!'

He stood, right arm through a hole in one of the display cases, trying, with some difficulty, to get a grip on the snake inside. 'I shall kill myself, kill myself,' he panted. 'I shall press the snake to my throat and let its fangs feed the venom through my body. Death is the only honourable course!'

All this was pronounced between grunting sobs as he struggled to move the unwilling snake from its cosy home.

Wishing to run but seeing that it was her duty to stay, Matilda approached him warily. Standing a yard or two away she soon saw it was the poor mother python he was trying to remove.

'Mr Plunkett! Mr Plunkett! She's an Indian python. She's not venomous and she's a mother. Just look at the lovely eggs. Oh, do be careful!'

Crying now with vexation – there is nothing more thwarting than being faced with an instrument of death that refuses to rise to the occasion – Mr Plunkett used his free hand to hammer the top of the stand. This was too much for the mother snake who opened her non-venomous mouth and nipped the unwelcome intruder sharply in the wrist.

'At last! My time has come!' Mr Plunkett staggered back, clutching his hand. 'He's bitten me.'

'She,' Matilda corrected wearily. It seemed she was to be nothing but a spectator in this whole lunatic scene. 'It can be quite nasty even without poison. Why don't you sit down?'

Convinced he had achieved a fatal bite, Mr Plunkett did not take her advice but continued to stagger about.

Picking up the chair Matilda followed him doggedly. It struck her that if he thought he was dying, he might like to do it quietly after the first shock wore off. Sure enough, Mr Plunkett decided to sit down uttering the lugubrious words, not untinged with satisfaction, 'I shall sit here and let death sweep me away on his black chariot. O, ever-merciful God, have pity on my soul!' With which he closed his eyes.

Quick as a flash Matilda was out of the conservatory and speeding along the passages that always seemed to come between her and the resolution of any drama. One servant was dispatched to summon Dr Rebew, two more to watch over Mr Plunkett until the doctor arrived. 'Do not approach him,' they were advised by Lady Hope whose indecorous manner shocked them. 'Merely see he does himself no injury!'

'Yes, m'lady,' agreed Croke, who was so curious he must go himself although it was hardly his place.

'And let me know when Dr Rebew arrives.'

'Yes, m'lady.' Croke and his underling hurried off with barely concealed exhilaration.

Matilda went to her little drawing room, which seemed astonishingly peaceful, and summoned Elizabeth, Lily and Miss Waterville. 'Mr Plunkett is ill,' she told them when they arrived, eyes wide with anticipation – would life ever become normal again? (And

did they want it to be? Not that they wanted any more deaths . . .)
'He is in the conservatory. I would like you to stay upstairs until
Dr Rebew has taken him away.'

After their departure, no questions allowed, Matilda sat back in
her favourite chair and took a series of deep breaths. The baby,
she now realised, was strong, for although tired, her body gave
no symptoms of internal disorder. In fact, she felt well enough
to consider poor Mr Plunkett and wonder if his condition was
irreversible. Dr Rebew would know, mental derangement being his
special field. But how unfortunate that she should have committed
Hannah to Miss Plunkett's care. Gradually, as she sat upright and
waiting for further developments, she was forced to confront the
knowledge – with a truthfulness that marriage, nine babies and
twenty servants could not dilute – that she had encouraged him.
She had looked into his eyes, albeit in the name of charity, and let
him look into hers and the result was this unleashing of destructive
passion.

Matilda sat in her chair and allowed darkness to grow round
her. The maid who came to light the lamps was sent away and it
was only when Croke knocked to announce the arrival of Dr Rebew
that she came back to herself.

'Thank you, Croke. I will see him when he has seen Mr Plunkett.'

'He has gone along already, m'lady. I have also taken the liberty
to send for the snakes' keeper.'

'Good, Croke.' Matilda was irritated by her butler's manner.
Was he waiting for approbation? Or why did he stand there,
block-like, by the door? And yet when the house was in such a
turmoil, she must remain calm. 'Yes, Croke?'

'The snake, m'lady,' in the darkness Matilda could hear the
warm pleasure in his voice, 'the large one whose living quarters
Mr Plunkett had, er, broken into . . .'

'Yes, Croke. The Indian python.'

'Quite, m'lady. The python, m'lady. Ahem. In the time before
we arrived to succour poor Mr Plunkett, the python, er . . .' Croke
paused maddeningly.

'What, Croke?'

'The python, m'lady, became the mother of a large and active
family. That is, when we found the vicar, m'lady, he was covered
in all directions with little crawling snakes. I fear it did not help
his illness, m'lady, for from his words, panic-stricken words you
might say, I had a fair conviction that he thought he was in . . .
Hell!'

'Oh, no!' Croke's rich rendering of the last word was cut off by

227

Matilda's cry of horror. There was a small pause but since she said no more (for what more was there to say with him present?), Croke, message delivered, retreated, closing the door softly behind him.

'What hope that he recovers now?' whispered Matilda to herself. 'Must I blame it all on myself?' Pressing her hands together, she dropped to her knees. 'Dear God, I ask your forgiveness and, dear God, give me strength . . .'

Dr Rebew, understanding the urgency of the case, had brought an assistant with him. He was a strong young man who had no difficulty in persuading Mr Plunkett into the strait-jacket. 'It is only necessary until I give him a sedative,' explained the doctor who was training his assistant and, anyway, had a didactic turn of mind. In fact, there seemed little justification for it since Mr Plunkett had calmed down as soon as the baby snakes had been removed by the keeper.

'Such an unfortunate happening might drive anyone out of his wits,' said the keeper, sympathetically.

But Dr Rebew was experienced in such matters and could see the embers glowing in his patient's eyes. Now he muttered in dull tones, 'Oh, truly I am dead.' But a moment before he had been flailing his arms about and screaming, 'I am the devil for he has taken my soul!' The unpleasant truth was that when the doctor arrived at the conservatory he had found the poor vicar in the process of stuffing an unwilling baby snake into his mouth. A man who would do that might do anything.

The assistant led Mr Plunkett to a waiting carriage while Dr Rebew went to report to Lady Hope.

'You might say this house is cursed.' Matilda stared away from him.

'I would say no such thing.' The doctor congratulated himself on not having described the snake-eating incident. 'Mr Plunkett will recover. He is merely suffering at the moment from an overheated brain. A little peace, compresses, blood-letting, solitude. Soon he will be back in the world.'

'Oh, I'm so very relieved to hear it!' Some colour returned to Matilda's pale cheeks and she was able to look at the doctor for the first time since his entrance.

'And you, you are thriving. We have the birth of a new baby to look forward to. Do not forget that.'

'How could I?' Matilda bent her head again. 'The baby is well, as you say. But I am not thriving. I . . .' What was it she wanted to say? She could feel Dr Rebew's very dark eyes waiting attentively.

'Your baby is well so you are well,' he said eventually since she did not seem able to continue her thought. 'A mother cannot be separated from a baby at a time like this.'

'I wish. Oh, I wish . . .' But again she stopped.

'You wish Sir Theodore was at your side.' The doctor rose to his feet, for there was a limit to the time that he could keep his patient constrained in a cold, dark carriage. Above all, Dr Rebew was humanitarian in his outlook.

Was that what she had wanted to say? Matilda rose to her feet also, accepted the doctor's grave bow. Was it Theo's absence that gave her this longing? Yes. It must be so. It must. 'Please let me know how Mr Plunkett progresses.'

Chapter Seventeen

A letter, or rather a packet, arrived from Theo on Christmas Eve. Since it had been written in October, it had no seasonal message of goodwill, indeed little of goodwill at all, at least in the first pages. Matilda knew from the date he could not yet have received her letters informing him of the twins' death and her own new situation but, irrationally, she expected some charismatic acknowledgement of all she had suffered – and still suffered. He should have *felt* it.

But Theo's letter seemed mainly written as commentary on another enclosed within it. 'It is remarkable to me,' began one energetic sentence, 'that people who pretend to know about such things can be proved so disastrously wrong and that the innocent victim can have recourse to nothing but distant apologies and explanations to his long-suffering wife.' What was he talking about? Matilda turned to the enclosed letter, which was written in the hand of a secretary, smooth-flowing ink, upright letters and a regular march across the page.

Matilda had so little to do with the business interests of her family that it took her some time to understand the message that was being set out with such prolonged order. In short, the money that had been gained from selling her father-in-law's building company that, according to Theo's orders, had been invested in the shares of an aspiring South American railway company, had just crashed dramatically. The money had already lost eighty per cent of its value and looked likely to lose more. Sir William's lawyers, advised of the matter, pointed out that since the income from the Abbeyfields farmlands had dropped to almost non-existent proportions, they were concerned about his financial position. There were many more details, interesting to Matilda for what they revealed of a man's world but only substantiating the conclusion that they were in serious financial difficulties.

Matilda looked round the breakfast table where the letter had been brought to her and saw the cheerful expectant faces of

Elizabeth, Lily and Edward. Tom was under the table, feeding a dog on bacon scraps while his mother's attention was engaged elsewhere. In the last few weeks, the atmosphere in the house had brightened beyond what she would have thought possible. Hannah had returned home and was much stronger, although she did not yet attend breakfast. Mr Plunkett would shortly leave hospital and be despatched to a distant and kindly uncle. Matilda's coming baby had been accepted by all the children as a sign of a happy future. The twins were not forgotten but the girls, in particular, concentrated on the idea of another nursery era. They felt old enough now to help, they had told their mother, and intended to do so.

Oh, how I love them all! sighed Matilda to herself. But it was a sigh, not a smile.

'Is it from Father, Mama?' burst out Elizabeth, unable to contain herself any longer.

'Yes, my dear, and he is well. That is the main thing, he is well,' repeated Matilda, as if trying to convince herself.

'Will you read it to us, Mother?' asked Edward. That was the other change of atmosphere in the house – the boys' return for school holidays. They looked clear-eyed at events.

'Tom, come out from under the table!' Matilda sat up straight and folded the letter carefully. 'I'm afraid I cannot read this letter to you, children. It contains grave news which I must consider carefully.' As she saw Elizabeth's disappointed face, she added impulsively, 'Just a paragraph or two, then, where he describes his last journey into the desert.'

Matilda began to read a part of the letter she had skipped through before. ' "We had spent the night in a small town called Jaipur, enjoying – or more truly – suffering from the hospitality of the prince who rules this little kingdom. First of all he subjected us to a feast of vegetables, which had twenty-two courses, including peacock brain and—" '

'Peacocks aren't vegetables,' interrupted Tom loudly.

'But their brains are, stupid,' said Lily, so decisively that no one bothered to contradict her.

'He continues about the feast,' said Matilda, now longing to be allowed to go away quietly and think about this new blow of fortune. 'Then he describes the entertainment afterwards: "Knowing my interest in reptiles, they had set up a whole parade of charmers, each one of whom was induced to put his charge through its paces. As you know, I have never set store by such circus and, the Indian being patient beyond any European, the whole evening seemed interminable. The result was I set out at dawn after only three hours' sleep with a dreadful ache in my head and my legs so stiff from sitting cross-legged over four or five hours that I could hardly mount my horse . . ."'

Matilda's mind wandered. This life her husband led when he left her was too remote to be imagined; she knew certain wives followed their husbands on even wilder journeyings than Theo but she had never been tempted.

'There you are,' she said, laying down the letter. 'Enough for now.'

'So he only caught one little snake,' commented Tom who had been following more closely than anyone, 'and that died in the night.'

'It makes one appreciate what a remarkable collection we have here,' said Edward seriously.

'Oh, yes,' agreed Elizabeth eagerly. 'We had an expert from the London Zoological Society only a week or two ago come especially to see the baby pythons. Father's work is very important.'

Matilda found herself shuddering as she stood up. She could never think of those baby snakes without picturing Mr Plunkett in his living hell. 'Breakfast is over, children. Elizabeth, Lily and Edward, I would like to see you in the small drawing room before lunch.'

'But, Mama, we were taking the Christmas gifts down to the village.'

Despite garlands of holly in every corner of the dining room, Matilda had temporarily forgotten about Christmas. Normally this day would have been taken up with a grand party for the village. But the combination of Theo's absence, her pregnancy and the mourning period for the twins had absolved her of this responsibility. It would be held in the village school, thoroughly cleansed of scarlet fever, and the children had promised to take down gifts that morning. Matilda tucked the letter in her waistband where it stuck out oddly over her protuberant stomach.

Mr Lapidus, the lawyer, made the journey to Abbeyfields after Christmas. It was dark when he arrived, dressed, it seemed, in layers of coats and with news of snow on the Salisbury plain. Any hostess other than Matilda would have seen the longing for a fire in his room, a hot bath and a whisky. But she led him straight into Theo's study, where she thought this conversation should take place, and sat behind his desk. Behind her head, rows of leather-bound books, bore witness to the inheritance she was in danger of losing. In the corner a glass-fronted cabinet held some books Sir William had discovered behind a chimney in the old farmhouse before it was demolished. No one ever looked at them so they sat there gathering dust. History is being remade all the time, thought Matilda with her own situation in mind. The past only gathers dust.

'I fear this cannot be an agreeable interview.' Lapidus blew on his fingers and shuffled his feet. Quite clearly the fire had only just been lit for the room was freezing. Annoyingly Lady Hope looked conditioned to the right temperature, if her smooth complexion and brow were any indication. Lapidus did not like to deal with women and began to feel more and more irritable. What was Sir Theodore doing, leaving his wife the responsibility of such a house and a young family? Remembering suddenly that Lady Hope's black dress and shawl signified a family loss, he rubbed his head respectfully. 'Nor is this an appropriate time to bring you unwelcome news.'

'Sir Theodore wrote to me,' said Matilda, trying not to feel impatient for emotion could lead to tears and it would be humiliating to weep in front of this cold fish. 'I understand the situation.'

'Ah,' responded Lapidus, conveying the clear belief that only he understood the situation.

'But, please, do tell me more,' said Matilda. She must not antagonise him for he was the only one who could help her. With this thought it at last struck her that her guest might be thirsty or hungry. 'Perhaps you would like some refreshment?' Not waiting for an answer, she rang the bell for Croke.

With a glass in his hand and the fire blazing, Lapidus settled much more comfortably into his task of describing the financial mismanagement and bad luck that had led to the Hope money, created so painstakingly over thirty years, disappearing without any trouble at all in less than thirty weeks.

Matilda, fatalistic in temperament particularly after her own experiences over the last several months, did not blame Lapidus. She assumed, with wifely lack of confidence, that it was Theo's fault. The best summary seemed to be, 'The business was sold unwisely and the money invested unwisely.' But so much money? Money that had created the vast world of Abbeyfields? That, she must realise, was part of the business. When the Hope Building Company disappeared, then it must stand alone, unless, of course, supported by the income from the farmland. But that had been losing money for the last two years ever since the fall of the corn prices had been followed by the shocking harvest . . .

Matilda put her elbows on Theo's desk and rested her head in her hands. It was an untypical posture and caught Lapidus's attention. He stopped in mid-sentence and rethought what he wished to say. 'You will not be rich but you will by no means be poor. Nevertheless, Abbeyfields Hall will be such a drain on your resources that I would advise that you sell and move to a smaller residence.' His speech slowed, for Lady Hope was standing in front of him and even he could no longer avoid noticing the altered shape of her usually pencil-slim body. He bowed his head quickly, giving Matilda the occasion for a very small smile.

'We will continue our conversation over the dinner table,' she said briskly, and then turned. 'Perhaps we should live in London,' she went on almost gaily.

But in the evening the aunts graced the table once again so further conversation on a financial subject was impossible.

That night Matilda dismissed her maid and undressed herself. It was a difficult job, although nothing like the early days of her marriage when the unbuttoning and unlacing could take twenty minutes. Nevertheless she took off garment by garment slowly. It was another cold night but her fire burned boldly. Eventually she stood naked, her smooth, rounded stomach silhouetted against its red brightness. Matilda had never been afraid of her nakedness. The warmth on her skin was soothing, even if the further parts of her body began to show signs of goose-flesh. Crouching down so that all of her was in line with the heat, she stared into the flames. She was remembering Mr Plunkett, how he had been during the two years of his happiness and how he had become during the two hours of his madness. How quickly a man could change! How quickly all things could change! It was impossible to resist thoughts of the bouncy little twins now lying, at best, like pale marble statues under the frosty earth.

Trying very hard to substitute an image of Heavenly cherubs for decaying mortal flesh, Matilda found she had begun to shiver violently. It was too much, too much. Moving swiftly, she put on her heavy nightdress and burrowed into bed. She should have put a guard on the fire but it required too much effort. Sleep would restore her. A prayer and then sleep. She had always been strong. Strong enough. What was it Mr Plunkett had said in one of his sermons? God gives everyone precisely the strength he needs to face the tribulations in his life. She must place her faith in His mercy. That was tonight's brief prayer. Matilda closed her eyes with profound gratitude that the day was over.

At night, in the moonlight, Abbeyfields Hall spread over the side of the valley like a dark stain. Its towers and battlements, exuberant expression of Sir William's pride in his capabilities as a builder, were flattened and turned into insignificant squiggles. Only one part of the house reflected the silver in the air and made itself visible. This was the oldest part of the building. The wall of stone that had stood in the same bit of land for hundreds of years shimmered, ghostly bright, in the surrounding dark.

Matilda turned over in her bed. She never slept well in pregnancy but eventually, at about two or three, exhaustion overcame her restlessness and she sank into a sleep near unconsciousness. A few minutes later a lump of coal slipped down in the fire and relit the end of a sharp dry twig. Crackling into flame, it shot out a spark from the grate and into the soft, fireside rug that Sir Theodore had brought back from his last travels to Ceylon. The rug smouldered gently but made an inexorable trail to where Matilda's quest for sleep had tossed the bedclothes to the floor. The flicker burst upwards like a yellow flower, dahlia or chrysanthemum, pushing for air. At the same time smoke from the rug began to fill the room.

Mr Lapidus, due to nervous anxiety that he might not receive an appropriate alcohol intake, had drunk far too much. He woke at three with a dry mouth and throbbing head. He drank the water at his bedside and then rose in search of more. When he detected the bitter odour of smoke, he was filled with rage. In this house crammed with servants and people, was there no one else to spend the night hours sniffing down icy corridors? Clearly not. In the stillness the beat of his over-stimulated heart sounded like the thud of elephants.

With extreme reluctance, Lapidus drew on his surprisingly garish dressing robe, his button boots – his slippers were hiding somewhere – and set out from his room.

Matilda's eyelids were as heavy as a copper lid on a saucepan. When she forced them open a crack, she saw a vision of steam so she closed them again. Next time she forced a wider crack and saw a devilish figure patterned in red and purple swirls bending over her with mouth askew. Naturally she shut her eyes once more. But she was not allowed to rest for long as hard fingers snatched at her arms. Matilda fought to stay where she was. Refusing to try another look at an unwelcoming world, she put her hands above her head and clasped the ornate bed rails.

'I cannot believe it! I cannot credit my eyes!' Lapidus was not a man of action; what he liked was words, preferably on paper. Yet here he found himself trying to save a woman's life, who

236

seemed even more reluctant to be saved than he was to save. It was true the flames were more threatening than enveloping but the smoke choked and made his eyes sting. Perhaps he should try to put out the fire first, then open a window, then fetch help. While Lapidus considered alternatives (which was more in his line) he gave a desultory pull or two on Matilda's arm and thus failed to keep a proper eye on the flames.

Suddenly an orange giant, purple-tipped and corkscrewing dangerously, roared to the ceiling.

'Oh, my!' Lapidus gaped with terror and now an instinct for self-preservation gave him the energy he had previously lacked. 'Lady Hope! You are leaving. At once! With me!'

He had her out of bed in a moment, wide awake too and staring accusingly. 'Mr Lapidus, have you been smoking?'

'Ha!'

But now she saw the flames and simultaneously a crowd of servants arrived at the run. Under Croke's command they heaved buckets of sand on to the fire, often losing a bucket in their enthusiasm. At the height of the excitement two of the dogs somehow got loose and came barking and bounding to join the fun. Lapidus, who had been very frightened, realised he had lost both his shoes under the sand and flame and began to cry. Luckily no one noticed so he wiped his eyes and tried to look like the hero without whose timely arrival Lady Hope (and her unborn child) would have been burned to a crisp in her bed.

She was shouting orders now almost gaily and apparently oblivious to her red, streaming eyes, bare feet, rumpled nightgown and dangling hanks of hair.

'Croke!' she cried. 'Water is not necessary. The genie of the fire is thoroughly quelled. I do not want my bedroom turned into a pond.'

Mr Lapidus sat on a wooden chair in the corridor and looked at his thin white feet. It was strange to be in such close proximity to what was nearly a conflagration and see your feet shrivelling from cold. He felt too upset to return to his bedroom and, besides, he was a hero. If temporarily forgotten.

Matilda, with the stance of Boadicea, was thinking that such dramas came as a relief from her anxieties. Recalling Lapidus's role, she managed to stifle a laugh at his solitary woebegone appearance.

'Thank you, Lapidus, thank you. Now you must try and get some sleep.'

She was so commanding that Lapidus did not like to mention

his shoes. He went down the corridor obediently and thought that, at very least, he had ensured his place as lawyer to the Hope family for ever more – although that post might not be as remunerative as it had been six months ago. Not so remunerative at all.

It was impossible for Matilda to go to sleep again, even though she could choose from eight or nine guest rooms. The knowledge of a near escape from death gave her a restless excitement in living. Summoning her sleepy maid, she dressed quickly and went down to Theo's study. Although it was still dark, an under housemaid was already cleaning the grate. For a flash, she put herself in the girl's position, wondering if when they moved house, which they must do – she was certain of that now – she would get to know the shape and size of a grate. That was unimaginable. But the image of her bedroom, singed and burned and full of embers and sand, made her shiver, although she smiled too. She was well. Well! The baby was well, too. Ordering the housemaid to lay a new fire, she found the big book of accounts that Lapidus had pulled out to show her the night before – she had not looked – and opened it solemnly at the first page. She must take in hand this renewed moment of her destiny.

Croke had taken it on himself to send a message to Dr Rebew. A fire. A near escape from tragedy. Her ladyship in an interesting condition. He knew it was not his place but there are times when your place is not what it seems.

Dr Rebew was ushered along to Lady Hope just as the steaming breakfast tureens were being carried from kitchen to dining room. The speed at which the servants proceeded, black-coated and silent, reminded him of some ceremony more important than the provision of devilled kidneys and coddled eggs to people already overfed. It might have been part of a religious service or doctors hastening to an emergency. Dr Rebew felt impatient this morning for his little hospital was overcrowded and due to overcrowding there had been an incident during the night. Fevered minds must have peace, not the pressure of cramped dormitories and enforced incarceration. Without making a conscious link, he became more irritable at the distance he had to travel to reach Lady Hope who, for some unaccountable reason, had removed herself to the male wing of Abbeyfields. Dr Rebew, who had always looked on Sir Theodore as a fellow spirit, suddenly found himself muttering uncharitable words like 'selfish', 'egocentric', which led him to gain relief from his feelings in a spiteful mutter, 'It would have served him right if his house had burned down!'

'Dr Rebew. I do not believe I called for you!' Matilda was startled by the arrival of a frowning black figure who had not even had the manners to remove his top coat. It crossed her mind that this scene had been often repeated lately. 'So early too!' She shifted backwards defensively. 'I am in perfect health, I can assure you.'

Ignoring her, the doctor snatched her pulse and made it his own.

'Moreover, I will not lie down,' continued Matilda although helpless in his grasp.

'From what I have been told, you are without a place to lie.' Dr Rebew dropped her wrist and fixed his plummy dark eyes on her with curious humanity.

'I hope Mrs Rebew keeps well,' said Matilda, pulling her sleeve down over her wrist. She kept her eyes fixed downwards for never again would she look into a man's eyes. She had wished to ask about Mr Plunkett, whether he was enjoying a coastal recuperation with his uncle.

'Mrs Rebew is in excellent health, thank you, your ladyship. But my hospital, ah, my hospital!' Dejectedly, the doctor sank into the large chair facing the desk but bounded up almost at once as the breakfast gong rolled like thunder towards them.

'What a merry sound!' Matilda was up, too. 'I find I have an indelicate appetite. I hope you will give us the pleasure of your company?'

Lady Hope and her doctor walked at a dignified pace to the dining room, which was already crowded with people, talking more than eating. The children and the aunts had only just learned of the fire and were questioning Mr Lapidus, who stood, at last enjoying a hero's recognition, with his back against the laden sideboard. Heroic stature was denied him by the strange sight of his head apparently steaming like a chimney (the steam actually issuing from the open tureen behind him) and by his extraordinary footwear.

'Slippers at breakfast,' Matilda could not help remarking as she entered his circle. Softly though she spoke, the sensitive Mr Lapidus heard and a blush spread through his whiskers. He could say nothing, however, since the explanation could only sound like a reproach.

'Good morning, m'lady. We are all overjoyed to see you descend.'

'Descend?' repeated Matilda, raising her eyes to Dr Rebew. 'I have been downstairs for some time. Studying the accounts, but we will talk of that later.'

The dining room had never looked so cheerful. The mahogany table reflected rows of gleaming teeth and shiny eyes. The richly patterned wallpaper stood background for the pots of cream and red orchids, which the gardener had made his speciality since the funeral lilies disgrace. At one end of the room burned a huge but well-disciplined fire, at the other the Tudor window, incorporated by Sir William into his new house, acted as a channel for lozenges of light. Since some of the panes were coloured, red, blue and a green as pale as water, they reflected on to the dark rug like a giant's necklace. There had been so many days of drab greyness that the brilliance of the room seemed unreal, dazzling.

Dr Rebew, sour-humoured though he was, found himself attacking his plate of gammon with ardour. But he must not forget. Laying down his silver knife and fork, the price of a monthly stay for a patient in his hospital, he leaned across the aunt on his left. Whether by accident or design Lady Hope had placed him between the two aunts whose acquaintance he preferred to limit to the professional. It was also unfortunate from his point of view that the aunt on his left side, beyond which Lady Hope bit gracefully into her toast, was the one with the low protruding bosom. It was not easy to gain a view round such an obstacle.

'Ah, doctor, you are always pressed for time.' Matilda had judged his contortions prelude to departure.

'Not at all, my lady.' To make his point, he picked up his fork again.

Mr Lapidus looked on this brutish rival with disapproval. He was too intimate in this household of women. But it was always the way with doctors. Lapidus, who was not married and who had no working knowledge of a woman, returned the kidney speared on his fork to his plate. It was a disagreeable thought that those black-haired hands examined the secret places of a woman's body.

'This is a magnificent house!' Dr Rebew's loud-voiced exclamation did not sound like a compliment. He had just experienced a vision of this glowing room filled with the poor deranged people he looked after – not that they were necessarily financially poor and, anyway, in exceptionally interesting cases he took them without charge. But they were poor in the way the healthy inhabitants of this room could never conceive. Even the succubus aunts, occupied with vacuous inactivity to the end of their days, were rich compared to his patients. They lived in torture, every hour, every minute of their lives and yet they could not even be given

240

the consolation of decent living conditions. How could he help their minds when their bodies were so neglected?

'If only I had a house like this for my hospital!' Unable to restrain himself, the doctor rose to his feet and banged the table.

Matilda, whose head had begun to ache from her sleepless night, looked at him vaguely. It crossed her mind that the difference between women and men was the latter's ability to put forceful expression to their needs. She sighed and said nothing.

Lapidus, severely agitated and also suffering from a headache, began to expostulate on his hostess's behalf. 'If I may say so, doctor, this is hardly the moment to express such feelings. We are at the breakfast table, in the midst of the family—'

'No. No. I apologise.' Dr Rebew, coming to himself, rubbed his hand over his thick hair. 'Indeed. I should not have stayed. Breakfast. So charming.' His words came in bursts and his eyes turned to the door.

Croke, catching his look, took the opportunity to open the massive door as invitingly wide as possible. The guilty knowledge that it was he who had summoned the erring doctor made him even keener to see him once more astride his sturdy black cob.

'This house was built by my grandfather and it's the biggest house in the country.' Tom's strident voice cut through the air of tension.

'The biggest house built this century in the West Country,' corrected Edward.

Dr Rebew looked at them wonderingly. He had looked after them since first coming to this area when even Edward was only two or three but he had never before been so aware of their absolute confidence. This was their house, built by their grandfather for them. They crowed on top of their possession like a cock on a dung heap. The doctor shook his head, bowed low to Matilda and sped out through the door.

'He didn't even finish his gammon,' commented Lily disapprovingly.

'If I may ask,' Lapidus leaned deferentially towards her ladyship, 'what is his hospital?'

'It's for the mad,' shouted Tom, before his mother could answer. 'They have shaven heads which they bang against the wall and some of them are so dangerous that they have to be chained by the ankles. Dr Rebew loves it, though. He cuts them up to see what makes them lunatic!'

'Thomas!' Matilda summoned energy. 'You will leave the room at once. Miss Waterville, please see that Master Thomas spends the morning in the schoolroom translating four pages of Pliny. Croke, I believe breakfast is over.'

Why did she not burst into tears? Matilda leaned against the wall of her little sitting room. 'Little' as it seemed to her now, she thought bitterly, it would seem palatial from the viewpoint of whatever house in London they might be able to afford. Tom had always been difficult to discipline but how would the others be, crowded all together like prisoners in a gaol? If only there were someone she could consult. But her confidantes were all correspondents and they, an aunt, a cousin and an old friend, looked to her for advice and support. None of them would be able to cope with this sad turning of tables. In a fit of despair, encouraged by her utter exhaustion, Matilda wished that she had not let Lapidus remove her from her burning bedroom.

Lapidus was feeling better. After breakfast he had taken a little walk to clear his head and prepare himself for the resumption of his interview with Lady Hope. As he took short quick strides along the path above the house, his eyes were soothed by the smooth expanse of the winter-cropped valley. Unconsciously, he took in the pleasant sight of the little village with the smoke, white in the cold air, curling from the chimneys of the rows of cottages. He saw and did not see the stone church, which looked older than it was, and the solid square-cut vicarage beside it. He expected countryside to give him such pastoral order and, for all he understood of it, it might as well have been a painting on a wall.

His entire mental activity was reserved for working out a future for the Hopes. This was his moment of power. Out of ill-management and disorder, he must make sense and stability. This was the village he must create, out of sound advice and legally binding contracts. The crux of the matter was a sale of the house that was both profitable and acceptable to his client. It would not be easy. He looked down at the great pile of stone and bricks below him. Too many of the newly rich had enlarged or built themselves houses beyond their present means. The market had never been wide for such a structure as Abbeyfields and now seemed to be shrinking. He would take advice, of course, and somewhere they would find the right buyer. Lapidus clapped his hands together and wondered if Lady Hope had yet given the orders to light the study fire, which reminded him to relive once again his heroism in saving her. Poor lady! She had much to bear at the moment. Lapidus's somewhat inhuman heart warmed with protective pity. She had looked so defenceless with her hair down and her nightdress crumpled to the shape of her presently inelegant body. He must do his best for her.

Matilda's despair had been interrupted by Elizabeth and Lily wanting to bring down Hannah to sit with her. The sight of her invalid daughter raised her spirits at once. Here was someone who needed her.

'My dear Hannah, come and sit by the fire.' She looked closely into her face. 'You are pale, certainly, but then you are always pale in the winter.'

'Oh, Mama.' Hannah blushed red and looked as if she might cry. So much attention from her usually distant mother was almost too much. 'I was so concerned for you. To think you might have been burned in your bed.'

'Nonsense, dear. Merely suffocated.' This was Matilda's habitual style with her children and Hannah's blush subsided. She sat down docilely in the chair indicated and took out the book she had brought down with her.

'No! No!' cried Matilda, unwilling to lose her role as concerned mother. She whisked the book away and appealed to Elizabeth and Lily, who stood by with the usual deep interest that sisters feel in each other's relationship with their mother. 'Hannah reads far too much, don't you agree, my dears? And what is it now?' Not waiting for an answer, there was seldom time in her relationship with her bevy of children for more than rhetorical questions, she read from the spine of the book, '*The Mad Woman of the Moors.* Oh, Hannah, Hannah, what are you reading now?'

'No, Mama,' replied Hannah earnestly. 'It is a good book, a serious book. Dr Rebew recommended it. He says it has much to say that is true and informative about the sort of poor people he takes care of in his hospital. He says we should all try and understand such things and I agree with him. He says one of his patients is a frail little girl of eight but when she becomes violent it takes two male nurses to hold her down. He says that the violent side of her nature is matched by another delicate, imaginative side. If he puts a vase by her bed she'll watch it for hours, unmoving, just staring in – in wonderment.' Hannah's eyes stared, too, as if she could picture this wonderful scene. 'I would like to take fresh flowers to that little girl.'

'I think Dr Rebew says too much,' commented Lily anxiously. 'He should not fill Hannah's head with such ideas when she is not well.'

Matilda looked at Lily indulgently. She was so pretty and fresh, so determined to see only the happy side of life. It was she who felt threatened by violent little girls who saw more in flowers than a neat posy. 'Dr Rebew longs to fill our corridors with his patients,' she began teasingly. But her attention was caught by a black shadow passing across one tall window and then another. When it passed the third she recognised it as Lapidus, heavily coated, hatted and wound into a long scarf.

'Mr Lapidus!' she cried, starting forward. He half heard her and his long pale face wavered round like a fish coming up for air. But then he moved onwards, either too respectful or too stupid to look into the windows of the house.

'I must go!' The girls watched, not very surprised, as their mother dashed from the room. They had already enjoyed more than their fair share of attention.

The fire in Sir Theodore's study had only just been lit. Lapidus saw it with depression the moment he entered the room. It was freezing just as before. But there was Lady Hope, her shawl dangling from the chair, her cheeks, normally so pale, slightly pink.

'Ah, Mr Lapidus, Mr Lapidus.' She half rose in her enthusiasm and then her gaze fell. She seemed to stifle a laugh. 'Your slippers are most serviceable. I see you never allow yourself to be parted from them. Do you not possess something more solid?'

Torn by the desire to appear silent in the face of such effrontery, and the longing to divulge how his shoes had been sacrificed, Lapidus did not at first answer and thus lost his chance of recalling his heroism.

'Oh, I apologise. Pray accept my apologies. I am not myself. I have had such an idea, such an idea and you must help me effect it!'

'Good, good.' Lapidus drew his chair as close to the fire as he was able. 'I await your ladyship's commands.'

'We must turn Abbeyfields Hall into a lunatic asylum!' cried Matilda, hands clasped and eyes flashing. 'That way everything will be worthwhile.'

Chapter Eighteen

Theo had little sense of his own importance. Yet he was utterly self-centred. This was an odd combination, which made him hard to deal with. He did not, for example, announce his arrival home, he merely appeared one delightful May evening with his hand luggage and a particularly favoured snake in a basket. He was, roughly speaking, a year ahead of his expected return date. On the long carriage journey from the station to the house he had struck up a relationship with his driver, who had endeared himself by not showing disgust when he learned of the contents of the basket. As a reward, Theo promised to give him a tour of his snakes when they reached Abbeyfields.

Typically, this was in the forefront of his mind when the carriage stopped. 'Follow me,' he instructed the driver.

'What about the horses?'

'They won't go far.' Theo looked about him vaguely. 'The grooms spring out the moment they hear hoofs.' That the grooms had not sprung out did not seem to worry Theo but preyed on the driver's mind as they entered the great house, thus diminishing what should have been an extraordinary treat.

Croke, whose ear was never deceived, appeared in time to see the easily recognisable form of his master and companion disappearing down a corridor. Sir Theodore, he could tell even from the back, was thinner, which was always the case when he returned from foreign parts. His beard, though, had grown so long that it turned the corner of his face and flew over his left shoulder.

'Sir Theodore!' hallooed Croke, for the times were exceptional, but only the companion's head turned briefly. Mustering his energy, Croke set off in pursuit.

'This is a shambles! A disgrace! A travesty of zoological practice! An insult to the honour of an ophiophile! An insult to the honour of all these honourable reptiles!'

Sir Theodore had reached the conservatory and found it, only just created in its glory on his departure nine months ago, now, as he said, a shambles. Cases were stacked on cases, plants had been dug out and discarded, labels were removed and disfigured, the walkway partially dismantled.

'Someone will be punished for this,' bellowed Theo.

'I think I should go to the horses,' said the driver, giving up any pretence at peering into the glass-framed cases. He would have fled at once were it not for the matter of payment due.

'Croke!' shouted Theo, catching sight of his butler with no look of surprise. 'Pay my driver and then return at once with an explanation for the holocaust that has overwhelmed my beautiful snakes.'

Croke had a message to impart so he came back with alacrity. 'Her ladyship,' he begged bravely, even though perturbed by the long yellow mamba that Sir Theodore had drawn caressingly from its basket. 'Her ladyship,' he paused again, for although Sir Theodore always insisted he did not keep poisonous snakes, this new arrival had just opened its mouth, revealing something that looked unpleasantly like a fang.

'Her ladyship is important, of course,' said Sir Theodore impatiently. 'I trust she is in good health. But first I must have an explanation for this – this devastation.'

Croke was not a man who gave in easily; he was a man of few words and those he knew were inappropriate to his present needs. Eyes fixed on the snake's ever-widening jaws, he gave up the effort of a butler's pedantic delivery and gulped out, 'The house is to be turned into a lunatic asylum and at this very moment her ladyship is giving birth to a baby.'

'Lunatics? *A baby?*' Thrusting the mamba at Croke, Theo was off down the corridor again. The letter telling of the twins' death had reached him but not this announcement. Death was worthy of sorrow, of course, but hardly of comment; it was an ending, natural and inescapable, even in the very young. Theo thought such things as he sped along to Matilda's bedroom. For birth was a wonder, a joy, a splendour, a glory that could almost make one believe in God! Oh, Matilda. Matilda, thought Theo, as he mounted the stairs, what a welcome, what a homecoming, what a magnificent celebration of our reunion! Any memory of words like 'lunatic asylum' or his despoiled conservatory were overwhelmed in a rush of love and excitement.

The baby was already born, a large healthy boy carried away to be cleaned and dressed. Matilda, half-unconscious, found tears slipping from under her closed eyelids. This was happiness of a sublime, unearthly sort. To partake in the act of creation, to be part of God's mighty plan. There could be nothing more perfect, nothing more satisfying. She was truly in ecstasy, her body wiped out by all the pain and hard work, her mind floating in blue skies. Even as the tears wet the pillow, she was smiling and smiling and smiling.

Theo entered a small room in which six of the eight occupants were crying. They stood, sat or leaned in various attitudes of dejection. Even their astonishment at his sudden presence in their midst did not stem the flow. Eventually, Edward, though tearless, said in a low, despondent voice, 'Mama has had a healthy baby boy and we're all so happy.'

Theo looked with understanding and affection at his sons, his three daughters, their governess and his two old aunts. This was family life. He must pay more attention to it.

'And your mother?' he asked Edward. 'How is she?'

'Well,' gulped Edward, on the point of succumbing. This was a birth after months of deaths, illness and, if you counted the Reverend Oswald Plunkett, madness.

Theo patted his elder son on the shoulder. 'Has anyone seen the baby yet?'

'No.' Edward looked at his father for strength. Bright winter light shone through Theo's greying hair and beard making his sunburned face seem darker than ever. He had come from far away. 'Dr Rebew made the announcement,' said Edward, 'and then the girls began to cry. Oh, Father, why is everything so difficult?'

'Nonsense,' responded Theo abstractedly. He was trying to remember if he had ever been in this room before. It was an upper sitting room, part of the nursery wing. Even so, it was furnished with solid mahogany. 'In India,' he said, kissing each of his daughters on the top of their heads, 'I lived most of the time in a tent. A most commodious tent, well equipped with furniture. But still a tent made of canvas. And now I shall go and see your mother.' Bowing at the aunts who had begun, at last, to wipe their eyes, he retreated as rapidly as he had come.

Matilda lay in a clean white nightdress between fresh cool linen. She had been left alone to sleep and she was waiting for her exhilaration to let her down, as she knew it would, breath by breath. She did not hear the door open but, through closed eyelids, she sensed a shadow bending over her. A hand touched her forehead in a kind of benediction. In her dreamy, self-satisfied state, she half imagined the face of Oswald Plunkett, before he had lost his wits, of course. She smiled and sighed.

Theo looked down on his wife and his large frame seemed to expand with love and admiration. She was perfection at this moment, her absolute pallor giving her a look of spiritual beauty. He bent closer, meaning to kiss the smoothness of her cheek. This aim disregarded his traveller's whiskers and beard which lay across Matilda like a prickly hedge.

Matilda gasped, opened her eyes and screamed. It was only a little scream, partly out of exhaustion and partly because she saw at once that it was Theo and that there was no point in carrying on. Just for a second he had seemed like God, the Father, come down for a visit. Matilda recovered herself and even smiled.

'Dear Theo. We have a son.'

'Oh, my dear. My dove. My duck!' Theo was overcome with emotion and laid his huge hairy head on the bed beside her. Slowly he lowered himself on to his knees.

Without moving from her supine position on her back, her body was best kept still after all it had been through, she patted his head. 'You have come back.'

'I have come back.' Tears rolled out of Theo's eyes. He could not imagine why he had ever left this ideal of womanhood. And to find she had presented him with a son, almost, as it seemed, on her own! It was too much.

'The baby is healthy,' murmured Matilda.

'Oh, yes indeed. I saw him before I came here. Dr Rebew insisted. He says you are well, too?'

'Oh, yes.' Matilda's lids flickered. Strangely the sleep that had not come before, now, with Theo's presence, threatened to overwhelm her. Why should he affect her like this, as if his return was security? When had Theo's presence ever given her security? Yet that was how it was. She could not think any more, she could not speak, she must close her eyes.

Theo lifted his big head so he could see her face. 'Yes. Yes,' he said dotingly. 'You sleep. You have earned a long sleep. A long sleep. A long rest. I shall guard you.'

Making a final effort, Matilda patted her husband's head again. He was her giant guard dog, her mastiff, she could sleep safely with him on her bed.

Croke was still trying to catch up with his master. The mamba had been an upsetting diversion, winding itself round his arm, apparently in mistake for a branch, and only allowing itself to be unwound when it spied a rat hiding under a flowering oleander tree. It disappeared then with the speed of lightning. In the end Croke shut the conservatory door and left the appalling scene. He had decided that, with his mistress relatively *hors de combat*, the children too young for such responsibility and the aunts too old, he should be the one to explain the changes in the household – with worse to come. At the back of Croke's dutiful mind was the hope that it might not be too late to reverse the gathering flood of lunatics. Despite nearly twenty years of evidence almost entirely to the contrary, he persisted in believing that Sir Theodore would appreciate the rationale of the *status quo*.

'Uhum,' said Croke, arriving at the open door of the same room where Theo had met the celebrating relatives. Then they had been lamenting in happiness, now they were busily chatting, estimating each for the other the possibilities within Theo's return. 'Uhum,' repeated Croke with more authority. It was a sound he had devised over the years as substitute for a knock on a door, impossible when it was already open. But either the occupants were too much engaged with speculation or Croke's recent mamba experiences had diminished his vocal power for he was not noticed.

Since Sir Theodore was not present, it hardly seemed worth a third try. Croke removed himself quietly and made a closer approach to her ladyship's bedroom. This was not his sphere of influence but his need drove him forward. The truth was that he wanted to speak to Sir Theodore before his ears were stopped by the wild plans of that black villain Dr Rebew.

'Doctor, good afternoon.' Croke stepped sideways on the landing he had reached, dangerously rocking a vase standing on a chest behind him. The doctor did not stop. He was in a hurry, of course; he had been there all night and it was now late in the day. He would be dashing to his hospital. Had he already spoken to Sir Theodore?

Theo had fallen asleep. He had been travelling for weeks. Although he had stopped in London for a couple of nights, staying at his club, he had been busy making a report to the Royal Zoological Society and finding a temporary home for his catches, most of which would not arrive for several weeks – even months. Now he slept, still on his knees, his massive head pillowed in his arms.

Croke arrived outside the door. The nurses had gone to the nursery. The maid was taking a rest. Croke listened. There were no voices and at first all was perfectly quiet. But soon an irregular but repeated rumble, sometimes developing into a shrill whistle, made him press closer. There was no doubt about it. Croke started back and clawed the air furiously. Those were Sir Theodore's snores. At this hour of drama and threatened disintegration, he was sleeping!

Pale and not at all himself, Croke fled back along the landings, corridors and stairways. If he had been a woman when he reached his small yet dignified room, he would have thrown himself across it and wept. Instead, he got out his valiant but untravelled case and began to pack it with exemplary neatness.

Theo woke refreshed. He touched Matilda's face and saw that she would not stir for hours yet. Forgetting his guard dog duties he crept, as far as a man of his size and clumsiness could creep, from the room. Outside he was met with an impenetrable blackness. Holding on to a wall, he thought of the Indian nights which, even in the middle of a desert, were never as black as this. He tried to remember why not and pictured a brilliant starlit roof and the dull red of a cow-dung fire.

'Why is it dark?' he shouted, before remembering his sleeping wife. The reason, of course, was that Croke, who usually gave the order for the lighting of the gas, was packing his case, and Matilda, who might have reminded him, was dreaming of floating and flying, twirling and whirling.

A three-pronged flame approached along the corridor. Behind it appeared the scared face of Elizabeth, followed by Lily and Hannah, who held her skirts.

'Where are the servants?' asked Theo, irritated by their fear. He took the candelabrum too roughly so that wax dripped on to Elizabeth's hand.

'Edward and Tom have gone to find Croke.' Elizabeth picked the wax off her finger and under the cover of darkness began to suck the burned spot.

'I am glad you are here, Papa,' said Lily. 'Ever since Mama decided to sell the house, the servants have been most awkward.'

Theo raised the candelabrum to look at the faces of his three daughters. The candlelight flickered over their staring eyes, their tight little-girls' mouths, their cheeks, which should have been round and rosy but now seemed pale and, in Hannah's case, unbecomingly drawn.

'We are all tired,' he said. 'A baby and a homecoming is too much on one day.'

One of the girls sighed, or it could have been all three together, a long-drawn-out sigh expressing relief. Their father had appreciated

250

the situation and even agreed that he played a part in it. Along the corridor they heard two servants approaching; they were lighting the gas as they came. Soon the glow spread ahead of them, an unrolling wave of normality.

'I hope at least Cook is on good form.' Theo began to walk briskly towards the light and the main part of the house.

'Cook wants to come with us to London,' said Lily, 'so she is on top form.'

'Good. Good.' Theo, who seldom bothered to hide his feelings, now took his watch out of his pocket so that he could bend his head away from his children's watchful eyes. What more had happened in his absence? What was this talk of London? Where could his snakes live in London? 'It is already six. I must change for dinner.'

They were past the servants with the tapers now so he squeezed out the candles. A nurse scurried by, on her way to Matilda; the children's maid came wanting to help them change. Miss Waterville emerged from a side corridor and joined their train. Theo said to no one in particular, 'Are the fires lit?' He had changed his mind about dressing for dinner and now wished to stand in front of a hearth blazing with sweet-smelling logs. What did all these people expect of him? As was his habit in moments of distress, he pictured his snakes, but that only reminded him of the despoiled conservatory and his latest much-prized acquisition, so irresponsibly handed over to Croke.

'Croke! Where is Croke?' bellowed Theo, and since he now stood in the great hall the cry roared upwards, flung itself round the arched ceiling and returned, still unanswered.

The girls, urged by Miss Waterville and their maid, disappeared leaving him all alone. Unwilling to face the conservatory, he opened the door to the main drawing room but no fire blazed in its hearth and all the furniture was robed in white and pushed back into a circle, turning it into a dismal drawing-room Stonehenge. Wishing he had remained on Matilda's warm coverlet, Theo re-called his study, his own place, his inner sanctum.

'When Croke makes an appearance,' he said to a young servant he did not recognise who was just then dashing across the hall, 'tell him to see me in my study.'

A deep anxiety of a sort never before faced by Theo was gaining a hold. He had married Matilda when he was nineteen, she twenty. He had loved her. She sat on a pedestal of perfection and even when he began to see a more human side – irritability, impatience and what he perceived as narrowing interests – he did not take

251

her off the pedestal, he merely moved it a little further away so that the imperfections should be less obvious.

He did not allow his love, of which he was proud and protective, to clash with his zoological passions for which he had already left Cambridge, finding it too narrow a discipline. He saw no problem; she had more feminine occupations, as was right, he supposed, if not very interesting. He had given up talking about reptiles in the early years of their marriage when Matilda's dutiful expression of listening had reminded him of his mother. He had not liked his mother, who had died when he was fifteen, mostly because she had not appeared to like him.

His wife, of course, could never really resemble his mother for his marriage, in contrast to his childhood, was a source of strength and happiness. So he believed. What he did not appreciate was how much it was based on the material circumstances provided by the wealth of his father. Theo did not trouble to appreciate it because it did not interest him, because he did not think it important . . . because he did not altogether approve. He was the beneficiary, certainly, but hardly by choice. It was Sir William's choice to build this great house and Matilda's to live in it. Theo truly believed, and would have told anyone who asked him, that he was just as happy in a tent.

He opened the door of his inner sanctum and saw glumly that neither had the fire been lit here. Worse still, the desk was piled high with papers, which were certainly nothing to do with him. The clawing hand moved from his arm to his stomach. Was life as he had known it about to end? Furious with the evidence of practical and physical responsibilities, Theo threw first the papers off his desk and then began to tear the old books from their shelves. 'There is nothing here for me!' he wailed but as he spoke his eye was caught by a speck of brightness in the cabinet where more decrepit books lay gathering dust. Glad to divert himself, he opened the glass front and took out the one whose cover had partially broken away, revealing the coloured illuminations in the margin, that had held his attention.

Theo took the pages to his desk and sat down. As he did so, a sheet of vellum, plainly written upon, fell unnoticed to the floor. It settled among the discarded estate papers and books as if at home. The volume at which Theo looked was a prayer book, small and personal, written in Latin; probably it had come from the monastery in the sixteenth century. Theo found himself so moved that tears began to glaze his eyes. Its survival, over so many centuries, seemed almost as miraculous as the birth of his new son. He could make no sense of either but it made him feel tender-hearted and the tears rolled down his cheeks. He had thought his own survival depended on ruthless selfishness but perhaps, after all, there was another way. If the lunatics must take over Abbeyfields and he and Matilda remove to London then he must play a part in it himself. It struck him, with his first recognition of the importance of money, that there was a market for such rare beauties as the little prayer book.

Croke sat beside his packed case, muttering grimly, 'Hunting . . . I should have known when they didn't hunt . . . no hunting . . . entertaining . . . who do we see now? One month to the next . . . now Sir William . . .' Croke closed his eyes wearily. It was all Sir William's fault that he was here. 'Hardly dead a year . . .' he continued to himself, muttering and moaning.

Upstairs in their bedrooms the girls held their heads still to have their hair dressed by the maid. They had stopped talking now, oppressed and exhausted by the atmosphere in the house. Yet every now and again, quite frequently, one of them would remember their beautiful baby brother and a look of wild, inexpressible happiness would appear on her face. The future was full of hope, after all. And even the removal to a small house in London seemed capable of unknown but not unexciting possibilities. The image of the baby's pink shiny face and tuft of hair even wiped out the thought of their own dear bedrooms being taken over by lunatics.

They smiled and then they sighed and then they tried to look resolute. 'Thank you, Mary,' said Elizabeth. 'We should go down now. Papa will be waiting.'

Edward and Tom had decided that Croke must be ill; they could hear him muttering in his room in a very unCrokelike way. Neither of them liked to admit just how unwilling they were to disturb him. He had been a more important figure of authority in their lives than their father and they were more frightened of him. They could not think why they had assumed this responsibility of bearding the lion – in his own den, too.

Croke made up his mind and stood up. He patted himself all over carefully but nothing was out of its place. He must not act hastily. It was not in his own interests to leave without proper notice, reference and another situation. The case, however, would remain packed.

Taking three firm steps out of his small room, Croke caught sight of Master Edward and Master Tom fleeing down the shadowy corridor.

He was about to call but thought better of it. Let them go. Doubtless they had come in search of him, which was hardly surprising since without him the house would come to a standstill. He preened himself for a moment. But he would not take responsibility for them any more. Let them go.

Edward and Tom looked at each other when they got back to the main part of the house. Although Edward was six years older, almost a young man, he was the more tentative of the two. 'Perhaps he was sick and now is recovered.'

'Perhaps. Perhaps.' Tom skipped three paces. 'At least it's better than school.'

Dinner was late but not remarkably so. It could have been a delay caused by the birth of a new son. Croke made his usual impassive appearance and Theo ordered up some old claret to toast his new son's health. The aunts, not used to their nephew's presence, forgot to hide in their wing so the dining-room table was full, even festive. Only that morning the girls had competed with each other to make spring flower arrangements.

However, once soup had been served, no one found very much to say. Theo became aware that his glass was being refilled not between sentences but between silences.

'Tell us about your travels, please, Papa,' said Tom, who would have spoken earlier had he not been concentrating on his food.

'Oh, yes, dear Papa!' There seemed to be tears in Lily's eyes and indeed she was finding the strain of the meal almost intolerable. Did anyone else of her age have to put up with an eccentric father, two revolting old aunts who positively wallowed in their soup and a poor, sweet mother who was far too old to have another baby? London must be more ordinary.

'Ah, yes. I am glad you are interested.' But now tears filled Theo's eyes for the third time that day as he remembered with a full flood of misery the dreadful sight of his once-beautiful conservatory.

'Mother did read us a little of your letters,' said Elizabeth, 'but there was so much to distract her.' Elizabeth did not wish to hear about India or reptile hunts. She wanted to talk about what was happening to them now but did not dare broach the subject. 'Hannah has only recovered quite lately,' she said as a hint, receiving a reproachful look from her sister who hated any public attention.

She need not have worried. Beyond giving her an identifying glance, Theo said nothing. There was too much here pressing for attention, too many people, too many mysteries, too many changes. Even the aunts, whose existence he had always found particularly easy to ignore, hung over him in an assuming way. Since Elizabeth had taken her mother's place at the further end of the table, he was between the two old ladies, steering his frail craft between Scylla and Charybdis. Their silence, or rather, noisy intake of food, only made them more menacing. Theo felt himself under attack.

'When you went into the desert, was anyone killed?' asked Tom, perseveringly.

'Papa is very tired,' said Lily, with a look of desperation as Theo still did not speak. Was he going mad, too? Would he end up here with all Dr Rebew's lunatics – in her bedroom, perhaps?

Matilda woke slowly into a glowing semi-darkness. The nurse sat sewing beside the one lamp lit. She was young and her face was gentle. Matilda was glad of her presence and glad that she need not move or act in any way. She had no particular desire, even, to see her baby until the morning. She knew he would be well looked after by Lulworth, who had returned at the new birth. She no longer felt the ecstasy of earlier in the evening but she still enjoyed a supine contentment.

From far away she heard the faint sound of piano music and recognised one of Elizabeth's pieces. 'Open the door, nurse,' she said.

The nurse, who had thought her charge asleep, dropped her sewing with surprise but stood up obediently. With the door open Matilda could hear a little more clearly and realised it was Lily playing not Elizabeth; her touch was less sure and yet too lingering. As she listened a sadness grew, for Elizabeth had played the same piece, over and over again, a couple of years ago when the twins had been no more than fat babies, sitting like little Buddhas on the carpet. How could she forget them so easily and feel such happiness in a new little boy whom she did not know at all? The soreness and ache in her body, which she had hardly felt before, now came as a reproach to her disloyalty. Was she just a mother, a womb, with fewer feelings even than a ewe who loses her lamb? 'Tell them to stop playing. It disturbs me.'

The nurse once more rose obediently.

Lady Hope was not recovering from her confinement as quickly as was to be expected. The servants who lived in the house talked of it, the servants who came from the village took the news back to their cottages. The gardener, planting a young tree in honour of the baby boy's christening, told the lad who was digging, who told the stable boy. Miss Plunkett told the village school to pray for their patron's quick return to good health and, after some thought, informed her brother, the Reverend Oswald Plunkett, who had recently returned to his post, a quieter man but steadier. It was the beginning of August, three months since the baby, whose name was Gilbert, was born. He flourished, fat and golden-headed, as strong as the corn ripening in the fields, the flowers standing heavy-headed in the borders, the trees turning themselves into shady parasols against the sun. It was a very hot August. Almost every day the children set out for picnics in the governess cart or on foot or on horseback. They knew this was their last summer in the country and the things they had taken for granted now took on a special significance. Edward accompanied them often, forgetting that picnics were 'girlish pursuits'. Even Theo came several times, loading his horse with equipment as if it were a mule in the Himalayas.

'We must make use of our surroundings,' he ordered his children, who had not been included in his attention previously. 'We do not hunt, we do not fish, we do not shoot. We are in the country but not of it. We must explore, penetrate and observe.'

None of the children referred to their imminent departure. Like their mother's continuing as an invalid, it was not spoken about although underlying all their activities and behaviour.

Matilda lay in bed, not ill in any way she could define but waning. Gilbert's birth, which had made her temporarily so happy, was now the excuse that kept her away from the family. Perhaps it had begun with the conscious realisation that she had never had time to mourn the twins, so much piling on her at that time. But she did not otherwise analyse her condition.

'I am perfectly well,' she told Dr Rebew who visited regularly, looking more anxious each time, 'merely tired and perhaps a little weak.' The doctor's anxiety was understandable, not just because he was a sympathetic human being and sorry for Matilda but because he must keep in mind the greater good for the greater number. His patients were due to move into Abbeyfields in October. The bedroom in which Lady Hope convalesced was to be converted into a dormitory for twelve old ladies.

One morning Matilda caught Dr Rebew pacing the length of the bay window. She understood at once, particularly when the doctor tugged guiltily at his dark beard. 'I shall be gone soon,' she said smiling, for though passive and sometimes gloomy she was not angry.

256

'Not at all. Not at all.' Dr Rebew thought he understood Matilda better than she did herself. He had seen her through Sir William's sudden death, her unhappy school experiments, her disastrous alliance with the Plunketts, her husband's departure, Hannah's illness, the twins' deaths, her own narrow escape when her bedroom had caught fire, pregnancy and the introduction of yet another life and finally, with the Hope money wasted, the need for a new life in London. She was worn out. Rebew understood this and felt guilty. But he had carried a dream for twenty years and that dream was about to become reality. At Abbeyfields he would have the space to run a hospital as he had always planned it. His patients, those who could leave their beds – and he knew they would grow in number – would enter rooms through which light beamed in gracious curves. There would be real furniture, carpets, hanging baskets of flowers. The wardens would be instructed to treat them as human beings who were merely ill in the mind instead of the body.

'I understand that the charitable monies accruing to you are very considerable.' Matilda spoke with remote interest.

'Certainly. Indeed. It is all most gratifying.' The doctor looked up from his dreams. 'It is such a particularly fine day. Can I not persuade you into the garden?'

Matilda pulled herself up on her pillows. It was a fine day. She had watched the sun raise itself, pinkly glowing, over one window sill and now it had moved to the other window, turning to a duller yellow but still full of warmth and reassurance. She had heard the children and Theo clatter off on some expedition or other. She pictured the silver birch trees above the house, the delicately spotted shade and soothing green view across the valley. 'Could you stay and help me downstairs?'

The doctor agreed heartily. He called her maid himself, chose the strong shoes and loose clothes she should wear and explained that a bath chair might be needed at the foot of the stairs.

I am an invalid, realised Matilda with resignation.

Dr Rebew pushed Matilda up the steep pathway. He was a small man and soon he began to pant. 'There's a bench half-way up,' suggested Matilda sympathetically. But when they reached the bench, coolly shaded by a young oak, it was already occupied by a nursemaid and perambulator.

'Oh, I'm sorry, m'lady.' The nursemaid jumped up.

'Let me see Gilbert. Help me to stand, please, Dr Rebew.'

Matilda peered over the edge of the perambulator, which was as large as a small coach. The hood was pushed back but a square canopy, tasselled at the edges and lined with green, shaded the baby from the sun.

'He is a very healthy child,' said the doctor, taking off his hat to wipe his perspiring forehead.

'He is fat,' commented Matilda, delightedly. Gilbert was asleep, loudly asleep, his cheeks bright red and shiny, his thumb half fallen from its place in his mouth, his long golden eyelashes twitching. He was sleeping like a well-fed animal, full of happy dreams and digestive experiences. As Matilda watched, the eyelids stopped twitching and lifted quite suddenly, revealing gleaming blue eyes. Immediately the thumb was thrust deep into the mouth, which began to suck voraciously. Matilda laughed out loud. 'He's just exactly like Theo.' She bent forward and stroked the damp curls on the top of his head.

Dr Rebew looked at this motherly demonstration and despite all its fondness, was struck by something removed about it. Matilda did not seem to be admiring Gilbert as something she had created but as a wonderful creature all on his own.

As suddenly as the eyelids had risen, they dropped again and soon the thumb-sucking began to lessen. 'It's the heat, m'lady,' explained the nurse, as if the sleepiness of her charge were reprehensible.

'I know.' Matilda sat back in her chair and stared across to the blue-yellow sky. The nursemaid took a good grip on the perambulator's handle and started off down the hill.

'You can go now.' Dr Rebew's dark presence was spoiling Matilda's pastoral idyll. He smelt of chloroform.

'But how will you get back?'

'Someone will collect me.' Matilda undid the top two hooks of her linen coat as if she were already on her own.

Dr Rebew marched briskly after the perambulator, thinking that a characteristic of those who had always lived surrounded by servants was a confidence verging on arrogance. Doubtless someone would collect her and, if not, she might just find she could walk. Yet he must not think critically of her for she was helping him to fulfil his life-long ambition.

Theo was stung by a hornet while investigating a cow pat in a stream. The sting came up in a huge bump on his forehead. When travelling abroad he was stung by far worse things and made no fuss at all, but he did not expect pain from the dulcet English countryside. He left the children and trudged crossly home across

258

the low-lying meadowlands. The beauty of the scene no longer appealed to him.

When he reached Abbeyfields, he looked for his manservant who rubbed on Reckitts Blue, he looked for Croke to order tea and brandy and he looked for Matilda to comfort him.

'Her ladyship has gone out,' said Croke, who was counting the days until his departure and enjoyed anyone's discomfiture.

'*Out?*' bellowed Theo, who appreciated Croke's mood.

'Dr Rebew wheeled her out,' said Croke calmly.

'Bring the bottle and a glass here at once,' he ordered, and reflected that he had enjoyed Dr Rebew's company before he became the architect of their removal.

The sun was sinking below the flank of the valley on which Matilda sat. It still had strength enough to throw its rays to the opposite flank, which was gradually changing colour from a pale, dried, summer green to a rich copper. Matilda was almost uncomfortably cool now but she was far too content to think of moving. When she saw Theo's bulk filling the pathway, it took quite an effort not to seem interrupted and cross.

'So! I find you at last. "Out", Croke says, without defining the "out". Was it likely I should look for you so far away from the house?'

Matilda let him sit and settle down beside her. He immediately poured himself a brandy – he had taken the precaution of bringing the bottle and glass with him – and commented, since she said nothing, 'I am suffering. I am in pain. I have been stung by a hornet who is a close relation to a swordfish!'

'I thought that blue bump couldn't be mere chance.'

Theo took another swig of brandy. 'Who would think it in the peace of an English meadow! A hornet the size of a swordfish! We are all at risk.' He gave her a quick sidelong glance. 'Your children are at risk.'

'Oh. Were they attacked too?'

'Of course not.'

There was a pause. 'I'm afraid I'm not better,' said Matilda. 'I'm afraid I may not get better at all.'

'Nonsense!' cried Theo, jumping up and then sitting down again. He took her hand gently. 'You will never give in.'

'It's something wrong inside me,' said Matilda, looking at the valley which was now the colour of dead bracken. 'Dr Rebew thinks it is merely the after-effects of the troubles last year—'

259

'Troubles? What troubles?' interrupted Theo, before catching Matilda's wide look and subsiding again. 'The poison's reaching my brain,' he said, rubbing his head and then adding, 'My snakes are in trouble, that's true.'

'You'll manage very well on your own,' said Matilda smiling. 'Particularly once you're all together in London. There'll be women lining up to look after you.'

'I don't know why you talk like this! You know how I love you. How I need you. How we all need you.'

'I know. I do know,' whispered Matilda. 'I love you, too, but I can't stop what's happening. It's God's will.'

'God's will!' Theo's face blushed as darkly as his blue bump. He stamped like an angry child until he was several paces from his wife.

'Hush, Theo,' said Matilda. 'It is God's will and I'd like you to send for the vicar.'

'What! That nincompoop! That lily-livered minion of a non-proven deity! That village Plunkett!' Theo's rage carried him, gesticulating, further down the path.

'Mr Plunkett back?' But Matilda was not strong enough to call and now Theo had turned his back on her and was striding downwards.

Down the hill galloped Theo, his prophet's head – of an unbeliever – lit from behind in a reddish halo. From beyond the huge block of the house the voices of the returning children competed with the rooks, the pigeons and an out-of-order cockerel. Further below, the village was now completely enveloped by the blue cloak of evening.

Only a few figures still moved, slowly for it had been a long hot day, shutting up the last of the animals, checking gates for those who stayed out, collecting forgotten tools. Most were already inside, hungrily eating their meal.

A door opened in the house beside the church. The Reverend Oswald Plunkett looked out, took another pace and turned his face towards Abbeyfields Hall.

'Do come in, brother dear,' called Miss Plunkett anxiously from inside the house. 'You know how treacherous these summer evenings can be and your constitution is no longer strong.'

'I should pay my respects,' he muttered, and then a little louder, 'I shall pay my respects.' And before his sister could capture him, he had set off briskly towards the great house.

A few minutes later Miss Plunkett followed, a man's coat flapping over her arm and her hat insecurely pinned on her head so that it bobbed excitedly for a while and then took itself off into a hedge.

Theo reached the conservatory panting, dishevelled, smelling of brandy. His two helpers, who had just finished sealing the snakes into their travelling cases, opened the door to their master with some surprise.

'Hammers!' ordered Theo. 'Crow-bars! Arm yourselves, the time has come to end an empire!'

The bewildered men watched as Theo began to smash the glass and wondered if it had anything to do with his swollen blue forehead. Like a man possessed, he swung at any window within reach and then began to attack the supports too.

'This is a matter of life and death!' yelled Theo. 'Do not stand amazed, follow your leader's example.'

Soon, all three men were doing their best to demolish the conservatory. Attracted by the noise the children approached and were joined by those inside the house. 'It is for your mother!' cried Theo, stopping to take breath and becoming aware of their gaping faces.

Up on the hillside Matilda sat under her tree and smiled. Theo loved her.

Along the edge of the house slid the dark shadow of Mr Plunkett. He was too far away for Matilda to recognise him and everybody was busy. Sidling along by himself, he prayed that God's will should not direct Sir Theodore to let loose the serpents from their boxes. His heart beat dangerously fast and his hands sweated. Deciding he could not risk misreading God's will, he retreated as silently as he had come.

'Oh, my dear brother!' Miss Plunkett embraced him out of the dusk. Oswald gasped and trembled but did not struggle. He was safe now. Miss Plunkett, keeping a firm grip on his arm, cast about for her hat. It had been newly trimmed that summer.

Darkness came now entirely and with it dew and dampness and calm. Theo mopped his sweating brow with his sleeve, leaving a large blue mark, and went up to rescue Matilda. He found her by her pale coat with its pearl buttons and by her white face.

'There!' he announced. 'Now you cannot leave me. I have nothing but you.'

'You can push me home, dearest.'

'No!' Theo grabbed Matilda, light as a feather, and held her tight in his arms. 'I love you my own dearest, my own beloved wife, and now I have you I will never let you go.'

261

Matilda breathed in the bitterness of Theo's sweat and wondered if she were giving up too easily. But it no longer felt as if she had any choice in the matter. She felt removed and incapable of action. 'My dear,' she twisted her thin white fingers in his bristly beard, 'I have tried to be a true wife.'

PART FOUR

A well-known scientist (some say it was Bertrand Russell) once gave a public lecture on astronomy. He described how the earth orbits around the sun and how the sun, in turn, orbits around the center of a vast collection of stars called our galaxy. At the end of the lecture, a little old lady at the back of the room got up and said: 'What you have told us is rubbish. The world is really a flat plate supported on the back of a giant tortoise.' The scientist gave a superior smile before replying, 'What is the tortoise standing on?' 'You're very clever young man, very clever,' said the old lady. 'But it's turtles all the way down!'

Stephen W. Hawking, *A Brief History of Time* (1988)

Chapter Nineteen

In 1980, or whenever . . .

Theo heard Matilda make her entrance into Abbeyfields. At least, he heard the siren on the ambulance that brought her. It was an odd time for a siren, four o'clock on a winter's morning not long after Christmas, although that meant little to Theo. He was awake because he had begun to hide some of his sleeping pills. He liked the night hours because they were normally more peaceful than the day – even though his room-mates sometimes defied all drugs to achieve some vicious manifestation of self-hatred such as poking a biro into Theo's ears.

But usually night was quiet enough for him to hear the muffled chat of the nurses on duty, to listen to the noises of the countryside, for the hospital was sited in a remote valley, and, if he had time, to think serious thoughts. This last was usually too much for him, fuddled as his mind was in his present circumstances, but at least the possibility was there.

He had been on the verge of a serious thought breakthrough (his doctors disapproved of thought) at the moment Matilda's ambulance had interrupted him. His dormitory was situated above the main entrance so he could hear quite clearly the voices of the men who carried in the stretcher. They didn't worry about waking patients.

'She's out cold,' said one, as if surprised.

'Sedated, that's all.' The other had an older voice. 'Otherwise we wouldn't have been told to bring her here.'

He was right. This hospital did not have intensive care facilities: if someone was seriously injured they must go to the nearest big town, fifteen miles away. This new entrant, being a woman, had probably ineffectually slit her wrists. It was strange how many women chose that way to broach death, as if blood-letting were an essential part of the procedure. Perhaps it was their monthly bleeding that suggested such an unpleasant way out.

267

Theo shuddered. Women were a fearful threat to him in certain moods.

On both occasions when he had attempted to cast himself off from life, he had chosen an overdose of pills. Indeed, rather than coveting death, he had merely wanted to knock himself out of life for a bit. He had never been angry, like some patients, when reawakened and kicked back into gear. On the whole, he was thankful, suicide being such a terrible sin against God. No, he did not think of himself as a suicide. Yet he had to admit that his collection of unused sleeping pills – quite a feat when the rule book insisted patients must be watched as they took their proper dosage – was an insurance against too much pain. He might need to bow out again sometime.

Outside his window the doors of the ambulance were banged shut and he heard it move off at great speed down the drive. The men would be looking forward to a cup of tea. Theo considered whether he would like to join them in the world outside but knew that he lay in the bed he had chosen. Without too much unhappiness at all, he could lie back and imagine the progress of the woman on the stretcher. By now she'd be in the big lift, on her way upstairs to the women's wing where she'd be put in a side room for what remained of the night. She'd wake up there hardly knowing where she was, angry or resigned according to her temperament. The walls were pink Theo knew from what other patients had told him but there were no decorations and no curtains since it was an inside room. This was a National Health hospital, all mod cons but nothing fancy.

Matilda knew at once where she was when she woke up. She'd pictured such a room so often, the emptiness, the defeat, the misery and relief of giving up all responsibility for herself or anyone else. She had waited so long for this moment and now she was here, secure in defeat and humiliation. It had been so easy, too. She lifted her bandaged wrists. Not the years before, but the action of cutting through the skin, which had brought her to this pale room. If only they'd let her lie in this bed for ever. Matilda closed her eyes with the nearest feeling to hope she'd had for ten years.

The doctor was a woman, which was an unwelcome surprise. She came with two young male assistant doctors or nurses, Matilda did not know which. The doctor introduced herself as Dr Fairweather as she unwound the bandages.

'Ha,' she said. 'Not much to worry about here.'

'I'm sorry,' said Matilda, who'd been brought up to be polite to doctors.

'Your husband seems to think you should stay in a little while, anyway.'

'My ex-husband.' Matilda had planned to say nothing more than 'I'm sorry', but some facts had to be put straight at once.

'Of course.' Dr Fairweather looked knowingly at a folder. Matilda shut her eyes. 'Do you want to stay in?'

Matilda's eyes jerked open. Hadn't she done enough? Was slitting your wrists not a clear indication that . . . ?

'You see, the beds here are in great demand. You can imagine the cost per week. I have to be sure—'

Matilda began to scream. An hour later, when all sensible talk had failed to prevail, she was given another knock-out injection.

'It's my duty to the tax payers,' Dr Fairweather explained a little defensively to her students. 'There're thousands of people who'd give anything for a nice quiet life.'

In the morning Theo followed the usual pattern of his day. Since he had been awake so long he was always first in the breakfast queue, first in the pill queue. He was ready to talk then, too.

'Good morning, Sergeant.' He had nicknamed a young female nurse 'Sergeant' to keep everyone's spirits up, and often followed it with a salute, not that he had ever been in the army – unless you counted God's troops. 'Morning, Theo. In good spirits, I see.' Sergeant was friendlier than some who seemed to think a smile would cause a revolution.

'Exciting night. Young woman, was she? Suicide? Slit wrists?'

'You were supposed to be sound asleep.' She smiled as she dealt with the next in line, an old man called Lenny, too old, you would think, to need any subjugation by drugs.

'Go on, tell me. Who was she?' Theo persevered. In a place like this any newcomer was a welcome stir.

'You'll find out for yourself soon enough.'

'You mean, she's coming on this ward?' Theo tried to hide some of his excitement. They didn't like it if he became too excited. 'Then she can't have been much hurt. These silly women, they all—'

'Ssh, now, and go and find something to do.' Sergeant was serving an obese young girl called Linda. What should have been a round pretty face was disfigured by a shrunken eye and a puckered scar where she had attempted to blind herself with a meat skewer.

269

'Good morning, Linda,' said Theo cheerfully, but as usual she turned away. She hadn't spoken since she'd been transferred to the hospital ten weeks ago. Theo's only real objection to her was that she smelt. 'Why don't you make Linda wash, Sergeant?' he asked over the top of another patient, a young black boy who had tried to strangle his brother.

'I told you to go away, Theo. Now off! Some of us have jobs to do.'

Usually Theo enjoyed being treated like a child. At first it had felt a little strange, a big, hulking, middle-aged man like himself being ordered about by young creatures half his age but soon he had accepted it, as he did everything else, and even grown to enjoy the sense of security it gave him.

Today, however, his almost entirely sleepless night had left him restless. If he had been sensible he would have returned to bed but instead he went down the corridor for a second breakfast. Food was a solace to be enjoyed now that he had lost any interest in his physical appearance. In that sense he had come full circle to his days at the monastery when his body had been second in importance to his long black habit. His habit was his body with his head on the top like a face through a cardboard cut-out at a seaside fair. What an extraordinary shock it had been the first time he had felt Jenny's hand through his robe. He had felt the pressure on his leg like a burn.

Theo gave the same sort of shudder that he had produced in the middle of the night when reminded of women's menstruation, and then took a large jam doughnut from the counter. Jam dough-nuts so early in the day were quite a treat.

Matilda came round in her little pale room less willingly than the first time. Without exactly recalling her brush with Dr Fairweather, memory of someone aggressive, someone expectant encouraged her to put off the moment of reawakening as long as possible. From under partially closed lids, she twice watched nurses come to inspect and leave. The third time a girl nearly as young as her own daughter lifted her hand to take her pulse. She had to push the bandage aside to do it. When she had finished she put it down gently and said, 'You're awake now, aren't you?'

'Yes,' agreed Matilda, always ready to take the easiest line.

'Are you hungry?'

'No.'

'Do you want to wash?'

'No.'

'Do you want to go to the toilet?'

Matilda turned her face into the pillow. The nurse went out. All Matilda wanted was to be left alone. That happened for several more hours during which she half slept. Blissfully, her head remained empty of dreams. She felt that if she was allowed to keep absolutely still she might, just possibly, become intact again.

A nurse reappeared – or at least a young man in a white coat. 'I'm told you're awake but won't move.'

Matilda said nothing, shut her eyes firmly. The man bent over and took one of her hands from under the bedclothes. 'Oh, you've wet the bed.'

Matilda heard the disgust in his voice. 'I'm sorry,' she said, although she didn't really feel it. Far the most important thing was not to move.

'I'll get it changed.'

'No, thank you.' She tried to make her voice a little clearer, a little firmer, but the young man was already out of the door. Soon he returned with two other assistants. One carried a rubber sheet.

'Out you get,' commanded the original young man, as if she might actually do it.

'There's nothing wrong with your legs.' He began to sound cross when she took no notice. The best thing, Matilda decided, was not to speak or move. Maybe they would understand then that it was essential she stayed where she was. After all, this was a hospital and they wanted her to get better.

'That's right. Get a good grip under her armpits.'

Matilda could hardly believe what was happening. She hung on to the bedclothes and held herself completely rigid, but it was clear they would have her out in a minute. Matilda began to scream.

Theo looked at his lunch with disappointment. 'We had bangers and mash yesterday.'

'There's moussaka or vegetarian curry.'

'Foreign filth.' Theo did not really have such a view but hospital life led one to cliché. Spotting Sergeant scuttling to the television room, he abandoned his lunch and dashed after her. 'Where is she, then? Last night's suicide.'

'Don't be so nosy. The hospital's not run for your entertainment, you know.'

'She's not so well, after all. I expect that's it.' Theo grabbed Sergeant's arm so she could not escape.

'You know what, Theo, you're becoming a bit of a pest. Don't you have a group therapy session or something to keep you busy?'

271

'I slept all morning,' said Theo, becoming sulky. 'What do you want me to do? Get rid of myself? I was looking forward to a new face, that's all.'

'Sorry, sorry.' Sergeant stopped now, seeing Theo's real depression. What seemed like mere boredom could become something more dangerous in here. 'I'll tell you what, we'll have a game of draughts when I've sorted out Mrs C.'

'Right,' agreed Theo brightening. 'Wipe Mrs C's bottom and then find me in the games room.'

So Theo did not see Matilda on her first day nor find out what had happened to her.

On the second morning when Matilda awoke – although she wasn't counting in days or even hours, rather in some abstract of absent time – she knew she was settled in this place, this hospital, and the worst that could happen had happened: they had yanked her out of bed. But afterwards they had let her crawl back in. She was here to stay. No one would make her go back to her house, her children, her work, her ex-husband or her lover – or rather, ex-lover. This conviction brought with it a sense of security so that she dared to move her body a little. A little stretch, a little turn. The action, though so slight, made her stomach speak plainly for food. The noise was loud and disconcerting in the silent room. Nor did it carry with it any sensation. She didn't feel hungry, although the angry noises made it clear that she was.

Soon, one of the nurses who had heaved her upright the day before stood at the door. 'Do you want a wash before breakfast?' she asked.

Matilda didn't answer. She debated whether to answer 'no' would result in forcible washing as the previous day. Was it a real question or a disguised command? Did she have to wash? Did she have to have breakfast? If that was the case she would go quietly. 'I would like breakfast here,' she said, testing the ground.

'This isn't a hotel, you know.' The nurse's attitude was not unfriendly but Matilda found she had begun to cry. It was a sentence much used by her mother, now dead ten years, in her childhood.

The crying didn't seem to make much impression on the nurse who left the room briskly, saying over her shoulder, 'Press the button if you want help.'

Matilda cried for another ten minutes, which temporarily drowned the noise of her stomach. She couldn't move. They might as well recognise that. She had broken down, in the sense that a car breaks down, and only now did she understand how aptly the term described a human being in her condition. Her motor would no longer turn, her batteries were flat, her big end gone. Matilda pulled the bedclothes over her head and considered the image of herself as a broken-down car without the smallest sense of humour.

Theo followed Sergeant round as she visited the various patients who had not left their rooms.

'You're like a terrible big dog,' she said irritably, finding him waiting outside the door for the third time.

'Woof, woof,' replied Theo politely.

'I'm too busy for you. Can't you see that? You know I am at this time of the morning. Perhaps later I'll get my own back at draughts.'

'I didn't sleep all night thinking of her,' said Theo.

'What? What?' Sergeant was preparing to enter the next room. 'What do you mean?'

'The day-before-yesterday suicide. Have you seen her? How is she? What does she look like?'

Sergeant turned to face Theo. She had a sensible face, short fair hair, small square nose, hazel eyes. It was a thoroughly agreeable, unthreatening face, which had comforted many patients more disturbed than Theo. When Theo had thought he could fly she had closed the window so pleasantly and yet so firmly that he had not dared to open it again.

'You've got an appointment with Dr Rebew this morning, haven't you? I'm off this afternoon. Come to the door at one and I'll take you for a walk.'

'You'll tell me about her?' Theo was too anxious to get his own way to thank her for giving up her free time.

'Yes. Yes. She's just a sad middle-aged woman with plasters on her wrists.' Sergeant was impatient again. 'Now, off you go and find something useful to do.'

Theo went and joined those sitting in front of the television set watching morning *Playschool*. There was the silent fat girl, Linda. She didn't smell as bad as usual. Perhaps someone had persuaded her to wash or perhaps it was the cold. It was very cold. Theo wondered whether to find a nurse and complain about the lack of heating. Before he had made up his mind that too much aggravation could become counter-productive, he found himself confronted by the black youth who had tried to kill his brother.

'You stink.' This was a distinctly hostile overture from a boy who usually spent the day slumped and inactive. It didn't particularly worry Theo, who was bigger and stronger. The smell theme was an interesting coincidence, given his train of thought, and a spot of aggression would cheer up a dull morning.

'Sorry,' he said mildly.

'You stink of piss,' elaborated the boy, whose name was Edward.

It was a surprising attack since they had always got on rather well, playing snooker several times, drugs permitting. Then Theo remembered he had received a visit from his family the evening before. The last time they'd come he had thrown a chair at one of the nurses.

'Look,' said Theo, standing up so that he could make his height felt. It was a pity about his slack gut but that was an inevitable result of not enough exercise, too much food and too many pills. 'You're a good boy. If I smell of piss, I apologise—'

'Don't call me boy!'

It had been untactful, Theo saw it now, for Edward had taken a kitchen knife from his shirt and was pointing it at him.

'Sorry, mate—'

'Don't call me mate!' His voice had become very high and his eyes unfocused. Theo wondered if Linda might find the energy to fetch a nurse but her eyes were fixed on the television set. Even though the knife was neither sharp-edged nor pointed, Theo didn't fancy it in his throat. The trouble was, he didn't trust his own sense of timing enough to attempt to take it from the boy. Drugs made you so clumsy. Out of the corner of his eye he saw another patient sitting at the far end of the room pretending to read a newspaper. No one really read a newspaper here.

'What is it, Edward? What's wrong?'

'I told you, you stink. That's what's wrong. I'm going to carve a hole in your fat belly.'

'Quite honestly, I don't think that's the knife to – er – carve holes.' The newspaper had been put down and the patient, whether to fetch help or merely avoid trouble (a perfectly possible alternative), slunk out.

'You think I can't, do you? You fucking, bloody . . .'

Theo cut his mind out as the swear words, inevitable as water from a tap, gushed out. It was the aspect of the hospital he found most distasteful. Even six years after his exit from the monastery he couldn't get used to the taking of the Lord's or Lady's name in vain, 'by Our Lady', 'bloody', the use of sex as a swear word, although that, in a sense, was appropriate . . .

Theo refocused abruptly as he felt the knife poking at his chest. Instinctively, he put up his hand to grab the wrist that held it and with his other struck out at Edward's intent face.

274

Edward fell backwards instantly, dropping the knife. At the same moment two nurses rushed in. They looked at Edward rolling about the floor, yowling and clutching his nose from which blood poured. They looked at Theo standing over him. Their expressions made it clear whom they thought was guilty.

'He menaced me with a knife,' said Theo, defensively, although he didn't really care. The scene had passed time better than *Playschool*, which Linda was still watching.

One of the nurses picked up the knife. 'Menaced,' he said ironically. 'You couldn't menace a mouse with this.'

'I know, that's what I told him.'

'Then why did you hit him?'

'Why don't you stop him making that noise and bleeding all over the carpet?' asked Theo. 'I hit him because he stuck a knife in my chest. My reaction was reasonable, moderate and humane, which is more than can be said for most people round here!' Feeling this would have most impact as an exit line, he walked with as much dignity as possible towards the door.

It was annoying to hear the same stupid nurse, obviously unimpressed, call after him, 'It'll go on your notes to Dr Rebew.'

'Fuck you!' Sometimes even Theo had to resort to the devil.

Theo had been lying on his bed for an hour trying to read *The Bridge over San Luis Rey* when he was called to Dr Rebew. Dr Rebew's room and Dr Rebew himself always had the same depressing effect on Theo. Over the years he had learned to know them with his eyes shut: the square cream walls, the orange blind at the window – he particularly hated this – the spider plant introduced by a secretary, the two prints (one of a Picasso horse, dating him to the fifties) and one of a woodland scene, presumably bought for its soothing qualities. Dr Rebew's face had more character, although was no more appealing – to Theo, at least. He had a high broad forehead, a thinnish fuzz of brownish grey hair, a long elegant nose with a depression on either side of the tip, smallish black eyes disguised by recently acquired film-producer-style glasses, a broad flat mouth and a strong chin. This had been covered by a black beard when Theo had first come before him but it had disappeared so quickly that he sometimes wondered if it had been a product of his deranged imagination. He had never asked Dr Rebew because their relationship was based on Dr Rebew knowing everything about Theo and Theo knowing nothing about Dr Rebew. For all Theo knew the doctor had been married three times and had twenty-three children. Or perhaps his life was full

275

of tragedy, a beloved wife dying of cancer. Occasionally Theo fantasised but not often. During a weekend away from the hospital he had once seen the doctor at a party in London and had fled quickly to the other side of the room. It was bad enough to be in his care and have to suffer these regular gloomy interviews. At least he could avoid him socially.

'Good morning, Dr Rebew,' said Theo, with almost ingratiating cheerfulness. 'Lovely sunny morning, if cold.'

The doctor allowed a moment to elapse before saying in his usual doleful voice, 'I see you've been in a fight with another patient.'

It was his dolefulness that most irritated Theo, no, insulted him. If he who had so much more reason to moan, managed to smile, why couldn't the doctor make a stab at it, at least once in a while? 'It was nothing, doctor,' he said politely. 'Poor old Edward came at me with a knife so I disarmed him.'

'Oh, I see.' The doctor made a note. 'So you weren't the instigator?'

'Certainly not!' Theo was indignant. 'When have I ever been violent?'

Dr Rebew did not answer this. One of his most maddening traits was never revealing his opinion. 'Did you want me to be violent?' asked Theo, knowing he would get no answer.

'Ah,' said Dr Rebew, and after another pause, 'I hear you're not sleeping.'

'Fine,' said Theo, avoiding a lie.

'Are you taking the pills I prescribed?'

This was awkward. A direct question. Of course he did take some, sometimes.

'If you were, you would sleep.'

'Ah,' said Theo, imitating the doctor.

'If you don't sleep, your brain will become over-active and soon you will start hearing those voices you dislike so much.'

This was a blow below the belt. Said in such a cold unsympathetic voice, too. Theo wondered if his irritation with Dr Rebew was turning to hatred. But, in either case, his long training as a monk had accustomed him to accepting authority. Yet the way he had pronounced the word 'voices', as if it were some childish ailment like measles or chicken-pox, instead of a terrifying hallucination of aural disharmony, a connection with outer spheres, of worlds unseen and unknown, except linked through devilish agents into . . .

For once he was happy to hear Dr Rebew's voice calling for

attention. 'You seem restless.' He looked down. 'It says here you've been restless.'

'I'm sitting still, aren't I?' Theo repressed an urge to leap up and pull the horse off the wall. 'You'd be restless if you were cooped up twenty-four hours a day.'

'Ah. You think you're well enough to go out, do you?'

Now this was serious. Theo thought hard. 'Not well enough to go right out. But perhaps the odd exeat.'

'I see. No problems, then?'

His time with the doctor must be nearly up and now he was unwilling to leave. 'I've become obsessed by this girl,' he said, hoping to catch his interest. 'This woman. A suicide.' Perhaps it was true; he was obsessed.

Dr Rebew leaned forward across his desk but didn't seem really interested. Time was up. 'You must tell me about it next week.'

Theo didn't blame the doctor for wanting to get rid of him. He had only raised the subject of the woman as a kind of tease. He expected nothing helpful from Dr Rebew. He was commandant of the camp but of little use in the regulation of Theo's thoughts. Theo had realised this the moment he identified Dr Rebew as Welsh and, although almost certainly agnostic, not likely to understand or be sympathetic to the nature of his Catholic preoccupations. In fact, they were as remote as two human beings could be.

'Thank you, doctor.'

The sun was hard and sharp at one o'clock. Theo could see it, even through the murky window-panes. He went and stood by the door leading downstairs and outside. His heart fluttered a little as it did after a long spell on the ward. He was well enough to know that there was nothing to frighten him outside where, after all, there were only garden and trees and winding pathways, but his irrational self linked to the one who screamed in pain or lay comatose, immobilised by terrible thoughts, and made his heart flutter and the blood come up in his cheeks.

'I'm sorry I'm late.' Sergeant wore a heavy coat and two or three scarves wound round her neck and shoulders.

Theo, who wore nothing but a sweater, bowed gallantly. 'It's my pleasure.'

Carefully Sergeant unlocked and relocked the door. Theo put down his head and gripped the banisters.

'Round the block?' asked Sergeant cheerily when they reached the bottom of the stairs and the door to the outside world.

Theo nodded, unable to speak. The air was so fresh, the light so bright, the sky so high, the distance in front of him so immense. Understanding his feelings, Sergeant took his arm supportively. 'It is a beautiful valley,' she said.

The hospital had been built on the remnants of a large Victorian house which, in its turn, had been constructed over what remained of an old monastery. The Victorian house had been surrounded by a landscaped garden with walled kitchen garden, an ancient yew avenue, a birch grove and wild garden, ornate balustrades round a rose garden below and, dotted about, magnificent trees. Much of this still remained, although the stonework had been allowed to fall and crumble and garden care only existed to mow the grass into a more manageable length. The walled garden was now covered with new buildings and what had once been ornamental terrace had been turned into a tennis court. The only untouched survivors were the huge wellingtonias and monkey puzzles, chestnuts and copper beeches and great, spreading, oak trees. They dwarfed and put in their place the council signposts: 'King Cynewulf House. Wards A to C'.

All three houses and fifteen wards bore the names of Anglo-Saxon kings. This fancy labelling arose because the most ancient building on the site had been an early Christian monastery. It was traditionally supposed to have been built over a mammoth stone brought from a Roman ruin. No one had ever seen the stone and Theo had imagined when he first came to the hospital that he would find it, uncover its solidity from wood and felt and lino and cry, 'Eureka!' or, even, a more appropriate Latin tag. The heart of the hospital was the way he had thought of that stone. The heart of a monastery beating still in a modern centre for lost secular souls. Or was a secular soul a contradiction in terms? At any rate, he didn't think of such nonsense now.

'Let's walk.' Sergeant shivered despite her scarves.

Theo never felt the cold. His monastery, way up north, had been decorated with ice on the inside of the window-panes. Sergeant's suggested 'Round the block', described the path that skirted the wall enclosing the central part of the old garden. It was built to keep patients in and was ugly and depressing. Nevertheless, it was the longest walk and therefore a privilege. From where they stood, half-way up the side of the valley, they could see beyond the wall to the other flank, which was farmed in a fairly desultory way by a couple of farmers living in the village at the bottom of the valley. The land's appearance was unchanged over hundreds of years for it was too steep to plough into subservience, like most of the countryside round about. In the summer much of it was

278

overgrown by nettles, which were taller than the sheep that nibbled among them. In the winter its green grew thin and dull until the gorse bushes pushed out yellow shoots. Because Theo had almost never seen a man up there, he thought of it as remote, even mysterious, although it was hardly more than three miles away and less as the crow flies.

'Once, long ago, those hills were heavily wooded,' said Sergeant, seeing where Theo was looking. It was always surprising when a patient saw something outside himself. 'They've got a history of the place in the office. Old engravings.'

'I've seen them.' Theo's attention had not been held for long. 'How is she?' he asked intently.

'I don't know why you care,' replied Sergeant, guessing he was back with the new patient.

'What does she look like?'

'Dark curly hair, greying, pale skin. Light eyes, possibly blue, but she doesn't open them much. Middle-aged. Your age. Battered.'

'Battered! Battered?' exclaimed Theo excitedly. 'Her husband swings one, does he?'

'No. I don't know. I just meant in the usual way. Battered by being in existence for fifty-odd years.'

'Oh, that. But it must be more than that. Or why would she end up here?'

'You're right. But I don't know. I'm only the nurse. You should have asked Dr Rebew.'

'I did raise the subject.'

'Well?'

'He took no notice.'

They had almost reached the lowest slope of the garden so that they were enclosed and without a view. 'Jenny is younger than me.' Theo stopped walking and began to swing at an imaginary golf ball.

'She hasn't visited you much lately.'

'She's threatening . . . threatening. Actually, she's found herself a more satisfactory man.'

'Is that bad?' Sergeant began walking again, puffing as they started the uphill curve.

'She's a peroxide-blonde scrubber.'

'I see,' said Sergeant, who had formed just this impression on Jenny's few visits. She had seemed an odd girlfriend for an ex-priest.

'She worked in the monks' laundry and, believe it or not, she was captivated by my extreme good looks. I was younger, of course, and didn't carry this camel's lump around.' Theo patted his protuberant stomach, accentuated by his overtight yellow sweater, 'She loved me because I was handsome, well born, well educated.'

'And dressed in a monk's habit.'

'Oh, no. Jenny isn't at all kinky. Very stupid. I don't think she properly understood what the habit meant. She saw me as a man in his thirties who looked at her with lusting eyes. She saw her simple womanly duty.'

'And did you love her?'

'I wanted sex with a woman. I wanted to sleep at night with a woman. I wanted close contact with a human body that wasn't my own. When she was in a room I felt completely different. I shook till my teeth rattled when she came near.'

Theo stopped again to swing his imaginary golf club. Above their heads loomed one of the biggest oak trees, dating well back beyond the Victorian garden, perhaps even three or four hundred years. Neither Theo nor Sergeant looked up. Sergeant was curious to hear the full story of the laundry girl and the monk.

'My family said she was vulgar and uneducated and out for my money. But I didn't have any money. I'd given it all to the monastery. They said she didn't know that. And it's true she made me press my brother to give me some of the family money. But, after all, we had to live on something. They just hated her.'

'Surely they were upset she'd taken you from the Church?'

'Possibly.' Theo began to walk so fast that, matching his long legs, Sergeant had to run to keep up. 'My mother never wanted me to be a monk.'

'Aren't they Catholics?' Sergeant puffed out determinedly. Above her head a swirl of birds flew in formation to the other side of the valley. The sun was behind her so she could see each beating wing.

Theo didn't answer her last question. He was thinking of the few months immediately after Jenny and he ran away from the monastery. They had found a small cottage not far from this valley where she still lived. His home, too, he supposed. The feeling of freedom had been extraordinary. Jenny had taught him to make love. She had laughed at him, calling him a fastidious bachelor. At first he had continued to pray to God on his knees night and morning but one night he had been too tired and another morning too involved and after that it had struck him that God had had an awful lot of him over the last twenty years and a little break might be a good thing for both of them.

He had been happy. Jenny was warm-hearted, easy-going and

generous. He hadn't seen her as a scrubber then. It was she who had kept them in those first few months, working in the big supermarket in the nearest local town. She had bought herself a moped and he had waved her off every morning. She was a touching and absurd sight with her blonde hair streaming out from under her helmet and her rather large bottom in the tight black trousers. He must have loved her.

Sergeant's curiosity was now overtaken by a desire to put Theo back inside the hospital and get away. She knew only too well how patients hated that moment of parting, of rejoining the same enclosed world which less than an hour ago seemed so difficult and dangerous to leave.

As she feared, Theo reached the door of the hospital and stood rigid, gazing at the sky. 'I'm afraid I must go.'

Theo took his time. 'Got a date, have you?'

'None of your business.' Lightness of tone, joking acerbity, might galvanise him.

Theo brought his attention back from the sky. 'I might stay out a bit.'

'You know you can't without a nurse.'

'I might go to the shop and buy some chocolate.'

'Come in or I won't take you out again.'

Theo supposed he should have felt humiliated as she pushed him in and up the stairs. However, it was important not to lose her good will and he had noticed how his story had interested her. 'You look like Jenny,' he said, making his blue eyes smile.

'A peroxide-blonde scrubber?'

He'd forgotten he'd said that. But Sergeant was laughing. She didn't mind. She was a good sport. 'I'll tell you the rest of the story sometime,' he said.

'Goodbye!' Sergeant shoved him through the final door and then locked it carefully.

'See you tomorrow!' called Theo.

'I'm off tomorrow,' mouthed Sergeant, half-way down the stairs.

Faithless girl, thought Theo without rancour, and pottered off towards the television set.

'You haven't eaten all day.' A nurse stood accusingly over Matilda. 'You don't want us to push tubes down your throat, do you?'

'No,' agreed Matilda, blinking her eyes open.

'You must be hungry.'

'Yes,' agreed Matilda.

'Then why don't you eat?' The nurse was young, male, and

fairly new to psychiatric care. He still brought common sense to bear as if it was relevant. Occasionally his approach worked when other more sophisticated techniques had failed.

Matilda began the movements of getting out of bed.

'There's cottage pie or ham salad,' encouraged the nurse, pleased by his success.

But cottage pie and ham salad was a counter-productive piece of information. Matilda returned to the horizontal and pulled the sheets tight over her head like a cover over a jam pot. Thoughts of all the meals she had given to her children shut out any further pleading from the nurse. In the interests of their healthy growth she had presided over mountains of cottage pie, herds of pigs. A good-sized hill and several pigs had ended in the waste bin, for her children were a perfect example of the Western hemisphere's over-production and misuse of food resources. At one point Matilda had worked for Oxfam. She had loved her children with a vitamin A and B and C.

From a distant place a stern voice advised, 'If you don't start eating tomorrow, we will have to take steps.'

Matilda felt a light-headed giggle bubbling upwards. Throwing back her bedclothes, she cried, 'Caught you!'

The giggle burst at the sight of the astonished doctor and nurse. 'You were moving,' she explained, 'I saw you moving so now you've got to go back to the beginning.'

'Interesting,' said the doctor, making a note. 'She's playing Grandmother's Footsteps.'

Chapter Twenty

Men and women ate in the same canteen. Breakfast time was usually a mournful scene for most of the patients had hardly thrown off their pacifying night-time drugs and moved with the muffled glide of the sleep walker. Only Theo, who had once more managed to avoid taking all but the first sleeping pill – a negligible tranquilliser to a man of his strength and size – spoke and moved like a man of action.

'Bacon and eggs!' he shouted. 'Preceded by Frosties and accompanied by a double-dose cup of coffee.' He did this more to annoy than out of real desire. Food passed the time. Shouting raised his spirits and even lifted a few other heavy heads. He was a cheer-leader, a heroic figure in this place of pale ghosts.

Matilda first saw him like that. He caught her attention with his bellicose stance, his protuberant stomach, his shock of grey curly hair, his dare-devil brilliant greenish-blue eyes. He reminded her of a little boy of four or five who dares the world because he knows he can still run to Mummy. Because he was in this place Matilda immediately knew he was both brave and pathetic. Trying not to draw his notice, for she shuffled even worse than the other patients and her head hung lower, she edged her way towards a table.

'Welcome!' cried Theo, spotting her at once. He knew he was becoming too excited but happiness was a rare bird and must not be instantly caged. She was the new woman – even without seeing the plasters on her wrists he could tell that. As described by Sergeant, she was pale, thin, dark, battered but there was also an appealing bounce to her curly grey-threaded hair, a shine to her murky blue eyes. He must not play the buffoon too far. Yet even as he thought that, he found himself sweeping a bow and crying, 'Let me draw out your chair, dear lady, and take your order.'

'Leave her alone, Theo,' interrupted a nurse, following along behind Matilda.

'Theodore to you,' said Theo with dignity. 'Father Theodore.' It was best getting these things out in the open at once, he thought, and noticed that his words had produced a little lifting in the woman's head. Self-absorption, the curse of the mad, had not entirely killed curiosity, then.

'Sit here, Matilda,' said the nurse, pulling out a chair as far as possible from Theo.

Matilda. She was called Matilda. Well, he supposed it was no odder than Theo. Bent now on conversation, Theo sat himself by fat Linda and asked her, with an engaging smile, whether she had enjoyed last night's showing of the world snooker championship. She had watched it for several hours the night before, showing such unusual fury whenever anyone had tried to switch channels that she had been victorious until pill time.

Since she didn't look up from her natural yoghurt – poor Linda was supposed to be on a diet although everyone knew she guzzled sweets at all times except meals – Theo imitated hitting a ball into a hole.

'Go away! You're filthy!' Her protest was so violent that Theo obliged her swiftly. Surely she couldn't imagine he was making an overture? This day was beginning badly. Taking his plate, he retired to a solitary corner where he could watch Matilda and not draw any more attention to himself. Already he had a nasty feeling that those two nurses by the door were agreeing that his level of energy was rising above normal.

An ex-priest. A priest. Matilda's imagination was caught by this piece of personal information. She had left the peaceful vacuum of her bed only wishing to return as soon as allowed, but now her condition had subtly altered. Surreptitiously she glanced at Theo. As she watched, he carefully lifted his fried egg, now leathery, and laid it across his cup. He then picked up his two slices of bacon, stiff as card, and balanced one against the other on top of the egg. He contemplated this still-life for a few seconds and then raised the cup as if to drink from it. Bacon, eggs and coffee showered into his lap. He seemed surprised by this and slightly irritated, wiping the mess away on to the floor and then tucking into his Frosties voraciously.

Watching Theo, Matilda failed to approach her own yoghurt and toast. 'Come on, now,' said a nurse over her shoulder.

Matilda ate the yoghurt, which slipped down perfectly easily. It wasn't food she objected to, merely the action necessary to obtain and eat it. When she looked up again she couldn't see the priest or ex-priest for a moment until she spotted him crawling round the floor.

'Had a little accident,' she heard him explain airily to the lady from behind the bar.

'But it wasn't an accident,' said Matilda.

'Showing off again, was he?' The nurse seemed uninterested.

'Is he really a priest?'

'A monk. At a big public school. He ran away with the laundry girl.'

Matilda found she had eaten her toast without thinking. Sometimes she thought it was the dullness of her breakdown that was most distressing. She was a housewife who couldn't cope. A wife who turned against her husband and lost him, a mother who felt despised by her children, a lover who couldn't believe in the reality of her lover, a working woman who loathed feminism. She was a mismatched product of a colour supplement, a woman without substance who cried in the same way over a burned casserole as the discovery that her husband had left her. She was not a serious person. Tears began to roll so fast down Matilda's cheeks that one dived off the edge of her chin and plopped into the empty yoghurt pot. Tears were such a solace, she had thought at first – until they became uncontrollable. 'Control yourself,' Martin had said with his disdainful dark eyes but that had increased a trickle to a flood. Tobias, her lover, the man who loved her, or so he said, forced her to her feet when she cried and held her there as if the vertical would stiffen her sinews, turn her from watery self-pity to brave strength. But that didn't really work either, although she tried hard for him, gulping back and holding in. But it only came out later when she was alone, from deeper cisterns, ballcock stuck interminably down.

The nurse led the weepy Matilda back to her room. But not before Linda had seen her and started a quiet sympathetic trickling from her good eye. Theo, half-risen from the floor, saw her go, too, but she seemed to be upside down from his point of view, giving a surrealistic quality to her exit. Straightening himself too hurriedly for hereditary low blood pressure, the room became suffused with black ink and he flopped down suddenly in a chair, head between knees. When he dared raise himself it was to face a stern Dr Rebew. This was unusual for he seldom tracked down patients to the general rooms. Theo adopted what he trusted to be a sober and pliable air.

'It seems fairly clear you haven't been taking your pills.' The doctor looked impatient as if diverted here from other pressing duties.

'Ah,' said Theo putting his hands together with a hint of prayer. 'Indeed.'

'"Indeed" meaning no, you haven't been taking them.' He peered closely at Theo, who thought discretion the better part of valour and said nothing. After all, he was in this man's power.

'You must decide for yourself,' continued Dr Rebew brusquely. 'I can only tell you what's best for you. It's your will that counts.'

Theo thought his years at the monastery had taught him more about 'will' than Rebew would ever know. He had left it to be free of Free Will. 'Can we talk in your office?' he said, playing for time.

'No,' said the doctor. 'Just take the pills, otherwise I'll have to arrange for injections.' Away he swept, sure in his health and confidence.

Theo left the canteen and penetrated the corridor that led to the little room where the nurses gathered for coffee. He rat-a-tat-tatted on the frosted-glass door. 'I've come to confess,' he said when the door was opened. 'Who's the priest on duty?'

'What is it you want?' Only Sergeant of the nurses had a sense of humour and she wasn't there.

'I've been a naughty boy and the big chief doctor is cross with me.'

'Oh, yes. You've been hiding your tranqs. Here. Take these now.' The nurse watched as he tossed the pills into his mouth and swallowed them with a debonair flourish.

After that there was nothing else to do but go and become a zombie in his bed.

Theo slept for eight hours until just before supper-time. It had the virtue of being a knock-out, dreamless sleep in which he undid the restlessness of three nights without. However, such is the imbalance of artificially righted nature, that he woke up not cheerful and refreshed but miserable and heavy-eyed.

Falling to his knees beside his bed, he prayed aloud. 'Give me, O Lord, a reason to continue, for my life is in your hands. Give me a love that is a reflection of your love. But only as you will, not . . .'

'Will.' There it was again. Theo put his head in his hands.

Sergeant found him there fifteen minutes later. 'There you are! Getting yourself into trouble the moment my back is turned.'

'My little ray of sunshine! My pink-cheeked chickadee!' Theo lumbered gratefully off his knees and kissed Sergeant on both cheeks. 'Without you, life is a drear and awful place.'

'Nonsense. And I hear you met Matilda.'

'Ah. Matilda.' His long sleep had almost wiped the memory of breakfast. 'How is Matilda?'

'Not much better than you. Heavily into bed rest.'

Oh, the wondrous matter-of-factness of Sergeant! For her alone, Theo could stay for ever in the hospital. If they'd let him, that is. Together, they strolled towards the canteen.

'So, what were you doing on your knees? Not more wicked thoughts, I hope?'

Once, Theo had confided in her the tests placed in his way by Beelzebub's foul minions. The awful compulsions to will the death and injury of his family and monkish ex-colleagues. The terror of it had been so great, for he knew the power would be given to him if he had accepted the temptation, that he had to tell someone. Her matter-of-factness then had been like the grace of angels.

'No wicked thoughts, no tempting voices,' said Theo. 'Only a few intercessions to the Almighty Father.'

'You haven't asked to see Father Donahue, lately,' commented Sergeant.

'A foolish prelate whose mind is gummed up with shamrocks. Actually, I prefer the Blessed Oswald Plunkett. Anglican or no, at least he doesn't think Proust's a liver complaint and Waugh pronounced "Wuff".'

'You are a snob.'

'Thank you.' Even Sergeant had her limitations. A young girl of little education.

Theo sighed and began to feel a little better. 'Tell the Blessed Plunkett next time he's here I'd like a visit.'

'Talking of visits.' Sergeant had come to Theo's room because he had a visitor. But when she had seen him on his knees she had felt misgivings about leading him to the nervous woman waiting hand in hand with a man dressed in a policeman's uniform without the hat. A warning would be appropriate.

'Jenny is here,' said Theo.

'How did you guess?'

'Your anxiety.'

'She has brought her friend.'

'What's that? Her friend. Ho ho.' Desperately Theo tried to break through the cotton wool of drugs. If she had brought her friend then he wanted to parade like a peacock, make his feathers stand up and glow, impress with the sharpness and precision of his pecking ability, strut like the king of birds when presented with a modest relation of brownish hue.

'Shall I tell them you're otherwise engaged?'

'Certainly not. But first I'll return to my room for a little wash and brush up.'

Jenny and her friend, Robert, sat in the recreation room and whispered together. Robert was nervous and felt inhibited by his policeman's uniform in such a place. Jenny should have given him time to change out of it but she was so impetuous – impetuous and warm-hearted. He gave her hand a squeeze. 'He has to see you,' she had said, 'or he'll never believe in your existence. He doesn't want me, he doesn't even like me but he feels tied to me by our sexual relationship.' Robert had not much enjoyed this reference for Jenny's body was too close to his own to allow of intimate contact with another, even in the past. But she had made things better by continuing cheerily, 'Of course, unlike you, dear, he was a beginner in that area.' She had not added that he had been a pretty fast learner, too, and Robert would never have guessed it. 'Mad as a hatter' was the way he liked to dismiss his predecessor. Sitting in the grubby recreation room with a half-witted, scarred fat girl on one side and an old drooling man on the other, it was easy to feel sorry for Theo.

'Voilà, la belle Jenny! Or is it voici?' Theo made an entrance. He had wound a metallic blue-green scarf, which matched the colour of his eyes, round his throat and donned a pair of black and white chequered trousers. The effect with his usual overtight yellow sweater was dramatic, to say the least. Robert, who had stood right arm outstretched, gaped.

Theo, having made his entrance, gaped back. A policeman. Jenny had chosen a policeman to take his place. The idea struck him as exquisitely ironic and appropriate. Would he, too, fling off his uniform as their association progressed? Although, he supposed, one couldn't altogether equate the discipline of a monk with the discipline of an officer of the law. For one thing you would have to cast the Home Secretary as God.

'How nice of you to come.' Theo kissed Jenny on both cheeks. The smell of sweet scent rose off her like steam off a kettle. It was nice of her to come. Admittedly she was living in his cottage, bought with his money squeezed at her urgent pleading from his reluctant family. Perhaps she would tell him she was to move in with the policeman. They had been holding hands when he came in, although that didn't necessarily mean much since Jenny was a great one for physical contact. Theo looked at Jenny's protuberant front and imagined her breasts released from the lurex thread sweater. The idea was too exciting for a man on fasting and abstinence. He turned his attention to the policeman's plain face, the bristly beige-coloured moustache had a particularly detumescent effect.

'You do look better,' said Jenny, who had an optimistic nature.

'And how are the snowdrops?' asked Theo, irritated by her patronage. When he had loved her he had loved her personal references but in the present circumstances he preferred a certain distance between them.

Sensibly ignoring the snowdrops, Jenny took Robert's hand. 'And of course I wanted to introduce you to Robert.'

'Of course,' said Theo. 'Shall we sit down? Or would you rather', he turned to Robert, 'play snooker?'

'We've come to talk to you, Theo.' Jenny's voice was gentle as if humouring a child.

Theo felt a strong urge to behave badly. It was amazing that he had the spirit, considering all the pills inside him. Perhaps he could allow himself to behave slightly badly. After all, it was this complacent amalgam of flesh and bone who had driven him off his head.

'Are you a believer, officer?' he said politely.

'Sssh, Theo,' responded Jenny looking upset.

He must control himself for, in all honesty, he could not blame Jenny for acceding to the needs of a thirsting man and then turning out to be nothing more than a stupid peroxide scrubber. She had behaved well enough unless you counted her money-squeezing activities. But even then she must be given the sympathy due to a working girl, making her way in the world, no concerned mummy and daddy to be milked.

'Perhaps you'll be setting up home together?' Theo asked Robert with the same polite interest.

'We've come to see how you are,' said Jenny cutting across Robert, who announced in firm tones, 'We are to be married.'

They exchanged anxious glances.

'How nice!' said Theo. 'Congratulations. As for me, I'm thriving, as you see. Thriving.'

'Well, yes. We do see.' Theo knew by the unclamped look of Jenny's glistening mouth that she had something more to say. He prompted her. 'This hospital has certain qualities of home: food, a bed, companionship.'

'You don't expect to be out for a bit, then?' Jenny tripped over the words in her anxiety. Robert looked embarrassed and stroked his moustache.

So that was it. They wanted to move into his cottage. 'You'll have to ask the dictator Rebew that.' Theo paused, and gave Robert

289

an appealing smile. 'One of the joys of my miserable life is knowing that my little cottage, snug and well appointed, complete with outside larder, electric blanket and open wood-burning fire, is waiting for my emergence. Your clever fiancée persuaded me to buy it and I shall treasure it as much as a memorial to her – now she's leaving me to cleave to you – as I will for the afore-mentioned amenities. It is a monument to a love that burned too bright to last.'

'Theo! Shut up!' Theo had been enjoying the bewilderment on the policeman's face caused by his moving rhetoric and thus failed to notice Jenny's rising fury. In the face of it, his only option was to capitulate entirely.

'Please, move into my cottage,' he said spreading his hands in bonhomous and rather priestly manner. 'Peace be with you.'

'Of course we wouldn't—' began the policeman until quelled by one of what Theo thought of as Jenny's searing looks. Perhaps it really was her who had driven him mad.

'You are good, Theo darling. Of course you are welcome to visit whenever you wish. There will always be a place, a welcome . . .'

'How kind you are!' Theo began to sense the atmosphere of an eighteenth-century farce. 'But what if I, too, should find a life companion?'

'I wish you wouldn't talk in this silly way,' said Jenny.

'Ah. You used to love my conversation. So stylish, you said. So classy. You particularly enjoyed my Latin. And my rendition of the Metaphysical poets. Lying in bed, lust temporarily satisfied, I used to read—'

'Ahem.' Robert cleared his throat with a distressed look.

Theo saw it would be cruel to continue. Jenny must be allowed to win, as she always did. She had the supreme power of the unimaginative. 'I would be happy to think of you living in my cottage,' he said to the policeman in a quite ordinary voice. 'And now, if you'll forgive me, I'll return to my room!'

Stumbling a little, a wounded beast of the jungle, Theo headed back to the security of his lair.

'Good!' said Jenny, smoothing down her tight skirt as she stood up. 'That went as well as can be expected.'

'Are you sure it's—?' began Robert.

'I could have sued him for breach of promise,' said Jenny fiercely. 'Five years I cared for him, kept him financially for the first year or more. And what did I get at the end? Marriage? Not at all. A lunatic who throws my clothes out of the window and tries to dry the snowdrops with my hair dryer. He owes me more than a cottage. He owes me my youth, my—'

'Yes. Yes,' agreed Robert, eyes fixed on the exit sign at the other side of the room. He knew that everything she said was true. She had suffered terribly, been humiliated by Theo's family who treated her like a gold digger. A lesser woman would have ended up in hospital herself. Keen to get out, Robert more or less pushed his future bride through the door.

'Do come back soon,' said a young nurse to their departing backs. 'He has so few visitors.'

But neither turned.

Theo was too exhausted to attend supper, and unlike Matilda, no one tried to make him. He could live off his stomach for weeks. Matilda, sitting in front of her tomato soup, looked for him to cheer herself with his ebullience and was disappointed when he didn't appear.

'Where's Theo, the big man?' she found herself asking a nurse.

'Resting. He had visitors. Theo's not as strong as he looks.' She paused. 'You look better this evening.'

'Just because I'm eating.' Matilda's white face looked calm but she was resisting a desire to crawl under the table and cry. If she was better they would send her home and then the nightmare would begin again and she would have to cut her wrists for a second time or do something even more desperate.

'You need to get strong.'

Matilda thought how strong she used to be, as a young wife, a young mother, bearing the weight of Martin's uncertain ambition, of her children's constant needs, of house-moving, of cooking, cleaning, loving. It made her dizzy to think how long she'd coped and how well. When had the reverse trend started until she'd reached the point where she was now, being able to do nothing? Certainly it had little to do with Martin's infidelities, although he, guiltily and self-centredly, thought so. She had probably begun to break down about ten years after their marriage, when Martin was more confident and the children spent more time at their school and with their friends than with her. But that was too simple because by then she had found work and a lover so that one way and another she was just as busy as before and managing just as well. Her market garden earned sums Martin boasted about to his friends with less energetic wives. She had been a superwoman until her Big End went. Nervous exhaustion was what they called it, until she slashed Martin's and her bed and then slashed her wrists – ineffectually, in one sense, but providing enough of a reason to remove her from the world.

'Like a game of draughts?' A big-boned girl with tattoos visible below her T-shirt, three earrings in one ear and bad acne, stood in front of Matilda. Feeling threatened, she looked for support from a nurse but none was near. Out in the world, this tattooed girl would have stayed safely in the distance, on the back of a motorbike or the corner of a street.

'I'll teach you if you can't play.' This was friendly enough. Judging by appearances was a dreadful middle-class habit.

'I'm called Nora.'

'I'm called Matilda.' In this place, Nora and she were equals even if all they had in common was parents with terrible taste in Christian names.

Nora went and fetched the draughts board and set it up on the table. They began to play silently. When Nora had jumped several of Matilda's pieces, she lifted her head and said, 'Haven't seen you at therapy.'

Matilda realised she had a Scottish accent and wondered how she had ended up in this remote corner of south-west England. 'I haven't been to therapy,' she explained.

'Everyone goes to therapy,' said the girl in a less friendly manner.

'Then I expect I'll go,' agreed Matilda, praying she wouldn't have to. Memories of Californian group awareness parties started a faint sense of panic.

'I like therapy,' announced Nora. 'You can say exactly what you think. If you don't like someone, you can say it as loud as you like.'

Matilda felt her skin turn to goose-flesh. Nora's remark exactly pinpointed her worst fears. She must be brave. 'Do you dislike a lot of people?'

'I *hate* a lot of people, if that's what you mean.'

'In the hospital?' asked Matilda faintly.

'I hate my husband worst, then my boyfriend and then my boyfriend's mother. She tried to kill me.'

'No wonder, then,' murmured Matilda sympathetically, though inwardly relieved that the hatred seemed turned outwards.

'I do hate people here, too,' Nora jumped three of Matilda's pieces and crowned her victor with another. 'The women, in particular. They're all so jealous.'

'Oh,' said Matilda, wondering whatever there was in this unattractive woman of which to be jealous.

'They're jealous because they know Dr Rebew is in love with me. They know he comes to my bed at night.'

Matilda began to long for her quiet bedroom.

'You've probably met Dr Rebew,' said Nora, leaning forward intensely. 'He likes dark, slim women like you and me.'

Despite her lethargy, Matilda recognised the danger in the black eyes waiting excitedly for her response.

'No, I don't think so,' she said calmly. 'At least I don't remember.' She pushed back her chair. 'If you don't mind, I feel rather tired.'

She had reached the door before footsteps sounded behind her and Nora's voice, raised to a scream. 'You won't take him from me, however fucking hard you try! You're too fucking old! Too fucking withered! Too fucking grey! Fucking you would be worse than fucking a fucking corpse!'

Shaking so much that her teeth clattered together audibly, Matilda nevertheless managed to move away down the corridor. Behind her, the screams subsided to muffled oaths as Nora was taken in hand by the nurses.

Back in bed, Matilda pulled the sheet over her head but found that her shaking, instead of decreasing, began to hold her in painful spasms. Her head throbbed and burned as it had at home. In order to break through before it split her apart, she began to scream as loudly as possible.

A new day in the hospital could bring relief or greater pain. Theo woke up with the feeling that today couldn't be worse than yesterday and therefore might even be slightly better. In effect, yesterday's visit had released him from the life he had created with Jenny after leaving the monastery. The monks had already let him go, although he knew they still offered up prayers and said masses for his soul. His family had withdrawn almost entirely or, as they thought, been chased away by Jenny. He was alone or, at least, alone in the hospital. Perhaps the nearest to a friend was Sergeant, a nurse fifteen years or more younger than he, who was in any case merely doing her job. Her real life was doubtless carried on in her off-duty hours. So Theo was alone. Alone. The idea was vertiginous but simple. He was answerable to no one, possibly not even to God.

Theo's stomach rumbled thunderously, reminding him that he had missed supper. Swinging himself out of bed – he was still fully dressed from the night before – he lumbered hastily to the canteen.

*

293

Matilda's inability and unwillingness to act was now compounded by her fear of the other patients on the ward.

'You got out of bed yesterday,' said the nurse in fairly agreeable tones.

'She attacked me,' muttered Matilda from under her bedclothes.

'Nora, you mean. She wouldn't hurt a fly. Poor Nora.'

'She assaulted me verbally.'

'Sticks and stones. Sticks and stones. You can't live in an ivory castle.' Firmly, the bedclothes were removed.

An ivory castle was just about what she fancied, thought Matilda as she trundled down the corridor.

The canteen was fuller than usual, cigarette smoke already wafting above the smell of bacon, few vacant chairs – and two of them on either side of Nora, who sat looking morosely at a bowl of Rice Krispies.

'Be my guest,' boomed a voice to her right. It was the ex-monk, his grey hair peaking like whipped cream, his clothes crumpled and his bright eyes directed warmly towards her.

'Thank you,' said Matilda, sinking weakly into the chair he held out for her. Was it because he was middle class that she felt more secure in his presence? Or a feeling that once a priest always priestly? Or did she just like him because he looked so unlike her thrusting ex-husband and her charming, untrustworthy ex-lover? At least he was a bulwark against Nora.

'You will be joining us this morning, I expect?' Theo asked after she had settled herself with toast and tea.

'I'm very tired.'

'It's usually for everyone.'

What was he talking about. 'What?'

'Once a week. I find it a silly game. But perhaps it benefits some poor soul. The good doctor has fun, of course.'

Matilda realised he must be talking about the group therapy session referred to by Nora. 'Oh dear,' she said.

'Never mind.' Theo patted her hand sympathetically. 'Beginners can keep as quiet as mice. I usually try and get in a few funny stories but Dr Rebew has no sense of humour.'

'Do I have to go?'

'It's not so bad. Breaks the monotony of the day. Linda, that's the fat one, cries. Edward, the black boy, runs about a bit and Nora shouts but no one takes much notice. On the whole, it's like bad TV.'

The therapy session was held in the recreation room, a dismal setting that seemed to have sucked depression into its blue walls and orange and blue curtains. Despite three outside windows it was also lit by two neon strips, which cast a purplish air of unreality. The trees outside the window, grand and dark against the further hillside, took on the semblance of a painted backdrop. Besides, the winter countryside was so quiet that not a bird or sheep hinted at a real world outside. Matilda, sitting nervously in the circle of chairs, tried to think of her market garden plants on which she had lavished so much love and attention, but found it impossible.

'In my view this was the monks' chapter house,' said Theo, who had placed himself, guardianlike, beside her.

'Oh,' said Matilda, assuming he was inventing this piece of information for personal reasons.

'Much rebuilt, of course.'

'Of course,' agreed Matilda, whose eyes were fixed on Dr Rebew who had joined the circle of chairs athletically springing over the legs of an old man. Perhaps he played tennis in that other world that didn't exist.

'Good. Good.' He waved his hand to Matilda. 'Matilda is new to us. Matilda, meet Theo, Edward, Nora, Linda, Oscar, Jim and Maria. There's nothing formal here. It's just an opportunity for a general chat between yourselves. I'm here, of course, but as the least important member of the group. As you see, there's a nurse or two outside the magic circle but that's just because they're nosy. OK, who wants to start?'

'I want to ask Edward why he said I smelt and drew a knife on me.' Theo was in with his question so quickly that Matilda jumped. So did most of the other slower-thinking patients. Edward, in particular, looked quite bemused.

'I, uhm, like you, man. You don't, uhm, stink.' As he fought for words it became clear that he had totally forgotten the incident. Searching for a rational memory he eventually came out loud and clear. 'Fucking Linda stinks.' As it happened, Linda was sitting right next to him so his words were delivered full into her face.

Wordless, as usual, Linda began to cry, reminding Matilda, with a certain relief, of Theo's prediction on the course of the session. She had no place in neurotic outpourings. All she had to do was sit tight with her head down.

Half an hour or more passed in this way until Matilda felt safe enough to raise her eyes slightly. The movement was instantly caught by Dr Rebew, who up until now had controlled his energy. Smiling as if host at a difficult cocktail party, he interrupted Nora in mid-flow. 'Matilda, I'm sure we'd all like to know why you're here.'

Matilda began to shake and felt a hot flush wash up her neck and face. How dare he ask her that in front of everyone? He said he stayed out of things. Now her hands were shaking and sweating.

Theo poked her in the side and said in what he must have supposed to be a whisper, 'Just say the first rubbish that comes into your head.'

'My Big End went,' whispered Matilda, loud enough for everyone to hear.

Edward began the laughter, followed by the old man, Oscar, who repeated the words 'big end' over and over again. Linda became immediately hysterical, tears streaming down her face, while even Nora, who had begun by looking furious at all this attention turned to a rival, found it impossible to resist the relentless tide of mirth. Even Dr Rebew smiled merrily and Theo gave a guffaw or two, at least until he saw Matilda's stricken expression.

'Don't worry,' he whispered under cover of the noise, 'laughter usually turns sour here. With any luck a drama will follow and then, clap hands, silly game over and back to real life.'

Matilda was sufficiently in control enough to appreciate his concern for her and sure enough, Linda had an accident, urine trickling down the chair legs, and the young South American girl, Maria, began to wail heartbrokenly. Dr Rebew clapped his hands and the nurses entered the circle to lead off their most disturbed charges. The rest dispersed, give or take a hiccup, in a subdued manner.

Matilda sat where she was, reverting to her earlier policy of letting the storm wash over her.

'I'm sorry about that.' Dr Rebew sat beside her.

Raising her head, she saw Theo still seated the other side. His eyes were bright, his nose lifted as if to catch every nuance of their conversation. 'I'm sorry,' she said. 'It was an idiotic thing to say.'

'True, perhaps?' questioned the doctor.

Matilda sensed more than saw Theo nodding his head frantically. 'Yes,' she said.

'People often laugh at true statements. Particularly when they're very personal. It's a mixture of shock and embarrassment, actually, a form of politeness.'

'Oh,' said Matilda, thinking of the distorted faces turned towards her. She would have thought it was nearer rudeness than politeness but the doctor must know better.

'Dr Rebew has a very sophisticated attitude to human nature,' volunteered Theo, unable to restrain himself any longer from entering the conversation.

'Theodore', the doctor was the only one in the hospital who ever used his proper name, 'is a nosy parker.'

'Ha! Ha!' It was seldom Theo managed a successful provocation. 'As a matter of fact the whole thing was my fault. I told this young lady to say the first rubbish that came into her head.'

Dr Rebew ignored this and instead turned a brooding look on Matilda. After a moment or two, he seemed to come to a decision. 'Go for a walk in the garden,' he said firmly. 'Theo will show you the way.' He stood up before either of his surprised patients had time to speak. 'It's a fine sunny day,' he added, already in retreat. 'I'll tell the nurse in charge.'

Theo and Matilda looked at each other nervously. He was thinking that only two days ago he had not been trusted outside without a nurse and now he was being asked to look after a suicidal patient. She was thinking that this command must be preliminary to dismissing her from the hospital and that she was nowhere near ready for that.

'Typical Dr Rebew,' said Theo eventually. 'He can't stand me, you know.'

'Oh,' said Matilda, wondering why, if that were so, she had been entrusted to his care. 'I think he isn't a very liking person,' she suggested tentatively.

'A thoroughly unpleasant piece of work.' Theo heaved himself upright. 'We'd better get this walk over.'

'I suppose it's a sort of test.' Matilda looked doubtfully at her thin legs dressed in faded corduroy trousers. 'I used to be quite strong, you know,' she said in unconvinced tones.

'We were all something or other, I suppose.' Theo had regained some courage. 'I was a priest, a man of religion, a teacher, a lover of poetry with particular reference to the Metaphysical poets. If I had only recognised my response to the human side of Donne's inspiration, I could have forecast what some might call my undoing, although I don't take such a tragic view. One must develop as best one may, even if the outcome is painful. I could not regret Jenny even if her physical allure in conflict with my spiritual notions of man's role in the universe probably sent me off my rocker. I am what I am!'

'Yes,' agreed Matilda as Theo stood in front of her expectantly.

Not knowing who Jenny was, she had only understood part of what he said but it seemed safe to add, 'It must be very difficult to be a priest.'

'An understatement,' replied Theo briskly, but he looked pleased with her all the same and took her arm into his. 'We shall totter round the garden, clinging to each other for support like two frail barks in a storm.'

Considering their relative dimensions, this seemed a romanticised picture except that he did give a feeling of physical instability, a swaying and rocking which appeared to be outside his control. He was rather like a ship, whose ballast swung from one side to the other. With her arm in his, Matilda found their progress altered between a lengthy stride, part side-step and something nearer a run.

'The air will do us good,' remarked Theo as if to convince himself.

Matilda and Theo stood silently in front of the hospital's main outer door. Matilda, who had arrived in an ambulance by night, was overwhelmed by the grandeur of the tall trees – mostly evergreen, although an oak spread spiky fingers against the sky – by the strange sensation of the other flank of the valley rising opposite them and by the icy coldness of the air and light. She pressed her gloved hands against her face as if to pummel the flesh into life.

'It makes your head spin?' suggested Theo sympathetically. But he felt brave and strong.

'It's ridiculous,' whispered Matilda. 'I grow plants and even trees. But these trees are so enormous. They must be hundreds of years old.'

'Most of them are only a hundred years old but one or two are supposed to date back to the sixteenth century.' Theo had an idea. 'You're not ready for a walk.' He took her arm and led her slowly round the edge of the building. Soon they reached a battered door set below a fire escape. At first it seemed to be locked but it gave way under a kick from Theo.

'I discovered this last year when I paid a short visit to the hospital after taking off all my clothes in our village hall.'

Matilda's heart began to beat rapidly. She recalled that she was in the company of a madman, a lunatic. Maybe he had brought her here to rape her or beat her to death.

Theo found a light switch. They were in a cavernous space employed, obviously, as a dumping ground for anything that was not presently used. Near at hand was a pile of deckchairs without canvas, an armchair with coiled springs bursting through the seat, a huge broken chandelier, an old-fashioned lawn roller, a furled Union Jack and all kinds of rusty iron equipment for which Matilda could imagine no application, even when new.

'They've shoved in more stuff.' Theo peered about eagerly as if he were looking for something special. 'I call the mountains of old papers the lavatory rolls of history.'

Matilda wanted to leave but felt it would be impolite to Theo, whose manic qualities did not, after all, seemed turned towards her. She perched instead on an arm of the chair.

'There's junk here dating back to eternity,' cried Theo who was receding into the gloomier recesses. 'I found a halberd last time and the burned remains of a splendid piece of oak carving. That seems to have vanished now. Probably this was the undercroft of the monastery. Imagine it, living down here.'

'I expect they had windows.' Matilda looked at the walls but the light from the two dangling bulbs did not reach so far.

'Follow me!'

Reluctantly, Matilda left the security of the door and chair. Why had she been put in the charge of this ex-monk? Where were the nurses, the doctors, the guardians of those who could no longer look after themselves? Junk shops had always filled her with depression and a kind of guilt. Why should she be voyeur to the humiliations wrought by time? Who was she to patronise the rusty wringer, the mildewed painting, the legless table, the cases of unwanted books and papers? Perhaps, on the other hand, her depression was not caused by patronage but a too-close identification.

'Here they are, battered but unbowed – well, no more bowed than they always were.'

Matilda could just discern that Theo stood between what seemed to be two walls of stone. As she approached, a little warily, she saw that they were not walls but gigantic carvings of figures reclining in an almost horizontal position. They lay on stone plinths and were taller than Theo and twice the length of any man.

'Let me introduce you!' Theo grabbed her and made her stand like him between the two figures. 'To your left you will see "Melancholy Madness". You will notice his semi-naked condition, his shaven head, his vacant and doleful expression, his languor, as he scarcely manages to lift his head from his mat, his lolling tongue. Here is a human being reduced to the intelligence and activity of a worm.'

Without pausing for a reaction from Matilda, who stared with a horrified fascination at the vast stone limbs and terrible face, Theo

299

whipped round to the other effigy. 'And here we have his partner, rather his *alter ego*, "Raving Madness". You will notice immediately the manacles and chains that bind him to his pallet. You see he does not even wear the pantaloons of poor old Melancholy – although I should say that both of these men are in the prime of life. Raving here has the strength of a brutish animal and his face, although well featured, has the stunned incomprehension of a wild beast only temporarily resigned to his cage.'

Theo watched Matilda as she walked slowly round the figures with the air of a successful showman.

'What are they?' asked Matilda.

'They used to adorn the grand entrance to a famous seventeenth century madhouse. In those days the populace of England was tougher, they didn't mind passing by such fearful images. The Victorian founder of the first asylum here took them inside and put curtains round them. He was an enlightened man. Now we have banished them altogether. Anguish of such an order is too upsetting and counter-productive to a sensible and positive approach. Everybody knows that there is nothing now that can't be sorted out with a little self-control and a bottle of pills.'

'They are very upsetting,' said Matilda, trying to lessen their impact. 'But I'm glad you showed me. They are great works of art and it is odd they should be stuck away like this.'

'Works of art, ha! They are true, that's what they are.'

'Yes,' agreed Matilda and, unable to bear more, she hastened away, stumbling against broken inanimate objects.

'Don't flee!' cried Theo dramatically. 'It solves nothing!'

Ignoring him, Matilda arrived panting at the door and pushing it outward with all her strength, half fell into the wintry sunshine.

When Theo arrived beside her, she wrapped her arms round herself and said, 'I felt faint.'

He nodded. 'An understandable reaction. Perhaps you saw yourself as Melancholy and me as Raving?'

'No!' screamed Matilda. 'No, I did not!'

'I was only joking,' said Theo, looking hurt.

They moved together but in silence in the direction of the main entrance to the hospital. They turned the corner at the same time as a car pulled up. Matilda stopped walking. She watched as a dark, well-dressed man and a boy and girl of about nineteen and twenty got out.

'What's the matter?' asked Theo with interest.

'My ex-husband and children.' Matilda pointed, for tears were impeding her sense of communication.

'Poor you.' Theo took her arm. 'At least I haven't any ghastly children to torture me.'

'But I love them!'

'You don't look as if you love them. You look as if you want them to get into the car and drive away again. They look terribly spoiled to me. Does your daughter always wear a tailcoat?'

'Lucy's very keen on fashion.'

'And your son seems to be carrying a tennis racket.'

'Tom's very keen on tennis.'

'Aren't you going to go off for hugs and kisses, then?'

'Oh, Theo . . .' It was the first time that Matilda had pronounced his name and he was glad it should be in an appeal of this order.

'We will hide in the Friends' sweets and crisps caravan,' he said decisively.

'Oh, thank you, thank you.' Matilda's tears were already drying as they scurried back the way they had come, passed quickly through a pathway between ragged yews, took a right across the driveway and a left round the back of an old cedar tree until they were in sight of a caravan parked by the back exit gates.

'I am their favourite client,' said Theo, patting his stomach, 'their best client. I, alone, give them a sense of charitable purpose. They will not let us down.'

'I am so grateful,' said Matilda, wiping her eyes and blowing her nose.

'We loonies must stick together,' agreed Theo grandly.

Chapter Twenty-One

Dr Rebew wondered what instinct had made him throw Theo and Matilda into each other's arms. It was dangerous for patients to become involved; their sense of individuality was fragile and their ability to understand or sympathise with anyone outside themselves minimal. They were self-absorbed, usually self-hating and never self-possessed. Dr Rebew looked with dislike at his Picasso horse. Today was a bad day when he felt the hopelessness of his profession. When had he ever cured anyone? He should have become a surgeon and mended people's bones. Thinking his mood could hardly be worsened, he pulled over a District Health Authority report on proposed cuts in their support grant for the hospital.

Matilda looked at her face in the mirror. She had been in the hospital for ten days and this was the first time she had thought of her appearance. This surprised and pleased her. She couldn't say quite the same for her face, which was thinner and paler than she had ever known it although there was a luminosity about it which she had noticed on friends returning from health farms. It was the look of a nun – due, she supposed, to no alcohol, little food, little air and no responsibility. Her hair, the grey no longer camouflaged by coloured rinses, had become streaky like animal fur. In the last weeks at home she had thought of herself as horribly ugly, wrinkled like the witch in Hansel and Gretel, as though enseamed with the dirt of fifty years. She had hated particularly her breasts and vaginal folds, which were only there to age and wither. She perceived herself as something disgusting.

Even now, in her more tranquil state of mind, she couldn't bear the thought of looking at her body. She kept her head up when she stood in the shower and stayed there for as few moments as the nurse would allow her.

*

Theo strode about the garden. Now and again he swung an imaginary golf club or raised an imaginary gun at a scurry of pigeons. Some chose freedom and others had freedom thrust upon them. He was getting well too quickly. It was an artificial health since it relied on regular pill-taking but, then, Dr Rebew was always trying to impress on him that someone with his problems should consider drugs no more but no less important than bread at breakfast or tea at tea-time. What the silly doctor failed to realise was that taking pills was the equivalent of putting him in a padded cell. It curtailed his personality as securely as poor Raving Madness had been manacled to the ground. Pills were useful for the times in anguish when his thoughts raged and turned themselves into demonic voices, but they could not be a way of life. Besides, there was now Matilda to consider. She would hardly care for association with a dopey zombie.

'Bang!' shouted Theo, pleased with his decision. As long as he took his sleeping pills, they would hardly notice a diminution of the rest. God gave us each a certain amount of life and we who have more than average should be grateful. 'Bang! Bang! Bang!' screamed Theo so that a robin which had inherited absolute security in this part of the garden from generations of forebears was suddenly as nervous as a lark. 'I think,' said Theo, aloud, but in gentle tones, 'I think I'm in love.' The robin, reassured, returned to pecking busily for worms.

Matilda, though still despising her body, nevertheless became more capable of action. Dr Rebew asked whether her husband or children or lover had concerned themselves with the market garden and when she had said no, they had thought it a silly hobby until it started making money, he had suggested she spend some time each day working in the hospital's garden. He had seemed surprised by Matilda's vehement refusal, so much so that she had ducked her head and murmured, 'I sell fucking plants, not grow them.'

Dr Rebew had been even more obviously surprised by the 'fucking' and made a note in his file. Or perhaps that was about her refusal. 'I am ill!' Matilda had suddenly felt inspired to insist. 'You cannot make me do anything!'

Now it was Dr Rebew's turn to bow his head.

All the same Matilda liked the doctor. The very characteristics that irritated Theo appealed to her. She liked his dingy, anonymous manner, his lack of expression, his inability to smile. Her husband had been a cornucopia of expressions, a veritable Pandora's box of emotional variations. His face wasn't still even in sleep. Her lover, too, although she was now beginning to think of him more in terms of a younger brother – he was four years younger – had a lively face, filled with energy and positive thinking. He was an estate agent, which possibly explained the readiness with which he smiled. Dr Rebew's face would have driven away anyone except the certified insane.

The first afternoon that Matilda returned out into the garden to do the doctor's bidding was extremely cold. The clouds were dark and heavy, possibly with snow. Matilda realised that Dr Rebew was madder than she.

'It's February,' she told Sergeant, who had been detailed to accompany her, a task she was carrying out with a distinct lack of enthusiasm. 'The ground is like rock. Nothing's growing except snowdrops. What "work" does he expect me to do?'

Sergeant shivered. 'Perhaps he considers the countryside healing,' she suggested since Matilda seemed to need an answer.

'Rubbish!' Matilda's cheeks turned red and then back to white. 'He's a sadist.'

'Let's go back, then.' Sergeant's loyalty to her medical superior was tempered by an instinct for self-preservation. It was too cold to snow, she thought.

'He has been corrupted by power,' cried Matilda with unusual animation. 'I thought I trusted him but now I see he has not got my best interests at heart.'

'You've a point there,' agreed Sergeant in her sensible voice, 'but I wouldn't make too much of it. Dr Rebew is not a country man. In fact—'

She seemed about to elaborate further when her attention was diverted to a commotion coming from the direction of a fine old chestnut tree.

Matilda, undiverted, shouted, 'Dr Rebew is a loony sadist!' Her breath turned white and unfurled upwards.

'Bravo!' the chestnut tree replied in a jovial halloo.

'Oh dear,' said Sergeant, advancing wearily. From the middle of the much-agitated branches, a yellow object fluttered like a flag and then fell to the ground. It was Theo's sweater, although Sergeant only realised this when a large blue and white checked shirt followed.

'What a funny place to do a strip-tease,' commented Matilda, who felt petulant about not being allowed to concentrate on Dr Rebew's iniquity. It had been fun, a breakthrough in honesty.

As the two women approached the tree they could just see Theo's large semi-clad body, half-hidden by shaking branches.

'The tree must be awfully strong,' said Matilda.

'Let's hope so.'

'Hosanna in excelsis!' cried Theo, hurling his trousers upwards where they caught on a broken bit of wood and remained suspended like legs without a torso.

Sergeant wondered whether to dash to the hospital for help but she would hate to return and find Theo dead on the winter-hard ground. 'You are behaving like an idiot,' she said.

'Not surprising, since I am one!' called Theo. He was now entirely naked, his huge pink body standing within a wall of branches.

'Actually he looks quite safe,' said Matilda, echoing Sergeant's thoughts.

'I am going for help.' The nurse made up her mind.

'I'm staying here,' announced Matilda, ducking out of her grasp.

Theo heard Matilda's voice and pushed through a layer of branches. He looked down at her and she looked up at him. Despite his stomach he was well proportioned although his male organ was clearly suffering from the cold.

'Do I look like a god?' asked Theo, striking an attitude. 'My full name means gift of God, you know.'

'Yes. Sort of. Like a Blake painting, I think.'

'You are like a pale flower. Your face is turned up towards me like a daisy looking for the sun.'

'You don't look like the sun,' objected Matilda, even though she was touched by his romantic image.

'Soon I shall spread my wings and fly to you.'

'Oh, I wouldn't do that.' Matilda suppressed a feeling that she would enjoy seeing such a performance.

'You see, you are my lover. I love you!'

'Oh.' Matilda sat down. She crossed her legs neatly. His declaration could not be taken standing up.

'Where are you? I can't see you.' Theo's anxiety made the boughs dip and sway.

'I'm on the ground,' said Matilda in a small voice. 'I'm afraid I'm not too good on love.'

'Don't worry about that! I have enough love for both of us. As you know, God's love is infinite and he gives each of us as much as we need. I am bursting with love, overflowing with it, powered by it, like a speed boat is powered by its engine, I am all combustion, all energy . . .'

In his excitement Theo had shifted his position so that his weight, instead of being distributed over several branches, was entirely supported by one. Shouting, exulting, he began to bounce, working up a rhythm as a child might in his cot. Inevitably, the much-tried branch lost patience and slowly severed its connection with the trunk.

'You're falling,' warned Matilda, daisy-face filled with fear.

'I'm flying!' exulted Theo, waving his arms beatifically.

Branch and man dropped suddenly, crashing to the ground with so much elasticity that Matilda barely managed to avoid the rebound.

'That was glorious, heavenly.' Theo spoke through gritted teeth and then gave a loud groan.

'I think you've broken your leg.' Matilda looked at his right leg, which stuck out at a very unusual angle.

'It was worth it,' said Theo gallantly before fainting.

'Is he alive?' asked Sergeant, arriving in great haste with two other nurses.

'He was flying,' explained Matilda loyally. She didn't add that he was flying to her because he loved her; the idea needed further examination.

'I'll take Matilda in and get a stretcher,' said one of the nurses.

'Ambulance, too,' said another.

Head bowed, Matilda was led away. 'It wasn't my fault,' she mumbled as they reached the hospital entrance. 'Not entirely.'

'Of course not. Theo always does exactly what he wants.'

Theo was away in the general hospital for nearly a week. He should have been there longer for he had two operations on his leg and was still in traction when he returned. He was, in fact, expelled for bad behaviour. Even immobile in a side room, he managed to spread panic among the old men in for prostate operations and the young men who had tried to kill themselves on motor bicycles.

'It's his bellowing voice,' complained one.

'He rings his bell at all hours,' moaned another.

'He plays his television like a trumpet,' commented a third, who was a member of the local brass band.

But worst of all were the cigars. 'I took them up as a pacifier,' Theo explained to Matilda, on the day of his return. 'Like a baby's dummy.'

'It may have pacified you but it seems to have infuriated every-one else.' Matilda sat beside Theo's bed and felt an undeniable glow of pleasure at his return. Without him the hospital had been dull and drab – even Nora seemed too sunk in apathy to be jealous of her. She had struck up a sort of friendship with Linda, who turned out to have an interest in numbers, but after a while she had to admit that prime factors had their limit as a subject of conversation. Moreover, the icy weather had continued so she had not been tempted to another garden visit. Her only excitement was a successful repelling of her lover. Her ex-lover. She had refused to leave her room and eventually he retired, defeated, although planning a return attack.

'It's strange they won't leave me alone now,' she said, breaking into a monologue by Theo in which he was explaining that his cheerful manner was due to the medical inadvisability of giving him tranquillisers when he was having general anaesthetics and antibiotics, etc, etc.

'You see,' Matilda continued, finding she had spoken aloud, 'when I was at home and utterly available, they had no interest in me. No serious interest, at least. They saw only my functions as wife, mother, worker, lover, not me.'

'How interesting,' commented Theo, who despised this kind of talk. To his mind, it smacked of unhealthy self-pity. Much better to accept that the world is a cruel place filled with cruel people and then make the best of it. That's what Dr Rebew never understood about him, his Christian acceptance of a sinful world coupled with a pagan ability to throw a few wreaths on the water.

Matilda saw that Theo had no more interest in her real self than anyone else but found herself curiously unresentful. She was finding lately that her attitudes brought to the hospital from the outside world were dissolving gradually just as her memories and even nightmares of that world were dissolving. All she knew certainly was that she did not wish to go back to it nor see anyone from it.

'We missed you at therapy yesterday,' she told Theo encouragingly.

'I'm not surprised.' Theo wiggled the toes on his plastered leg. 'I shall not disappoint you next week.'

Matilda leaned forward. 'What's that written all over your cast?'

'Aha. I thought you'd never ask. That says "I love you, Matilda" in fifteen languages.'

'Oh,' said Matilda, much taken aback.

'The foreign language was a master stroke, of course. Knowing your feelings about love, I would not wish to embarrass you.'

'Oh,' repeated Matilda, even more weakly. What had she told him about love?

'It did present a challenge, however, because the nurse I'd bribed to do the writing turned out to be completely illiterate in anything but Welsh. Welsh is there, incidentally, you see, *cwnnymwllanelly*, or something like. Our doctor is Welsh, you know, though he pretends to be Jewish. We used so much Tipp-Ex that I could fairly claim to be the proud possessor of the first Tipp-Ex cast.'

As Theo talked on, Matilda decided to slip out of the room. She could not believe he would care too much and the pressure of remaining in the little room with that vast erect leg coated in Tower of Babel declarations of love was becoming too great to bear.

Theo, still pouring out words, watched Matilda's departure with sadness. Doubtless the world was bloody. Leaning over with a wince, for he had been badly bruised as well as broken in his flight from the tree, he chose his biggest and smelliest cigar. It would guarantee the arrival of a nurse in five minutes.

'You are filled with self-hatred,' said Dr Rebew, wearily. It was only his tiredness that led him to such a categorical statement to Theo, who seized it with the same joy as a cat pounces on a mouse. Here was something to play with, toss into the air, sink his teeth into. 'Self-hatred is a fundamental sin, leading inexorably to suicide. Oh, Dr Rebew, are you saying I do not love my neighbour as myself?'

Dr Rebew saw his mistake. It was not only his tiredness, for it was late afternoon and already dark outside, but this claustrophobic little room, which smelt of cigars and a large man. Besides, that leg looked so threatening raised up like a great club, like . . . The doctor rubbed his head mournfully.

'I love all parts of myself,' said Theo, having no pity. 'I particularly love this leg, which is a tribute to my love for Matilda. It is a living sculpture, incarcerated in loving words. It is a paean of praise! It is physical refutation of your charge of self-hatred.'

'Is it mending well?' asked Dr Rebew, like a mouse who plays dead.

'I am not interested in its mending,' said Theo grandly. 'My heart, you might say, is in that leg and my heart does not wish to be in a mending situation. Love is heart-breaking and I am in love!'

Dr Rebew sighed. If he was honest with himself, he had given up trying to help Theo, who was too much for him, a natural force he could contain with therapeutic levels of drugs but not overwhelm. Actually, before Theo decided to break his leg, he had been reasonably well. It seemed that association with Matilda had precipitated him into a manic phase, although now, once again, he merely seemed a little bullying, a little over-excited.

'Are you sleeping?' he asked.

'Are you sleeping, he asks! A man pours out his emotional core only to be asked if he's sleeping. Of course I'm not sleeping. How could I sleep when my heart burns, my leg throbs and my whole body's black and blue?'

'Absolutely,' said Dr Rebew, standing up. 'I'll tell the nurse.'

'Thank you, thank you. I shall look forward to Monday.'

'Monday?'

'Group therapy. My bed and I will find an unobtrusive little corner. Or perhaps we'll provide a talking point . . .'

Dr Rebew left, slipping out in much the same way as Matilda.

Now I'll have no more visits today, thought Theo, and a fearsome sense of loneliness took hold of him. He scrabbled for the stub of a cigar and a newspaper by his bed but his hands shook and his brain raced. Dr Rebew, although a Welsh git, was right. Sleep was the only thing of importance, a healing, soothing sleep. If only his huge and unwieldy carcass would let him sink a little below the surface.

Matilda walked the long corridors of despair. She hardly knew if she was in her bed or out of it, asleep or awake. In the darkness she felt her face wet with tears, which ran from her eyes unprompted. When she felt the damp pillow against her skin she knew she was awake and in bed and not walking anywhere at all. She was now in a room with two other patients but they didn't stir as, trembling with anxiety and shivering with cold, she rose, ghostlike, and slid out of the room. The corridor outside was lit brightly and at the far end she could hear a nurse talking on the telephone. She moved towards the noise and only then realised it was coming from the recreation room behind her and that the staff room ahead was empty. A blissful idea took hold of her.

The nurse on duty was a young man called Ray and he was watching a video on how to make your own sailing boat since his ambition was to be a psychotherapist on a big ship. He was taking notes as he watched, which explained why Matilda had to make as much noise as she did before she caught his attention.

Her plan had been to raid the pills, which she imagined in rows of glass jars as if in a sweet shop. She merely wished to end the pain of the night. But the room had cupboards and the cupboards were bare or locked. Eventually she became angry and grabbing the telephone receiver began to batter it at the glass front of one of the cupboards. The glass shattered under her fury but revealed no pills. It was only then that she felt frustrated enough to slash a shard along her barely healed left wrist, pulling it up and down several times. The pain was much greater than she expected – she remembered no pain from her last attempt – and she was terribly shocked. It was a cheat, for she had been planning to escape from pain not increase it.

'Cheat!' she screamed holding her dripping fingers away from her nightdress. 'Cheat! Liar! Cheat!'

The men's ward and private bedrooms were the other side of the staff room, which served both male and female patients. The nurse attached to the men was out of the office attending to an old man who had wet his bed. Theo had heard the nurse go by and liked the sound of another human being in a night when he was threatened by descending voices. Later he might risk an attempt at conversation even though it would enter his report card as a sleepless night. He did not hear Matilda's first break-in attempts but could hardly miss her subsequent yells. As they continued, he felt compelled to take action. He had already discovered how to unhook his weight from the end of his leg so it was the work of a moment to hoist himself out of bed and, cursing the nurses for not trusting him with crutches, hop along the corridor.

Theo and Ray, the would-be sailor, arrived in the staff room at the same time.

'My dear Matilda!' cried Theo, unable to avoid a sense of pleasure in the scene for, after all it was perfectly clear she wasn't going to die of a few little scratches like that even if they were dripping blood like an advertisement for paint. 'My dear foolish girl, whatever possessed you to carve up your pretty self like that?'

'Theo!' screamed Ray, furious that he would be discovered in dereliction of duty. 'Go back to bed!'

'Shouldn't you do something about her?' Theo waved his hand, which caused him to sway dangerously.

Ray could not deny this so Theo was able to sit on a chair and watch while he dealt with the cut. Matilda, meantime, had stopped screaming and stared downwards, mesmerised apparently by Theo's plaster-cast leg.

'Still there,' he offered in a consoling voice. 'Love without frontiers.'

Matilda shifted her gaze but still did not speak.

By the time Ray had finished bandaging and given out a soothing pill, the other nurse returned.

'Oh, God!' he exclaimed.

'That's me,' said Theo. 'You know, you night staff are much more understanding than the daytime lot so why don't we all have a nice friendly cup of tea with plenty of sugar?'

Since they could do nothing until the doctor arrived and Matilda was quiet and Theo easier to agree with than disagree, Ray plugged in the kettle.

'So, how did she get in here?' asked Alan, the other and more conscientious nurse.

'Ahmmm,' said Ray, looking nervously at Theo.

'I'd like you to know', said Theo cheerily, 'I'm not above blackmail. When you reach my position in life you can't afford to be above anything.'

'She flew in when I was on a round,' said Ray, unconvincingly.

'Which doctor's on duty?' asked Alan.

'Fairweather,' said Ray gloomily.

'She'll have your necktie for garters.' Alan smiled unsympathetically. 'You'd better think up a better story and don't forget to remove the video.'

'Oho!' said Theo. 'I'll tell you what. I'm a man of good heart, an ex-servant of God, a spiritual comforter—'

'Shut up, Theo.' Ray stood up unhappily. Visions of a berth on the high sea blurred with his nasty bedsit.

'I fell out of bed, you see. Alan was otherwise engaged with the king of the rubber sheets so you had to rush to my succour. Forgetting to lock the office is a venial sin under the circumstances.'

'I'd buy it, Ray,' advised Alan who, although above reproach himself, enjoyed the fall of others.

'What's more,' cried Theo, 'since I'm in need of nothing – always excluding God's favour – you can have it on credit.'

'Done,' agreed Ray, without enthusiasm. As he spoke, the brisk sounds of a woman's step approached along the corridor.

'Hark!' Theo cupped his ear theatrically. 'Something wicked this way comes.'

'You fell out, remember,' Ray whispered fiercely, 'and I came running.'

'Exactly that and if I may remind—'

'Sssh!'

'—remind you of your—'

'Be quiet!'

'—video—'

'Oh, Christ!'

312

As Dr Fairweather strode in, a small woman, weary but battling, Ray shot out.

'Chaos!' responded the doctor, recovering from Ray's exist to see the monolithic figure of Theo, plaster leg outstretched. 'I thought it was a woman patient.'

'I fell out of bed,' explained Theo.

'It must have been a very high bed,' said Dr Fairweather absent-mindedly, for now she caught sight of the hunched figure of Matilda.

'A tree came first,' Theo smiled understandingly at her mistake. 'The bed was this evening.'

'Oh dear,' said Dr Fairweather, who had just stepped in the trail of Matilda's blood.

'I'm pretty sure she won't need stitches,' said Ray, returning in a hurry with one hand behind his back.

'A tissue would be most useful,' said the doctor. 'Blood goes such a long way.'

'Ugh!' exclaimed Theo, wishing to draw attention to himself.

'You can go to bed now.' Ray felt able to turn on Theo since it seemed that Dr Fairweather was not in a mood to apportion blame. She sat beside Matilda wiping off her shoe.

'Can I go to bed, too?' asked Matilda sleepily.

'I gave her a hundred milligrams of Largactil,' said Ray. 'It was on her PRN.'

'Take off the bandage, then, and I'll have a look.' The cuts had stopped bleeding already. Everybody in the room peered at them and then at Matilda. She shut her eyes. Dr Fairweather stood up briskly. 'No need for stitches. I'll just give her an anti-tetanus shot, then we can do the reports.'

'She must have had anti-tetanus when she first came in.'

'Then it's only the report. There'll be questions about how she got into the office.'

Theo stood up and began to hop.

'Heavens, man,' said Dr Fairweather, as the room began to shake, 'you're not a stork. Where are your crutches?'

'*Verboten*—' began Theo, before seeing his opportunity. 'Nurse,' he said, gripping Ray's arm tightly. 'Where are my crutches? What I need are some crutches.'

'You aren't allowed—'

'Ah, nurse, what's the black object you've just put in that drawer?'

'Not crutches, surely?' said the dazed doctor. 'I'll write a slip and you'll have them in the morning. A big chap like you needs a support.'

'Thank you, doctor.' Theo winked smugly at Ray and graciously accepted his arm from the room.

'Can I go to bed now?' repeated Matilda plaintively.

'Yes, dear.' At last the doctor turned her full attention to the patient. The two women were about the same age and physical type – slim to stringy, pale skin beginning to crisp into wrinkles, large eyes with slightly too much white round the pupils. 'You're too tired and I'm too tired to talk about it now,' the doctor said after a second in which they gazed at each other recognising their similarities and the perfect possibility of a reversal in their roles. 'In the morning Dr Rebew will talk it through with you. You are not suffering any pain now, I presume?'

'Pain', muttered Matilda, eyelids dropping, 'is in the eye of the beholder.'

The day after a night of dramatic climax is always a sad and irritable one for patients. Neither Matilda nor Theo found the strength to address a word to one another although the hours had to be passed in the normal way. Since Dr Rebew was away at a conference in London, Matilda could have no therapeutic, or otherwise, session with him or his Picasso horse. Her wrist hurt surprisingly little so that were it not for the bandage and a sense of disgrace among the nurses she could hardly believe what she had done – or attempted to do.

'Have another go? Did you?' This was Nora's lunchtime comment and seemed to sum up the general reaction in the hospital: lack of interest combined with half-hearted disapproval.

'I couldn't sleep,' she said to Nora.

'You should get more pills. Nights are the worst. Nights, my husband comes and fights over me with Dr Rebew. Sometimes I hear them screeching at each other like tom-cats. Luckily the doctor's stronger.'

'Good,' said Matilda, although she found the conversation discouraging. Was madness catching? she wondered.

Possibly it was this anxiously diminishing grip on reality that weakened her resistance to a six o'clock visitor.

It was her ex-lover, Tobias. He sat in a corner of the recreation room, looking much smaller and paler than she remembered. In her life he had been cast as the solid, good-humoured one, not too sensitive perhaps but filled, almost puffed up, with the milk of human kindness. It was disconcerting, therefore, to see him

314

looking thin and anxious. She sat on a chair as far away as she could without being rude.

'I heard you . . .' He looked at her bandage.

'I just scraped the bark,' replied Matilda.

'Ah.' Tobias avoided her eyes. 'I came before, you know.'

'Yes. Of course, I came here to avoid you. Not just you,' she added kindly, seeing, as if through fronds of leaves, his sad expression. 'All of you. It was that or the great chopper in the sky.'

'Chopper?' repeated Tobias picturing helicopters since he had no way of knowing that Matilda's continuing association of Theo with a tree had led her to imagine divine providence in the form of a superhuman wood chopper. 'If we had married, we wouldn't have been happy,' he said all in a rush.

A look of distaste passed over Matilda's face. 'You never asked me to marry you.'

'I know, I know. But if I had it would all have been a disaster so that's why I didn't.'

Dimly and unwillingly, Matilda perceived he was apologising. 'You are younger than me and not very important,' she said disdainfully. 'I liked your smile and your physical dissimilarity to Martin.'

'You loved me!' cried Tobias in the tone of voice of someone who is making a declaration on his own behalf.

Matilda shut her eyes.

Tobias, realising more was needed, conducted a heroic battle between common sense and loving warmth. He did love her – but not enough to sustain her through this crisis. That was a husband's job. Yet he would have liked to get close enough to hold her hand – he had always liked her hands, so fine-boned, fanning out from such delicate wrists. When her fingers fluttered over his body, he had become aroused immediately. Embarrassed, Tobias realised the same thing was happening now even at the thought of it.

'You her husband?' A large girl with cropped hair and acne stood straddle-legged in front of him. Sexual deflation was immediate.

'No, her brother.'

'Her brother?' The girl, Nora, detected the lie at once. 'You shit.'

'I mean, her friend.' Tobias lost his nerve. He wondered how Matilda, who was so reliant on good manners, could bear this place. Another girl, fat like a monster and with a horribly scarred face, had come in behind. Matilda must be very unwell not to go off her head in a place like this. Tobias blushed at the complications to which such a thought led him.

'She doesn't seem very pleased to see you,' commented Nora with satisfaction. 'She's in a sulk because she loves Dr Rebew but he loves me.'

'I see.' Linda approached now, making Tobias jump foolishly. She stared at him and then turned away as if disappointed.

Tobias stood up for now all kinds of freaks were crowding through the door. In the lead was a huge, scowling, cigar-smoking man on crutches. Tobias had always been frightened of crutches, not so much the fear of being cracked over the head but of the moral dilemma they presented: should one defend oneself against an attack from the disabled? Would an unconscious one-legged man rightly condemn him to the moral outrage of the world?

Tobias thought of this as Theo swung towards him but came to no decision.

'You are a swine, a wart-hog, a piece of bird shit!' This was still Nora speaking but he needed to keep his eye on Theo, who had a nasty, purposeful air.

'Don't you have any nurses here?' Tobias appealed to Matilda.

'It's supper-time,' she explained, without raising her eyes from the table.

A second later Theo raised his crutch in anger. Despite forecasting such an eventuality from his first appearance, Tobias was slow to take evasive action. He bent, however, so that Theo, expecting to target his head, made contact a couple of feet lower on his back. This caused Theo to lose his balance and tip on to the floor like a statue.

'This is too much!' cried Tobias, tears stinging at his eyes for the blow had been a mighty one.

Theo groaned from the floor.

'Jolly good! Jolly good! Jolly good show!' shrieked Nora, reverting to an unsuspected childhood vocabulary of the games field.

Matilda, who had looked up just in time to see her gallant defender take action, now began to laugh. Theo stopped groaning and Tobias stopped moaning. One was delighted, a look of pride overtaking the grimace of pain, the other was furious, rising to his feet and hobbling to the door.

'Well, that's it! Matilda. I'm going now and I shan't come back.' Tobias pushed past a bevy of arriving nurses.

'Good,' responded Theo from the floor as Matilda didn't even try to contain her laughter. 'I can assure you, you won't be missed.'

Theo had rebroken his leg. 'Every bit of fun must be paid for,' he noted philosophically as the ambulance took him away for another operation.

Once more Matilda found his absence made the days longer and more dreary. After all, he had made her laugh spontaneously, which she couldn't remember doing for years. He was grotesque, of course, pathetic, deranged, obese and self-indulgent, but she still missed him.

Chapter Twenty-Two

Theo and Matilda made assignations to meet at the Friends' sweets and crisps caravan. The hospital seemed to have given up the idea of imprisoning Theo in traction and soon the ward became used to the crash of his crutch-borne approach for he manipulated himself like a trapeze artist so that he could swing or gallop – one-legged – or fly. His bulk, stomach prominent but, as he proudly informed anyone prepared to listen, decreasing, made him a formidable obstacle if met in a narrow corridor and encouraged the nurses to propel him outward into the grounds.

The Friends' sweets and crisps caravan was an obvious destination on Mondays, Wednesdays and Fridays between 1.30 and 3.30 p.m. Theo drank diet Coke and ate Maltesers, with the less-fattening centre, and on the first afternoon that Matilda passed wanly by, he shouted commandingly, 'Come in! Come into Paradise!'

Matilda, who found obedience a pleasure, entered at once. There was not much room, what with Theo and his crutches and his fuming cigar and the good woman – either Gillian or Jocelyn, although singly personified by Theo as Lily. In theory, they were served outside through a little hatch but Theo disdained such a vulgar concept.

'This is Matilda, Lily. Lily, Matilda.' He introduced her that first afternoon. 'She, unlike you, Lily, who are cheerful always owing to your good works, is filled with depression. You will notice her nasty scabs on her left wrist. We must improve her mood with a cherry Coke.'

'I have been here before,' began Matilda.

But Theo who had clearly forgotten the incident, waved this aside with his cigar. 'We will meet here three times a week,' he informed her firmly. 'We will talk of God and Lily's family, who give her a lot of trouble and are not as grateful as we are, and you will get fatter and I will get thinner.'

319

'Only if you give up cigars,' gasped Matilda while he paused for breath.

'Your word is my command!' The cigar sailed over her head and out through the open door of the caravan.

'Thank you, dear,' signed Lily to Matilda.

Since the hospital, despite the constant threat of financial cuts, still employed enough nurses to watch over the patients' behaviour, Dr Rebew was soon told about the meetings of his two patients. He took the information seriously enough to keep another patient waiting while he studied their two files side by side. Although he had now forgotten that it was his original impulse which had sent them into the garden together, he retained a sense that, for some inexplicable reason – he was not a romantic man – he was on their side. It was, he tried out the idea and it did not seem too ridiculous, a kind of group therapy, chaperoned, as he knew, by a good woman – who must, in his view, be fairly mad herself to sit for hours in a caravan parked at the back gate of a psychiatric hospital.

Theo, Dr Rebew continued his analysis, was a mental-hospital recidivist but harmless, an ex-priest who had found the pressure of saving his own and others' souls too great. Besides, he was presently incapacitated. Matilda was both a simpler and yet more complicated case. She was a middle-aged woman, previously married to a normally selfish husband, with two normally selfish children. Turned from them in some desperation to a job and a normally selfish lover, she had discovered a total emptiness in herself. Quite rightly, she did not particularly blame anyone for this but struggled with a sense of worthlessness at best, non-existence at worst. For someone of her age, Dr Rebew checked the file, this was both ordinary and serious. Contact with Theo, whose lunatic bravura and self-centredness disguised a desperate longing for human love (to replace, presumably, the intensity of his love for God), might at best stimulate her into a new awareness of her role as a living human being and at worst provide a jolly umbrella under which she could function unnoticed. In short, they might do each other good.

More than satisfied with himself, Dr Rebew shut the two files and dictated a memo. His voice, slow and profound, linked the two names as if in formal ceremony.

Several weeks passed uneventfully. Matilda found enough interest in living to send home for some clothes. She even managed to kiss the daughter who brought them and tell her that she loved her and it wasn't her fault that her mother had broken down.

320

This act of unselfishness led to another and she wrote to Tobias, apologising for the incident in the hospital and saying that she was better and her arm had healed nicely but she felt it would be sensible if their relationship discontinued. The finality of this caused a pang for she had loved the honey-gold taste and touch of his young body, but the relief overcame the sorrow.

Theo, leg healing and in regular communication with a woman upon whom he had fixed all his undefined hopes, felt himself in danger of becoming too happy. Happiness in his case led to flying from trees. Terrified of manic folly, he paid regular sobering visits to poor Raving Madness and, perhaps more usefully, became the first in the pill queue.

Dr Rebew, watching on, congratulated himself on his daring and discernment. It even inspired him to take down the Picasso horse, which had depressed him for years, and replace it with a print by John Martin, whose brother had been mad as a hatter and burned down York Minster because he didn't like the services. The print was exciting, too, and showed Byron standing at the bottom of an Italian waterfall. It would remind him that psychiatry, even in a state-run hospital, need not be only a matter of lithium and Largactil.

Then came Theo's birthday. Twenty years in a monastery had taught Theo that only Christ's birthday was worth celebrating. All this had changed, however, with the advent of Jenny. She was scandalised by the discovery that he hardly remembered the date of his birth, said it was an insult to his mother and explained that without regular celebrations life was hardly worth living. In the good early years of their association, Theo believed everything she told him and, besides, was not averse to an excuse for cracking open a bottle of champagne.

Birthdays, celebrations of all sorts, had become one of the jolliest features of living with Jenny. On such occasions their love-making was prodigious, their drinking as prodigious as finances allowed and their happiness pagan and untrammelled. It was after one such glorious occasion that he had gone into overdrive and had his first breakdown. But this was forgotten.

'We will enlist Lily's support,' he informed Matilda, 'and hold a proper birthday party under the trees.'

'How old are you?' asked Matilda. Since it was raining they were sitting side by side in the recreation room feeling rather drear.

It only then struck Theo that he was to be fifty. The idea excited him further, although under the excitement was a deep current of depression.

'I'm older than you,' said Matilda, with no feeling of regret. 'You shouldn't boss me about so much.'

'You like it,' responded Theo, leaning forward with glittering eyes.

'Kiss! Kiss!' shouted Nora from across the room. It had taken her a long time to admit that Matilda did not want to take Dr Rebew from her and she still had not lost the habit of watching her closely.

'Kiss! Kiss! Kiss! Kiss!' cried Theo, surging forward in his bounding hobble and kissing Nora's spotty cheek. 'We are going to have a party!'

In the event 28 March proved too cold for outdoor celebration, aside from the matter of those patients who were not allowed from the ward. Edward, the murderous black boy, had not left the hospital building for a year and old man Oscar was recovering from a nasty bout of pneumonia.

The kitchen staff, however, produced a blue cake with white icing and a batch of fairy cakes with a violet sugared almond on the top of each one. At the last minute, Lily appeared with a magnum of champagne. 'It looks like my christening,' Theo just had time to comment before the champagne was whisked away by a nurse. Alcohol on the ward was strictly forbidden.

Matilda, wearing make-up, high heels and a skirt, watched the retreat of the champagne with regret. It reminded her, like a snatch of music, of a time when she had been happy and, rather successfully, drowned her sorrows. 'Nunc est bibendum, nunc pede libero pulsanda tellus!' she cried, striking a pose of defiant gaiety.

Theo was thrilled by such unexpected enthusiasm and, catching her round the waist, swung her in a wide circle.

'Oh, for a draught of the warm south!' trilled Matilda, legs kicking freely like a doll's. Unfortunately, the party-going had been reduced latterly to vodka swilled surreptitiously from egg cups although she only had herself to hide from. But this image she dismissed and saw that Theo, too, regretted the passing of the champagne.

'We will steal it back,' he whispered into her ear, 'and drink it secretly together.'

Self-control is a dull exercise, depression not much different, although it is unwilled. Theo's cheeks flushed and Matilda's heart pounded as they crept, as far as a large man on crutches can creep, to the kitchen cupboard. There, behind the bottles of orange squash, the cartons of long-life milk, the tins of cocoa, Theo divined that the champagne would be hidden.

The hospital was quiet in this interval between tea and supper. The nurses had retired and the patients rested or watched television.

Matilda's admiration for Theo's almost superhuman understanding of everything increased when he triumphantly pulled out the magnum of champagne. 'Where will we drink it?' she whispered.

'I will put it under my coat,' said Theo, 'and we will go for a walk in the garden.'

'But it's dark.'

'Dusky. No more than dusk. They will give me permission because it's my birthday.'

'And they like some peace,' added Matilda, with a momentary wilting of the spirit.

'Peace is for the dead,' said Theo firmly, taking her arm.

The garden had never seemed more mysterious. It was indeed 'dusky', the trees wreathed like giants in mufflers of white mist. The other side of the valley, usually reared sharply up like a picture hung on a sloping wall, had receded into the ghostly colours of abstraction. The grass was damp but still springy, a corporal reality under their feet. Out of habit, they began to make their way towards the back gate where the caravan stood but then Theo changed direction and led Matilda to a path leading up behind the hospital. They reached the edge of a straggling grove of silver birch where one large oak gave umbrella protection. Matilda leaned against a trunk while Theo eased off the champagne top.

'I come from a quite grand family,' he said. 'Quite wealthy. Country rich, a large house, garden, not too much ready cash. We never drank champagne. On the other hand, when the need arose they bought me the cottage that Jenny's now pinched for her lover.'

'I like looking at the hospital from up here,' said Matilda. 'You can see the Victorian bits and the monastery bits and even the really ancient bits.'

'A little Tudor manor house stood over to the right. Most of it burned down and whatever remained was incorporated into the big house. Those two shattered-looking yews are the remains of an avenue. There're stumps too, under the grass.'

'Oh dear!' exclaimed Matilda. 'We forgot to bring glasses.'

'My dear lady, have you no faith?' Handing over the champagne, which was now steaming and bubbling, Theo produced a plastic mug from either pocket.

Matilda laughed and was disconcerted to find tears coming into her eyes. She was not used to feeling happy.

'I love you,' commented Theo.

'Oh, no! Please not.'

Theo quickly poured the champagne and the awkwardness of Matilda's instinctive reaction passed. She was with him, after all, and laughing till she cried.

The champagne entered their bloodstream and turned it to a glittering river of exhilaration. After a few moments they could not stand up, so they sat down and leaned their backs against the tree. It was nearly dark and their pale faces glistened mysteriously.

Theo bent forward and kissed Matilda on the mouth. He was still holding a full mug of champagne and, as the kiss continued, he let it tip so that a waterfall of bubbles hit his knee and then ran down his plaster-cast leg.

Matilda pulled back slowly, afraid she might faint. 'I have to breathe,' she said.

'I don't.' Theo put down his empty mug and the bottle, which he had gripped all through the kiss in his other hand. 'Why don't you take off your coat?'

'I'm too thin.' Matilda tried to think of her piteous ageing body for a moment but it didn't feel like that. 'You take it off for me.'

'On condition I can take off the rest of your clothes.'

Matilda saw no reason why he shouldn't if that was what he wanted. She smiled and leaned her head back comfortably. She had never felt so comfortable, so at ease. When Theo stroked her, she shut her eyes and put her hand out blindly to his face. She touched his thick hair and felt his strong neck and when her fingers reached his sweater, she murmured, 'It's not fair. You should take off your clothes, too.'

This was pretty difficult, given the matter of the encased leg, but was eventually effected with the maximum good humour.

'Adam and Eve,' boasted Theo, which allowed for a certain amount of romantic licence.

'You are silly,' said Matilda. 'But I like your body even with that filthy plaster of Paris. You're so solid. I saw you naked as a baby before you flew from the tree. Now you look even better because you're all nice and warm.' Matilda put out her hand to touch him.

It was very dark now, a starless moonless evening with the few country sounds muffled by the mist. The ground was wet but

Matilda laid out her coat and, besides, they could only feel the comfort and tenderness of being together.

'I always fall asleep after I've made love,' apologised Theo, 'and then I snore.'

'I'll dig you in the ribs,' muttered Matilda.

But instead she kissed him and soon fell asleep herself.

The lovers – more like giant babes in the wood than Adam and Eve – were missed when they didn't turn up for supper. Two nurses, cold and cross, set off to find them. Luckily, one was Sergeant. When she saw them cuddled together on the ground – the white plaster cast acted like a beacon – she commented wryly, 'What a triumph of love over matter.'

But the other nurse was scandalised, furious and guilty, because she had been the one to let them out. 'It's disgusting,' she cried loud enough to wake up Theo and Matilda. 'A paunchy man with one leg and an old woman. It's a frightful sight!'

'It's my birthday.' Theo sat up without bothering to cover himself.

'You should know better,' said the bad-tempered nurse to Matilda, dressed her quickly and stood her on her feet as if she were a small child.

'I am free,' said Matilda, still happy. And since this received no response she added, 'I don't know why you're making such a fuss, anyway, I'm far too old to have a baby.'

This made Theo laugh and they marched down to the hospital in good spirits. Theo insisted on giving his arm to Matilda for, as he pointed out, she was his beloved, his star of the night, his sweet flower, his apogee of goodness.

'I'm glad,' said Matilda, when she managed to get a word in, 'because you're my beacon of light, my mountain of goodness—'

'My orb and sceptre and crown,' continued Theo till they both began to laugh with such drunken lack of control that they could no longer walk.

'A price must always be paid for happiness.' Theo, waking up in the middle of the night, tried to reassure himself. Physical pain, in this case throbbing head, aching leg and churning stomach, had long ago ceased seriously to trouble him. 'But that does not mean the happiness is false or may not return again,' he muttered to himself, trying desperately to stave off the black thoughts of sin and guilt and death. Unfortunately, it was not the moment to pray to the Virgin who was usually so sympathetic, so forgiving. 'It was my birthday,' he said in a whine, which ended abruptly as he realised that his stomach, after all, needed serious attention. Too late, he stumbled out of bed, and charged blindly for the lavatory.

Sickness overwhelmed, the evacuation necessary and immediate. He could not even get his plaster cast out of the way so that it received, in a multi-coloured torrent, the supper he had been forced to eat. Even the birthday cake was visible, yellow marzipan, always indigestible. Theo rang for the nurse, sure, at least, that the black thoughts were at bay.

'I don't believe my eyes!' The nurse, female, who had been lightly slumbering, looked as startled as a rabbit.

'You don't want to believe it,' commented Theo. 'Nor would I if I were you. It's at moments like these that I think the patient has a better deal than the nurse although, of course, we're not being paid.' Theo sat on his bed and stuck out his revolting leg.

Since no words could express her emotions, and the job must be done, the nurse retired in search of the strongest disinfectant in the hospital.

Theo now had a moment to contemplate Matilda and for a horrible flash feared that their union, so perfect, so exhilarating, may have compromised their future relationship.

'I am sorry, I am truly sorry,' he pleaded when the nurse returned, for she was the nearest woman to be placated.

'I don't know what to do with this leg.' The nurse, refusing to listen, poured most of the contents of the bucket over the plaster.

'Cut it off, if I were you. After all, it only gets in the way.'

'You're too heavy to hop for the rest of your life,' said the nurse without looking up.

Theo, who had meant the cast not the leg, thought, with a very slight lifting of spirit, that he had always known the nurses were madder than the patients. 'Anyway,' he said, 'I should never have been made to eat such a filthy supper. You can see for yourself, pimento, spaghetti—'

'Shut up!' cried the nurse. 'Or I shall go and fill up this bucket with pure disinfectant and pour it over your head.'

Serious at heart, Theo hoped to himself that Matilda's morning reaction would be kinder.

Matilda had a good night's sleep and felt physically well when she woke. She refused to consider what had happened the night before, since all considerations seemed to turn bad in her head, and dressed quickly. Her hands were shaking, true, but she liked it as a sign of quickening life. Allowing herself support from the walls of the corridor, she tottered at speed towards breakfast.

*

Dr Rebew looked at the report on his desk and found he could not recall the appropriate response. He supposed it was a school-masterly carpeting. 'You are here to regain your mental equilibrium, which does not include copulating under trees.' Theo would never allow him to use such words. His monk's puritanism invested everything with an aura of morality. 'You have sinned.' Perhaps he could invest such an accusation with an aura of reality. Sighing, Dr Rebew rang to ask that Theo and Matilda should be brought to him.

Matilda had missed Theo at breakfast although, if she were honest, there was a certain relief in her reaction. How would he treat her after last night?

Matilda entered Dr Rebew's office without having seen Theo.

'Well, where is he?' Dr Rebew was saying impatiently on the telephone. 'You can't have lost him again.'

A few minutes later Theo shambled in. 'I was asleep,' he said before he spotted Matilda, 'in bed. But for you, Dr Rebew, I drop everything.'

'Ahem,' responded the doctor, drawing Theo's attention to Matilda. For a second, a look of embarrassment and fear froze his face but then he rallied nobly. It was time for truth without the aid of champagne. 'Are you well, darling Matilda?' he began in tones of the utmost seriousness.

But Dr Rebew was not there to listen to the carolling of ancient love-birds, however moving, however life-enhancing. He had a purpose and a busy schedule. 'Intimate relations are forbidden in this hospital,' he said.

Matilda, mesmerised by the pastel shades of Theo's plaster leg as fully revealed beneath the pair of extraordinary red shorts he was wearing, did not hear Dr Rebew's pronouncement and her attention was only captured when Theo repeated, 'Intimate relations,' in a tone of wonderment.

Ah, thought Matilda, that is indeed a perfect description of our relationship. We are intimately related. Having missed Dr Rebew's reproof, she beamed sunnily at Theo.

The warmth of her regard is almost unbearable, thought Theo, for once bereft of words.

He is my Caliban, decided Matilda, and then, remembering how she had come to him growing, as it were, out of a tree, she felt the image even more satisfyingly apt. 'Your leg,' she said. 'Have you been painting?'

Unfortunately, she interrupted Dr Rebew, who had been talking interestingly about the responsibilities of the mentally unstable to their psyche. Glowering at both patients, he stood up, gripping the edge of the desk. 'I cannot help you,' he shouted, 'if you will not help yourselves!'

The words amazed both Theo and Matilda, who thought that that was exactly what they had been doing. Seeing their faces, the doctor understood what they were thinking and was forced to admit to himself that they were absolutely right. Sitting down again, he drew a sheet of paper towards him. 'What day would be convenient for your departure from the hospital?' He looked at Matilda, his face apparently kindly.

'You can't chuck her out because she submits to my fond embraces!' cried Theo, eyes on Matilda's shocked face.

'It's nothing to do with that. She is ready to leave, that's all. The National Health is not a charity. I'm not sure about you, however.'

'I can leave when I like.' Theo's face, pale and bland before, was now red as a beetroot. 'I'm not sectioned.'

'Quite,' agreed Dr Rebew. 'But do you think yourself ready to cope with the world outside?'

Matilda began to cry. It was nothing more serious than the thought of home, for she had not yet conceived a future with Theo.

'You have made her cry,' Theo accused Dr Rebew.

'She makes herself cry,' said the doctor wearily.

'She never cries when she's with me.' Theo stood beside Matilda and rested his hand on the top of her head and indeed she stopped crying – more out of surprise than anything else.

'You see,' boasted Theo.

'If you really feel like that,' suddenly Dr Rebew had lost all patience, influenced possibly, although certainly unconsciously, by the priestlike blessing of Theo's flat palm, 'if you really feel like that, you should bunk off together in a little love nest and live happily ever after.' Once more he stood up and gripped the edge of the table.

Theo and Matilda stared anxiously. This was a display of emotion beyond the level of their bad behaviour. Theo, who had always tried so hard to provoke a sign of life in Dr Rebew, now found he didn't like it, after all.

'We are in your hands, doctor,' he said soothingly.

'No, you're not. You're in each other's arms.'

This was odder and odder. Dr Rebew felt it, too, but was powerless to stop himself.

'We'd better go.' Matilda, decisive in her turn, stood up and marched to the door. Theo followed, although not without a backward look at the avenging spirit behind the desk.

Once in the corridor, the lovers, for they had been sealed together by their doctor, leaned against each other momentarily.

'As far as a madman can promise anything, I promise I will always love you,' said Theo.

Matilda found tears in her eyes, a common experience for her but in this case, inspired by a daring happiness.

Breaking apart, they allowed a nurse to pass through them and enter Dr Rebew's office. Using the same angry voice, they heard him shout, 'The same morning I am told to cut my costs by a third, I am faced by sex between patients. Am I an administrator or a doctor?'

Sensibly, the nurse made no answer but Theo and Matilda looked at each other with the same expression. It had struck both of them that Dr Rebew must cope with the world outside their world and they felt sorry for him.

'I wonder if he has a wife,' whispered Matilda.

'Everybody has a wife but not everybody has a good wife,' responded Theo, and he led Matilda firmly along the corridor.

But the spectre of the outside world was upon them, of financial arrangements, of living arrangements, of people who didn't understand. Matilda gripped Theo's hand tighter. 'I am not going,' she said. 'I love my children and I have a residual affection for my ex-husband and ex-lover but I'm not going home.'

'We may all have to go home.' Reaching the glass partition between kitchen and corridor, Theo stared gloomily. 'You may note that we are no longer provided with Nescafé Gold Blend. Soon there will be no butter and then our delightful kitchen will be dismantled and we will be served travelling plastic boxes of food consisting entirely of numbers and colours. The gravy train will stop here no more!'

'I wish you'd be serious.' Matilda shuddered.

'Never more so. Three years ago the cuts were just threatened. Jab. Jab. Two years ago they first appeared. Slice. Slice. Nescafé Gold Blend was a symbol like the Union Jack, flying over the great houses of Empire. We are doomed. That's why Dr Rebew was in such a bad temper. He will have to go and work in London. All his work here will be wiped out. Melancholy and Raving Madness will be buried under the rubble of a demolished building.'

Matilda sighed. Words, however filled with frightfulness, seemed to cheer Theo. She only wondered if Dr Rebew really meant to turn her out.

'Let's sit down somewhere,' she said.

'First I must have a pee.' Theo squeezed Matilda's hand and

then let it go. 'The demands of the body are usually, but not always, boring. While I'm away, don't forget I love you.'

This time Matilda neither denied him nor felt tears in her eyes. In truth, she had to admit she believed him. Watching his extraordinary progress away from her, his lopsided red shorts, his too-long silvery curls, his height and width, she called out, 'You remind me of Salisbury Cathedral!'

Theo acknowledged he had heard by raising his arm but did not pause. Apart from other pressing needs, a cathedral had a different connotation for him than for her.

Chapter Twenty-Three

Dr Rebew looked out of his office window. Spring had changed the colours from black, green and grey to lime green, yellow and blue. They were the colours of hope and a new beginning. Across on the other hillside he could see bunches of young lambs, their coats too white to be true. Below them grew a spread of yellow gorse and below that, in the valley, a tall line of unfurling chestnuts.

Dr Rebew sighed, somewhat theatrically, for he would have liked someone to share his depression. This time the cuts amounted to a chop. The hospital was not meant to survive. It had always existed for historical rather than practical reasons. It was too remote to be a sensible regional centre and was only chosen because of the existence of a private mental hospital in a converted Victorian house. He had seen the erection of modern wings and three independent new buildings. What would happen to them now? What would happen to him?

Leaning further out of the window, Dr Rebew spotted Theo and Matilda strolling hand in hand. This prompted him to add, rather belatedly, a further question to his list. What would happen to his patients? This accurately reflected his growing sense that patients ultimately looked after themselves or, if they could not do that, were not seriously open to be looked after by anyone else. It was true that he had deflected some from suicide, raised others from depression, calmed down still others but as to curing . . .

'Theo! Matilda!' Giving in to an uncharacteristic need for reassurance, the doctor waved and shouted. Unfortunately, Theo and Matilda were discussing important matters.

'Jenny has no rights – particularly with the policeman in her bed,' said Theo.

'There will be room for my children to visit but possibly not to stay.'

'Perhaps in a tent in the garden,' suggested Theo kindly. 'I will find a teaching job in the local school where my boys will become—'

'And girls,' interrupted Matilda.

'My boys and girls,' agreed Theo obligingly, 'will become enthused by the depth and breadth of my knowledge of Greek and Latin with particular reference to the monastic writings of medieval Europe.'

'I didn't know you knew about that.' Matilda's voice was admiring. Her ex-husband thought history began with Harold Wilson.

'Theo! Matilda!' screamed Dr Rebew, aware that he was in danger of making a fool of himself but unwilling to fall into the trough of self-control.

'We will become prominent members of the local Catholic community,' continued Theo.

'Prominent?' queried Matilda, not wanting to sound discouraging but she wasn't a Catholic, barely even a Christian.

'You're right. Prominent is out – at least to begin with. We will become humble members of the Catholic community. Backbenchers, as it were, on the pews of God's house.'

This image was beyond the scope of Matilda's imagination but she had faith and thought of the long summer evenings in which they would untangle the meaning of life.

'Since we have been together,' Theo illustrated his point by holding up Matilda's hand as if she were a boxing champion, 'I have not been tormented by the devil.'

Dr Rebew, who had been about to try one last appealing yodel, saw this action and choked down his voice into a froggy croak. They were deaf to him. Not as deaf as when they had first arrived at the hospital for then they had been able to hear nothing and now they could hear each other.

'And what will I do when you're teaching?' asked Matilda, for now Theo had let down her hand and they were walking forward again in quiet harmony.

'You will teach, too,' suggested Theo, enthusiastically.

'Oh, no. No, thank you.'

'Then what will you do? Women must not be allowed to hang around. My mother hung around and became mean and bitter. The first day Jenny left off working at the supermarket, she made me chop wood, fill up the coal scuttle and wash my hair, despite the fact I'd been out teaching.'

Glad at this level of realism, Matilda ventured shyly, 'I do have a little market garden I started.'

'A market garden! A market garden with fruit and veg – things that grow!' Theo was ecstatic. His hands chopped the air and his pace quickened.

Dr Rebew turned his back on the window. They were off their heads, of course. One must not overlook that. Theo would forget to take his pills and drink too much and break his other leg by trying to stop a moving car. Matilda would mourn the failure of her marriage and the loss of motherhood so that even Theo would not be able to make her believe in her existence. Eventually, she would become dissatisfied with scratching her wrists and swallow a whole bottle of paracetamol.

Dr Rebew sat at his desk with the gloomy satisfaction of a kill-joy. The following morning he was to attend a conference in London. That was where his future lay now, with new medical breakthroughs coated in sugar. He was a psychiatrist not an analyst, which this quiet fold of the countryside was leading him to forget. His wife, who had an interest in music, would enjoy London. So would his two clever, sociable children who, up until now, had spent much of their time at boarding school. Perhaps they could be removed to an appropriate day school and he would get to know them better.

Lost in positive forward thinking, Dr Rebew no longer watched Matilda and Theo, who were heading off for their favourite walk to the tree at the end of the back drive. Strangely, although no one would now object if they had left the grounds for a longer exploration, they stayed within the hospital's boundaries. They were partly limited, it is true, by Theo's plaster cast – now demurely painted white – but, as he said, he had never allowed the body to dictate to the heart.

'That's one of the reasons I love you,' said Matilda, who had become shameless and brave. 'You are the first person to give me a sense of freedom.'

'God's freedom,' annotated Theo in a reproving tone of voice.

'Whatever you like,' agreed Matilda sweetly. 'What I mean to say is . . .' But she stopped, for whatever she meant to say was inexpressible.

They walked on in silence, which was unusual for Theo but even he was affected by the symptoms of spring around them. It made him want to hug Matilda, crush her to the ground in loving embrace so that she became one with the grass and then lie on top of her. Luckily, he was beginning to learn some self-control. Instead he squeezed her hand so tightly that the knuckles cracked together.

333

'Ouch!' cried Matilda, delightedly.

'If you only knew what you're missing. I suppose you are too old to have children?'

'Oh, yes.' Matilda's response was quick as a flash and anxious. 'Quite right. I am not a fit father.'

'But that's not the reason—'

'No. No. One must not be carried away by the wiles of spring. Permit me.' Disengaging hands, Theo held Matilda's face and kissed her gently. 'We stand outside time, outside space,' he began in a sing-song voice, as if reciting poetry, 'we are here enclosed and freely here. We hold together, although we know we are apart. We are good and bad and thoroughly stupid. You are you and I am me. Or is it I? We give each other hope, although we are both perfectly hopeless. We . . .'

Running out of steam slightly, Theo looked for Matilda's approbation. Unfortunately she had been distracted by the discovery of a white violet among the grasses. 'There is nothing in the world,' she muttered, 'nothing so beautiful as this violet.'

Seeing her enchantment, Theo forgave her lack of attention. 'You are my violet,' he announced gallantly. 'If you were crystallised and on top of a cake, I would eat you.'

'Oh, thank you,' responded Matilda, not really hearing. But then an echo of his earlier words came back to her. 'Is it possible to be happy inside time, inside space?'

'Amen,' replied Theo firmly, knowing hers was a silly question.

'Now I've met you I want a future,' persisted Matilda. She had picked the violet, which she twirled between her fingers.

'You need wiser heads than mine. Aha. Follow me.'

Obediently, Matilda followed Theo all the way back to the hospital and to the subterranean storehouse. It was as smelly and depressing as ever. 'No, thank you,' said Matilda.

'But old Raving and Melancholy are sure to know the answer to your questions.' Theo stood like the ring-master in a circus. 'Besides, they must be desperately lonely. I haven't visited them for ages.'

Matilda laughed at his persuasive face. Why did she love him – a madman?

Hand in hand, they made their way to the stone giants. 'We will plight our troth in front of them. They are witnesses of distinction.' He began solemnly 'I plight my troth—'

'Why would anyone keep this box of papers?' interrupted Matilda. 'Piles of old papers.'

'You should attend.' Theo was severe. 'I am disappointed in you.'

But Matilda bent over the piles of musty papers, some rolled and tied with ribbon, some scattered loose.

'Survival is boring.' Theo put his face close to Raving Madness and snarled in imitation.

'They're to do with the house, I think, or the estate . . . 1867, this one's dated. But here's a sheet so very ancient it's not even written on paper.'

'I told you already, survival is boring.' Theo stretched his eyes and mouth with his fingers. 'I love you because you are a suicide. You see through the petty guiles of life.'

'Lovely writing. Strange writing. On vellum.'

'I, of course, am a life-force. Some people believe women represent the life-force but personally I find them tending to gloom, although that could reflect my immediate venue. The female manic is rare at Abbeyfields, you may have noticed.'

'It might be Anglo-Saxon, I think, or Celtic,' said Matilda.

'You sound sane and commanding.' At last Theo came over to her. 'Did your husband, or indeed lover, appreciate these qualities? Are you sure we'll get on? It is fair to say, I'm highly educated myself.'

'Oh dear.' Matilda was now sitting cross-legged like a child among the dirt and mouse droppings. 'I can't understand what it says and I expect it'll fall to pieces any moment.'

'That wouldn't surprise me one bit.' Theo laid a consoling hand on her shoulder. 'When you come to think about it, that's just like life. First, you can't understand it and then it bloody well falls to pieces.'

Matilda looked up. Theo's large reddish face with its framing of bouncy silver-glitter hair, wore a simple, kindly expression. She took his big hand and pulled herself up. In her other hand she still held her findings. 'I might keep it all the same, to remind me of Abbeyfields.'

Theo raised his eyes heavenwards as if at an erring child. 'You might just as well give me a kiss and forget all about it.'

'And now I've dropped my violet,' said Matilda, a little wildly.

'Nonsense,' contradicted Theo and, in order to spare her distress, made munching noises. 'I told you I was going to eat it. It's absolutely safe.' Since she seemed unconvinced, he patted his stomach appreciatively. 'Yum. Yum.'

'Oh, Theo!' Matilda put down the page of writing and hugged him round his substantial middle. 'You are my tree and I am your ivy, and if we are only partly convincing, then what does it matter?'

The sheet of vellum, discarded on Melancholy Madness's big toe, balanced precariously for a while and then, caught in a draught from the closing door, fell to the ground. It was still perfectly intact.

EPILOGUE

Time past and time future
Allow but a little consciousness.
To be conscious is not to be in time
But only in time can the moment in the rose-garden,
The moment in the arbour where the rain beat,
The moment in the draughty church at smokefall
Be remembered; involved with past and future.
Only through time time is conquered.

T. S. Eliot – 'Burnt Norton'
from *The Four Quartets*

The sun was coming up above the eastern flank of the valley. Although it was a spring sun, sharp and energetic, it found it hard work piercing the soft strings of mist which stretched along the horizon. Below, in the folds of the valley, the mist still muffled everything in thick whiteness.

Matilda, watching from her bedroom window, wanted to see the sun break through, bring outline and colour to the sky and the grass and the trees. Yet the mystery of the only partially seen was what was actually making her stand there in her nightdress, face pressed close to the glass. In those vague shapes and half-formed images, she felt something of herself undiscovered and only partly understood.

It was the past, she thought, reminding her that even at this most daring time she was still part of everything that had gone before, unseen and incomprehensible as it was.

'Come to bed, Matilda.' Theo had been watching his wife for some time. She had not slept well lately, although the baby was not due for several more weeks.

'It's going to be a beautiful day.' Matilda turned and smiled, but her eyes were blank for she was still waiting for the battle between sun and mist to be resolved. She would have been confident in the sun's victory except that sometimes in this westerly part of the country, the mist gathered forces and rolled up more heavily, suffocating the sun in its dankness. Suddenly she was altogether on the side of brightness and light.

'What are you doing?'

'Encouraging the sun.'

'The sun can come up perfectly well without your help.'

Matilda did not move. 'What a day to go to London.'

'Come back to bed. We can keep watch together.'

Matilda turned from the window and walked towards her husband. The moment she turned her back, a gilded fan of light spread through the glass.

341

Theo stared. The rays burned out Matilda's nightdress so she seemed to be walking towards him naked. The beauty of her smooth body with its white stomach as gently sloping as the hill outside made him blink his eyes. 'Turn sideways and come to me.'

Matilda stood by him obediently for, although the sun had no warmth yet, she could feel its light around her and through her.

Slowly Theo ran his hands down her body. Neither of them spoke, for they felt themselves united in the triumph of the sunrise and the countryside it was revealing outside their room.

'What a day to go to London,' Matilda repeated eventually, and she got back into bed. But it was only a sigh like the sighs caught in the mists below her window.

The door was varnished too glossily like the twenty-four others in the complex of buildings. But beside it leaned a stone tablet on which Theo had carved the number seven. It distinguished their house from all the others, Matilda thought.

'Theo! We'll miss the train if you don't hurry!' Each house had its little garden although the estate was set in its own grounds of tall trees and thick shrubs. Matilda had watched over the conversion wall by wall and had been pleased when she saw the great arch, which Theo said was Roman, set into a courtyard and in the middle of the courtyard the foundation stone she had stood on during their first visit.

Even Theo, who seemed to feel himself in competition with these stone-makers of the past, had admitted the old parts gave an atmosphere to the place quite unlike any other estate that they had seen.

'At last!' He was there behind her, dangling the car keys.

The keeper of early manuscripts looked at the young couple in their anoraks and jeans. They were not foreign, they were not even tourists, nor were they academics. They were from the country, with colour in their cheeks, bristling hair and the slightly dazed look such people have when they come up to spend a day in London.

'How can I help?' he asked. He had come to them in a corridor with a blue-suited security guard at his desk.

'We have something to show you.' The man's voice was confident, untainted by the majesty of the British Museum.

The keeper drooped and looked away. He did not encourage people to bring in granny's little treasures. 'You need an auction house.'

But the girl began to unwrap a package. Layer after layer of tinfoil and Kleenex. The keeper looked at his watch and sighed.

'We found it a year ago on a demolished site. It has a long history.

We've done some research in the local library and we think it must be Anglo-Saxon. We don't want money. We just want it to be properly cared for. It seems to be poetry…'

Matilda looked up from the revealed page of vellum and saw the keeper's face. He seemed to be on the edge of tears. His face, which had been smooth and greyish, had turned crimson and his hand, when he stretched it out to take the page, was shaking.

'We'll leave it with you,' announced Theo. 'As my wife says, we just want to see its future secure.'

'My colleagues…' The keeper gasped. 'Have you shown it to—?'

'No one else has seen it,' said Theo.

'We've been busy.' Matilda smiled, thinking of their wedding, the move to Abbeyfields, the start of the baby.

'Kingston Lacey.' The keeper muttered mostly to himself.

'It didn't come from Kingston Lacey,' said Theo, 'although we do live in the same part of England.'

'No. I'll tell you what.' Now the keeper smiled manically. 'You wait here a moment and I'll just—' Without finishing his sentence he disappeared through a side door. A moment later his head popped back. 'I should tell you, this is—this may be—a very interesting find. In the vernacular, Anglo-Saxon, you see, not Latin. Quite rare. It looks like—it might be—over a thousand years old.'

When he had gone again, Matilda laughed. 'I suppose it's like his dream come true. And you thought it was a piece of newspaper!'

'It's history, that's what it is.' Theo peered down the corridor with its shelves full of leatherbound books. To arrive in this corridor, they had passed through room after room of cases and cabinets all filled with books or manuscripts. 'That's why he's so excited, this whole place is a graveyard of history.'

Great puffs of smoke billowed up from the churchyard at the bottom of the hill. It reminded Matilda, looking from her kitchen window, that Theo had told her that one of his tombstones had been recently erected there. He had wanted her to admire it, she knew, but the baby had taken all her attention.

'Come, Lucy, time for a walk.' She lifted her from the floor, felt the satisfaction of her weight and the shiny dampness of her skin. 'You're heavier than me, I do believe,' she grumbled, and the baby laughed at her and snatched a dangling strand of hair.

Outside, the air smelled heavy from the summer grasses and flowers and trees but the bonfire smelled strongest of all. It was a sweet yet acrid smell, mossy yet dry. 'We're going to see what your clever father's made.' Matilda leant over the pram and looked into Lucy's glassy blue eyes.

It took less than half an hour to walk down to the little village where the old school-house with the fish-tail roof and the vicarage stood beside the rather characterless stone church. But to Matilda it seemed like another world to their own home halfway up the valley. This afternoon she opened the iron gate to the churchyard having met no-one. She wheeled the pram up the grassy path and then, since it was a hot afternoon, set it in the shade of the single yew tree. Lucy's fingers were already in her mouth and her head lolled as if she planned to sleep.

Matilda glanced around. Most of the tombstones were old, simple stone crosses, upright rectangles or horizontal slabs. There were one or two in silver granite or white marble but nothing that could be Theo's work. Enjoying the peace and the unaccustomed feeling of being alone, she wandered among the tombs, reading the inscriptions when they weren't too weathered or encrusted with lichen.

'Mary Coffin,' she read out loud, 'Beloved wife of Frederick Coffin.' Next door lay Edward Squibb, whose wife was also called Mary. The repetition of the name interested her and, wondering if it might be a local favourite, she began to look along the tombs for other names beginning with M.

She had found another Mary, Mary Chaffey, by the time she reached the westerly end of the church beyond which the fire was still puffing like a lazy geni. There were more tombstones here, so Matilda continued round, walking slowly, feeling slightly trance-like in her sense of the quiet all round her. There were noises but they were all natural, the cooing of pigeons, the occasional crowing of a cock, the scrabblings and twitterings of smaller birds. A faraway tractor only increased her sense of peacefulness. It was as if everybody else in the world had disappeared, leaving her entirely on her own. It even affected her body, giving her the sensation that her heartbeat was slowing down.

It struck her then to glance upwards to Abbeyfields Hall. But the sun had moved from the south to the west so that it pierced her eyes painfully and made her blink and turn away. It was then she saw the name Matilda. It was inscribed on a large square tomb, surrounded by low iron railings, clearly the property of a grander family than the Coffins and Squibbs. The carving had crumbled badly but she could just make out a list of four or five names which ended with Matilda and the date of her birth and death, 1840 to 1882. 'May she rest in God's Peace.' Further down she traced with her finger another name, "Abbeyfields Hall."

Matilda sank down on a neighbouring horizontal tomb and bowed her head. It seemed right to sit there beside this other Matilda in a modest act of recognition. Even though Lucy was out of sight on the other side of the church, she did not feel at all

344

anxious but still enjoyed an extraordinary sense of calm.

Perhaps it was partly due to the smell of the bonfire which, although lower now, continued to pump pungent billows into the air, but she soon found it impossible to keep her eyes open.

Theo was riding home from work on a bicycle. On sunny days he enjoyed the exercise and the feeling of being enclosed by the countryside. When he reached the steep hill leading up to Abbeyfields, he dismounted as usual and began to walk up slowly, pushing his bike. He passed the church almost at once and saw with astonishment Lucy's pram, unattended. Dropping the bicycle, he ran, with all the concern of a new father, into the graveyard.

'Lucy! Lucy!' He bent over his daughter, who was wide awake and concentrating on blowing bubbles. Panic no longer appropriate, he straightened and looked around. 'Where's your mother then?'

Leaving the pram, he too wandered round the other side of the church, where he immediately saw Matilda fast asleep on a tombstone.

Matilda smiled as she opened her eyes. She was glad to see Theo there, even though he was frowning. 'I wanted to see your headstone,' she explained.

'My head-stone?' Theo stared at her in astonishment. 'You're still asleep. I don't have a head-stone here.'

'You told me about it. That's why I came.'

Theo sat down beside her. She looked so soft and lazy. The fire was hardly smoking at all now and the evening sun cast a yellow glow reflected from the warm stone of the church. 'My head-stone, if you mean the last one I carved, is at Hazelbury Compton, not here.'

Matilda looked up at him and beyond. 'That's lucky because I never saw it. I found a Matilda from Abbeyfields Hall instead. There, behind you. The big one with the railings.'

So Theo looked. He studied the big tomb and the tombstones beside and behind and around but, for all his efforts, he never found "Matilda" inscribed anywhere at all.

'That's silly!' cried Matilda, coming to life again. And she too began to peer, even scraping at the rough stone where there were words but crumbled away and quite unintelligible. It was hardly easy for her to concentrate because Theo had stopped looking and was jumping from tomb to tomb, crying out mockingly, 'Matilda fell asleep and had a dream and guess what she dreamed about? MATILDA!'

'Stop it, Theo. I did see it.' Then Lucy began to cry, bawling loudly

345

from the other side of the church so there was no time to carry on looking. 'I'll find it next time I come down,' Matilda said and ran round to her baby. As soon as she rocked the pram Lucy stopped crying and peace was restored, but it was no longer the extra-ordinary peace of earlier.

Theo pushed his bicycle up the hill with one hand and put his other round his wife's waist. He was hungry and all the jumping around had made his heart pound. 'If I have a heart attack, you'll have your dream to blame.'

But Matilda only leant forward to make a funny face at Lucy.

'If you have a heart attack it will be because you showed no respect for the dead.'

'And who will carve my head-stone?'

'Sshh.' As they rose up the hillside, Matilda felt as she always did, the sky coming to meet her. She only thought of what she wanted to say as they turned into the driveway of Abbeyfields. 'When I die, I shall be buried in that churchyard and then there will be a Matilda.'

'And what about me? What about your beloved husband?'

'Oh, you wouldn't lie quietly enough.'

Theo became serious suddenly. He took Matilda's hand from the handlebars and held it tightly against his face. 'You are everything to me,' he said formally. 'And when I'm drawn away from you, as is sure to happen, you must remember it is only a temporary separation.'

They did not look at each other as he spoke but stared ahead at their home, now burning with a reddish gold from the setting sun on one side and cast in blackest shadow on the other. It seemed like a painting or a stage-set waiting for the actors.